World and Town

World and Town

A NOVEL

Gish Jen

ALFRED A. KNOPF   NEW YORK   2010

THIS IS A BORZOI BOOK
PUBLISHED BY ALFRED A. KNOPF

www.aaknopf.com

Library of Congress
Cataloging-in-Publication Data
Jen, Gish.
World and town : a novel / by Gish Jen.—1st ed.
p.   cm.
ISBN 978-0-307-27219-5
1. Chinese-American women—Fiction.   2. Widows—Fiction.   3. Cambodian
Americans—Fiction.   4. Refugee families—Fiction.   5. City and town life—
United States—Fiction.   I. Title.
PS3560.E474W67 2010
813'.54—dc22   2010007057

Manufactured in the United States of America
First Edition

For Maryann Thompson

The American attaches himself to his little community for the same reason that the mountaineer clings to his hills, because the characteristic features of his country are there more distinctly marked; it has a more striking physiognomy.

—ALEXIS DE TOCQUEVILLE, *Democracy in America*

Although the eye is the first stage in vision, remember that it is actually the brain that "sees."

—NEIL CAMPBELL, JANE REECE, et al., *Biology*

With our thoughts, we make the world.

—GAUTAMA BUDDHA

Contents

World and Town

A Lost World

It's the bǎi shù *you'd notice most—the thousand-year-old cypresses— some of them upright, some of them leaning. And their bark, you'd see, if you visited—upward-spiraling, deeply grooved, on these straight trunks that rise and rise. They look as though someone took a rake to them, then gave them a twist, who knows why. Just having that idea about what made a fine tree, maybe. And jumbled up at their feet: acres and acres of grave mounds. Not one succeeding the next, in orderly rows and avenues with each inhabitant duly lined up and noted, but rather newer mounds piled up, willy-nilly, on top of others, so that as far as you could see it would be Kongs, Kongs, Kongs! All of them descendants of Kǒngzi—Confucius. Even now, at age sixty-eight, it is something for Hattie Kong, American citizen, to recall. Two thousand years of relatives, plopped down to rest in a single old forest.*

Said forest lying in the town of Qufu, in Shandong province, in China—not far from where Hattie grew up, and yet a world away. For Hattie grew up in Qingdao, also in Shandong, but on the ocean— a port city. A cosmopolitan city, occupied by the Germans before the Japanese, and a city known therefore for its "charming Bavarian architecture" and for its beer, which its residents drink from plastic bags, with straws.

Qufu is not about beer.

Confucius's mound, naturally, is the biggest of the mounds—maybe ten feet high—and the most distinct. It's set off some from the others. There's some stone this-and-that and scrub grass around it, but mostly it is an eminent pile of dirt. If you saw it in a natural history exhibit, you might think it a wonder of nature—something the termites made, bugs being so much more of a force than we give them credit for, and so on. Nothing could be more modest, or of this earth, so to speak. It was an anti-monument, really; who knows why Hattie's mother loved to stop in front of it. But yángrén that she was—foreigner—she would pause, tuck her hair behind her ears, fold her hands, and then lower, with reverence, her blue sun hat. Never mind that she was no longer a missionary, but a Chinaman's wife. Never mind that she had, as people so kindly put it, "gone native." Standing there in her Chinese dress—and she would, of course, be wearing a Chinese dress—she would strike the same attitude she might have had she been standing in a church, and had not been disowned and disavowed by the civilized world.

"This is worth taking in," she would say, in English. "This is worth taking away." Then she would nod as if in deep agreement with herself, and look to Hattie, who—eight years old then, and brown-haired like her mother—was supposed to reply in English. (Her mother not having given up on civilizing entirely, of course, just on the civilizing of strangers.) And so it was that Hattie replied—naturally—in Chinese. Shénme? What? What was worth taking away?

"Hattie! Please!" Her mother waited with her freckled hands folded. "Hattie?"

(And her hands could stay like that a long time, Hattie knew. Her hands could stay and stay and stay.)

"Hattie?"

Until finally Hattie folded her hands, too, and said, "Yes?"

"Do you see?"

(The dirt and grass were dusty, like the air and clouds and sun.)

"I don't."

Her mother frowned at first. But a moment later, the shade on her face drew up; there was a smile of light, and then—look—a real smile. "But of course not." The shade came back down. Hattie's mother hummed. Then Hattie and her mother dutifully joined the rest of the family in their grave sweeping and clearing, though—modern people that they were—her mother and father were far more interested in Hu Shih and Darwin than in the Old Sage. Ritual! The Five Relationships! What a lot of hogwash it all was. Should women really obey their husbands as children obeyed their parents? And why could only male Kongs and their wives be buried in Qufu?

"That is, if they had hair!" Hattie's father would exclaim—Confucius, in his wisdom, having specifically banned from the family forest, the bald.

Hattie's mother shook her head. It was no better than what she used to teach at the mission school, really, if not worse. Worse! Still Hattie grew up dutifully sweeping the Qufu graves, too—every spring, on Qīngmíng, as well as on her ancestors' birthdays and death days—until one day, when Hattie was fifteen, her father's mother announced a solution to the problem of Hattie having to be buried elsewhere: She'd found some distant Kong cousins willing to marry their son to a hùn xúc'er—*a mixed blood.*

"Isn't that good news?" finished Nǎi-nai. *Her dry eyes that did not shine much anymore somehow shone; outside the latticed window, even the moon seemed to brighten, and the blue night clouds. And Hattie was glad to behold that brightening, even as she was relieved, a minute later, to hear her mother switch to English.*

"I will not see her married off," she said, as soon as Nǎi-nai *left the room. "I will not." People said she was growing more American all the time instead of less—so earnest—and now, as if to prove their point, her knuckle hit the table on "I" and "will" and "not." She leaned forward, her wattley neck straining hard against her collar. "She has to have a choice."*

More raps with "has" and "have" and "choice."

Hattie's father raised his smooth hand. Though his wife was the Westerner in the family, he was the one in Western clothes—pants and a shirt. He wore a length of rope for a belt, and answered in English.

"Excuse me. Teacher." He spoke softly, as everyone could hear everything in their old house—and tuned in, too, of course. "I did not know today we have class."

"Very funny."

"No, no. Really." He winked at Hattie. "I haven't my book."

"I don't have," corrected Hattie. "I don't have my book."

Her mother did not even tell her that children, excuse me, did not speak to their fathers that way.

"You are siding with your mother," she said instead—in Chinese, now, though not in the lispy, fat-tongued Qingdao dialect their family all spoke, but in Mandarin.

Hattie's father nodded. "I'm afraid of her," he agreed disarmingly, speaking Mandarin, too—meeting his wife, as if on a bridge. Wǒ pà tā. He winked again, sitting back on his stool. They were partners still; they were forging something together. A little family.

They were partners.

Two months later, though, he had stopped wearing Western clothes. He had stopped eating Western food. He had stopped reading the Bible.

Family English lessons had gone up to five hours a day.

And Hattie found herself having a sit in the Qufu graveyard. She had never done any such thing before. But one brown spring day she made herself a seat out of newspaper, set it in a far corner of the graveyard, and then sat herself down on it, with the aim of thinking things through.

The graveyard was no help.

Yet since she was sitting there anyway, she took the place in—the reassurance of it. The appeal of it—a world with membership, it seemed, in an eternal order. She watched the sun move. She watched the shadows darken and grow. She watched the ants work, and the birds zip back and forth—what strangely urgent lives they led. She thought about their all-important nests, their frenzy over crumbs and worms; she thought about her grandparents, and her great-grandparents, and her great-great-grandparents, and her great-great-great-grandparents. People called for her—Hǎi dì! Hǎi dì!—their voices ringing and rising; and yet still she sat. How close she had come to occupying that great peace! How naturally and thoughtlessly she might have dwelt there as a bird dwells in its errands.

For thine is the power and the hogwash.

She stood up concerned mostly about the newsprint on her pì-pì.

And yet, decades later, when she heard that the graveyard had been dug up, she found herself yelling in her sleep, Stop! But this was the Cultural Revolution; the Red Guards just went on, of course, not only robbing the graves, but stealing the very dirt in the mounds. And there are the villagers, helping—carting the soil out to the field. That soil being rich and unfarmed, after all. They replace the mounds with their old depleted soil—throwing the dirt in every which way, just to get rid of it. Heaping it however, wherever.

Imagine.

Villagers Hattie's family had thought they knew well—had thought they'd treated well—now shā qì téng téng. *Seething fit to kill. And there, too's their handiwork: Thousands of years of tradition, destroyed. Even now, in America, Hattie sees the scene sometimes. The villagers with their trowels; the wagons shuttling back and forth as the old mounds are bitten up. In the side of each roundness, there are new ragged edged chews. It's sickening. Though underneath the ancient cracked surface, sure enough—look—there's something rich and crumbly. Black. Fertile. Many years later, a* zǔ zhǎng *will tell the Kongs who went where, that they might try to reconstruct the graves; Hattie and her brothers will hear about it from a great-aunt. In the meanwhile, there is so much dust in the air, the leaves of the trees look to have survived a strange storm. And there is the man whose idea all this was—a coarse man, in a new shirt.*

At least Confucius's steles have been saved—"tombstones" they'd probably be called here, though they are bigger than that. Steles. They're broken, sadly, but at least the pieces have been saved. And though this villager and that claims to have gotten hold of some bones, some poor ancient bones, the bones have only lasted days, people say, before disintegrating.

Is that true? Did the bones really disintegrate, just like that? The former scientist in Hattie—the former researcher in her, the former biology teacher—can't help but think, Hogwash!

*Though, well, blessed be decomposition, if they did. Today for a couple of hundred yuan, Kongs can be buried in the family forest again. Yet here sits this bag of protoplasm still, mulling over those two thousand years in Qufu. A misogynist tradition, a gerontocratic tradition; and what an obsessive-compulsive, her ancestor, in truth. If the mat is not straight, he does not sit on it. A nut. Confucius did, to be fair, speak of sincerity, too, and humility. Integrity—what made a noble man. (There were no noble women, of course.) And as an important counterweight to ritual, human-heartedness—*rén. *Goodness, capital G, that was, which people were born with but, in his sensible view, needed training to hang on to; today Hattie, too, is in favor of people cultivating their* rén. *All that clutching of the past, though— all that resurrecting of ancient rites and texts, some say for his own purposes—was he not a kind of fundamentalist? A godless fundamentalist, but a fundamentalist nonetheless.*

Well, never mind. Hattie looks at herself in the mirror now and sees her parents' break with all that—with the old ways in general. It's in her face: in her pale skin and flat nose. It's in her straight hair (bright white now, and trimmed even all around, like a topiary tree). Thanks to her father, she is not as wrinkly as she could be—she has some of that Asian fattiness to her skin. And she has him to thank, too, for her tadpole eyes—or should she say her formerly tadpole eyes. What with her eyelid fat breaking down a little now, her eyes are actually growing rounder and larger all the time. (And of course, they always were, like her mother's, hazel.) Not that this is what Hattie sees when she looks in the mirror. What Hattie sees, when she looks in the mirror, are her parents' youth and hope, even as she feels the pull of all they pushed away. For what has there been to replace that old world, with its rituals and certitudes, its guide posts and goalposts? Where will Hattie be buried, when her day comes?

It's a question, since her husband, Joe, had his ashes sprinkled from a hang glider, and her best friend, Lee, had hers dug into a peony bed. And since her closest companions these days—closer by far than her globetrotting son—are her dear dogs: Cato and Reveille and Annie, her puppy.

Maybe she should be buried in the pet cemetery?

Hattie I: I'll But Lie and Bleed Awhile

Last week, a family moved in down the hill—Cambodian. They plan to build themselves a little house, people say. Hoping that that house will—*ta daah!*—become a home. Well, that's not so simple, Hattie happens to know. But never mind; this is an age of flux. She, Hattie Kong, came from China; her neighbors from Cambodia; is there anyone not coming from somewhere? And not necessarily to a city with a cozy unhygienic ghetto, but sometimes—if not immediately, then eventually—to a fresh-aired town like Riverlake. A town that would have pink cheeks, if a town had cheeks. Riverlake being a good town, an independent town—a town that dates to before the Revolution. A town that was American before America was American, people claim—though, well, it's facing change now, and not just from the Cambodian family. Of course, there's always been change. In fact, if you want to talk about change, the old-timers will tell you how Riverlake wasn't Riverlake to begin with—how Brick Lake overflowed its banks a hundred years ago and came pouring down in a flood to here, and how the resulting body of water had to be renamed to avoid confusion. Riverlake, they dubbed it then—a lake born of a river. And the town that went with the lake was called that, too. Riverlake—a town born of change.

One thing will become another; and Hattie's neighbors are at least living for now in a double-wide trailer such as many around here would not sniff at. For some flatlanders bought property on the lake with this trailer on it; and seeing as they were going to build themselves a vacation place with radiant heat and a standing-seam roof, they gave the thing to the Cambodian family for free. Worked with the powers-that-be on the Internet, it seems. Had an interest in that part of the world, having marched—and marched and marched—against this and that in their youth. (As did Hattie, too, by the way, it wasn't such a big distinction.) The powers-that-be contacted a church, which in turn had the trailer moved to that triangle field at the bottom of the cliff behind Hattie. An odd lot the church was left in an odd will, and which odd lot the church has been trying to sell off for way longer than Hattie's been living in Riverlake, anyway. Which would be—what?—some two years now. Ever since Joe died and then Lee, in a kind of one-two Hattie still can't quite believe. It was like having twins; at one point they were even both in the recovery room together. She got to book the same church with the same pianist for both funerals, and did think she should have gotten some sort of twofer from the crematorium. And now, well, *Come back, come back,* she still begs them, in her half-sleep, sometimes. *Come back. Come back.* Though sometimes she's as mad at them as if they'd gone and had an affair on her.

How could you? How could you?

As if they could explain it.

And, *What now? What now?*

There being whole days, still, when she more or less lives to feed the dogs. Hers is a loneliness almost beyond words.

What now.

As dear Lee, that fountain of pith, used to say, *The unlived life isn't worth living.*

Her new neighbors.

And that lot, which was still the Lord's free and clear, awkwardly placed as it was—right in the crotch of a three-hill scrunch-up. It wasn't like Hattie's place, open and cleared and up on a granite knoll, with a little lake view. There was some clearing, but mostly the place was woods, and not the picturesque kind. These were real woods, impassable woods, with trees leaning and lying all over. A lot of sodden logs and lichen and toadstools, and even on the live trees, dead branches that stuck out all around the trunks like thorns. There was no view, and no light. And being sunk in a pocket like that, most of the clearing, aside from the trailer site proper, was wet. What the place really needed was divine intervention in the form of an in-ground dehumidifier. That did not, unfortunately, seem forthcoming. The good Lord did appear to be providing, though, if not for deliverance exactly, then a use for the place—about which, living as close as she did, Hattie was not thrilled. But, well, who could stop Him?

Hattie having heard that the church was going to do something someday, but having somehow envisioned that someday to be like the Rapture—a day that might or might not be on the immediate horizon. One week, though, the trailer sat as normal in its old site near town. The next its yard looked like a truck trade show. Hattie, out walking the dogs, stopped more or less dead as a churchload of folks jacked up the trailer and split it right down the middle, then with considerable adjusting and cranking and readjusting, opened it up like a child's pack-'n'-go dollhouse. Things snapped and sank; things leaned and bowed and split. This was not the growth of a crystal or a protein—some natural process bordering on dance. No, this was manmade inelegance itself. Still, only one worker swore (*cussed to make the heavens blush,* Hattie's mother would have said), namely baby-faced Everett, husband of Hattie's walking-group friend, Ginny. Whom someone had up and volunteered, unchurched though he was, on account of his size; never mind that the poor man was bound to incur more ambivalence than gratitude for his pain. Hattie knew him as a guy who would shovel her out in a storm—a man who'd show up without her asking and refuse to be paid, and a regular snow mason to boot, who over the course of the winter would produce path walls so plumb, you could have checked a spirit level against them. He was a kind man, an obliging man. And yet said kind and obliging man would not leave off cussing when people gave him the eye, quite the contrary. Said kind and obliging man seemed, if anything, to cuss all the louder for the looks—a man after Hattie's own heart in that way, but less dear to his coworkers, she could imagine, as the day wore on. For hear tell a jack gave, a hitch snapped. The coffee ran out. The cold got colder. One man just about took his thumb off, and had to go to Emergency with his hand in a bandanna tourniquet. So who knows but that Everett's mouth might have proved contagious—who knows but that he might have led others into Error—had the Lord not eventually gotten those trailer halves up on wheels.

There they were, though, finally, up up—at last—hallelujah! The group disbanded; heathen Everett disappeared. Then down the road the trailer halves rolled, one after the other, their private parts all in public. Did not a body have to wonder how intelligently designed we can be when none of us has so much as a wheel-like option? Well, never mind. The most intriguing part of all this, to Hattie's mind, had nothing to do with the brute grunting and heaving-ho—or even the dawning realization that the halves were headed toward her house. (Which was not *intriguing*, by the way—which was a shock!) It was rather when one of the trailer halves passed her on the road. For in the kitchen, as it rumbled by, was a blink of a girl, holding up the cabinets. Young—fourteen or fifteen, Hattie guessed—a tea-skinned pip-squeak of a thing with a swingy black ponytail and a shocking-pink jacket. Some cabinets had gotten knocked loose when the work was being done; the girl was put in there, it seemed, to keep them from coming down completely. Never mind that her spindly legs were wholly inadequate for the job—there she was all the same, gamely holding them up. Having taught high school for the better part of her life, Hattie waved at the poor thing; this being one of the things teaching's made of her, besides a habitual hoarder of chalk: a compulsive supporter of gumption. True, she'd retired right after Joe and Lee died. (As she had had to, being unable to bear the campus at which they'd all taught—being unable to climb the hill with the crocuses, or to set foot in the teachers' lounge, anything.) But never mind. That the girl did not wave back is the thing—that she could not begin to think about waving back, probably. Still, Hattie waved anyway—as the girl might never have even noticed, had the trailer not happened to hit a pothole.

A well-known pothole, this was, more famous in these parts than any movie star. It was top of the summer list for the road repair crew—a gap big enough to make you fear for your car axle. If locals had drawn up the map, this thing would have been on it in red. But that driver hailing from parts unknown, he failed to slow down— making for a jolt. The top of the trailer tilted like a fair ride; the girl was slammed askew. She lost her footing; a door sprang open; some cabinets tore off and a drawer shot out, sailing with surprising aplomb out onto the road, where it landed, spinning.

"Help!" the girl shouted.

"I've got it!" Hattie called back.

Did the girl hear? In any case, as the trailer pulled back level, the dogs and Hattie went and rescued the drawer—a wood-veneer affair, with a pitted, copper-tone, Mediterranean-look pull. Empty. The sort of thing you don't even see as a thing unless it's lying in the road and about to get run over. The dogs sniffed it immediately, of course. Wise Cato dropping his tail even as Annie the puppy attacked it; Reveille the glutton nosed an inside corner. For the thing did smell of cinnamon—someone's ex-spice drawer, guessed Hattie, as she picked it up. A thing worth something on its own, but a thing you'd have to say had suffered a loss, too. Its fellow drawers, after all—not to say all the cabinetry it had ever known.

Ah, but what has happened to her that she can find herself feeling sorry for a kitchen drawer?

Hattie gone batty!

Anyway, there the thing was, still in one piece.

She would have brought it back the very next day, except for the rain attack—these huge drops leaving the sky with murderous intent. Anyone foolish enough to pit an umbrella against them would only meet defeat even before the onslaught turned, like this one, into something resembling concrete aggregate. Of course, it will let up soon enough. Soon enough, Hattie's friend Greta will be whizzing by again, her white braid flying and her back baskets full—honking Hi! at Hattie's house, midwestern-style, as if to remind her of the music series, the dam project, the water quality patrol! So many ways to Get Involved, so many ways to Prove an Exemplary Citizen!

For a blessed few days, though, Hattie the Less Exemplary sits painting bamboo. One stalk, two.

Wind. Sleet. Hail.

She dips her *máobǐ* in the ink.

Rain.

Until finally comes a big blue sky, solid as wallboard.

Hattie admires the mountains as she crosses her side yard—the mountains in Riverlake being neither the highest hills around, nor the most dramatic, but quite possibly the most beguiling. Folding into one another like dunes, if you can imagine dunes dark with trees and sprinkled with farms. The west side of the lake, where Hattie lives, tends to the plunging and irregular—irrepressible granite heaves with drifts of unidentified other matter in between. (Including, this time of year, a few last gray amoebae of snow.) The east side, though—which she can see from her side yard and back porch—is rolling and dotted with some of the big old farms that used to be everywhere around here. They're squares of spring green today, like handkerchiefs dropped down from someplace they use green handkerchiefs; Hattie likes the barns, especially. It's hard to say why plain nature would be improved by a red barn or two, but she does feel it so. Maybe it is just the Chinese in her, always partial to the civilized, but she likes silver-capped silos, too, and farmhouses.

Peace.

Though look what's floating from the crest of the hill today: the trial balloon for the proposed cell phone tower. A long long string with a white balloon bobbing at its top—the whole deal a-waft like a ghost in a kids' play now, but just wait until it's a lunky metal affair with trusses and uprights and baubled appendages. There's a family hoping to make a killing on the thing, people say, as well as a big select board meeting on the subject coming up, to which—meeting-ed out as she was by her fervent youth—even Hattie will go.

But first, her neighbors.

The land is a swamp, but the trailer site itself isn't bad. As nobody has built steps up to the front door yet, though, she has to step up onto a milk crate to knock, and even so finds herself knocking at the door's knees. An awkward thing to do while holding a drawer, especially if you have a bag of cookies set in the drawer, as she does—butterscotch chip, nothing too extraordinary, though Hattie did use turbinado sugar in them instead of regular, seeing as how it was on special one week. Whatever turbinado even is or means. Anyway, the sugar gave the cookies a chew; and now here the door is opening, with a scrape—a half-gone hinge. The air has the mushroomy smell of rot.

"Hello," she says from her pedestal. She hoists the drawer before her like a popcorn vendor at a baseball game. "I've come to welcome you to the neighborhood."

Her audience being a half-stick of a man—looming over her at the moment, but not actually much taller than she is, which last she dared measure was all of five foot two. He has on a blue buttoned-up polo shirt, a black leather belt, and blue denim pants that look as though they are meant to be jeans but somehow look like slacks. His hair is white and thin, his skin pale and loose, and his face the fine result, she guesses, of a Pol Pot facial: One of his cheekbones sits a half-step high. She shivers. The man's nose is likewise misaligned; his pupils are tiny; and his gaze has a wander, as if possessed of a curiosity independent of its owner. Nystagmus, she thinks—damage to the abducens nerve. (Recalling old science terms more easily than she recalls her grocery list, naturally.) His gaze lists left, like a car out of alignment, then jerks back—left left left again, and back. It is strange to think him around her age—younger than her, even. Mid-sixties, people have said. He looks, she thinks, to belong to his own reality; and who knows but that he thinks something similar of her, for he beholds her with a blankness so adamant that the closed door he's replaced does seem, in retrospect, to have been friendlier.

"Hello," Hattie says, all the same. And, when he does not answer, "Do you speak English?"

He gazes at the top of her head as if she is growing something there.

"Do you speak English?" Slower this time.

A pause.

"Lit-tle," he says finally. He pronounces the word with equal stress on both syllables.

"Well, welcome to town," she says, trying not to speed up. Half the trick with English language learners, she knows, being the maintenance of a certain stateliness. "My name is Hattie. Hattie Kong. I live across the way, in the red house. See it over there? The red one."

She inclines her head in the general direction of her place—a two-bedroom cottage, one floor, with aluminum roof flashing that does, well, flash in the sun. She isn't the kind of city close where you can chat just fine without availing yourself of a phone, but by country standards they are cheek by jowl. Nobody would have picked it. Her neighbors' front door faces west, like hers, and if they'd been set the same distance from the road, she'd probably have found it intolerable. It is just lucky her new neighbors are set downhill and a little farther back than she is. They can't see into her place; nor she, she doesn't think, into theirs. Of course, with a little figuring she could probably set a basketball to roll from her back porch down to the milk crate, but never mind.

"I came to say hello and welcome," she says again, politely enough. "And to give you back your drawer."

Nothing.

"I came to return your drawer." Repeating herself like a record with a skip in it, if anyone even knows what a record is anymore. But there, at last: He glances down. Belatedly registering, it seems, that there is a white-haired lady bearing a kitchen drawer at his door.

"It's yours. It belongs to you. Part of the trailer. I believe it fell out while they were moving it. The trailer, I mean." She motions with her chin in case "trailer" is new vocabulary. "My name is Hattie Kong. I saw the men bring your house here."

Silence.

Somewhere in the woods a woodpecker pecks its brains out.

"Chi-nee?" he asks finally.

A stress on both syllables again.

"Half," she says, with a twinge. She has no earthly right, of course, to expect others, Asian or not, to perceive what she is. But having been asked all her life—well, there it is, a well-established little neural pathway, or should she say rut. "My father was Chinese, my mother was white."

"Peo-ple say you Chi-nee," he says.

"Well, that is half true."

"Half Viet-nam," says the man.

Viet-nam, accent on the first syllable—Vietnamese?

"No no no," Hattie says. "My mother was American, my father was Chinese. Do you know what a mutt is?"

"You speak Chi-nee?"

"I do. I grew up in China—a city called Qingdao. When I was growing up they spelled it T-S-I-N-G-T-A-O. Like the beer."

He does not appear to have heard of the beer.

"I came to the U.S. when I was sixteen. Ten years ago," she jokes.

No laugh. His eyes go on with their roving.

"You speak English good," he says.

"My mother was an English teacher at a Methodist mission. Before she married my father, that is. So I guess I got the phonemes when I was a baby."

Phonemes.

"Sounds, I mean," she says. "I heard the sounds."

"You speak Chi-nee too," says the man. "Boat."

Boat. Both.

"Yes," she says. "I speak both."

"Amm-erri-ken."

Amm-erri-Ken, with a rolled *r*—American.

"I'm American now. Yes."

The woodpecker pecks.

"Eat Chi-nee food?"

"Do I eat Chinese food? Of course."

He brightens. "Chi-nee food number one." He puts his thumb up. His eyes seem to focus, his face to broaden and regularize—a handsome man, once upon a time. For a moment she can see him in a suit and tie, with slicked-back hair and a cell phone.

She changes her grip on the drawer. "And your name is?"

"Ratanak Chhung."

Ra-tanak. Ra-tanak. She repeats it to herself to fix in her memory. Accent on the first syllable. *Chhung* is easy.

"Chhung is your surname?" Checking because though Asian surnames usually come first, people do often switch things around when they come here.

He nods, but with nothing like the woodpecker's energy, she has to say. He is more like the tree being pecked.

"May I call you Mr. Chhung?" Somewhere she has gotten the idea that respectful forms of address are important to Cambodians—from Greta, probably. Greta the well informed.

"American call me Chhung," he says. "Just Chhung."

"Ratanak is too hard," she guesses. "Not that hard, but too hard for some. Too long."

A delay. But then finally he nods, as if in accordance with an order sent from afar.

"Americans can be so lazy," she goes on. "Hardworking as they are."

A more definite bob.

Such an odd sound, pecking.

Hattie did not teach English as a Second Language back when she taught high school; she taught Biology and Mandarin. Still, in-house immigrant that she was, she'd been called in to help with the English Language Learners all the time, and had heard, over the years, all manner of accent. And yet she'd never encountered one quite like Chhung's. The chop of his speech, certain features of his grammar, that trouble with ending consonants—all these resemble problems native Chinese speakers have. Problems her father had, and that she probably had too, fifty or sixty years ago. But Chhung has that bit of a rolled *r,* in addition—kind of a Spanish-lite deal. Also those very short syllables, and an odd stress pattern. She has to still herself to understand him. Concentrate.

And so it is that she is concentrating—carefully casually asking about his wife and children or some such—when a corner of the crate sinks. She shoots her hand toward the doorframe but still half steps, half falls off the crate, turning her bad ankle and dropping her drawer clean into the mud. Her bad ankle!—she works it a bit, to make sure it's all right; this being her right foot, her bad foot—one of the reasons she always wears lace-ups with real support, though don't those sheepskin jobs look easy on.

Chhung diplomatically says nothing. But then he answers, "One boy, one girl"—as if that information, like the instruction to nod, has finally reached him. He forwards it on with a gentler voice than before, though—not wanting to go knocking her over again, maybe. "One baby. And two udder one, not here."

Two other whats? And why aren't they here? Well, never mind. Hattie goes on with her joint trials.

"Please say hello," she says. "Please tell them welcome to the neighborhood. Tell them they can drop by anytime. Okay if I leave you your drawer?"

It does seem unmannerly to leave it there on the ground, but then this Chhung is not exactly Mr. Manners himself.

"I'm going to leave you your drawer," she says. (A good helping of her mother's *sorry-to-do-this* in her voice, she notices.) "The cookies are for you and your family."

He nods, more or less.

Pecking.

A porta-potty sits in a dry spot up behind the trailer—a ladies' toilet they have, for some reason, with a little triangle-skirted figure on its green door. Did zoning okay that? And how are they going to get a septic in, what with the ground so wet? The trailer is quiet except for the *shush-rat-tat* of a mop or towel being wrung out into a pail. *Shush-rat-tat. Shush-rat-tat.*

That roof seam must have leaked something terrible.

Shush-rat-tat.

An interesting counterpoint to the woodpecker.

Shush-rat-tat.

Is that the girl mopping?

The sorrows of the rich are not real sorrows. Hattie does not hear her father's voice too often, but she hears it now. *The sorrows of the rich are not real sorrows; the comforts of the poor are not real comforts.* Was that a Chinese saying or something her father just liked to say? She doesn't even know.

And never will, now, probably.

Mud. The mud sucks so hard at her boots as she tromps uphill, she is just glad they are tied on. Then there she is again, returned to her own damp but springy grass. Down below the white lake glitters; the treetops toss. Some advanced clouds are already starting to move back in, and somewhere far off a car beeps in a way you don't hear much around here.

Hattie's no artist. Joe used to call her Miss Combustible, and probably in her day she was indeed lit more by the blindness of the world than its beauty. Vietnam! Staff firings! Library closings! She fought them all. But her chief job these days is to reconstitute herself. (*That you might rise and fight again,* Lee would say—one of her favorite quotes being from some old warrior who is said to have said, as he lay a-drip on a field, *I'll but lie and bleed awhile. Then I will rise and fight again!*) And, well, the painting has been a help with that—especially on bad days it's been a help. Maybe just because it's something Hattie did growing up—her childhood associations tied to her muscle motions—who knows. Anyhow, it's gotten her up out of the voracious depths of Joe's reclin-o-matic—her official mourning chair—starting with the slow making of ink in her father's old inkwell. That inkwell being a mini-doorstop of a thing, into which she pours a bit of water, and above which she circles her wrist, ink stick in hand. Circling and circling. The best ink being made *wú wéi*—by acquainting the stick with the water, never pressing. Dissolving the fine particles of lampblack one by one, practically. Who needs meditation? By the time she's ready to dip her *máobǐ* in the dark ink, Hattie's full, not so much of Western-style contentment as of detachment—what the old Chinese scholars used to seek. *Dá guān*— a feeling that one has risen above life, seen through it. Attained a monklike lightness by sitting the proper way—back straight—and by holding her goat-hair *máobǐ,* likewise, not at an angle like a pen, but straight up, like a lightning rod. She pauses, poised. And then—the judicious pressure, the traveling lightness, the slowing, pressing lift that produces a segment of bamboo. The segments narrow through the middle of the stalk, then grow wider and darker again; each stroke *shēng yì,* as her father used to say—a living idea.

Bamboo: the plant that, as every Chinese knows, bends but does not break.

It's absorbing. Still she does listen, a little, for her neighbors as she paints. Finding, as she does, that if she opens a window in the right wind, she can sometimes hear chopping and washing. Frying, pounding—a lot of pounding. Meaning spices, probably. Who knows what Cambodians eat, or with what. Do they use their hands, like Indians? Hattie's delighted to hear the noises in any case, if only because of what it says about her hearing. Studies say the hairs of a young inner ear can detect motion the breadth of a hydrogen atom. Well, hers are nothing like that. What with the loss of some of her higher frequencies, in fact, she's finding even mouse squeaks sounding different these days—more sonorous, as if their little mouse chests have been getting bigger.

Thanks to the inevitable sad stiffening of your basilar membrane, Lee would say.

Something she learned from Hattie, actually, who used to measure the highest frequencies her kids could hear and chart them, showing how they lowered every year.

But Hattie's neighbors. She's delighted to be able to hear them and delighted, too, that she can glimpse a portion of their doings, it turns out, from various windows as she crosses the room to wash out her brushes. Not spying, exactly.

Hattie nose full of beeswax.

She does try not to spy. Trained in observation as she's been, though, she can't help but notice how in the mornings there's only the outside of the trailer to see: that black plastic crate; that beat-up front paneling; those small metal windows with their oversized louvers; and that one good-sized picture window, mullioned tic-tac-toe style. In the afternoons, though, she can see both inside and out by the low west sun. Nothing too much through the ruffle-curtained bedroom windows, but the picture window affords a fine view, and by night the living room lights up clear enough that she's begun keeping her spare distance glasses on the windowsill. She has, nota bene, stopped short of parking her binoculars there, too; she does have some pride.

And yet somehow she soon knows that right around four the girl is almost always out front, swatting flies. She sits sideways on the milk crate, keeping the light out of her eyes—which position puts her body half in shadow, half in light, as she works her glinting knife or gray mortar and pestle. There's a colander beside her, usually, and a bunch of plastic bowls—green and yellow and fish-belly white. Assorted dish towels, too, for the heaps of peels. All of which helps perk up the otherwise bleak scene, like her shocking-pink jacket, which she generally leaves open.

Today, though, it's zipped shut like Hattie's fleece—Hattie having moved her painting table onto the back porch for fun, only to find some winter teeth left in the early-spring air. She's had to warm up her red hands several times—tucking them into a spot under her breasts, right in the fold there, as she likes to do. It's a private pleasure. For though she is mostly an old lady with an old lady's epithelial cells, that part of her body, if she may boast, is still soft and new. Of course, if she had gone out running in her underwear the way the girls do these days, well, who knows. But never mind. The girl's jacket is zipped up, is the thing, half on account of the cold, and half because the baby is with her, and zipped up in it. Hattie watches the bouncing going on in the girl's lap—a live pink jiggling—the baby poking its head out every now and then so that its face is right in front of the girl's. It pats her face and pulls her hair; that's when it doesn't look to be trying to eat her. And has she ducked into her jacket now, too? All Hattie can see is squirming—the hood flapping up and down and the two armless sleeves flying around like a scarecrow's. How loud the girl and baby squeal! Hattie couldn't block them out if she wanted to.

But here comes Chhung, now, opening the door. He looms in the doorway over them and, just like that, the squealing lets up. The girl's head pops out from the neck of her jacket; her hands pop out from the sleeves. The torso does keep on heaving, but now with a loud, frustrated wail as the girl leans awkwardly forward to pick up a carrot. She peels away with something half kitchen knife, half machete—an enormous, curved blade that glows in the late-day sun like something just forged for a mountain king.

Chhung closes the door shut behind him.

A brown truck rumbles up the road. Never mind that it's mud season, with vehicles stuck all over town, this thing heads unhesitatingly down the mire of the Chhungs' drive. There's a ratcheting up of the hand brake; then a loud *bong* as a deliveryman appears. He's dressed all in brown, to go with his truck. The girl jabs her bright knife into the ground, jumps up from the crate, and shouts; she's bundling up her peels, stacking up her bowls, unzipping her jacket so the baby can see—the baby holding close but leaning out, too, and affording Hattie, as it does, a good glimpse of its thick black hair (something she would probably never have noticed, had she never come to the States and found the babies bald as melons). A woman appears briefly in the door—younger than Chhung, by the looks of her; or maybe she just dyes her hair, which is soot-black, like the girl's and baby's. Anyway, she's tiny and lithe. And there's Chhung, and the boy Chhung mentioned—a hair-dyer for sure, with a low, blond ponytail. He runs to help the deliveryman wheel a box down the truck ramp. A gargantuan box, this is—so big the men have to unpack it outside the trailer. They strew around an ungodly amount of Styrofoam as they do, the enormous chunks multiplying like the calves of an iceberg; their lively white bobs in the brown of the caked-mud sea. And what's this screened thing emerging from it all like a weird rectangular sea monster? A TV, Hattie would say, except that this is so much bigger than any TV she's ever seen. If there were another one like it, the town would have to build a bar to put it in, for ball games. It is hard to imagine the thing fitting into the Chhungs' living room.

And sure enough, when a little later Hattie sees—cannot help but see—one part of the screen shining through the window, it does look to take up the better part of a wall. She hesitates, but finally goes to fetch her binoculars from inside. Is that a videotape they're watching? Some kind of MTV? Asian guys with cars, anyway, Asian girls with long hair. A perpetual wind. Back out on the chilly porch, Hattie adjusts her focus wheel and makes out an abandoned girl, heartbreak, rain. Then a cell phone call; a change in the weather; and off the girl goes on the boy's motorcycle, her arms around his waist. Just like in real life. They head into a neon sunset, leaving the city for something very like a prairie. Hattie is half expecting to behold, in the background, not a water buffalo, but a buffalo buffalo, when the dogs start to bark—Reveille and Annie with five-alarm excitement, but judicious old Cato more alarming than alarmed. He barks twice, gives Hattie a look through the screen door, then barks twice more. An incremental approach. Hattie nods a quick thanks. She has only just stashed the binoculars away under her seat cushion when Judy Tell-All appears.

"You painting?" Judy Tell-All is a large woman with blunt bangs. "You never told me you painted."

Hattie shrugs and sniffs. Judy's wearing a musky scent Lee would have called *Eau de Pheromone.*

"Those bones?"

"Bamboo," says Hattie.

"I thought you might be doing the lake."

"Well, I'm not."

"Because most people do do the lake," observes Judy, batting her stiff lashes, "when they're looking straight at it. That some kind of Chinese brush?"

Hattie takes her time answering.

"And how can you paint with both your glasses up? I can see your driving glasses, but don't you need your readers?"

Hattie sighs—trying to compensate for the lump under her *pī-pī,* though it's like trying to walk with one high heel—an awkward business. Judy, dammit, is about to catch her out.

But Judy, luckily, is too full up with news to catch anything. Because guess who's in town—the middle son great professor! she blurts. Expelling the rest like something under pressure: Here for a spell and retired, it seems—as a body might expect a sixty-seven-year-old to be, if you didn't know the Hatches. But, well, everyone does know the Hatches, never mind that they moved away some ten years ago now, right after the real Dr. Hatch died. And never mind that they sold off that great old Adirondack lodge of theirs in the process, either, with that fireplace that looked to have been practice for Fort Knox. (And to city folk, get that!—city folk who took down everything but the fireplace!) Still, seeing as how the Hatches go back to the Revolution—seeing as how they're as much of a local feature as the town green, practically—people talk about them just the same. How the real Dr. Hatch died at a lab bench at ninety-nine, and how Carter's older brother Anderson's still going strong. Starting up a start-up, in fact, in his seventies. People talk and hear less about little Reedie, for some reason—always have. But Carter, now—Carter! No one but no one would have expected the middle son to up and retire.

Yet such be the mystery and miracle of human change, as Lee would say. He's hanging out for the first time in his life, apparently— and having a crisis as a result—but then, aren't we all, says Judy with feeling. What's more, he knows that Hattie is here—Judy having dropped in with a loaf of date nut bread and told him. Told him that Joe died a few years ago, too—lung cancer, never smoked, and so on. Gave him the whole scoop.

"Though I didn't have to," she says. "You know why?"

Hattie swishes a brush in some water.

"Because he already knew," she says. "He knew it all— everything! And do you know why he knew?"

The Turners told him?

"Because he was interested, that's why. Because he was driven to know! Consciously or unconsciously." Judy lifts her painted brows.

Hattie blots her brush.

"Not that he would ever say so. He's like his father that way—a clam of a man. Keeps his cards close to his chest."

"Like any card-playing clam."

"Exactly. Just like his father!" Judy bats her stiff lashes once more.

And of course, Hattie knows she's being baited. Can she just let people make of others what they will, though? Eyes on the far-off lake, she says, "He is not like his father."

"Is that so." Judy's eyebrows are painted kind of a fox red; they look like a bison's brow from a Neolithic cave painting. "Well, I had an inkling you might want to know that he's here, and I can see I was right."

You are not right, Hattie starts to say, but then—realizing that this is match point—already—she stops, puts her brush down, and laughs. How did she, Hattie Kong, come to be a woman worked over by Judy Tell-All?

Judy frowns.

"Is Hattie coming to the cell tower meeting?" she asks, after a moment.

"Probably."

Save her a seat?

Hattie shrugs—all right.

As for whether she can guess who's coming, though, Hattie just laughs again and declines to respond—to that, or to Judy's *And Ginny has news!—she and Everett have news!,* either. Instead Hattie focuses, a few minutes later, on the happy sound of Judy leaving. Can gravel crunch happily? It does seem so to her.

Judy nose full of beeswax.

She liberates her binoculars. Then it's down with her reading glasses and up with her jacket zipper—the metal a cold, hard press on her chin. A returning bittern flies on by; and there's the one-note warble of the winter-hardy hermit thrush. If she sits long enough she could just hear a veery thrush and a wood thrush, too—kind of a trifecta. It's happened before. And so Hattie listens as she paints, shutting her wandering thoughts out. *Carter. Everett. Carter. Carter.* Her stalks are rising fat but dry and light today—a bold shadowy vertical up the left side of her sheet. Not that she's chosen that, exactly. It's more *bǐyì,* the will of the brush. But there they go, in any case, with her hand's blind help, one segment after another. They grow clear up through the top of the page.

Town Hall was not made to hold so many. The lights of the suspended ceiling blink as if with surprise at the crowd, and up front, the cell tower people are blinking hard, too. They came during mud season on purpose, Hattie heard. Scheduled a meeting before the summerlings were back, so as to keep the turnout down. But look now how people keep coming—wave after wave of them, like something the lake's washing up. Folding chairs are getting set up along the back and sides of the room, and there are extra chairs all along the front, too. Every last one of them squeaking as it's opened until the metal chairs run short. Then it's clatter you hear; those old wooden chairs do clatter. And there's the family that stands to make out like bandits, right in the first row. The Wrights. A moat of empty chairs all around them, though cozied up with them does sit—can that be right?—Hattie's walking group friend, Ginny. Who does not actually walk with the walking group—who actually only meets them later for coffee or lunch at the Come 'n' Eat—but never mind. Hattie feels for her distance glasses even as Judy Tell-All waves her over. And sure enough: There indeed sits a certain pink turtleneck with bleached-blond do—that artichoke cut always reminding Hattie of how Ginny's hairdresser does dog grooming, too. A versatile type. Maybe Ginny's sitting up front on account of her hip? How uncomfortable the Wrights might feel, in any case, were it not for her. How marooned on their very own folding-chair island. Instead, Ginny leans in, saving them. They nod and joke and guffaw—Jim Wright proving himself a wit, it seems. A born funnyman.

"When is a snake not a snake?" asks Judy as Hattie sits down.

"When she has God on her side?" guesses Hattie.

Judy smiles, but normally good-natured Greta, whom Judy has somehow managed to ensnare, too, is frowning. Her still-dark eyebrows all but meet over her straight, long nose.

"Though, well, why shouldn't Ginny sit with her relatives?" Judy goes on. "Maybe she just feels sorry for them. And they are her third cousins twice removed, after all." She winks.

"She wants something," says Greta. Greta could almost be a Shaker, dressed as she is today in a handmade blouse and skirt, except that she brandishes the end of her braid like a police baton. "Ginny wants something."

"Do you think?" says Judy, innocently.

Hattie gives Judy a look.

"Well, hmm, let me think," continues Judy. She's wearing a floral print, but the flowers are all black and gray, as if grown without chlorophyll. "How about that new hip she needs?"

"But of course!" Greta's gray eyes flash. "Her hip!"

"Do you really think they'd pay for a new hip?" Hattie waves at some people, wishing she could remember their names—*Hattie gone batty!*—then realizes, disconcertingly, that she does.

"Maybe not, but they could help with health care, right?" says Judy. "Being family? They could put her on the feed store payroll and get her the employee rate."

Hattie stops waving.

"That's illegal!" says Greta.

"How creative," says Hattie, after a moment. "If it's true."

Judy waves her hand. "You'd be creative, too, if you were in her shoes," she observes. "If you had a hip like hers and were leaving Everett on top of it. You'd be creative, too."

Leaving Everett?

"Giving him the heave-ho," confirms Judy as Greta gasps. "Dumping him flat. Get that!" Judy folds her program up into a fan; and indeed, what with the crowd, the room is getting warm. She looks at Hattie as she crimps the bottom into a handle. "I told you Ginny had news."

Hattie makes her own fan then, thinking. For what Everett put into Ginny's dad's place!—everyone knew it. Obliging man that he was. And that farm being the oldest of the family farms and worth it, in his view. As in the view of many: Even Hattie the newcomer's heard how the farm broke up when Rex died, and how something in the town broke, too. And now, for all of Everett's effort, this fine reward. Ginny leaving Everett!—and without a word to the walking group, either. The fluorescent lights blink. Hattie uncrosses her legs so she can recross them the other way—these old wooden chairs being designed, it does seem, to put you in touch with your god-given overhang.

Judy fans and smiles.

Just about everyone is here. Not only the rest of the walking group—Grace and Beth and Candy—but other townsfolk, in addition. Jill Jenkins and Jed Jamison, among others, and a lot of the farmers from the far side of the lake, too. Old-timers Ginny and Rex would have probably known forever, but that Hattie knows mostly by the way they talk: quick and with a lot of *oors* and *ahhns*, as if, spending as much time around it as they do, they've picked up the sounds of their machinery. They're the real thing, people say, not like the hippie farmers from the commune—people like Belle Tollman with the parrot and her husband, Paxton, with the dreadlocks. Who are keeping a low profile today, though what with their torn clothes and low-concept hair control, they'll bother some people anyway. Ginny, for instance—they'll bother Ginny. Hattie herself is more bothered that she didn't think to bring along her new neighbors—Chhung and family—even as she thinks, Those eyes. That jitter. That knife. And despite her best efforts not to think about it: Pol Pot. The killing fields.

It's the world come to town, Joe would have said. *As it will, you know, as it will.*

"It's not that Everett's not Christian," Judy is saying now. "He's just not the right kind."

"Eastern Orthodox, you mean?" says Greta. "Because of his father?"

Judy nods, readjusting her waistband. "Meaning *baptized at birth.*"

As opposed to born again, apparently he promised to recommit years ago but never did, etc. So that finally the Lord told her, Enough! That he was like the rock that had to be rolled away before Lazarus could even do something about his bandages! An obstacle!

Not exactly the story as Hattie knew it, but never mind.

"And how exactly did the Lord tell her?" inquires Greta.

"E-mail?" guesses Hattie.

Judy just fans, her shirt sleeve falling back from her henna-tattooed arm.

As for who's going to bring in her firewood when Ginny can barely walk:

"That's why the Lord's helping get her hip done. So she can bring in her own wood," says Judy. "Hey, look, there's Lukens!"

Hattie throws her gaze left, using her peripheral vision. It's the way she used to teach kids how to spot shooting stars—their rod photoreceptors picking up the low light, their retinal ganglion cells, the movement. And sure enough, there he is, a tall man with something of the look of a cell tower himself. Lukens, the big-deal retired judge, scratching his chin in the shadows.

"And look over there!" whispers Judy again.

For here comes huge Everett, his cherub cheeks rising incongruously from a camouflage shirt. And right behind him—more hidden by the camouflage than its wearer—the middle son great professor. Hattie lowers her distance glasses.

Carter, denuded!

She drops her fan.

He looks a little as though someone has pulled a white hula skirt over his head, only to have it get stuck around his ears. Which in one way is no surprise—Carter's father, too, had a notable egg. And how shocked should Hattie be to behold Carter beardless in addition, when she did glimpse the shave ten years ago, at Dr. Hatch's burial? She must not have filed that face away, though, because Carter's features seem not only repositioned—as if they have slid south in some Great Facial Drift—but caricatured: Everything is more plainly itself. The fine nose and high cheekbones of his youth are like line drawings redone in marker; his mother's egret neck has gone a bit pelican. As for his father's eyes—those preternaturally blue eyes—can they really be even brighter than they were? Maybe they just seem so, set off as they are by a now predominantly pink face, as well as by what appear to be shadows—hollows—around his eyes. Which could just be the lighting. But then again, maybe not. For Hattie knows this man well, or did once; and this is a studiously unhaunted Carter who strolls down the side aisle in a chamois shirt and jeans, his limbs loose. Carter holding on to himself as if on to a kite.

Carter, looking a bit like her poor denuded, post-chemo Joe.

He shoots a smile and a wink at her, then goes to stand, in provocative fashion, on the other side of the room. Talking with such apparent sincerity to this one and that, even as he affords a fine view of his profile, that she can't help but laugh a little. For she remembers this game, of course—the neural pathway is still there. And—as he no doubt intends—it renders her, for a moment, seventeen again. She is not usually aware of her age, any more than she is aware of the number of steps she walks in a day, or the number of times she pulls down her glasses. But now, somehow, she feels it—how she's been living shoulder-to-shoulder with time. It is not so much on account of her white hair, or two sets of glasses that she feels it—*Hattie six eyes*— shocks to Carter that those things must be. It is not even the fact that when the word *energy* occurs to her now, it is mostly in reference to herself, rather than to a reaction or an equation. No, it's the mark of experience she feels most keenly—how much she would like never to have seen Joe yellow with bile once his liver failed. How much she would like never to have watched him itch himself until he bled every- where. How much she would like never to have heard Lee rant the way she did, toward the end—her gumption still there but come heart- breakingly unhitched. Time's marched Hattie hard. And as for Carter, Time's reminder—Carter who brought so much *before* and *after,* in his day—is this Carter even Carter? Isn't Carter the man who changed others more than he himself changed? A catalyst. A man she would have thought outside time, if anyone was. And yet Carter was still Carter in being unable to simply say hello. Anyone but Carter would have simply said hello.

(Next to her, Judy watches and fans.)

Carter, though, always did disdain convention; he was like Hat- tie's parents that way. *You should try a new hat every day,* he used to say. *Think out of the box. It's the way every great thing gets made.*

Modest as they were, the Hatches did focus on achieving things about which to be modest.

But, well, who cares now? Who was modest, and about what— Hattie lifts her chin. All that is decades behind her now. Detaching herself, rising above herself—*dá guān*—Hattie turns her attention to the meeting, which is focused on questions like what can be seen from whose kitchen, and which has a greater effect on property values—one's view sitting down or one's view standing up. Greta tugs on her arm.

"This is so dysfunctional. You have to say something," she whis- pers. "You do."

Hattie demurs. Still, Greta keeps insisting—"You do, Hattie, you do"—until finally Hattie half raises her hand, only to be immediately called upon. And there she is suddenly, towering over a sea of heads. Blinking. Feeling the town gaze. She has not done this in a long time. But then she senses Carter's gaze and remembers: She has done it, though. Of course. Did it all the time, in fact, at the lab.

"It's hard not to notice the convenience of cell phones," she says, her voice clear and strong; she can feel the vibration in her thoracic cavity. "But ought there not be one place on earth that cell phones can't reach?"

And back down she sits; probably she should have said more. Opined the way the men do, as if they own the air. Though as it is— what a roar of applause. People are hooting and stomping; Greta is whispering Thank you and You see? And look how Neddy Needham is standing up in Hattie's place, inspired. He's a high-tech person—a puffball of a guy, only starting to gray, whose particular kind of soft- ware, people used to say, could never be done in India. But now he has time to drive up if he wants; and so here he stands with his mag- pie hair and high-diopter glasses. Quietly pointing out that from a radiation safety point of view, there is only one usable corner of the property, and that a cell tower at that site isn't even going to provide good coverage.

"There are going to be holes in the service," he says. "It's going to be Swiss cheese. Rescue is not going to be able to count on it; no one is going to be able to count on it. It is going to be a joke."

The lawyer for the cell tower company lowers the pitch of his voice. "Are you implying that this town is being misled?"

"This is not the best site in the area, sir," answers Neddy. "This is the site you think you can buy."

Applause.

"I beg your pardon," barks the lawyer, but Neddy just pushes his glasses up his nose.

"The question, it seems to me, is, Whose town is this?" He looks first at the cell tower reps, and then all around, at the audience, too. "Whose town is this?" It's a surprising show of rhetorical flair for a body people have always thought smart but shy; and even he blinks as he talks, as if surprised at himself. He takes his glasses off like a lawyer on TV but then, as if realizing he can't see without them, puts them back on. "It's not such an easy question to answer, is it? And yet if I may say so, sir, this much I know: Not yours. No, sir. Not yours."

This brings the most thunderous applause yet, replete with stamping and hooting. Hattie claps as loud as anyone, though is this town hers, either? She does wonder. *What now? What now?* There's no vote today, this meeting being strictly informational; the only leverage the town has is in zoning. Happily, though, the cell tower company will be needing a zoning permit; and even with Jim Wright head of the zoning board, well, there's only one conclusion it can really reach now. Because things are just clear. What's more, it's going to be free coffee for Neddy at the Come 'n' Eat as long as he lives in Riverlake, while the Wrights will be dining during off-peak hours.

Ginny, maybe, too, as she seems to realize. She sits a minute, contemplating the magic stretch material of her wrinkle-free jeans.

David beats Goliath! Down with the corporation! Judge Lukens stops to shake the hero's hand, whereupon people shed their discretion like a fast-molting snake. They form a ring around the pair; they gawk and crow with glee. The town celebrities! The judge and Neddy leave the room, nodding. Tall and short but seeing eye to eye, it seems—unlike the cell tower people, who clump up by the whiteboard, frowning. Though they brought every color dry marker, they somehow only used the blue. And look how, not far from them, Ginny stands in her walker now, waiting to leave. Everett makes his way to her, but she snaps her compartment lid shut as if she doesn't know who he is; and when he puts his hand out beseechingly, she slaps him flat in the face. People look up. But then off she rolls as if nothing's the matter, and people obligingly look away. A private matter, they're thinking, a spat, even as Everett stands there, stunned— huge and dressed in camouflage yet less prepared for combat than pink-clad Ginny, who holds her head high. Captain Ginny, some call her, though others call her the Power and the Glory, as in *For mine is the Power and the Glory.* Poor Everett! Hattie tries to catch his eye, but he's turned his back and doesn't see her. And so it is that she finds herself moving down the aisle, preoccupied, almost failing to realize it when someone gives her elbow a squeeze.

E-mail! There's no one to blame but herself, that when the town got DSL, Hattie did, too—ushering in the future, she did think then. Instead, though, it's been the past—the past, the past, the past. She half expects to be hearing from the dead direct, pretty soon—*Joe! Lee! I've been thinking about you!*—though let her say right now:

When that particular advance is upon humankind, she is not going to sign up for service.

E-mail is trouble enough.

For example, though a lot of her Chinese relatives have M.A.'s and M.B.A.'s and Ph.D.'s from the States—and though a lot of them have lived in the West, even live in White Plains and Quincy and Vancouver still—all the same, they e-mail on account of Hattie's parents. Or, more accurately, on account of Hattie's parents' remains, which they want to see moved from Iowa to Qufu. Of course, the Chinese have always sent bones home, having been brought up from birth to recite *Shù gāo qiān zhàng, luò yè gūi gēn:* Fallen leaves return to their roots. But to want to do it now! In the twenty-first century! Hattie's flabbergasted.

Yet they do. *The Kong family forest,* they write. *Ancestors. Luck. Tradition.* It's the kind of hogwash her parents turned their back on once, and that she did, too. And so it is she writes: *Over my dead body.*

But still her relatives keep at it. *Dear Auntie. Dear Auntie.* Never mind that she's only head of the family because her younger brothers have both died; never mind that her relatives have no real reason to listen to anyone at all, really. Still, they storm her—having gotten up at least a mild conspiracy among themselves, it does seem. For how else to explain it that everyone writes in English, when most of them, she knows, have character keyboards? How do they know, as they seem to, that her computer isn't set up for Unicode?

She replies, *This is the twenty-first century, excuse me.*

She replies, *I am a scientist of sorts, please recall. A retired scientist, but still a scientist.*

She replies, *This is hogwash, don't you see? Hogwash!*

To no avail.

Some of her correspondents are more superstitious than others. Some of them go to fortune-tellers, that's to say, while others just burn a little incense every now and then. Wear a Buddha or a Guanyin, if they're sick, or change the entrance to their house. There's as great a range among them as among churchgoers. But whatever their stripe, they write. This, for example, from the ringleader, Hattie's niece Tina, in Hong Kong:

Dear Auntie Hattie,

Internet says your spring is late this year because the ground hog saw its shadow and went back into its hole. Is that true?

Even with global warming? We think that is very strange. Americans are so superstitious!

Hong Kong now is start typhoon season, but that is not why we write to you. After all you can say we are used to the rain! We write to you because of our daughter Bobby. You remember her, number one. Went to Andover then MIT then Harvard Business School, got a nice job on Wall Street. But now all of a sudden, she quit that job to live with a drummer, and on top of it try to sell the apartment we give to her. Very nice place, upper East Side. Have a doorman, everything. But she do not care. All she think about is drum something. We worry. She is our number one daughter, how can this happen to our family? We analyze, in particular Johnson. Johnson is quite well known for his analysis. But in the end, there is only one thing we can guess. Only we can guess that the graves of Grandpa and Grandma are not auspicious. The story we always hear is how Grandpa and Grandma were not buried in Qufu, as they like to be . . .

Hogwash.

Instead because they died in Taiwan First Uncle bury them in Taiwan. And then when he himself leaving Taiwan, no one left to sweep the grave, he have to move them somewhere again. Mainland still closed, cannot bury them there. Impossible. So he say okay, how about Iowa? Never mind that Grandpa never visited Iowa once in his life. First Uncle said, at least they are go to Iowa together. And of course, when the bone picker open the graves, look like the bones are dry. That is true. So First Uncle say, you see? If the fengshui is no good the bones are not dry, even many years later. He say, I pick good place the first time, now I pick another good place. He say Iowa is good. Probably you already know this story, which is the story my father tell me. I just tell you in case you heard something else, over there in United States. My father say you are sent there to live as a girl, is that right? All by yourself, very brave, though my father always say how actually you have no choice, everyone else stuck in China and cannot get out.

But anyway, too bad. Now the Iowa fengshui is not so good as before and our family face difficulty again. We hear there is a shopping center moved in right next to our grandparents, not to say a train line. And that is why our family, our luck not so good. Everything leaking away. Not just our branch, many other cousins say it too. Our situation not even so serious as other cousins. Some of them are losing money—a lot of money. So now we are thinking, how do you feel about if Grandpa and Grandma should be moved to Qufu, which is their real home? We believe they are lonely in Iowa. No one can sweep grave there. Of course we understand there is some question whether Grandma can stay in the graveyard in Qufu too. But we feel confident someone can arrange it, really you just have to find out who you should pay. After all Grandpa is still have the name Kong, and who can even see Grandma is a foreign devil anymore? Now she is not even bones, only some ashes or pieces, something like that. No one can see anything. And by the way I do not think Confucius ever said a big nose cannot be buried in the family graveyard. He never even thought about that case. Probably he does not even know nose can get so big. Everyone say American people do not take care of their parents' grave, just let the weeds grow all over. Their thinking is different. You know better than anyone the kind of clothes they wear. They think that is normal. Anyway, we have been talking to some other family member, everyone agrees. Our family, something is wrong. Fallen leaves should return to their roots right? We should do something. But what do you think?

What does Hattie think? *If you are near red dye, you will turn red; if you are near black, you will turn black.* Who knows but that if she had grown up in Hong Kong, she'd be a superstitious nut, too. As it is, though, she just writes that she's sorry, but moving the graves is not an option. Not adding, as she would like to, *The dead are dead and can do nothing for us! We're on our lonesome own!* but pecking out the letters with one hand while she plays tug-of-war with Annie. Hoping Annie will not pee in her excitement, though of course, she does—a nice long fingerlake of a puddle in which she promptly steps. Hattie sighs.

SEND.

Good riddance!

Three days later, though, another e-mail arrives, and then another, both about money. *What is it about the Chinese and money?* Joe used to ask.

And then this one, also concerning the graves:

Dear Aunt Hattie,

You remember Vivian, what kind of girl she is. Like an angel, we always say she have wings, if you had special glasses you can see them. And beautiful besides, that is why she got such a good job in the karaoke bar even though she does not know how to sing. But you know what those local officials are—what kind of people. One of them ask her if she will take a bath with him. Of course, she say no, but he try again. So finally one day she take a fruit knife out of her bag and stab him. Not too bad, just in the leg, and she even put the bandaid on for him. Nice and neat. But now she lost her job.

Hattie sighs and moves to her painting table. And yet another e-mail, the next day:

I write concerning my son. My son is very good at drive car. He practice every day, also read some books. And he buy a car with some friends, all of them go in together, that car is some special kind car, have so-called four-wheel drive. Everyone say that car can go all over, that car can go everywhere. But my son took that car to Tibet in the mountains and got stuck there. Is that not some bad luck? He drove down someplace, in some kind of valley, then cannot drive back up. Even he ask ten men to help him, they cannot push out. So now his friends very mad, want him to pay them back.

Hattie shakes her head and writes:

I'm so sorry to hear of your troubles, but do you really think moving the graves will help you?

Outside, the sun is out later than it was even a week ago and setting farther in the west. As she walks her dogs, Hattie sees how it catches many more trees than it did, turning them orange and sepia and rust; the apparent world is broader. And look—down in the swamp—pussy willows! Showing their soft hermaphroditic catkins. Hattie feels them—furry but cold. She'll be back later in the day to pick some for a vase.

Riverlake's north. Making winter the basic fact here—wool and hot drinks, a fire in the evening, and, of course, ice. Even with global warming, the lake stays frozen as a rock until April; it's easy to see why people called it Brick Lake before it up and moved. But one day every year, there are cracks which one night fail to refreeze, turning instead into rivulets that turn into streams that turn into rivers, multiplying and crisscrossing until the whole white plain of the lake has come live. Giant shards of ice get thrown up onto the shore then—the sun patiently working its energy down into the surface of other things, too, until you start to feel a closeness in the air. A collecting. One afternoon you may even find your dashboard warm, especially if it's black, like Hattie's.

Hattie, though, is still keeping to her fleece—the state fabric—like most people; pretty much everyone's got a vest on, at least. Only Carter Hatch would be traipsing around with no hat and no hair, in just jeans and a flannel shirt, top buttons undone as if to show off his pelican neck. The shirt hangs away from him—no paunch—men his age tending to come in two models as they do, padded and not, Hattie's noticed, depending on their metabolisms.

Carter, dropping in like Judy Tell-All.

Hattie overfills her coffee mug and has to sponge up the mess.

Is he still running? She doesn't know, but somehow wouldn't be surprised to hear he's still taking home trophies in the occasional senior trot. That seven-league gait, after all, and that drive—that Carter Hatch drive. What with her house up on a knoll, she's watched people make their way up to her door all sorts of ways—some tackling the driveway with a little umph, some with a marked trudge. No one has ever taken it the way Carter is now, as if simply opposed to gravity. He's carrying one of those dark green book bags from the days before backpacks—his father's, if she had to guess—toting the rubberized thing so naturally that he looks not so much like Carter carrying his father's sack as—eerily—Dr. Hatch carrying his own. Of course, in one way, it's a surprise, looking back, that Carter didn't go into marine biology or some such—one of those fields where you battle cold climes and come home with a distant look in your eye. But in another way, where would he have made his expeditions but to the lab? At least as an undergrad he looked different in the summer than in the winter—more like his god-given self, ruddy and hale. Later he just stayed his winter self year round, too busy examining how people see to actually go out and see much himself; she never did behold him without wanting to offer him a cough drop.

Now, though, a thump on her front porch, and the start of a rap, but ha!—she's opened the door before he's knocked; and seeing as how she has yet to put up her front-door screen, there's nothing but her in the doorway. Surprise.

"Miss Confucius."

Dr. Hatch!

But no—it's Carter, who, if she hadn't surprised him with the door, or startled a bit herself, might well have relaxed enough to give her a kiss or a hug. Instead, he stands there with his book bag between his feet and his hands in his pockets, gazing at her as if he's about to have his mug snapped for an I.D. card.

"It's good to see you," he says.

"Well, and I've had worse surprises." She can still feel how she was about to step through the doorway and give him a hug back—that potential energy. But now she straightens up, too, the dogs gathering around Carter, who—can this be right?—appears to be wearing the very same hiking boots he used to wear back in the lab. That can't be, she knows. But these do seem an exact replica of his old Swiss boots, with their zigzag red laces and first-class padded collar; they even have the same lovingly beat-up look.

"Go on," she tells the dogs. "Out."

Eliciting a funny look from Cato, especially—this isn't their pattern. With a little more prodding, though, they do finally go sprinting down the hill and across the road to the sunny field, Reveille leading but Annie almost keeping up, and Old Cato, too; his hips must not be too bad today. As for whether Reveille will keep clear of that porcupine in the tree at the edge of the field, well, Hattie can only hope—Joe having been the expert quill-puller in the family. She never has gotten as plier-proficient.

"You've become a dog lover."

"Fit company for the old dog I've become myself," she says.

He laughs his old laugh, with a drop of his jaw—as if he just has to make a show of his hearty pink tongue and scattered gold crowns. "That's my Hattie, ever sweet and obliging. You know what I remember most about Chinese?"

When he arches his brows, they make little familiar tents, too—*pup tents* she always thought them. An expression Carter himself taught her, although not for his eyebrows, of course, but for the real pup tents he and his brothers used to pitch in their backyard.

"*Bú duì!*—wrong! You loved to say that. You never said, 'Try that one more time' or 'You need to purse your lips' or 'Try touching your tongue to your palate.' You just said, *Bú duì!*"

"Well," she says, collecting herself a little—Carter did always make you have to collect yourself. "I suppose no one else ever told you you were wrong, did they?"

"*Bú duì.*" His crow's-feet are more pronounced than his frown lines, she's happy to see; and his plaid shirt is missing its second button—so that's why the two unbuttoned buttons. White thread ends sprout from the flannel like the hairs that could be sprouting from his ears but, she sees, are not. "Many people told me. You just wanted to tell me yourself. Though here's what I've been meaning to ask you all these years—why you never said it to Reedie. He told me that to him you always said, *Hěn bàng!*"

"Well, you know." She gestures vaguely. "Reedie."

"Did you hear he got killed in a car accident last November?"

"Reedie?" She freezes.

"Driving drunk. Hit a beech tree. We tried to reach you, but no one knew where you were."

"Oh my god."

"I'm so sorry to be the one to tell you."

And indeed, where was Judy Tell-All to warn her? Shouldn't Judy Tell-All have warned her?

"No," she says. "No."

"I'm sorry," he says again. "And here you were right in Riverlake. As we would no doubt have heard had Reedie's ashes been buried here and not elsewhere."

"No."

"His wife said it was his unequivocal choice to be buried with her family." He looks off. "Dear Sheila. I heard about Joe, by the way." He stops. "The Turners told me."

She waves a hand.

"I'm so sorry. Two years ago?"

She nods.

"So young."

She nods again, or thinks she does. If there is any point in bringing up Lee, she can't anyway.

"Joe was a good man." Carter hesitates in his Carter-like way—not looking away, as other people do, but fixing on her again instead. "It was a shock, as I hardly need tell you."

Reedie's death, he must mean. Anyway, she cries and cries.

Really she should ask him in, but Carter has already settled himself, leaning back against the porch railing as if against his desk. His elbows are bent, and his shoulders raised up, one hand sitting to either side of his hips. Much the way that a dog or cat sits, according to a little neural sub-routine, he arranges himself the way he always has; he's ready to talk. And even as her chest heaves, she finds that her arms and legs have answered his on their own, crossing themselves and leaning sideways against the doorframe as if in his office doorway. It's the force of habit—these patterns embedded, no doubt, in their very Purkinje cells. A disconcerting idea, in a way. And yet what a comfort it is right now—knowing the same dance, and knowing that they know it. It's a comfort.

"I used to tell him it wasn't worth trying to catch up to me," he begins. "That there was nothing to catch up to. But he had that idea, and it made him feel pressured."

She nods, numb.

"He didn't care about Anderson. I guess Anderson was too far out of his league."

"Anderson he worshipped."

"Precisely. But me." He laughs a short laugh, pressing his long fingers into the railing, which flakes a bit; it needs paint. "I guess he thought anyone should be able to catch up to me."

"You really think it was your fault?"—her mouth talking without her.

"No."

"You just wonder"—her shirt sleeve is rough—"if you contributed."

"Yes." Carter's voice still falls like an ax, but there is something new in his gaze—something lanternlike and reflective. "There are few subjects about which one dares generalize these days, but if I may in this instance: The death of a brother does give one pause." He exhales. "And wonder how one contributed, as you put it. He had his own lab at the end, you know. He was doing good work—AIDS research. NIH loved him."

"So I guess he caught up to you, by the end."

"I would have said passed me. But as you know, we see what we see."

"World makers that we are, you mean."

"Yes." Carter hesitates, his eyes on her, then says again, "He always felt pressure"—a backtrack so uncharacteristic that, upset as she is, she can't help but notice. People used to say his train of thought really was like a train—that he made his stops and moved on. She's never known him to wander, as others do, after what he used to call *the wraith of an idea*. Not that it much matters if he does now—since when are the people we admire most like trains anyway?—except that Hattie remembers what people said about his father—*he's slipping*—and how that haunted Carter. *Dr. Hatch is slipping.* Is that why he retired? It is hard to believe that he'd be slipping in any noticeable way at sixty-seven. And yet maybe that was the idea, to get out before anyone noticed—before anyone could say that about him.

"I brought a towel," he announces suddenly. "And a wet suit." He toes his bag, leaving a dimple in it. "A concession to middle age."

"Are you thinking about a swim?" When there could still be ice floes in the water? Now this does make her wonder about his mental competence. He can't be serious.

But he is. "With company, I hope. Do you own a wet suit?"

"Maybe you'd like to come in first?"

A belated invitation, half hospitality, half avoidance: Whether or not Carter is still his old self, she is no longer the Hattie who would dive into any kind of water. Time's made a sensible creature out of her.

Carter gives a Carter Hatch shake of his head, though—with a back and forth so subtle, it could almost be a tic. How used to being read he is—to people divining his thoughts. (The Gnome, people called him in the lab; and later, she heard, the G-nome, though it was Anderson who was working on the genome, not he.)

"I heard you've retired from the saving of our nation's youth," he says suddenly.

Just teasing, she knows, and yet she bristles. "The youth do need our help, Professor."

He smiles. "You've grown testy in your old age, Hattie."

Testy.

"And what about you? What have you grown?" She's trying to tease—trying not to be *testy*.

"Stupid—I've grown stupid." Another smile. "Sweet and slow, as they say."

"Oh, Carter," she says. "You'll never be sweet."

Inviting return fire, she thinks. But he just sinks into himself a moment—his irises as blue as ever, though she can't help but look for the arcus senilis around his corneas, and finds it: that faintly milky edging that midlife will bring, like a sea of memory rimming one's worldview.

"And if I do not own a wet suit?" she goes on, more gently.

"But everyone knows that you do."

"So why did you ask?"

"Bashful, I guess."

To which she smiles in spite of herself—charmed and glad to have been charmed. Glad that he's managed to charm her. "And what if I had a cold? You are impossible."

"Unlike you, Miss Agreeability?"

"Yes."

"*Bú duì*," he says. "*Bú duì, bú duì, bú duì*." He winks. "How's my pronunciation?"

She laughs.

Her wet suit is packed away who knows where. For while she does start swimming early in the year, she doesn't start this early; whatever the neural circuits for sanity, hers are still firing. Bureaus. Baskets. Reedie. Reedie. It's worse than looking for her keys, which she brilliantly keeps on a designated hook, painted red. Reedie. Joe. Lee. Is it not too much, all this death? Reedie. But, ah—there. She changes self-consciously—feeling more naked than she has in many years—trying not to notice the clamminess of her crotch. Middle age! When one is not surprised by one's age, one is surprised by one's youth. This sudden alacrity of her body, for example, as unexpected as it is undignified. She'd have sworn herself past this, but there go her nipples, bobbing up from the soft of her breasts like corks. *My life's companion* Lee used to call her body, back when it was failing her; now Hattie squinches her own *life's companion* into the thick neoprene skin. She feels like an armored sausage as she hunts for the neoprene cap that goes with the suit. Neoprene aficionado that she's become, she even has insulated booties.

The complete walrus look, Lee would say.

"Sorry to be slow." Hattie finally reemerges.

But look: No Carter. No book bag.

Is it not just as well? She traipses over to the side yard and squints out past the Chhungs', toward the lake—sensing, through the dry chafe of the neoprene, the even pat of the sun. The life-giving sun, with which she began her fall, back when she taught. Her house has what's called a distant water view, and it is distant indeed—too far to make out a swimmer even if she had on her distance glasses, which she does not. She does not think of going in for them, though, or for her binoculars, either—having her pride, after all. Or, all right, call it *an emergent characteristic.* Still.

Hattie a tad less batty. She admires some willow trees across the way—their yellow-green flaring against the gray-brown of the other trees. And look at how the birches have woken up, too! Their white trunks spawning a bright mauve haze of new twigs and buds. How empty the house when she goes back in, though, without the dogs— how strangely big, as if it would echo if she were to say anything. Of course, it wouldn't, really; it's a small house. And what would she say anyway? *Behold my insulation—?* How much more likely that she'd start hearing other people's voices—Joe's, for example: *You always were well insulated, Hat. Probably you had to be.*

She works off her cap, then goes back out and calls the dogs.

Come back!

She unzips her suit.

Chhung is putting in a garden. It's back behind the trailer, so you can barely see it from the road, and from the house, Hattie can only make out the north end of the work. But there he is, sure enough, digging away with his son. On weekends in the beginning, but more recently on weekdays, too—a surprise. Shouldn't the boy be in school? And what a big garden they must be putting in—big enough to feed the family and more, if it works. She can't help but wonder if it will, though, given the light level down there; it's pretty dark. If they were anyone else, discouragement would be coming in by the cubic yard. But instead there they are, on their own. People hesitating a little to step forward, maybe—or so Hattie guesses, extrapolating from her own hesitation. Not that she's not sympathetic. She's sympathetic, of course. But she knows, too, from her teaching days how the troubles this family has seen are unlikely to have ended in America. Why would they have moved to Riverlake if they were thriving? And who knows, maybe the Chhungs know something the locals don't, anyway. What can be grown in a spot like that. Maybe they know.

Possessed as they may be of some ancient Cambodian wisdom?

The shovel is so much more substantial than Chhung, it looks to be wielding him. The boy is more equal to his spade. Not that he's so tall—Hattie puts him at maybe five foot six or seven. Still, taller and stockier than Chhung—and stronger, too—he digs easily. With a signature style, even, a certain exaggeration, as if he's not only working, but making a show of his work. Imagining, as workers will—*Imagine!* Joe would say—that he might not appear to be working hard enough. His whole body lifts; his elbow knifes high; his shovel bites hard. Chhung is wearing assorted sports clothes, including green nylon pants and a rust-and-white training jacket, as well as a straw hat with netting draped over it. The boy is wearing city clothes—no straw hat with netting for him. Instead, he wears a backward baseball cap over his ponytail, and to go with it a fat gold chain and earrings. A blue basketball jersey with some shine to it, and jeans so baggy they threaten to fall down. It's a city fashion Hattie never could understand. How do you walk with your crotch at your knees? But never mind. He's a handsome boy, with a chisel to his face and a slash to his brow—a boy who would break hearts, if there were any around to break. For now, he devastates the no-see-ums.

He and Chhung don't stop work often, but when they do, the boy generally jabs his shovel into the dirt the way Chhung does, so that it stands straight up. Every now and then, though, when his father's not looking, he stands it up on its point, steadies it with his palm, then lifts his hand free quick enough that the thing just thuds. Then he looks off. Relaxing the ciliary muscles of his eyes, Hattie guesses, not to say his back—and who could blame him? This is not an easy job, what with the soil so wet, and clay besides. Even uphill from the Chhungs', Hattie's had to lighten her soil, dig in some compost; roots rot on her all the time. Probably she'll put sand in under her garden one day, the way Greta did, for drainage. But how about Chhung? Who's going to tell Chhung how he should really try sand? Someone, she thinks, should tell Chhung.

The girl brings the baby over, and at first it just clings and clings.

When she sits it down in a pile of dirt, though, it begins to play and pretty soon wants to investigate the hole. Chhung yells and swats at himself; the girl tries to distract her charge, which is dressed in a frilly blue blouse and some overlong red pants, one leg of which stays rolled up fine. The other, though, seems bent on showing off its fine bunchy length. *Hecq!* the girl cries, swatting at the flies. *Hecq! Hecq! Hecq!* Clapping her hands, so the baby'll switch direction, which works. Everyone watches, relieved, as the child crawls on one knee and one foot, bottom high in the air, away from the pit.

Then it veers back toward it again.

Chhung throws a shovelful of dirt at the girl's toes, making her back away. He jabs at the ground, comes up with another shovelful, and for a moment seems about to heave that load at the baby. But instead, he stops and looks up at the sky, which is a wash of whitish blue—streaky, as if someone's just squeegeed it, and about as inspiring as a whiteboard, when you come right down to it. Still, Chhung sets his shovel aside, crosses a hump of dirt, and picks the baby up. The baby's crying and arching its back with frustration, but Chhung swings it like a pendulum, its pant legs a-dangle, as he calls up to the trailer. The woman hurries out with a bottle. She's a slip of a thing, in black pants and a white blouse; the blouse has puff sleeves. Her hair is shoulder-length and wavy, her skin darker and smoother than her husband's, and her face a little rounder, with hooped cheekbones like the fairy wings of a child's Halloween costume. A lovely woman, and yet not nearly as lovely in her features as in her movements—in that simple way she makes her way down onto the milk crate, for example, and then down again, watching where she steps. Careful even in her hurry. The earth is packed down at the bottom of the step now; it's not the mud pool it was when Hattie first went calling. Still, the woman picks her way across it as if across the mud she is aware is not there. Quickly—not wanting to appear to be dawdling, it seems—and yet somehow with the grace—the steady but light concentration—of a dancer.

She reaches the pit as the girl swoopingly reclaims the baby from Chhung, standing it up on its feet. The baby stops crying and, its fists gripping the girl's fingers, starts to step. One foot, then the other. Then the first foot again. Concentrating. Feet planted wide, and each step a stamp, as if there were a bug it wanted to shmush. Its hips loop around, hula hoop–style. Still, it goes on, determined; it doesn't seem to mind even the pant legs, though when they get caught underfoot, the waistband pulls and the girl has to stop to roll the things up—a bit of a project, now that they are caked with mud. Still, she rolls, only to have them fall back down; they drag like the ankle cuffs of a chain gang. More steps. Chhung says something. The woman nods reassuringly; the girl answers reassuringly. The boy swats. The girl walks the baby away from the pit, swiveling her body as if in imitation of it. Planting her feet so wide, she looks to be wearing a diaper, too. She holds her head down.

And with that, peace returns. Chhung and the boy work; the woman slips away. Hattie resumes painting—wetting her brush, contemplating her composition. *What now?* A moment of puzzlement, and then a *How about this?* It's no substitute for Joe and Lee, but it's something. Her hand begins to move; Annie launches a fierce and protracted attack on poor Reveille's tail as Cato takes a nap. He lies on his side with his legs stuck out straight—his arthritis. She'll get him a warm compress in a minute.

By day three, the hole—a trench, really—is a lot bigger. A car and a half long, maybe, and deep enough to bury a vehicle up to its windows. The dirt piles along its edge are so high that Chhung and the boy can't throw the dirt clear of them anymore; they're piling it onto a piece of cardboard instead, and sliding that up an incline. It's an excruciating procedure to watch—like farm life before not only the invention of the wheel, thinks Hattie, but the deployment of the ox.

She finishes her current composition with disappointment. *Three flat boards with thorns sticking out,* her father would have said—a graceless thing. Ah, well. She feeds the dogs, bags up some old *Nature* magazines for recycling, then ventures downhill with a wheelbarrow. The wheelbarrow's rusted out in one corner, an ancient thing left behind by Joe's uncle when he moved north some years ago—back when Joe was wondering if it was enough to have moved, first out of the city, and then out of the suburbs; back when he was wondering if they shouldn't move north like his uncle, too. Which Hattie did, of course, in the end: Here she is. But it was one of the differences between them that Joe was always looking to retreat from the world, whereas Hattie was looking for something else. *To regroup,* Lee said once. *To reconcile your contraries and, one day, to fructify.*

Fructify?

Well, whatever, as the students used to say. And who knows why Hattie brought the barrow with her when she moved. *A little retentive, are we?* Lee would have laughed—Lee who held on to nothing. *You know, I have no last will and testament,* she said, bald and weak, toward the end. *But I bequeath to you my comments; may you remember them always.* She opened her stick arms like a pontiff blessing a crowd; her I.V. line hung down.

Lee.

Anyway, for what it's worth, Hattie's always liked wheelbarrows. Their unassuming usefulness, and the feel of them, too. She's always liked the spread of their handles spreading her arms—opening her heart, Adelaide, the new yoga teacher, would probably say. As if in stretching one's pectorals one stretched one's spirit, too. This wheelbarrow squeaks and rattles the whole way down Hattie's driveway, though. Something's loose; the tire's flat; the handgrips have split. It's work to push the thing even downhill. She wouldn't give it to anyone else. So why give it to the Chhungs, then? Is it not insulting? She does not feel spiritually stretched by the idea, quite the contrary. She feels spiritually contracted, and by the time she reaches their drive, is half thinking to head back home.

The Chhung men, though, have already come around the side of the trailer to greet her. They stand side by side—the boy half a head taller than Chhung—resting their shovels in just the same way, as if per some regulation. Then Chhung says something, and the boy goes back to work. He doesn't slow down until Hattie actually approaches, and then it's the gauged pause of the underling: Chhung may be taking this chance for a break, but his son is aware that his interest is not called for, and certainly no excuse to slack off. Chhung, on the other hand, unties his net and flips it back over his hat. He casually lights up; the cigarette tip flares, the bright ring travels. A large crow flaps through, cawing way up high above them, where there's sun; Hattie can see the light on its wings when it banks, but it doesn't cast a shadow because they're already in shadow.

"Hello," she ventures. It's colder and damper down here than at her place; enormous white toadstools gleam in the dark woods. She shivers. "Excuse me. Sorry to bother you. But can I give you this?"

The boy watches, his fingers and clothes streaked with dirt. He sports dirt-edged Band-Aids on his hands, like Chhung.

"Thought maybe you could use it," she says.

"Tank you," says Chhung.

"I hope it will be a help." The flies are worse down here, too, with no wind. Hattie waves her hand in front of her face, but even so a no-see-um flies smack into her mouth. Of course, if she chose to reconceive the thing, she could probably find it not unlike a sesame seed. Instead, she spits it out.

Chhung takes a drag on his cigarette and, in a kind of answering gesture, blows smoke out his nose. Two wispy streams float up, obscuring his face. "Tank you," he says again.

"You're welcome." Hattie has a look at the work-in-progress. The layers of dirt are clear as the layers of a cake—an icing of topsoil atop a gravelly mix, then clay and clay and clay such as Hattie knows well. If you pick that clay up, you can squeeze it into a ball; and if you let go of the ball, you will behold a beautiful impression such as could make a real fossil find in a few million years. For now, though, the clay is mostly a premium seal-all. The bottom of the pit is about as dry as the floor of a car wash.

"That soil is heavy," Hattie starts to say. Before she can broach the subject of sand, though, Chhung has signaled to a window of the trailer. The girl peeks out from behind a lilac curtain; Chhung barks something, giving a swipe of a finger. The girl's head disappears then, only to materialize, complete with body, from around the corner; her mother and the baby accompany her. They present Hattie with a cardboard box of raisins, as well as a clear plastic box of something that looks like orange peels packed in sugar. The red Khmer script on the cover is all loops and squiggles, with an English translation below, in green: SWEET CHILI MANGO STRIPS.

"Thank you." Where the plastic box is sealed up with tape, Hattie pockets it and opens the raisins instead; she offers the girl and woman some. Naturally, they will not accept any until she's had one herself. But then they each take a couple, shyly. The girl rolls several between her fingers, as if making spitballs; the baby leaves off its bottle, leans out of the woman's arms, and opens up its molarless mouth. Aren't they concerned about choking? Apparently not. The baby kicks; the girl softens a few more raisins; the baby placidly picks the raisins out from the girl's outstretched hand. Not cramming them all in or hoarding them, as Josh would have, in those soft chipmunk cheeks of his. Just calmly picking them out, one by one, as if demonstrating the use of an opposable thumb; and what fine focus we Homo sapiens have! Courtesy of the foveal cells of our maculas.

Hattie watches, amazed.

"*A-muhmuhmuh,*" says the baby. The baby's drool is brown with raisin juice.

The woman is shy and still; *her spirit abides within,* Hattie's mother would say. A tiny woman—even Hattie dwarfs her. They exchange smiles as, between raisins, the baby goes back to drinking something that looks a lot like cola: some dark brown liquid, anyway, with lines of bubbles running up the length of the bottle. The girl is plain beautiful. She has her mother's smooth skin and hoop cheekbones, and her mother's high, wide forehead, too—a windshield of a forehead—but with lovely lifting brows of her own, and a decided lilt to her full mouth. She looks as though she were not born, originally, but somehow blown, still soft, down into the world through a tube. And then what life was blown into her! Her brows lift and fall, her nose wrinkles and smooths, her lips purse and pop wide. And behind those gestures something more flickers—wariness, interest, boredom, confusion—a liveliness of response Hattie remembers from her teaching days. How she's missed this, she realizes—how she's missed young people in general. *So many little gunning planes,* as Joe used to say, *on such highly interesting runways.*

"You're welcome!" the girl says now, even as she shrugs her shoulders and ducks her head—embarrassed to have been effusive. Hattie introduces herself. And, suddenly forthright, the girl introduces herself in return: So-PEE her name is. People call her Sophie all the time, because her name is spelled S-o-p-h-y, but actually her name is So-PEE, meaning "hard worker"—not exactly what she would have picked herself, but anyway. The woman is Mum.

"Which really is her whole name." The baby takes another raisin from Sophy's hand. "She's from the country, where they have names like that. Not like a real name. It just means like grown-up or something. Mature. Like, nothing."

Chhung retires to the trailer, swinging his arms; he has the air of an overseer headed to his desk. Sophy accepts some more raisins.

"I think I get what you're saying," Hattie says. "It's like 'Ma'am.'"

Sophy considers. "Yeah, like 'Ma'am.' It's a little like 'Ma'am.' Not exactly, but sort of. It's hard to explain."

"I think I get it," Hattie says again. She turns to Mum. "And where in Cambodia are you from?"

Mum tightens her arms around the baby and shakes her head.

"She doesn't speak English," Sophy explains. "And she doesn't read or write Khmer, either."

Kh-mai, she says, Hattie notices. Not *Kh-mer,* but *Kh-mai.*

"She's, what's that word?"

"Illiterate?"

"Illiterate. Yeah, that's it. She's *illiterate.* But she works hard, she knows you've got to work hard in America because, like, nothing grows on trees."

Mum says something then, holding the baby with one hand, and smoothing her shirt with the other. The shirt's close-fitting in a way you don't see much around here—a matter of tucks and darts. It doesn't move, the way Sophy's T-shirt does; it's formal. Both shirts, though, show their wearer's long waist and modest bust to advantage. Sophy tugs on hers with one hand behind each hip, as if adjusting a bustle.

"She says do you know anyone looking for a house cleaner, because, like, she can clean. And she does factory work, too. Like, if anyone around here is making electronics or medical equipment. Anything like that." Though Sophy shoos at the air with her raisinless hand, Mum, mysteriously, does not have to swat; the flies, for some reason, leave her alone. "She can do anything, she's really good, you should see."

"No medical equipment," answers Hattie. "But a lot of people do bake things."

Sophy translates. Looking in the air, thinking, speaking, looking in the air again. She gestures, swatting some more. Mum nods.

Hattie nods back.

And everyone smiles in the gray air—happy. In some basic, reasonless way, happy. A speckled pool of light—who knows where it's from, it must have bounced off something, somewhere—flickers at their feet, dancing and live.

The baby's name, it seems, is Gift.

"Because my mom thought he was, like, a gift," says Sophy.

He? The baby is wearing another frilly shirt today, with green-and-pink pants. Dangling its—or rather, his—legs on either side of Mum's hip, he is having a two-handed swig from the bottle, which really does look full of soda.

"*Mehmehmehmme,*" he says.

"Gift. What a lovely name," says Hattie. "Is he a boy?"

"Yes," says Sophy. "He's my brother."

"I see." Hattie does not ask why he's wearing girls' clothes.

Still, Sophy volunteers, "We dress him like that because some-body gave us that clothes." She shrugs. "And we don't care."

"Ah," says Hattie. "And here I don't care, either."

Sophy tilts her head, thinking about that. Mum murmurs.

"She says Cambodians can make—what?" says Sophy.

"Do-na," says Mum herself then, suddenly. Softly, but bravely. And again—a bit more slowly: "Do. Na." She holds her mouth open after the second syllable, like a singer drawing out her vowels. Lovely as she is, her bottom teeth do zigzag.

"Oh, right, doughnuts." Sophy's teeth are better than her mother's.

"Ah." Hattie smiles at Mum. "Very good."

"She's never made them herself, but Cambodians make, like, all the doughnuts in California. So it's definitely something Cambodians can do," says Sophy.

"Is that so," says Hattie.

Mum adds something quietly, from behind Gift, in Khmer, then lifts her chin in Hattie's direction.

"They also can make—what?" says Sophy.

"Ba-geh," says Mum.

"This French thing," says Sophy.

"Baguettes?" says Hattie.

An inspired guess. Mum nods and smiles, but with her lips pressed together, so that her smile is more a matter of her eyes than her mouth—a radiance.

"Yeah. If anyone around here likes that," says Sophy.

"I'll ask around."

Beside them, the pit yawns, dark and rough, all roots and rock.

"She's a great worker," Sophy says again. "Like she's fast, but she pays attention, too, you know? She doesn't make mistakes."

"She's accurate?" says Hattie.

"Yeah, accurate." Sophy nods, tilting her head. "She's, like, *accurate.* Where she used to work they always gave the most complicated stuff to her. They weren't ever things she'd want herself, if anyone gave her one of whatever it was she'd just give it to the monks at the temple. But she made them because she was supposed to—like it was her fate. She's Buddhist."

Hattie looks at Mum—keeping her in the conversation. Not that *paranoia is the human condition,* as Lee used to maintain. But Mum might just understand more English than she speaks.

"Is she observant?"

"What does that mean?"

" 'Observant'? It means, does she observe Buddhist rituals? Go to temple? Is she practicing?"

"Oh, I get it." Sophy nods. " Yeah, back in our old town, she went every week. Because she had to, like, bring the monks food so they could eat, to begin with. Like they'd leave this bowl out on the steps for people to put rice in, and my mom would always do that. Bring them stuff." Her eyes go to Gift, who's lost interest in the raisins; she pops what's left of them into her mouth, licks her open palm, and wipes it on her jeans. "And there were, like, all these festivals. Like to remember the dead, even if no one can really do it right because they don't have people's ashes." She licks her palm a second time—still sticky, apparently—and wipes it again. "But anyway, there's no temple around here. I mean, that's not full of hippies. And there aren't any meditation groups, either. So I guess she's not so *observant* anymore."

"Very good."

"Even if all she thinks about is *kam,* day and night, still. Is that what you mean?"

"*Kam?*"

"It means 'karma.' "

"Ah. *Kam,*" Hattie repeats—the student, instead of the teacher.

"She won't kill anything, even a fly," Sophy goes on. "Because she's trying to get out of this life."

"She believes life is suffering?"

"Yeah. But, like, it's all fake, too, it's hard to explain."

Gift throws his empty bottle to the ground and, when Sophy retrieves it, throws it to the ground again. This time Hattie returns it.

"I see you," she tells him, smiling. "I see you."

He coos adorably, then pitches the thing so hard he all but nails a chipmunk.

"What do you mean, it's all fake?" This time when Hattie rescues the projectile, she hides it behind her back. Gift squirms and cranes.

"Like we're all just fooled," says Sophy. "Like we think the world is real when it isn't."

"Like it's the veil of Maya?"

Sophy cocks her head. "How did you know that?"

Hattie shrugs—producing the bottle, to Gift's delight, before hiding it behind her back again. "I grew up in China, where a lot of people were Buddhist. Buddhist, Taoist, Confucian, Christian. And all of them at the same time, sometimes."

Sophy laughs.

Gift kicks with his chubby hand outstretched—clearer than his mother, maybe, about object permanence.

"Are you Buddhist, too?" Hattie goes on.

Sophy starts to answer but doesn't; Hattie looks up to see the ruffled curtain drawn aside.

Chhung, watching from the trailer.

The curtain shuts again.

Hattie returns the bottle to Gift once more but, rather than let him restart his game, Mum says something to Sophy, smiles at Hattie, and heads inside; never mind that Gift is reaching and kicking in protest, his pant legs dancing like puppets. Hattie is still waving when Sophy's blond brother saunters up.

"This is Sarun," says Sophy, rolling the *r*.

"How do you do, Sarun." Hattie rolls the *r*, too. "My name is Hattie. It's nice to meet you."

" 'S dope," he says.

"Cut it, *Bong*!" says Sophy immediately. Her eyebrows lift, her nostrils flare. "No talking ghetto!"

"It's a pleasure to meet you, too," says Sarun then, with mock manners. He has a deep, round scar on his cheek, as if someone poked him with an ice pick; his earrings are little pirate hoops.

"What does *Bong* mean?" asks Hattie.

"Just, like, I don't know. Older brother or sister," says Sophy. "Or cousin. Anything like that."

Sarun tries out the wheelbarrow.

" 'S ite," he says.

"*Bong!*" says Sophy.

"What does that mean, 'ite'?" says Hattie.

"It means 'all right,' " says Sarun. "All right, 'ite, get it?" He takes the wheelbarrow for a little test drive, trotting along behind it. Up one side of the pit, around the end, back. The wheel shrieks and squeals but no one seems to mind.

"He just has to, like, talk ghetto for some reason," says Sophy as his orbit swings their way.

"For your express benefit." Sarun skids to a dramatic halt.

Hattie starts to explain why it might be to his benefit, too, to speak standard English but stops herself. She is not, after all, responsible for this young person. She's retired. She smiles instead. "Talk however you want."

"With regard to this wheelbarrow," says Sarun, "I'd just like to say, it is just what I always wanted."

"Don't talk California, either!" Sophy tells him.

"How is that California?" asks Hattie.

"It's, like, Hollywood. The way rich people talk," says Sophy.

"Ah." Hattie nods. "Anyway, Merry Christmas," she says.

Sarun grins and doffs his baseball cap to her, his jewelry gleaming pale in the low light.

"Thanks," says Sophy, her cheeks flushed. She waves both her hands, holding their open palms out in front of her like airplane propellers. "Thanks for coming. Thanks for the wheelbarrow! And last time for the cookies, and the drawer! Everything!"

Hattie hesitates, but only a little. "You're welcome," she says, and waves a good-bye to them all, including Chhung, who reemerges just as she leaves. He nods, stubs out a cigarette, swats a few flies. Then he pulls the net down over his face and tries out the wheelbarrow himself, pushing coolly and with dignity.

Ginny's breakup is common knowledge, but as she doesn't seem to want to talk about it and as the walking group would rather sigh over Hattie anyway, they do, huddling at the Come 'n' Eat after their walk.

"Was he the love of your youth?" Beth runs a rock quarry, but she's the dreamiest of the group when it comes to romance. She ruffles her short hair as if trying to put a bend in it, then jabs a toothpick in her mouth.

"Yes and no," says Hattie.

Bringing gasps from some, and from even the avowedly postromantic, looks of interest. The love of her youth, sort of, returned in her late middle age to find her!

"I don't know that he's here to find me," says Hattie. "And I did marry another man." As everyone knows but red-haired Candy, the newest member of the group.

"And what happened to him?" she asks.

"Lung cancer," says Hattie. "Never smoked, but he got lung cancer."

It's hardly news at this point, and goodness knows they've all had their share of illnesses and accidents and shock; they're veterans of life. Still, it quiets things down. Other patrons push their chairs back; the front door opens and shuts, then opens but doesn't shut as Hattie steels herself to explain about radon, and about how the cancer had already spread by the time they found it—to his liver and brain before anyone knew a thing. His illness having been found late, and having only involved a chapter or two, Lee used to say, *Not like my Tale of Two Titties; it was just lucky I didn't have three.* That being the sort of joke only Lee would make—the sort even she stopped being able to make, some days; days when it was everything she could do to get herself out of bed and make herself walk. Walking, walking the drugs out of her system—walking, walking, in her pink punk wig. Candy does not ask about any of that, though. Instead, all she wants to know is, "Did you love him?" Her pale face washed out by her bright hair as she asks simply and sweetly. Unblinkingly.

"I did," says Hattie.

For she did love Joe, brusque as he could be—her fellow teacher, who taught World History and ran the bike club at school. Once, when a student was attacked by a pit bull, he jumped right off his bike onto the dog's back—that being the kind of thing he did, he said. What he lived for, even. *Those moments,* he used to say, *when you know what you're made of.* She did not believe she would ever know what she was made of. Sometimes, though, she did think she knew something, anyway, by the way she reached for him in her sleep— knows something, still. For even now she reaches, even now she dreams that she can feel him breathing—that they are breathing in synch, waking in synch, as they used to. One of the more nonsensical shocks of his death being that he ceased to have a rhythm, or a sense of hers. Of course, even autonomic responses require brain function. A working medulla oblongata; efferent nerves. She knew that. Still, theirs had been so unwilled, she had not quite registered, somehow, that they depended on life.

"Kids?" asks Candy.

"One," says Hattie. "His name is Josh."

"Grandchildren?"

"Not yet." Hattie picks the peas out of her Tuna Wiggle; she's partial to peas. The front door opens and sticks again; the new cook slams his pots on the stove as if he's used to a lower range and just can't get used to this one.

"So Carter disappeared?" Ginny's lips match her nails, match her shirt, but she has bags under her eyes, and her artichoke hair has a helmety look.

"I took too long looking for my wet suit."

"Don't you think he'll be back?" asks Greta.

"You don't know Carter."

"Here today, gone tomorrow." Beth removes her toothpick from her mouth, that she might jab at the air with it. "I know the type."

"He does dispense with a lot."

"And you hadn't seen him for how many years?" asks Candy.

"Oh, I don't know, maybe twenty-five? Thirty?" Hattie contemplates her thick plate. "Or no—I went to his father's burial ten years ago, but didn't talk to him. Does that count?"

She keeps forgetting about having gone to the burial, somehow—the interment of Dr. Hatch's ashes, really—though it was right here in Riverlake. And how surprised and pleased the Hatches were to see her—how could she forget that? *Floored,* they kept saying, a word they hadn't used to use much, but seemed to have taken up the way they'd once taken her up. They were *floored*—all of them. *Floored.*

Did she live with his family?

"When I first came to the States, yes."

And that was—?

"Oh, I don't know—some fifty years ago. I was kind of a permanent exchange student. Their live-in Chinese tutor and basket case." Hattie starts in on her noodles, which are, in truth, a bit gooey. "They were friends of some relatives on my mother's side. I don't think they realized they were going to end up stuck with me. But they took it in stride—put me up, made sure I got to college. And of course, they're a lot of how I ended up here in Riverlake—that summer house they had."

The Adirondack lodge—people nod. The one that was falling down and couldn't be saved. The one the Hatches couldn't bear to replace.

"Which I remembered when I was looking for somewhere I could live on my pension," she goes on. Something she doesn't have to explain; for who doesn't live with her means firmly in mind, after all?

"Were they Christian?" Ginny, perking up, asks as if the question just occurred to her, or as if it weren't hers, exactly—just something that popped into her head.

Greta, though, sets her spoon right down. Good Episcopalian that she is, gay bishops are fine with her but fundamentalists are something else. "What does that have to do with anything?" she demands.

Politely enough, really. Still, Candy, their evangelical, stiffens. Never mind that she disagrees with Ginny more often than she agrees; her mouth and chin stitch up.

"They were agnostic," says Hattie—precipitating vague, scattered nods.

"Did you say twenty-five years?" asks Beth. "Or twenty?"

"It may be more like thirty-five, now that I'm thinking about it," Hattie says. "Except for the burial."

"Isn't that something." Ginny straightens her cutlery.

They watch their favorite waitress put a knee on the lunch counter to redo the specials board. Flora is young and slight—a rock climber, dressed all in blue today, as her other job is in day care; probably she's off to be a whale in the afternoon, or the sky.

"Though it does sometimes happen, doesn't it?" says Beth. "That people reconnect with their sweethearts from high school or whatever? Years and years later. I read that in a magazine someplace."

"Did they say how often the guy needs taking care of?" asks Greta.

And people do laugh at that—no kidding.

"The healthy ones go for youth," Greta goes on. "Someone to—"

"Stoke the old poker," says Beth.

More laughs.

(*Men, men, men,* Lee used to say. *Always guarding their turgidity.*)

"What I want to know is why some of us can't be happy and single?" says Candy. People look at her in surprise. "I mean, if that is the Lord's plan? Why can't we just accept it?"

"Or how about if it's our own plan?" says Greta, warmly. "Might not some of us remain happily single even if it's our own plan?"

Scattered nods to that.

"Anyway, Hattie's not reconnecting. She married another man." Grace's wild gray hair is even wilder since she got a job in a greenhouse; the humidity brings up the frizz. "And didn't he marry someone else, too?"

Hattie nods. "Her name was Meredith." Dear Meredith.

"Kids?" asks Greta, helpfully.

"Two."

More pot banging.

"One of each?" asks Candy.

One of the meaner tricks of time being the turning of the sweet into the inane, Lee used to say. Anyway, Carter's two girls seem the proof some need that whatever Carter and Hattie were, it wasn't serious. The logic of this is not clear to Hattie, any more than why she would want to know where he is living and what he is doing.

But, well, the helpful will help.

"The Turners' cottage," puts in Candy. "You know how Dina hurt her knee? Right after they winterized? Well, they're renting it to him for the year. I guess he's writing a book."

"Thinks all day, writes things down, looks miserable," confirms Beth.

"Knows it wastes trees, but can't help himself," says Greta.

Hattie smiles. "I hope he at least recycles?"

Greta ought to smile back. Instead, she runs her braid through her hand as though reviewing a length of memory. "I'm trying to think," she begins.

Oh, where is Lee?

Though Greta, bless her, has at least registered that the kids in that Cambodian family aren't in school, as she brings up a few minutes later; and when others nominate Hattie to go talk to them, she does tactfully point out that it shouldn't be because Hattie is, like the family, a black-hair.

"Of course not," says Beth. "Her hair is white."

"And used to be brown anyway," says Grace. "Right?"

"You do not have to do this." Greta brandishes the end of her braid for emphasis. "As you do realize?"

Hattie contemplates a trapezoid of light on the table—picturing in it, like a holograph, Chhung. Those cheeks. Those eyes. *Why would they have moved to Riverlake if they were thriving?* Probably the Chhungs are trouble. On the other hand, didn't the Hatches take her in, once upon a time?

"I do live next door," she says.

"And can that really be a total coincidence?" says Ginny. "I mean, doesn't it just shout, Plan?"

"Do you mean as in God's plan?" asks Greta.

The ceiling fan whirrs. The register drawer closes, then pops back open the way it always does, and has to be pushed back in.

"Those kids should be thinking of the future," says Beth, finally. "That is just a fact."

"The future is important," agrees Candy. "It's what we all look forward to."

It is Grace, their ex-nun, who looks at Hattie and winks.

Outside of the school issue, things are looking up next door. Chhung and Sarun are making good use of the wheelbarrow; Grace and Greta are dropping off food. And Candy and Beth would be driving the family places, except that the family is already getting rides from a blue car with a WHAT WOULD JESUS DO? bumper sticker. It's not clear to Hattie where the car takes them besides to the grocery store. To a community center? A clinic? A church? Anyway, she is happy to think there's a shepherd around somewhere, looking in on these sheep—*ruminating on these ruminants,* as Lee would say. It's reassuring.

Of course, the kids are kids. Hattie sees Sarun out back behind Town Hall sometimes, shooting hoops at the netless basket there. People say his real sport is volleyball but that the kids around here aren't into it; he's retooling. Sophy has herself a guitar. She sits out on the milk crate, the big curves dwarfing her narrow lap; her strumming elbow is high as her ear. Every now and then she stops to rub her fingertips. But then she peers over the instrument, back down at her book, which lies flat on a towel on the ground. Never mind the still-chilly air; she holds the pages open with a bare foot. Checking her hand position, peering down at the book again, strumming a few measures. Turning the page with her dextrous toes.

A diligent girl, who ought to be in school.

Hattie sighs. Her painting is finally starting to show signs of one day having what her father would have called *yùn*—refinement. The white space is more charged—more part and parcel of the composition, less blank. And the stalks seem to have more to do with one another, as if they're acquainted from another picture—involved. She's learning. But will that relationship and charge be there the next time she sits down? It's hard for Hattie to stand up in the middle of this whatever-it-is—this new neuronal growth, probably.

On the other hand: a diligent girl, who ought to be in school.

Hattie packs away her brushes. She puts on her walking shoes; she bags up some cookies; she tells the dogs to stay. The wind is blowing downhill. Hattie walks as if submitting her will to a Greater Force, not that she believes in a greater force, exactly—certainly not one who talks to folks personal the way Ginny's does. Might there be *a superior reasoning power revealed in the incomprehensible universe,* as Joe believed, like Einstein? Well, maybe. Quite possibly. But never mind. Her cloth bag thumps softly against her leg; and as she approaches the trailer, the wind switches direction so that she hears, not Sophy strumming, but Chhung yelling in Khmer and Sarun yelling back, their voices choppy with anger. She thinks to turn around, but it's too late. They've seen her.

The yelling stops. Sarun pulls into himself. Sophy—her feet in sneakers now—smiles brightly, redoing her ponytail. Chhung's eyes jolt. He picks up a shovel but puts it back down. A Band-Aid on his thumb has flopped forward, revealing a raw popped blister; his forearms are hummocky with bug bites.

"Just wondering how you guys are doing." Hattie balls her hands up in her sweatshirt pocket. Though it is practically May, the air is still cold. "How's the wheelbarrow working out?"

"Great!" says Sophy.

Sarun toes the ground with his high-tops; Chhung glares. Hattie would never have believed that someone with such a wander to his eyes could glare, but Chhung is indeed glaring at his son's foot, as if daring it to go on moving.

It stops.

The trees creak and sway in the wind. A poplar flutters top to bottom, its tender new leaves all agitated, and when Chhung goes to light a cigarette, the matches go out. It takes three tries before he finally stands there, victorious.

He puffs.

For a thing dug by hand, the hole is huge—several car lengths now, and with claims to real depth. Looking at it through Greta's eyes, though *(Doesn't it look more like a foundation hole than a garden?),* Hattie does wonder about Chhung's approach.

"I hope you like peanut butter," she says, producing the cookie bag.

Chhung nods as he accepts the offering. Sarun looks on with interest, then glances at Hattie as if hoping she'll help him out in some way. And for a moment she's tempted to respond—give him a wink, at least. Feeling Chhung's eyes on her, though, too, she looks away.

"Thank you," says Sophy. Her voice is a normal voice and she's smiling a normal smile, but there are tears pin-striping her smooth cheeks. "Thank you!"

"You're welcome," says Hattie. "I brought you some insect repellent, too. It doesn't work for everyone, but it does for me. So maybe it'll work for you."

"Thank you!" says Sophy.

"It's herbal."

Chhung accepts the repellent much as he did the cookies, cradling them both in the crook of his free arm. His track pants have a tear in the knee.

"The pit looks great," Hattie goes on gamely. "A lot longer." She thinks. "Deeper."

"Thanks!" Sophy's still crying.

Hattie pulls out a still-folded but slightly crumpled tissue from her pocket. "It's no beauty," she says gently, "but at least it's not used."

"Thanks!" Sophy wipes her eyes with it.

Chhung watches.

There's no animal life today. No woodpeckers, no chipmunks, no birds. Just wind, and way up above them, clouds in a hurry.

"I hear your mother's cleaning houses for summer folk," says Hattie. "Helping Donna Legrand open cottages. It must be nice to see her working."

"It is!" Sophy says.

"Especially as there isn't a lot of work around here. She have enough?"

"No!" Sophy says. Her tears pool in the crescents of her lower lids, bright and full-bodied.

"That must be hard." Hattie tries to emanate understanding. Sympathy. Something. "I'll keep an ear out for more."

"We don't know what we'll do if Sarun doesn't pitch in the way he used to!"

The way he used to. Hattie isn't sure what to make of that but, what with Chhung hovering the way he is, doesn't dare ask. "I'll keep an ear out," she says again.

"Thanks!"

Sophy's still crying, Chhung's still watching; Sarun's digging. Hattie feels around in her pocket for another tissue but only finds lint and, embedded in the bottom seam, grit. A bike, meanwhile, appears up on the sunny road—Greta, who else, with her braid and her baskets. She honks as usual; Hattie waves back the way she always does, whether Greta can see her or not. It's nothing too fascinating. And yet the Chhungs watch intently—their three heads lifting along with their three noses and three chins, all in parallel. It is as if someone has just switched on an electromagnetic field, showing them to be polarized objects, and Hattie, not—as if some base difference has been made manifest.

Hattie stops waving.

"I came to see," she says, in a burst of inspiration, "whether any of you'd like to go up to the farmers' market." She explains how it's all kinds of people selling all kinds of things, actually, not just farmers and farm products. "If Mum ever gets around to baking her baguettes, for example, she could sell them up there."

"Bag—?" Though Chhung has been understanding Hattie just fine, he looks to Sophy to translate—buying time to make a decision, Hattie guesses. For, as it happens, she knows that space between languages very well—sees how Chhung barely listens, really, as Sophy translates, eyes on the ground. Sophy translates less haltingly for her father than she did for her mother, interestingly, although even now her Khmer is not as fluent as Sarun's; you can hear that she was born here, rather than in the camps. But finally, anyway, she's done. Her glance steals up, not to Chhung's face, but to Hattie's.

Hattie doesn't dare smile back. Instead, she receives Sophy's look, then looks up at the sky—focusing, not on the clouds, but on the shifting blue shapes between them. Something Carter taught her to do, way back when—to see the negative spaces—a way of *thinking outside the box*. She takes her time.

"I can take you all there," she offers, finally. "If you'd like to check it out."

"Sophy check it ow," says Chhung.

"Would you or Mum like to come, too?"

Chhung considers. Sarun grips and regrips his shovel handle, but Hattie knows better, somehow, than to offer to take him along. She can see what's plain out of the question, as can he, apparently. He does not try to make eye contact.

"Sophy go." Chhung turns away.

Sarun resumes digging until Chhung says something else. Then Sarun grasps the handles of the wheelbarrow and wheels it over to Hattie. He sets it down carefully, like a pilot showing off his landing skills.

"Oh, no," she says. "You can keep it. It's yours."

Chhung looks surprised.

"I'm giving it to you. It's yours. A present."

"Pres-en?"

"A present," she insists. "I don't need it."

There's a pause; then Chhung smiles a broad, if crooked, smile. "Cambodian say, You do good, good come back to you," he says.

"That's beautiful." Hattie gives a half-smile herself. "Hope it's true."

And not hogwash.

"True," says Chhung, looking her steadily in the eye. He can only manage it for a moment, but he does. He smiles.

Sophy's normally swingy ponytail rests flat on the nape of her neck; she studies the ground as if she has a test coming up on it. Just when Hattie is beginning to think their trip a mistake, though, she catches Sophy glancing down the hill.

"They like cookies," says Hattie.

"They do," agrees Sophy.

"I bet Sarun eats like a horse."

Sophy hesitates, but then says, "He does, he eats, like, everything." She wrinkles up her nose.

"He's that age," Hattie says. "My son, Josh, was the same way. The minute you slowed down on your meal, he'd lean in and say, 'You going to finish that?' "

Sophy laughs, her ponytail hanging free now. She stops to read Hattie's bumper stickers but doesn't ask what they mean, and climbs into the old Datsun naturally enough. Once they start driving, though, she stiffens, as if she needs to concentrate on her sitting.

Hattie pulls down her distance glasses. "How do you people manage without a car?"

"Sarun used to have a car," says Sophy. "He just smashed it up."

"In an accident?"

Sophy nods, sniffing. Up here at higher elevations, it's more clearly spring; even with the windows closed, the air smells of manure anywhere near the farms. "He smashed up two, actually," she says. Adding, "They weren't his, exactly. He shared one with a friend and one with a bunch of guys."

"Ah."

"He was racing."

"Was he. Well, if he ever borrows mine, I'll tell him no racing." Hattie peers over the top of her glasses at Sophy, whose broad forehead is bright with light, like a second windshield.

"There's nobody to race around here anyway," she says.

"I see. Was anyone hurt? In these accidents?"

"Yeah, but not Sarun, he was lucky."

"It sounds that way."

The market field is sunny and un-buggy, and warm enough that a few intrepid people are in T-shirts. Their spring arms are about as appealing as dug-up roots, but never mind—they swing them happily. Only Sophy hugs herself as if worried about hypothermia. She rubs her arms through her jacket sleeves as Hattie tries to get her to pick out some vegetables.

"They're fresh," Hattie says. "Organic. I'll treat."

But Sophy, it seems, likes her vegetables the way they have them in the supermarket.

"In plastic, you mean?"

"Organic means fifty cents a pound more, at *least*." Sophy's arms open at last, her outrage flowing out to her fingertips.

"Do you help your mom with the shopping?"

Sophy folds back up. "I'll be helping forever."

"Because she doesn't speak English."

"Because she is never going to speak English."

"I see." Hattie makes Sophy sniff some lilacs. "Now aren't those something?"

"They smell like soap," Sophy says.

A few stalls farther on they come, amazingly, upon some peonies—white with red flecks, *festiva maxima*. Most of them still in bud, but still—so early! It doesn't seem possible. Thanks to a south-facing stone wall, though, the stall owner's garden is a whole zone up from the rest of the area, maybe more.

"Can I buy you some?" Hattie asks. "These are something special."

Sophy shakes her head no. Still, when she makes a trip to the bathroom, Hattie, quick, nabs a bunch and stashes them on the passenger seat of the car. And when she finds them there, Sophy exclaims with delight. "Oh, thank you, thank you, thank you!" she says, sniffing them, then admiring them, then sniffing them some more. Her face opens as if blooming itself, and her smile is more than a matter of her mouth. The mounds of her cheeks rise up, her ears lift; the whole shape of her face changes. "What kind of flowers are they?"

"Peonies." Hattie starts the engine.

"Peonies. I've heard of those."

"They were my best friend's favorite flower before she died," says Hattie—then, "Ant," as an ant crawls out from between the petals of an open flower. "Ants do love peonies."

"Ants do love peonies," echoes Sophy. Rolling her window down, she coaxes the ant first onto her finger and then on outside, blowing at it and peering over the edge of the door to make sure it's safely off the metal and down onto the ground before they start moving.

"She used to say," says Hattie, "that they were the one thing she was never moved to joke about."

"Who?"

"My friend. Her name was Lee."

"Did she joke?" Sophy rolls her window back up a little.

"She did. But she said peonies were too beautiful to joke about. She said they were so ordinary and extraordinary, they gave even her hope."

"What do you mean, hope?"

"Hope that there were things even she would want to grow. Skeptic that she was. Hope that there were things that could turn even her into a fool for life." Hattie stops. *Oh, to be a fool for life!*

People like me take everything apart, you know, but secretly yearn to be corny.

Sophy looks bored.

"Do you have a vase?" asks Hattie.

"We have a bottle, I'm pretty sure."

"You need a real vase; peonies are so top-heavy. Can I lend you one?"

Sophy frowns. "My dad might not like it."

"Why not?"

She gives a little waggle of the head, as if she's drawing a figure eight with her nose. But then she sniffs and smiles again. "They're so . . . *luxurious*," she says.

And Hattie smiles, teacherly. She'd forgotten the satisfaction of occasioning a young person to reach for a word. *Luxurious.*

The car smells wonderful.

It's some work to persuade Sophy not only to borrow a vase, but to come in for a snack. But eventually she perches on a kitchen chair, her hands under her blue-jeaned thighs. The dogs sniff her over, then stand a moment, tails up—awaiting direction, event, something. When nothing like that comes, though, their shoulders relax and their heads drop as if some string has been snipped. Hattie introduces them.

"That's Reveille and that's Cato, my old man," she says. "See how gray he's gotten? He moves a little slow because he has arthritis in his hips. And this is the puppy, Annie."

Sophy pets the older ones gingerly. The puppy, though! It's soft, crazy Annie she falls for—all-black Annie, with her too-big head and too-big feet, who can still ball herself up, and who never starts one thing but that she starts another. She is the very picture of unobstructed energy—of *qì*, Hattie's father would say—unlike Sophy, who, fascinated as she is, braces herself, one hand grasping the edge of her seat, the other held out stiffly. Finally she sticks out a sneaker, only to have Annie attack it, growling—tugging so hard, she looks to be stretching the thing a half-size up.

Sophy does not laugh.

"She's from the pound in the city," Hattie says. "They called me because she was so young when they found her, and they knew I had everything you need."

"Like?"

"Like a hot water bottle, and a clock that ticks—that sort of thing. I gave her a pair of my pants to sleep on. She liked that." Hattie's coffee mug has some kind of a spot on it; she gives it a rub.

"I like that name, 'Annie.' Come here, Annie Annie."

Annie yelps, her tongue lolling out the side of her mouth.

"It's after Little Orphan Annie," says Hattie.

"Who's Little Orphan Annie?"

Hattie explains. "It was that or Jane as in 'plain Jane,' " she goes on. " 'Plain Jane' just being an expression. I guess because Jane is such an ordinary name, it's come to be associated with plainness."

"I like 'Annie.' "

Hattie sets Sophy to feeding Annie ice cream as she explains how the pound found Annie in a barn. "Someone abandoned her right in the dead of winter," she says. "Can you imagine? By the time they found her, her eyes were frozen open."

"Poor Annie!" Sophy's eyes seem to freeze in sympathy.

"Of course, no one knows what she is. But based on the dogs in the vicinity, the pound guessed half lab, half springer spaniel and border collie mixed. And that could be right. She'll chase mice, anyway, supporting the spaniel theory. Though she doesn't kill them, unfortunately. She was probably the runt."

"What's a runt?"

Pretty soon Annie is in Sophy's lap; and though her first cookie takes her a good ten minutes to nibble through, Sophy polishes off her second in two bites. She pops a third into her mouth whole as she tells Hattie how she has two sisters in foster homes.

"We're, like, so hoping they'll come here when they get out," she says, her mouth full.

Hattie nods. "I can understand that."

"Then our family will be together again."

"*Túan túan yúan yúan,*" says Hattie.

Sophy looks at her funny.

"It's what my grandmother would say every New Year's, as she held up an orange. *Túan túan yúan yúan*—the whole family together."

"That's Chinese, right?" Sophy lets Annie lick her face.

Hattie nods. Sophy still looks a little funny but, well, never mind.

"So why are your sisters in foster homes?" asks Hattie, finally.

"Because I was wild."

"Usually kids end up in foster homes because of something they did," says Hattie. "Not something their sister did."

"I was wild," Sophy insists. Adding, in a voice so quiet Hattie almost can't hear her, "I sinned."

"Is that so."

"I did," insists Sophy.

A surprise but not, thinks Hattie, a complete shock—the perennial themes of Lee's English class anthologies having been rainbows and baseball and feelings, of course, but also sin. And it's a whole lot churchier up here; they live, in fact, at the edge of a mini–Bible Belt. No megachurches, thankfully—people up here don't go in for that. But the churches with big crosses on their sides are cropping up like a new kind of weed, even as the steepled churches on the green appear to be following their congregations to their Maker: The last construction project in Hattie's own church was a wheelchair ramp.

"I'd like to hear more," she says, trying not to sound teacherly but failing, apparently; Sophy lets Annie scramble off her lap.

"Thank you," she says, standing.

"Don't forget your flowers."

"Oh. Thanks," Sophy says. "I mean, thanks a lot!"

She smiles a bright smile but races out, leaving half a cookie on her plate; it is everything Hattie can do to get to the slider before she does, opening it so that Sophy doesn't crash into it like a bird. Meanwhile, Reveille, of course, nabs the cookie before Hattie can turn back, then sits innocently by the table, yawning. He lies down.

Adelaide, the new yoga teacher, is quitting and moving to Nepal. Already! She's sorry; she had planned to put down some roots, she says. But this friend has e-mailed her about a trekking outfit looking for guides and, well, she's going. Sustainable tourism, after all, eco-sensitivity, the earth.

"Are you worried about the cold?" asks Hattie.

"I have down everything," says Adelaide. "Down comforter, down sleeping bag, down jacket, down vest. Down mittens."

"Well, send us a postcard. We'll miss you."

"I'll put up some prayer flags for you," she promises. "Send you good karma."

"Thanks. Are you Buddhist?"

"Namaste," she says, her hands in prayer position before her. Isn't that Hindu? Well, never mind. Behind her red glasses, Adelaide has pink sparkles on her eyelids.

Hattie does wish she would stay.

Now people are looking at yoga tapes, trying to find a program they can stand. Every last one of them, though, has some kind of a problem. Too fast. Too much schmaltz. That sunset! That ponytail! Several members of the class do not like the word "abs," especially Jill Jenkins, who teaches English at the high school. That's not a battle they can win, though; there is no yoga tape that does not use the word "abs." Finally, they put a "Help Wanted" sign up at the general store. And today at Millie's—look—there's an answering sign tacked right over it, offering a possible replacement teacher for the senior class, anyway. A temporary teacher. Not a professional, but a person with some experience and a willingness to try if the class members are. Hattie comes to class as curious as anyone.

Carter!

She tries to nod at him discreetly; it's yoga class, after all. Meaning that people take their shoes off quietly. Stuff their fee into a coffee can quietly. Unroll their special sticky mats quietly. It's a kind of church, in a way, and today they're extra quiet—excited to be starting again, but wanting things to be right, never mind that they didn't use to be so quiet. Before Adelaide, in truth, they were a whole lot more social. But Adelaide brought this hush with her from the city, and people liked it. They liked the idea that yoga was a way of life and not just exercise—a practice, Adelaide would have said. And they liked it that the first thing Adelaide did when she came was get the class moved out of the school gym and into her friend's sculpture studio, next door to Ginny's house. It's an old barn, really; it smells of clay. There are cloth-covered who-knows-what lined up toward the back of the room—plastic- and canvas-covered presences, wheeled out of the way. Ghosts. No one much minds, though. They love the high, high ceiling; they love the massive chestnut beams from the days when there were chestnut trees around here. It's the kind of setup hippies have made in surprising places, and that you have to know a hippie to get to see. Ginny, for example, has never seen this one.

But anyway, here the class is, anxious to be serious again. As is their habit, they say welcome to Carter, but otherwise carry on as if he is Adelaide. Carter, though, is nothing like Adelaide. Adelaide would start class by checking in with people—asking if they had any injuries or concerns, including spiritual concerns. There'd be a moment of silence; and then people would speak up like Quakers. Some of them complaining about their backs, of course, but some of the younger of the older people expressing desires—to be more open to experience, things like that. In truth, it took Hattie some getting used to; in truth, she could not help but feel that some bosoms were better left unbared. But after a while, she found herself touched by what people said: That they wanted to have more patience. That they wanted to have more compassion. That they wanted just to feel more. To know what they were living for. Hattie herself never said anything; even in this, the older-persons class, she'd thought of her classmates as somehow too young to address—too unacquainted, heaven help them, with life.

Where would she even begin? Time—what time is. Place. Home. And death—death! *A story no one would ever believe except for its handy hammering corroboration,* Lee used to say.

As some of them must already know, anyway, in which case they don't need reminding.

Now Carter sits cross-legged at the front of the room, hands on his knees, back straight, eyes closed. Asking nothing. Even balder, somehow, and all in black—black T-shirt, black yoga pants—he looks like an actor of some sort. A performer. He begins the class by simply opening his eyes—those intimidating eyes.

"Yoga is about our heads," he says, with no preliminaries. "That great underutilized organ, most critical to our practice. Does anyone here know what the hippocampus is? Or, to begin at the beginning, why we call it the *hippocampus*? Besides Hattie, that is."

No one answers.

"Hattie?"

"Well, being a part of the brain shaped something like a sea-horse," she answers dutifully, "we call it that. *Hippo* meaning 'horse.' *Campus* meaning 'of the sea.' "

"Thank you," he says. "You know, one of the things for which the hippocampus is responsible, besides memory, especially declarative memory, is route-finding. So that scientists have found, interestingly, that cabdrivers have enlarged posterior hippocampi, apparently from all their time finding the best route to the airport. And in similar fashion, Buddhist monks have enlarged left prefrontal cortexes, lucky beings, apparently from meditating. Does anyone know what the left prefrontal cortex is associated with? Or perhaps I should say what a differential between the left and right lobes is associated with, with the left being the larger of the two. Hattie?"

"Happiness."

"You've been keeping up." He smiles so spontaneously that for a moment she can see him completely bald and a monk himself. "Precisely. I bring all this up because it is impossible to do yoga, I find, without asking what this is doing to our brains. No one has done the study yet, to my knowledge. But I am confident that in engaging in this practice, we are shaping ourselves—generating synapses, altering our very brain structure, maybe enlarging that left prefrontal cortex the way the monks do. And, of course, increasing our strength and flexibility in the bargain. So let us begin. Legs in lotus position. You all know what this is, yes? Cross-legged is fine. Hands palms together. Spines pulling up to the ceiling and down to the floor, extending. Let's lift the tops of our heads even higher. Shoulders down, long neck. Think Modigliani. Longer. Inhale, exhale. Elbows a little more forward, please; this is yoga, not church. Did you ever see *The King and I*? You are wearing gold brocade, your costume is so stiff you have no choice but to stick your elbows out. There. Good. And of course you must keep your chin up; otherwise, that thing on your head will fall off."

Hattie steals a glance around the room. People are smiling.

And here they thought they could only love Adelaide.

Carter is not as flexible as Adelaide. Hattie is surprised, though, at how expert he is, and how limber—almost as limber as Jill Jenkins, who is fifty-two and a former gymnast, and only taking this class because she couldn't schedule Advanced. If Hattie had to guess, it would've been someone in the lab who got Carter started; those grad students do burst with interests. Still, his command is a thing to behold. Where Adelaide was all questions—*Have you tried it this way? Is that better?*—Carter is all directives.

"Spread your fingers. Pull up through the hips. Turn this."

And, disarmingly: "It's hard, isn't it. I've always had trouble with that myself. But here. Look."

And: "You need a block under that."

And: "I'll get you a strap."

Think about now, Adelaide would say. *Think about where you are now. What you have control over and what you don't. What is it that's bothering you? Can you make a picture of it? Can you ball up that picture and throw it far away?*

Carter does none of that. Instead, he says, "There. Good." Or: "No. Like this." "It is important to do this correctly," he says. And, "We are never too old to get things right." And, "We must try to connect things up."

He expands: "In yoga, our toes speak to our fingers speak to our spines, yes? The relationships between which may not be apparent in our everyday lives. But here our every part acknowledges its connection to the next. Here our heads speak to our hearts speak to our lips."

Did he say *lips* or *hips*? He stops in front of Hattie as he says it, in any case, and touches one hip, gently—pressing it back with two fingers.

"All in one plane, as if you are a slide specimen," he says. "There. Yes. Perfect. Now we can put you under a scope and see what became of you." He fixes his eyes on her; and though they both know how her image projects back from his macula to his lateral geniculate nucleus to his primary visual cortex, that path does not much describe, it seems, what is happening.

"Miss Confucius," he says. "Hattie."

Tears start to her eyes.

"Don't," he whispers. And, more loudly, "Spread your toes."

The class goes on forever.

"As I understand there is resistance to the term 'abs' in this class," says Carter finally, at the end of the hour, "we will employ their proper nomenclature, namely, 'abdominals.' We can also ban, if you like, the word 'washboard' unless it refers to a laundry aid or, metaphorically, a winter road."

Applause and cheering. Jill Jenkins is so overcome with joy, she misrolls her mat.

Next, headstands. Jill and some other class members join Carter, while the rest lie back, eyes closed, arms wide. Opening up their hearts to the sky. Hattie breathes. Relaxes. She feels her pectorals stretch, the muscles of her neck; the muscles of her face go slack. How heavy her head is. Her thoughts are starting to slacken, too—to unwind, like denatured proteins—when she senses a presence; and sure enough, there stands Carter, looming over her in principal investigator fashion. He offers her a hand to her feet, which she accepts. His hand is warm and a little papery, like a potato jacket.

"You've done some yoga over the years," she says, pulling on a sweatshirt.

"I have." He's put a flannel shirt on over his T-shirt.

"A hobby?"

She crosses her arms; he crosses his arms in answer—their mirror neurons at work.

"I needed to do something," he says. "My back. My sanity. One of my postdocs got me started."

As she guessed.

"You've had some tough years," she says.

"We all have."

"And you've always taken your hobbies seriously." She raises her chin.

"Too seriously, some would say." He raises his.

"Your father, you mean."

He gives a half-laugh. "Am I growing predictable in my old age?"

"You've always been predictable," she says. "Except, that is, when you're predictably unpredictable."

It's a kind of joke she hasn't made in decades, and comes out stumblingly; she is surprised when he laughs, and encouraged enough to ask, then, "May I ask what happened the other day?" Taking a tone she hasn't taken for a while, either—a restrained tone, with some cross-exam in it.

"I could see perfectly well you were not coming back."

"Could you."

A half-beat. "Would you like to see my boat?"

To which she has to smile—how agile—even as she answers with an aplomb of her own, "I'd love to. But—excuse me—what boat?"

"I'm building a boat."

"Of course you are. Though some people, you know, thought you were writing a book."

Her locution turning crisp like his, she notices.

"I have come to realize I have nothing to say, actually—that I am done saying things, if you can imagine the relief of my publisher and the reading world," he says.

"No more mindless deforestation on your behalf."

"Precisely. In fact, I am thinking of mounting an anti-writing campaign."

"That others might follow your fine example."

He laughs, his eyes lit. "Are there not too many books as it is? What we lack, it seems to me, is silence, especially attentive silence. Think what the world would be if one could get tenure based on the quality of one's silence."

She laughs, too.

"I should draw up a proposal for that," he goes on. "What with the advent of fMRIs, an appropriate metric is not altogether beyond our reach, you know. But first, my watercraft."

"A boat."

"A boat, yes." He smiles once more and—unusually for Carter—tilts his head.

. . .

The Turners' cottage is down the hill from yoga, on the lake path; they walk in a silence of some beauty. For here they are, after all these years—so much has happened, even as nothing has. They are walking, and that alone seems more than they could have asked for in this world. How well they would get along, probably, if they never talked at all—if they had no history. If instead all they had was this, their warm familiarity. It's been a while since Hattie's felt how the boundaries between people can go soft, but she feels it now, in the shortening of his gait to match hers, in the relaxing of his gaze. She doesn't remember his offering his arm to her, but somehow she's taken it. He's tightening the crook of his elbow around her hand, though that elbow's a little high; they've forgotten the difference in their heights, which is, as he used to say, *not negligible*. His hand digs into the pocket of his yoga pants now—old-fashioned ski pants, actually, she sees, with a raised seam down the front. His forearm drops, adjusting; and there—she can feel, between each two of her fingers, a creased-up fold of his shirt flannel. Joe and she used to walk like this, once upon a time; and wasn't it one of the best parts about being married, really—always having an arm to take when you felt like it?

Come back.

She'd forgotten.

"Look," says Carter.

Wildflowers! There, under some pine trees—a drift of purple hepatica—and not far from them, a patch of white bloodroot. Which, once upon a time, the Indians used for war paint, Hattie knows—having told her kids about it in school—those roots running with just what you'd expect from a thing called *bloodroot*. And beyond the flowers shine some new-leaved trees—those leaves *qīng qīng,* she wants to say—a fresh green with no translation she knows of, who knows if native English speakers even see it. And beyond the trees—the lake light, winking. It's late afternoon; the clouds are live and orange, burning and brooding. They move low and restless over the water—patrolling for something, it seems, by what's left of the day. But everything else is at rest. The light's gone soft; and the wind's a stir—a no-account conveyor of music, mostly: the chirp and caw of the birds; the rustle of the leaves and grass; the *glap, glap* of the water. And now a weird, warbly tremolo—a loon flying by with its mouth open, even as a brown weasely thing shoots across the road.

"Fisher," whispers Hattie. "See it?"

Carter nods.

"I've lost two dogs to fisher," she says.

"You've become an animal lover."

"You've gone bald."

"You wear two pairs of glasses."

"I still have my teeth, how about you?"

"Most of them."

"How extraordinary."

They laugh; the shadows of the balsams cross clear to the opposite shore.

Hattie has never noticed the shed back behind the Turners' cottage, though of course it's always been there—a stone's throw from the Hatches' place, but buried in brush way back when. Now all's been cleared out, and the shed is almost as visible as the new house. Look, the Hatches' chimney!—beautifully reused, and the whole house not bad, as modern houses go, though nothing like the Hatches' well-worn place, with its tree-trunk posts and extra-deep porch and gargantuan ice house. Now Carter slides the shed door open; and there's his wood shop—his tools hung up short to long beside a tool bench, and the whole room the very picture of order. It could almost be the lab—there's even a radio—except, of course, that it smells of sawdust. One wall is taken up by a window looking out onto a meadow and trees, in front of which sits a skin-on-frame kayak-in-progress, set on sawhorses. This is an upside-down canoe-shaped thing with a half-skeleton of ribs lashed to it now, but pretty soon it will be covered with nylon, says Carter; it won't always evoke road kill. Hattie laughs, admiring its long spine. A chordate, she says, and he laughs, too—yes—as he pulls a stool over, adjusting its height so she can experience its marvelous leather seat. She jounces a little while Carter points out how gradual the stern is; the boat's pivot point will be well toward the bow.

"Meaning it will fairly fly through the water," he goes on, "even as you feel everything—every current. Can you imagine what that will be? How live an experience?"

She shakes her head, smiling. Carter the enthusiast—how well she knows this man. When he was young it was bluegrass; later, it was yoga; now it's West Greenland Inuits. He pulls over a tottery wooden stool for himself.

"They would custom-fit every kayak with the rider himself as the measure. So that the cockpit would be the sitting width of your hips plus two fists, for example." He places his fists at his hips. "And the depth to sheer would be a *fistmele,* meaning the width of your fist plus an outstretched thumb." He extends his thumb like a hitchhiker; he always did have long thumbs. "These are really shallow boats."

"Wonderful." She swivels as she listens.

"Isn't it? I love the Inuit mind-set," he goes on. "So human-centered. Of course, it was still what Meredith—you remember Meredith—used to call a web of significance. Do you know what I mean?"

She shakes her head.

" 'Man is an animal suspended in webs of significance he himself has spun'—Max Weber. She loved that. 'Man is an animal suspended in webs of significance he himself has spun.' "

Not *slipping*—just repeating himself as if in lecture hall. Hattie smiles.

"Of course, we all do spin webs, but at least the Inuit web was more than a denial of death. As so many are," he goes on.

"Religious webs, especially."

"Yes. Not exclusively, of course." He gestures with his hands. "But religious webs, especially, yes, with all that emphasis on the afterlife. Whereas the Inuit web was about fish. Boats. Survival. This life."

"As opposed to immortal achievement?" She does not mean to sound cutting. Still, she is relieved when he does not answer but simply looks at her a moment with his mouth open, his fingers lightly pressing his lower lip against his teeth—a private thing he did all the time in his teens, but that she hasn't ever seen him do once since, not even at the lab.

"Do you see," he says suddenly, "what a waste of time all this is? How gloriously inefficient I've been?"

Attached to one sawhorse is a wooden placard, with what appears to be the boat's name branded on it: DISCONCERTED.

"I'm trying to force myself off task," he says. "My life having turned into one long concerted effort."

"You were turning into Anderson."

He laughs. "Who's waiting for his Nobel now, you know, for his genome work."

"The Nobel your dad didn't get."

"Miss Confucius!" He laughs again, open-mouthed. "How have I lived without you?"

"Though he didn't want it anyway, did he?" She swivels some more, stretching her back.

"He did and he didn't. He always said he wanted his picture to hang in the halls of his alma mater; you know how they have that long line of scientists. But with his picture facing in, he used to say, so that it wasn't about glory. So that it was about his contribution and his place."

"And was it?" She stops. "Hung face-in, I mean."

"Of course not. Though you know, I don't think he really would have minded. He wanted to be a person who didn't care about status. He admired people like that. But it was probably the one thing he failed at—getting past it."

"The way you're trying to get past it now."

He gazes at her in the half-dark, his arms crossed, one finger held up to his smiling lips. She is still, she can see, his favorite student.

"Unlike Anderson," she goes on, "who's picked up the torch for your father—even going on from cytogenetics to the genome."

"Isn't it almost too—what did you use to say in China?"

"Filial?"

"Precisely—*filial*. Isn't it almost too filial? I do love that word. Fil-i-al." He laughs. "The sort of translation that amounts to a nontranslation, don't you think? I mean, what does that mean to a Westerner? It was good to see you at Dad's burial, by the way, even if you left without saying hello."

She grips the soft saddle.

"Most un-Confucian of you."

"Well, you know, I was never the Confucian you all made me out to be, to begin with," she ventures casually.

More interest than surprise. "Did we push you?" He cups his knees with his hands.

She shrugs and swivels some more—the stool squeaking in one direction but not the other, she notices.

"Of course, our brains have a tendency to sharpen contrast, as you know," he begins, and she knows what he is going to say next before he says it: Witness lateral inhibition. The way the eye neatens up the edges of things. The way it suppresses any blurring data it may be receiving—any contradiction. And of course, it's all true—how the mind seeks clarity, how the sharpening goes down to the cellular level. And, more, how the brain makes "sense" of the cleaned-up data—how it constructs a "world" out of the world using certain rules of thumb. She hears him out. But then she says, "No one wants to be boxed up, Carter," and that's that. "Anyway, I survived." And it's true, of course. Whatever anger she once felt about this is distant and wavery now. Edgeless, as if some lateral inhibition for emotion's been turned off. "It was just plain rude to leave your father's burial the way I did. I'm sorry."

"You were avoiding me and ambivalent about my father."

There's no denying it.

"As were many, by the way," he says. "Legions, even, we might say."

A fly promenades down one of the boat's ribs; she shoos it away.

"But as you were saying."

"As I was saying. Yes. Meredith used to say, you know, that I worked on the eye in order to avoid seeing."

"Seeing what?"

"Any number of things. For example, that I didn't really care about science."

"But of course you cared about science."

" 'Happy is the man,' she used to say, 'who can wrap himself in his web of significance and die in it.' She said I was a man who didn't even make his own web. That I wrapped myself in my father's web, like Anderson. That I wanted my picture hung in the same hall as my father, because that was what mattered to him. She became a judge, you know."

"Meredith?"

"Appellate. Which she always said was the most boring kind, but if I ever knew why, I can't remember now." It's getting dark; he stands to pull the light cord, which is weighted at the bottom with what looks to be his old wooden pocket knife. "When she left me she left the bench, too, and became a Buddhist. Said she was becoming too compassionate to be a good judge anyway."

"Poor Meredith always was so helplessly kind."

He laughs again, his bald head lit up now, his shadowed face ghoulish. "Precisely. The Dalai Lama came to her school, and she became just fascinated—started going from one retreat to another. As if Buddhism isn't a web of significance? I don't know. She gave a lot of money away, saying she didn't see how there could ever be justice as long as we had capital accumulation. Possessions."

Hattie's toes kick against the inside of her walking shoes. "Do you think she was right?"

"I think she had the makings of a totalitarian," says Carter. "Then she died without asking for me once. As if I were this Terrible Mistake. This guy who refused to confront what his own research showed. You know the drill."

" 'Vision is a tool geared toward action, not truth.' " She straightens her back.

Carter lifts his chin. "Precisely. It distorts as much as it presents, giving but a most partial understanding of reality in toto. And so on."

"First lecture of the semester."

"I obviously don't disagree with her. Her take, though, was that we will do anything to maintain the illusion that the world we apprehend is reality. For example, I might believe myself to care about truth and the advancement of knowledge, but that would only be my self-serving illusion, beyond which lay a deeper truth. To wit—"

"Uh-oh."

"—that I wanted to be the brother with my picture in that hall."

"How kind."

"Don't let anyone tell you Buddhism breeds patsies." He sets his feet on a low rung of his stool. The knees of his yoga pants gleam yellow; the stitching of the raised seam has come undone here and there.

"How do you know she never asked for you?"

"Our kids were there." Carter looks out the window, though there is hardly anything left to see now—no individual trees, just movement. Shifting; the wind's picked up.

"I'm sorry."

"That was after our older daughter married a carpenter and didn't invite me to the wedding."

"Maisy."

"That's right, Maisy, very good. She said she didn't think I would want to be invited. That I considered weddings bourgeois and wouldn't approve of her choice, either, given that he didn't go to college. And of course she was correct about the latter."

"But still." Hattie turns her palms upward.

"Precisely. Her data were correct, but her conclusion was wrong. Influenced as it was by things Meredith told her."

"Divorced people will say anything."

"They should really warn you of that when you get married." He grimaces. "She told Maisy I was perfectly capable of grilling her intended at the rehearsal dinner. That I thought all young men were grad students."

"Aren't they?"

He laughs his big laugh. "She said that if she were Maisy, she would marry a carpenter, too. She loved that Einstein quote about how all knowledge just leads to further obscurity. But is that right?"

"What would life be if we didn't have knee surgery, you mean." Hattie works her shoes off.

He nods. "And doesn't Buddhism have limits? The Tibetan nomads have no antibiotics, but the tombs in the Potala Palace are solid gold. I saw them when I was in Llasa—one of them weighed thirty-seven hundred kilos. Can you imagine? A regular behemoth." He scratches his nose with his pinky—his digit moving with precision, almost elegance. "I don't mean the Tibetans should be oppressed, of course. I just mean I myself am not converting anytime soon."

"You mean, here you are. You got your work done and are now conducting a personal experiment."

He looks at her sheepishly—embarrassed to have been set back on track like a grad student, maybe. "Yes."

"Trying to live like an Inuit. And coming here to Riverlake to do it—to start over. As people will." She nods a little to herself. "You're here to spin your own web—get out of the rat race. See what there is to live for besides having your picture in that hall."

"Where it isn't going to hang anyway, by the way."

"You can't let that bother you, Carter."

He shrugs—his look not hard, the way it can be, but almost inquiring.

"You've done good work. You have," says Hattie.

"I was slipping by the end." His gaze drops to his lap. "I know you won't believe that, Hattie, but I was. I was making mistakes. At night—I was making mistakes at night."

So she was right about why he retired.

"Could you have just been exhausted? You've never gotten enough sleep."

"It's more than that."

"I'm sure you were functioning better than you thought."

"I was holding my e-mails until the morning, Hattie. So I could look them over before sending them."

The insistence.

"Make sure they weren't junk," she says finally. Gently.

"Precisely." There is something like relief in his voice. "In the daytime, I digressed."

Wandering after *the wraith of an idea.*

"And I was out of new ideas." He looks out the window. "I'd run out."

"You've done good work, all the same, Carter," she says again. "You have. And say you really have had a drop-off in invention. Say your grasp of detail isn't what it was or that you're slower or make little processing errors. You still have experience to make up for it. Judgment. You can still contribute." And wasn't his web just a web, as Meredith said? Something that served him for a while but was finally just a web, to be put aside when it no longer served him, like a boat? "Who knows what else you know, now that your left hemisphere's kicking in more," she goes on. "You can't only have become stupid."

"I'm becoming wise."

"Now there's a tragedy." She smiles. She's always been the older of them, but until now has never felt older. Though is she the more enlightened of them or can she simply not appreciate what this moment means to him—what it is, even, having never flown at his altitude?

"Anyway, the work will go on." He sets his hands on his thighs as if preparing to move out of its way.

"One cock dies, and others crow."

"As the Chinese say." He pauses. "If that's a consolation, to know how replaceable one is."

"It's good to change gears, Carter." She hears tenderness in her voice and wonders if he hears it, too—wonders if he'd want to hear it. "And you knew all along this moment would come."

"Did I?"

"You said it about your father. That a moment comes when you're past your prime—when your challenge is to accept it with grace."

"I said that?"

"That and 'The greater the man, the greater the fool he can make of himself at the end.' "

"Ouch." With his head bent, he is all shining scalp. "I do feel I at least did all the science I had it in me to do," he says, finally. "What I didn't do was simply beyond my capacity."

"And isn't that something? To be able to say that?" She is trying to help.

"If only everyone could, you mean."

"I didn't say that, Carter." She says this firmly.

Still, he plunges on. "You know, Hattie, I'm sorry about what happened. That we had that misunderstanding."

That misunderstanding.

"And that you left academia in the end," he goes on. "Left research."

It's the knees of her own yoga pants that catch her eye now—blue. "You knew. You saw me go."

"Yes and no. I knew, but I couldn't watch."

Outside, it's dark enough now that, though she can still see woods, the room is reflected in the window, too, so that she and Carter look for all the world like forest spirits, superimposed on the moving tree mass. How companionable they look! Chatting with no particular animus, it seems, about something the blue jays said.

"I don't blame you for what happened," she says. "You did what you had to do. What you were trained to do."

"You blame me for other things."

The floor is cold.

"You might have asked what happened to me," she says, finally—trying not to be *testy,* but the words are what they are. "Once you turned around."

"I thought you'd be in touch."

"You mean you assumed you'd stay in my picture whether or not I stayed in yours."

"I was in a position to help."

"And didn't you always help when you could."

"So you do blame me for what happened. That I didn't go to bat for you when that job came up."

Her chest tightens; she cannot respond.

"In any case, I did wonder, you know—my father, too. Where you went." He looks at her as if to keep her from disappearing again. "You joined Amy Fist's lab, didn't you?"

"So you knew." She wills herself to breathe.

"You guys were pretty hot for a while. Beat us out for a few grants, if I recall."

"Until Guy LaPoint told that review board that Amy was running a women's shelter, not a lab. That we were more about Title IX than about science."

"Good old Guy LaPoint Blank, as we called him."

"Your enemy turned hit man."

He shrugs. "Whom you confronted at a conference, I heard."

"I did."

"The Fist must have loved that."

"She said it had nothing to do with justice. She said an interest in justice showed itself in one's judgment. Of which I showed none. She said I showed indignation, which was something else altogether."

He laughs. "Leave it to Amy to eat her own young. And then what? Didn't she leave science?"

"She did. Saying it was a boys' club and always would be."

"A fine Fist jump from unsupported assertion to groundless speculation."

"Carter."

"All right, all right. It was a boys' club."

"Is, Carter. Is."

"Is. All right. Though there's been progress, you know. You and Amy were ahead of your time."

Hattie's turn to shrug; she tries. "She left to write a screenplay about Barbara McClintock. And I left to help her."

"But let me guess. No one in Hollywood knew what a transposon was or much cared, either."

"It was before Barbara got her Nobel."

"Bad timing." A nod. "And then?"

"Then I went to teach at a private school and married and had Josh."

"You dropped out."

"Got myself a new web of significance."

He clears his throat. "My mother would have gone hunting for you, I'm sure," he supplies, "had she not gotten depressed."

"It didn't by any chance depress her that hunting down missing foreign students was her job, did it?"

A pause. "I don't know if you realize this, Hattie, but she was hospitalized on and off for years."

Hattie stops. Sweet Mrs. Hatch? With her symphony work and her four-handed piano music and what Dr. Hatch used to call her maddening equanimity?

"Oh, I'm so sorry," says Hattie. "No, I didn't know. I'm sorry. And how is she now?" If she's even alive—Hattie's braced to hear that she's missed, not just Reedie's death, but Mrs. Hatch's, too.

"Better. It took the docs years to get her meds right, but they finally did. Of course, it's been hard for her, watching her friends die. For a while there she was going to two funerals a month. But now they're all dead, so that's over with. And people do make a fuss when you hit ninety-eight. She's finally a celebrity in her own right, now that she's losing her marbles. Her skin cracks in the winter like a dairy farmer's."

"Your poor mother. I'm so sorry—I've been remiss. I . . ."

"You were young and confused." He waves his hand, and this, too, comes to seem like a distant past with no real power now. "Never mind, Hattie. We lived. Though you really think we should've gone looking for you. That I should've."

She thinks of Lee and Joe—what she would have done. *Come back. Come back.* "You don't?"

He clears his throat again. "I suppose it's not clear to me what the point would have been, Hattie. Forgive me for saying so. But it's not as though we had a spare professorship for you."

"And that would have been the point, of course."

"Didn't you need a job?"

"What's more, you assumed, as you said, that I'd be in touch."

"If you needed something. Yes."

"Help, you mean—career help. If I needed career help."

"Yes."

"I was an associate of yours."

"Weren't you?"

His reply is quick, but he does not seem surprised that Hattie's is not. She runs a finger along an unlashed rib.

"You've wasted time in such a concerted fashion," she says finally.

He stands.

"You know who you remind me of?" she says. "My mother. Religiously getting rid of her religious past."

"You can't be angry with me still."

"Am I angry?"

"It was impossible, Hattie." He leans on the shallow sill.

"I'm delighted to see how you reached your conclusion," she says. "Whatever you're talking about. Which I'm sure I don't know."

"I'm talking about us, Hattie. You and me and what we were and weren't. Mainly weren't, I think you'll agree."

"I don't know what you mean."

"Hattie." He turns and throws his hands up. "You can't back away from a real talk now."

"I'm too old for this, Carter."

"You're not too old. Hattie. Look at me." His silhouette on the window is large and dramatic now, like a shadow puppet's. "You just haven't forgiven me and never will. You and Meredith and Maisy. None of you."

"*Bú duì.*"

"You think I put you on the altar of research."

"*Bú duì.*"

"You think I was a mindless whore who saw nothing but his work. His immortal work."

"*Bú duì.*"

"You think my lab was my world, in which you were never more than a guest. And now, on top of everything, I've come back. What is he doing here, you want to know. Just when you've gotten your own little world set up. Your dogs, your friends, your house." His silhouette is scarily still. "Well, now you know how it feels."

"To be disturbed, you mean?"

"To be torn, Hattie. Torn. As in torn asunder."

"I think I already knew that."

The windows are old; she can hear the wind outside them, blowing.

"Did you," he says. "Then tell me. Was it Joe who taught you to stonewall or has your old sweet reticence just hardened into something mean?"

She stares at the boat a moment—that crosshatch of shadows.

"If you want to know why Meredith left you, Carter, I can tell you," she says, finally.

He broods.

"If you want to know why Maisy won't speak to you, I can tell you that, too." She loosens the laces of a walking shoe and pulls up its tongue. "Why no one forgives you. I can tell you." She stretches down to the floor with her leg and seats her heel with a little wiggle.

"Can you," he says, glaring. "Can you. Well, I can tell you why, too. Because you don't want to." He steps toward her. "Because it's useful and familiar and pays more than moving on. That's why."

She is straightening up, half shod, her weight on her shoeless foot, when he grasps her, hard. How large men are—she had forgotten—the mass of them; his hands are iron hands, crushing her shoulders. She rocks back—throws the shoe but misses—her mouth grazing his warm shirt as he suddenly lets go, pulling the light cord so hard the pocket knife leaps. Then how loud her heart, and how loud his footsteps on the gravel—louder than the wind—everything pouring through the open door, everything blowing and rattling; everything louder in the dark. She breathes, circling a shoulder. The other one. Tests her bad ankle. She hears his heavy steps on his porch—those boots. Then her hand jumps—that light!—the Turners' floodlights—her hand instinctively shading her eyes thanks to her superior colliculus—the same quick-response center that enables frogs to catch flies, she used to tell her kids. The yard is lit up like a football stadium; her retinas need time. But there—now she can see again. How weird the light, though, and how cold the blowing air, almost as cold as the floor. Her walking shoe has gotten kicked under the stool. She bends down, shaking, and dumps the sawdust out.

A call! Will everything involving her child remain an event forever? Josh does e-mail to say what country he's in. What he's working on for the radio—he tells her that, too. An autistic boy who managed to wander over the border from Hong Kong to Shenzhen, only to clean disappear, for example—that's one story Hattie won't forget. She almost wrote back then to say that she could imagine how the boy's mother must feel—how nothing could be worse than realizing your child has vanished. But in the end she just said what a great story it was.

"This is Josh."

As if she might not realize. But all right. He has a new girlfriend, he reports. Well, not so new, actually. Actually, he's been seeing her for two months, but hadn't wanted to say anything until he could tell how it was going. Now, though, he can divulge that she's a journalist—a stringer right now, but with real prospects, he's sure. A diplomat's daughter, a third-culture kid. Went to school in the States, but her parents are Chinese-Brazilian. She has three passports.

"Wonderful." Hattie buries her fingers in Annie's soft scruff. "What's her name?"

"In English?"

"Sure."

Serena, age twenty-three.

"A little young?"

Silence. Maybe she shouldn't have said that? Or is it just the connection?

"I thought so, but she thinks my thinking about that is outmoded," he says, finally. "Dinosaur that I am at thirty-two." He is going to meet her parents in Delhi.

"Are you nervous?" Annie gives a play bow, then runs off; Cato and Reveille lie at Hattie's feet.

"Serena says I should just try not to drool. Which you did teach me, I told her. Of course, it wasn't easy," he goes on. "But I did learn."

Hattie laughs. Though the banter—she sometimes wonders if Josh doesn't hide behind his banter the way he hides behind his reporting. If it isn't a species of talking without talking—of being tough. When he was little, he and Joe would retreat to the woods for weeks at a time—a wonderful thing, except that Joe would sometimes take a retreat from the retreat, leaving Josh alone for a day or two. Hardening him, Joe said. Insisting that Josh could handle it, even when he was just nine or ten. And Josh used to insist he could handle it, too, never mind that he could fit three pairs of socks in the hiking boots Joe got him; his backpack hung down to his knees. He insisted he liked being left alone like that. *I did, Ma, except the time a snake came. I did.*

As for what Serena likes: "She's crazy about Pushkin—she loves Pushkin. She says it was worth learning Russian just to read Pushkin."

"And where's home for her?"

"She doesn't have one, really, but thinks my thinking about that is outmoded, too."

Hattie moves some copies of *Nature* off her reclin-o-matic. "Didn't Pushkin have a home?"

"That's what I said. I told her I thought we were programmed to be faithful to a place. Like storks with their—what's that German word?"

"*Ortstreue.*" A Carter word.

"*Ortstreue.* Thank you." His on-the-air voice. "I told her you developed different relationships. But she says how do I even know, when my parents could never settle down, and now look at me."

"That was your father."

He pauses then, as he always does, at the mention of Joe. And for a moment, they share the short silence; it's like a hallway they both use.

"She says we have Listserv to keep in touch with people," he goes on, "and that we journalists are like a floating village anyway. You ever see those? In Cambodia?"

"I have new neighbors from Cambodia."

"No kidding. And here I just did the decimation of the catfish in the Tonle Sap."

Would he have said more about his new girlfriend if she hadn't brought up her neighbors? Anyway, she explains about the trailer. The Chhungs.

"But you like the girl—this So-PEE."

"I like them all. But the girl, especially. Yes."

"Let me guess. The daughter you always wanted."

Joe's bluntness.

"Though why would you want a daughter when your son is everything you'd ever dreamed of?" he goes on.

"Oh, Josh," she says. "You're not so bad."

"As best you remember, you mean."

She tries to think what to say—still improvising with Josh, after all these years. Still feeling her way. "I do understand that coming home involves travel."

"Getting on an airplane, you mean."

Is that what she means?

"I'll come soon," he continues. "I know it's been over a year—"

"You're welcome anytime, Josh." Hattie doesn't mean to cut him off, but maybe she has? And is that *stonewalling*? "Anyway, good luck with your dinner."

"It's time for me to get married, you mean."

"I mean, don't drool and enjoy your food. If you like her."

"I like her."

Ah.

"Then, go. Live," she says.

"Don't waste time, you mean."

She sighs. "I mean, live." She stands back up and opens a window; outside, a half a dozen butterflies have crammed themselves into a nook between some rocks. "I mean, try and listen to your mother."

"You mean, the unlived life is not worth living."

She laughs. "Exactly! You remember! What Lee used to say."

"I thought it was what you used to say."

"No, no." Misattribution—the most common error of the memory. "It was Lee. Lee used to say that."

"Lee was great."

"She was. Lee was great."

She reaches down to pet Cato and Reveille at the same time, one with each hand.

Hattie does not visit the Chhungs for a week. Thinking to invite Sophy to the farmers' market again, though, Hattie finally tromps down their way, through the ferns. Which are, of course, pushing up everywhere now; the hillside's a veritable sea of curls, some of which will produce a trillion spores in their lifetime. As Hattie used to tell her kids in school, ferns are prolific. She'll have to take the same route repeatedly if she wants to have a path—encourage Sophy to take it, too.

That is, if there's going to be visiting.

The daughter you always wanted.

Why would they have moved to Riverlake if they were thriving?

Well, either way she's going to pick some fiddleheads to steam up. In the meanwhile, there's her tribute of cookies to present, and her compliments to pay on the pit. She produces, too, a new kind of insect repellent—a local product with a pen-and-ink mosquito on its label. Chhung nods in thanks, smiling and smoking.

"You speak Chi-nee," he says abruptly.

"Yes," she says. "I do."

"Grew up in Chi-nah."

"Yes. I grew up in China."

"Speak Chi-nee like English. Good."

She laughs. "Once upon a time I spoke better Chinese than English. But yes. Now I speak both equally poorly." She waves at Gift and Sophy.

"My grandparents Chi-nee. Come from Chi-nah. My father speak—Teochew dialect. But me, no . . ." He waves his free hand in front of his face.

Hattie stops; but of course. The oval face, the pale skin. How could she not have seen this? "Your grandparents were from China?"

"From Chi-nah." He holds up four fingers, all with Band-Aids; one has enough curve to qualify as a bandy leg if it were a leg. "All from Chi-nah."

"All four of your grandparents were from China. That makes you Chinese Cambodian, right? Overseas Chinese?"

He nods, smiling.

"Like me, sort of." She almost never thinks of herself as "overseas Chinese"—who knows what she is, or *what she's made of,* either— but never mind. It's a helpful enough category right now. "You don't speak Chinese, though?" She tries to ask in such a way so as not to make him feel bad.

"In city, children go to Chi-nee school. But where I grow up, no Chi-nee school."

"It's hard to hang on to a language you don't use."

He nods again, his cigarette ash growing into a fine little log; his hand is surprisingly steady. " 'Human strr-en cannot chain destiny,' " he says, enunciating carefully.

"Human strength cannot change destiny?"

He nods a third time. "Fate sent you for teach Sophy."

"Chinese? To teach her Chinese?"

"Chi-nee." A glowing hunk of ash falls from his cigarette onto a pile of leaves, but he does not seem unduly concerned.

"Is Mandarin okay?" Hattie keeps an eye on the leaves.

"Okay."

"I'd love to. But would she like to learn?"

He waves his hand. "Sophy smart. Learn fast. You teach her no problem."

Not exactly what she asked, but all right. He offers to pay her; Hattie insists it would be her pleasure. And in truth, she's been thinking of adding some calligraphy to her bamboo anyway—afraid as she is that she's losing her Chinese. Her characters, especially, in which was found *gúo cuì,* her father used to say—the essence of China. Though what does that matter here?

Who knows? Pretty soon she and Sophy have a routine. First they go to the farmers' market. Then they have their Chinese lesson. Then they play with Annie and have cookies. Sugar cookies, snowdrops, snickerdoodles—always something different, which Sophy likes even though Hattie is using whole-wheat flour now, trying to stay in step with their health-crazy time. Over the cookies, Hattie tells Sophy all kinds of things: How Annie is doing with her house-training. How little color dogs see. How Hattie once had a half-wolf dog, and how he really did wolf down his food. And how she got here, starting with how she came from China—Hattie tells Sophy that, too. How it was like being carried out to sea by a riptide. How she's been swimming for shore for fifty years.

She does not explain how she found an island in Joe and Lee.

Sophy nods thoughtfully in any case, and tells Hattie stuff in return, pulling at her hair. Her hair is straight like Chhung's, but she likes to pull it even straighter, then twirl it around her finger, then straighten it out all over again as she describes how her dad flips out sometimes, and how her mom misses Cambodia.

"My mom's family had a mango farm when she was growing up," she says. "They were, like, the mango family—people would come buy whole trees from them, because mango trees are easy to take care of and don't take a lot of water. And they sold mangos at a stand outside their house, too, and my mom and her sister were in charge of the selling. So, like, one of them could lie in the hammock under the house but not both of them, or if both of them did, one of them was supposed to at least stay awake. So they had all these tricks to keep awake but fell asleep all the time anyway."

"What do you mean, under the house?" asks Hattie, sipping coffee.

"I guess the whole house was, like, raised up on stilts. Because they had all this rain there, like in the monsoon season. So the fields were fields sometimes, but other times they were lakes. Like you couldn't ever just say something was land, it was only, like, land sometimes. That's why the house was on stilts. So it was always a place you could sleep, no matter what. But anyway, it got destroyed."

"It wasn't permanent, either."

"No, it wasn't. It wasn't *permanent.*" Sophy leaves off playing with her hair in favor of playing with Annie. "I guess the whole village got, like, destroyed in the end, my mom says because of their karma."

Annie pulls so hard on her chew toy, Sophy lets go.

"One thing I never understood," she says, tugging again, "is who Pol Pot was anyway. Like everyone's always saying during Pol Pot time whatever, and there's that movie."

"*The Killing Fields,* you mean."

Sophy nods. "But was Pol Pot like a regular person, or was he, like, a *k'maoch?*"

"Is a *k'maoch* a ghost?"

Sophy nods again.

Hattie explains as Sophy frowns, nods, wonders, then frowns some more. Her head is down, her brow flattened by the light of the open window. She plays with her hair, slips a sneaker half off, claps it against the callused heel of her foot.

"Whoa," she says at the end. Trying to take it in, but seeming to realize she can't, really. "Nobody ever told me that. I mean, I guess I sort of knew. But it's, like, so hard to believe."

"It is. It is hard to believe, you're right. It's so hard that some people have spent their whole lives trying to understand it. What humans are, and how it could happen."

Sophy picks up the chew toy, throwing it for Annie to fetch. Then she waggles her head thoughtfully and goes on. "My mom's family were farmers, but they were rich," she says. "I mean, not as rich as my uncle, who she was married to before she hooked up with my dad, but they had, like, a tile roof on their hut and . . ."

Hattie stops her. "Your mom was married to your uncle?"

"Yeah, it's kind of wack, but they were married until he died and then my dad's first wife died, too. Then my mom and dad sort of got stuck together."

"I see."

"It was, like, fate. Like I guess in the beginning they were just happy to find someone they knew in the refugee camp. And then they found Sarun, too, and had to take care of him, because of, like, the Thai soldiers and the mines." Sophy tries to make Annie walk on her hind legs.

"I see."

"And because, like, nobody else could, because everyone else was dead. Like one of my mom's brothers had a gold chain, and another had a gold ring, which was why they both died. Like they got killed right in front of my mom by some kid who'd always been jealous of them, and who took the chain and the ring, I guess he was Khmer Rouge. And then he got killed by somebody else jealous of him."

"That's terrible."

"And other people died other ways. Like, some starved. I don't know. They died a lot of ways. And on top of everything, my mom says if her family still had their house and their land, it would be worth, like, a million cows now. But anyway, they don't."

"Who does?" Hattie reseats her glasses on her head, one pair toward the back, one toward the front.

"I don't know. My dad thinks his family's house is probably worth a lot now, too, because everyone in Cambodia is, like, buying every-thing. But there's no way of even proving that it used to be his house because the Khmer Rouge took it over and everyone who knows whose it was before is dead now. And all the papers were destroyed, and anyway, my mom is sort of backward so it doesn't matter." Sophy dangles the chew toy so that Annie has to jump up for it.

"What do you mean, backward?"

Sophy shrugs, and though that makes her T-shirt bunch in her armpits and fold up above the shelf of her breasts, she does not tug at her shirt hem to pull it down, the way she usually does. "I mean, like, even if my mom got her family's house back, she'd probably give all the money to the temple. Or else to, like, her brother. Because she thought her whole family was dead but then found out this one brother was still alive, and that his job was clearing mines. I guess because they still have these mines all over Cambodia that explode if you step on them. So now my mom wants to buy him a car so he can have his own driving business and not do that work anymore. Because I guess he already lost one hand and only has one left, and anyway he's the only brother left of all her brothers and sisters so she doesn't want him, like, blown up. But my dad says we have to think of our family here, too. Because we've been here my whole life and still don't have anything because my dad can't work and if my mom isn't giving money to her brother, she's giving it to the temple. Which my dad doesn't believe will make a difference to our dead relatives or our next life or anything. He says it's just throwing money away."

"But she thinks it will?"

Sophy nods, though Annie is attacking her hand.

"And is she still doing that?" asks Hattie. "Giving away money?"

"I guess, because he's always asking her how much *lui* she made cleaning and she's always hiding it." Sophy eases Annie off her lap.

"*Lui* is money?"

Sophy nods again.

"Don't you need the money to live on?"

"Sarun has money."

"Sarun?"

Annie puts her front paws up on Sophy's knees. "He's not supposed to be in business anymore, but he has money anyway."

"In business? What do you mean? What kind of business?"

Sophy shrugs and looks off.

"And who's he in business with?"

"I don't know. With his old gang." Sophy wipes some crud from the inside corners of Annie's eyes.

Hattie thinks. "Is that where the TV came from?"

Sophy cleans her fingernail on a napkin. "Me and Sarun are, like, she makes the money, she can give it away if she wants. But you can't say that to my dad because he would be, like, so ashamed that she makes money and he doesn't. Because he was too tired to work when we came here, and now he's the age to retire already, so all he can do is tell everyone his wisdom. Like how we should be saving for a car or a house. Or, like, college. My dad is crazy about college. Like all day long it's college, college, college. Like it's his mantra."

Hattie nods encouragingly. "That's great."

Sophy flaps Annie's ears up and down.

"I don't know. My mom says college doesn't make people happy. Like she thinks it's more important to be good than smart, and anyway, that it's no use to push children. She says our fate is our fate—like college is our fate or it's not. I don't know. My dad says it's because of her background that she thinks that, I guess it goes with carrying stuff on her head the way she used to. And, like, how even though she's been here forever she still eats with her hands if she's in a hurry, my dad has to tell her she should eat with a spoon and fork every time. Or else with a fork and knife like an American, or chopsticks, like a Chinese. Anything. Unless it's, like, a sandwich. And otherwise off a plate, or from a bowl, you know how the Chinese hold the bowl right up to their mouths? Do you do that?"

"Sometimes." Hattie nods.

"And do you, like, make noise?" Annie nips Sophy's finger.

"Slurp? Probably." Hattie smiles.

Sophy makes a face and bops Annie gently on the nose. "He does that, too, the Chinese way. But I guess my mom forgets because she grew up eating from a bowl in the middle of the table, everyone just helping themselves. Or off banana leaves. And my dad says that isn't even the worst thing about farmers. He says the worst thing about them is the way they never think about the future. They're, like, the opposite of the Chinese. Like even his brother who died was the opposite of the Chinese, and he was Chinese.

"But anyway, she is trying harder, you should see, and my dad is, too. Like my dad used to say that if his real wife were alive, everything would be different. Like if his real wife were alive, we would respect our elders. If his real wife were alive, we would not be wild. But he's trying not to say it anymore."

"Isn't your mom his real wife now?"

Sophy shakes her head, letting Annie play with a sneaker; she has new, flowered sneakers. "They're only, what do you call it, common-law married. He calls my mom his camp wife."

"From the refugee camp."

"Yeah. And now she's his American wife. His first wife's his real wife—his Cambodian wife."

Hattie takes this in. "And is that true, do you think? That if your dad's first wife were still around, everything would be different?"

"Probably," says Sophy, reclaiming her sneaker before it gets destroyed. "But anyway, he's stopped saying it now that we're here, because we're trying to be different than we were. Like my mom is trying to learn English now, she really is, she watches this program on TV every day."

"That's great," says Hattie.

Sophy rubs Annie's tummy thoughtfully.

"You know, you should really be in school," Hattie says. "Your dad might be a little off, but he's right about college."

Sophy throws Annie's chew toy for Annie to fetch again.

"Aren't you bored hanging around? Don't you want to see other people?"

"I do see other people," says Sophy. "Like I take the car to the center and see people there."

"Ah." Hattie stops. "The blue car?"

"I felt sorry for the driver," Sophy explains. "Driving all the way out here, and then my mom won't even get in. I mean, she will go to the grocery store, but that's it."

"Because?"

Sophy shrugs. "It's just, like, one more backward thing. So sometimes I go. Me and Gift."

"To the center, you mean?"

She nods, kneading Annie's tummy with her bare feet now; she has long, smooth feet.

"Is that a church center?"

"It's Bible study."

Bible study—what Hattie's mother's mission school taught, long ago. "It's not school."

"No," says Sophy. "But I'm going to school in the fall, I think."

"That's great. Though—what do you mean, you think?"

"You've got to ask my dad." Hearing something they don't, Annie suddenly pricks up her ears and runs off. "I mean, he's been talking about home schooling, but I don't know."

"For Sarun, too?"

"Sarun?" Sophy looks surprised. "No, Sarun just wants to make money."

"Is his gang"—Hattie thinks how to put this—"is his gang—what they're doing—their business—is it legal?"

"Probably not. But anyway, he said he would quit that gang when we came here. He said it was no good and dangerous and that he was going to quit before he got shot by a goya." Sophy plays with her hair.

"A 'goya'?"

"You know, a Latino. We call them that because everything they eat has, like, 'Goya' on the can."

"Ah. And did he quit?"

"He must have, right? Because they're there and we're here. And because we're trying to be different than we were." Annie returns. "Because that's why we came."

"To start over, you mean?"

Sophy shrieks.

"Good girl!" cries Hattie—Annie has a mouse in her mouth. "Good girl! Good girl!"

Encouraging her because, though there aren't many mice in the house now, come winter there will be; it would be great to have a mouser. But Annie just drops the mouse and lifts her head to be petted. The mouse escapes. Hattie sighs.

"As you were saying," she says.

But Sophy just wants to know, was that a *mouse*?

All week long, people have been asking, How do you know him? and, Isn't he great? Professor Yoga, they call him. Are you going to class with Professor Yoga? And so it is that Hattie finds herself saluting the sun once again. Carter runs a good class with a focus on the spine and nice, clear instructions for both level one and level two—aware as he is, now, that there are different levels in this group. If he were anyone but Carter, Hattie would be singing the "Hallelujah" chorus like everyone else. And if Riverlake were not such a small town, she would simply ignore the fact that he does not look at her, much less touch her or address her. Instead, she approaches him at the end of class.

"This is ridiculous," she says. "We are not children."

"Indeed, we are too old to pretend we are not angry when we are. What was that you had written in your family mansion in Qufu? Wasn't there a little door you could literally open? Revealing a rock?"

"*Kāi mén jiàn shān*—open the door and see the mountain."

"Ah, yes. What happened to 'Open the door and see the mountain'? I know you weren't as Confucian as we made you out to be. Still, wasn't that one of your Confucian quotes?" Carter's mouth is grimly horizontal, though when some people in the class wave goodbye to him, he perks up and waves back.

"I'm just trying to act my age," says Hattie.

But Mr. Combustible betakes himself away.

In an ideal world, they wouldn't put it so high, now, would they." Hattie hears Everett's voice behind her in Millie's. "In an ideal world, they'd know you're the one who buys it."

Everett doesn't talk as fast as some of the locals do, but he does draw out the *orr* in *you're*, and he *oys* his *i*'s, too, as he takes some taco shells and puts them back up where the hoisin sauce was. The hoisin sauce comes down.

"I guess this isn't an ideal world, is it," she says.

"Guess it ain't."

"I'm not the only one who buys it, either, you know."

"But you're the main one, wouldn't you say? The most important one." His look is all baby-faced innocence, as if he's genuinely expecting her to say yes.

She laughs. "I don't think so but thanks for the intervention."

He nods and gallantly tips his hat at her, then winks. He has pale blue eyes and a pencil in his shirt pocket, pointy end up. What with the T-shirt barely fitting his huge chest, the pocket's stretched tight; wrinkles radiate in spokes from his armpits.

"I heard your news, by the way," she goes on. "I'm so sorry."

"My news." He thinks. "You mean 'Soul Saved—Husband Ditched'? You mean, 'Thirty-seven Years Wasted, You Could Say My Whole Life'?"

"I'm sorry," she says again. "Thirty-seven years. That's a long time." She's at a bit of a loss as to what to say next. "My husband and I were married for thirty-one before he died."

"Is that right. Thirty-one years." Everett shakes his head.

"Lung cancer," she volunteers then. It's not like her to bring it up, but somehow she wants to tell him—guesses he'd want to know, too. And that she won't be sorry she told him—she guesses that as well.

And sure enough he takes up the news with a certain enthusiastic sympathy. "Wish that hadn't happened to you, now. Wish it hadn't."

"It was a while ago," she says. And, surprising herself, "I think I'm starting to get over it. Or not over it. Accustomed to it. Like it's a past life, if you know what I mean."

Still, Everett shakes his head again. "Cancer. Where'd that even come from, cancer? Did cavemen have cancer?"

"That's a good question."

"A plague. It's a kind of plague, now, ain't it. Instead of locusts, we have cancer." He knits his brow hard, but just when he's starting to look like a spelling bee contestant in trouble, winks again.

Hattie laughs after a moment, and nods. "What do you think, Everett? Think we're being punished for something?"

"Maybe." He's serious once more. "Maybe. 'Cause in an ideal world, we wouldn't have cancer, now, would we." He puts his hand up on one of the gray support columns that stand smack in the middle of the aisle, and immediately takes on a structural look himself. "Cancer, heart trouble. In an ideal world, we wouldn't have none of it."

"You having heart trouble?"

He shakes his head no. "Ginny's pa had it, though."

"Rex, you mean."

"Know him?"

"Heard of him." Hattie hears herself picking up Everett's clip. "Rex the Farmer King."

"Old Rex," he confirms. "He was something, in his time, now. The real thing, folks said. He was the real thing. The kind of farmer you don't see much of anymore. In an ideal world, he'd have lived forever. In an ideal world he'd have lived and lived, with his cows—he'd have lived with his cows. But he died, Old Rex—heart gave out on him, see. Then we lost the farm and Ginny found Jesus—put Jesus up on the throne of her life. Put him right up where the farm used to be." He pauses. "The highlights, now. I'm just giving you the highlights."

"You're telling me what happened to your marriage."

He nods, thoughtful.

"You're telling how you attained the happy state you're in now."

"She put my stuff out in the rain, last week. Put my stuff out, but I moved it all back. Dripping wet as it was. I moved it all back and hung it to dry in the living room." He spreads his huge hands out, as if to help Hattie visualize the array.

She can't help but laugh.

"Let it drip dry, so as to make these little puddles on the floor," he elaborates. "Had to put in some nails to do it."

"Guess you were mad," she says.

"Guess I was."

"Guess you didn't stonewall."

"Stonewall?"

"Guess you got yourself across loud and clear."

"Guess I did."

Hattie smiles. "Your clothes still up?"

"Yes, ma'am, they are. They're still up. She would've taken 'em all down except that her hip was bothering her. Couldn't get herself up on a chair, now, see. And I hung 'em a little high. Just a little high." He gestures.

"Guess you were aiming to tantalize."

"Guess I was, Hattie. Guess I was." He looks embarrassed but proud. " 'Cause you can't just chuck a person out the way she wants, now. It ain't right." He shakes his head. "It ain't right."

"No," she says. "It's not."

"To be frank, Christians don't even act the way she's acting. So she's no kind of Christian anyway."

"No," agrees Hattie. "She doesn't sound it."

"Know what kind of Christian she is? The kind who sees the damned and the saved but can't see what's right in front of their nose. That's what kind. The kind that sees the sheep and the goats. Who's going to heaven, and who's going to toast. But suffering, now. They don't see suffering. People." His voice is quiet, his bearing light.

"*It's a blinding kind of vision,*" agrees Hattie.

He looks at her blankly.

"It's what my mother used to say. *They have a blinding way of seeing.*"

"Your ma said that?"

Hattie nods. "She was a missionary."

"You don't say."

"She was a missionary but didn't stay one."

Everett nods, then suddenly pushes up his visor and trains his pale eyes on her. "I want you to tell Ginny."

"Tell her—?"

"You see Ginny in that group, right?"

"I do."

"I want you to tell her she's no kind of Christian. I want you to tell her she's got a blinding kind of vision—a blinding kind of vision, just like you said. A blinding way of seeing."

We must see what we don't see, Hattie's mother used to say. *Starting with, that we don't see. We must see that we don't see.* How humble her mother was, in her definite way, and how scientifically correct, as it turns out. And yet Hattie hesitates.

"You know, I'm in a walking group with Ginny, you're right," she begins. "But—"

Everett's jaw tightens ominously; his eyes flash. "Hedging," he says immediately. "You're hedging."

And before she can finish, Everett's disappeared around the corner, disgusted. The aisle seems to widen; the fluorescent lights buzz. Hattie looks for him, but can't find him.

. . .

Dear Aunt Hattie,

Andrea is not the big one, she is our baby. Do you remember how early she began to read? Such a little girl with such big books, we were always so proud of her. She count very well too. But now we are sick with worry. I don't know if you have ever heard of this sick called anorexia. A kind of mental trouble. What happens is that a girl stops eating food. If she eats something, she makes herself throw it up. She takes a pill too, that pill is to help get rid of her food. So she becomes very very thin, but in her mind she thinks she is fat and wants to lose more weight.

The poor girl!

We don't know what to do.

The poor parents.

We tell her we can feed her some nutritious soup. George offer her $10,000 U.S. for every pound she gain. . . .

Hattie sighs. *What is it about the Chinese and money,* indeed.

But she says no. We beg her please, come back to Singapore. Please come home.

Suffering. Who don't see suffering.

Breakfast for the dogs, and then for herself. Coffee. Muesli for the fiber—roughage, they used to call it. She adds a little sugar, why not. Then there're the dishes to do, and the clean clothes to sort. Why does she fold her underwear? Never mind. Today, when the moment comes, she throws her panties in the drawer unfolded. Freedom! She puts off getting dressed, too—stays right in her nightgown and bathrobe. And who knows? Maybe she'll just stay in them all day.
The unlived life isn't worth living.
Is that a mouse?

She is busy adding leaves to her bamboo stalks—the leaves blowing pell-mell, flecked and pelted with rain—when Sophy bangs at the slider. "Hattie! Hattie! My dad is hurt!"

"Sophy?"

Hattie hurries over. The dogs are already there; Sophy's nose and chin are pushed up to the screen door.

"You have to come!" She runs off, her ponytail flying.

"I'm coming!" Hattie laces up her walking shoes and tells the dogs to stay. And who knows what it is about her voice or the situation—maybe it's just the sight of Hattie in a bathrobe and walking shoes—but even Annie sits like Cato and Reveille, and, though her feet dance madly, stays.

"Good girl," says Hattie.

She hurries.

The trailer door is open wide. "Sophy?" No answer. The milk crate has a wooden crate set next to it now—a second step. Still, it's at least two normal steps up from the higher crate into the trailer. Hattie is about to grab the doorjamb and lever herself in when Sophy appears. She puts out one hand, then bends her knees and digs in her heels, bracing with her other. Such a nothing of a chicken-boned wrist she has, but she's strong. Her feet slide forward in her flowered sneakers, a gap opening at her heel—those sneakers are a size too big at least, thinks Hattie, even as she feels a pull in her shoulder. Then smells wash over her—cigarette smoke, mildew, incense. And there— her first clear view of the entertainment center. An enormous, blaring TV, set on a low table, and showing some sort of space movie. Flashing panels, an emergency, floating astronauts racing time; and below them, assorted picture frames, plastic figures, Buddhas, vases, baskets, a pagoda-shaped lantern, a bowl bristling with incense sticks, white paper doilies. A sagging rust-colored couch faces all this—way too close for comfortable viewing, but there's no room to push the thing back. Calendar pictures of Angkor Wat on the walls, movie stars; ruffled curtains on the window. The kitchen counter features more kinds of chips than Hattie knew existed—the bags puffed-up and weightless, like the astronauts on TV and quite unlike Chhung, who lies in the larger of the bedrooms, on a mattress on the floor. He's gripping a pillow as if to strangle it; his eyes are frantic, his brow rucked and slick. His neck tendons stand out like the veins of a leaf. Mum, squatting near his head, looks up.

"He was digging," supplies Sophy.

"Where does it hurt?" asks Hattie.

Chhung gestures at his left buttock, and down the back of his leg.

"You have any ice? I'll call a doctor."

The phone's out. No one quite knows why, though, out in the living room, Sarun guesses that Chhung hasn't been paying the bill.

"Maybe he's over his credit card limit." He leans forward, his elbows on the kitchen counter, and gives Hattie a once-over: She's still in her bathrobe.

She blushes but carries on. "Does he have a credit card?"

"Excuse me, ma'am. That was a joke."

"He did have one once," says Sophy. "But the company cancelled it because he didn't ever pay."

"Do you have a doctor?" asks Hattie.

Sarun guffaws; Gift puts his hand in a floor vent and gets it stuck.

Back at her house, Hattie calls her internist and reaches the nurse practitioner. A herniated disk with resultant sciatica, Leah guesses, but he should really be seen. Does he have insurance? Medicaid? Sophy, standing next to Hattie, doesn't know. Hattie says she'll call back, and sends Sophy to the trailer with some ice and ibuprofen in the meantime. Then she calls the church agency that settled the Chhungs. Maybe somebody over there knows something? Or maybe they provide insurance, who knows. But, no. The church agency provides nothing and knows nothing. In fact, though the Chhungs are living on church property, the church does not consider them part of its ministry.

"I'm sorry to say these people are not our highest priority," says the lady on the phone.

"I see," says Hattie.

"In fact, they exemplify a carelessness characteristic of our former pastor and raised a ruckus of which they are perhaps not even aware. You might even call them something of a situation." The lady lowers her voice. "These people, you understand, aren't even Christian."

Hattie hangs up.

What about the church with the blue car? When Sophy returns, Hattie asks her about that church—the Heritage Bible Church, it turns out. Ginny's church. Hattie takes that in even as she calls and explains. There's no one but a girl with a head cold in the office, though; she sounds as if she's talking through a kazoo. Can someone call back? Hattie says of course, but is honestly surprised when, a few minutes later, a chirpy woman does call, and with good news: They happen to have a church member who can see Chhung for free. He's not a doctor, but he is an EMT, which could be better, says the woman.

Better than a doctor? Well, never mind.

"Isn't that lucky," says Hattie.

"It's the Lord's plan," the woman goes on. "We're sending him right down."

"In the blue car?"

"The car is blue, yes." If the woman is surprised, she doesn't let on.

"Well, thanks a bunch. You people do support each other."

"It's just neighbors helping neighbors," says the woman. "Spreading the Good News."

Anyway: no more digging, that much is clear.

Chhung and his rescue are center table at the Come 'n' Eat the next day. His rescuers, too, as the Power and the Glory, it seems, knows both the kazoo girl who answered the phone and the chirpy woman who called back, as well as the EMT who came down in the blue car and gave Chhung a used back brace to wear. The brace is a little big, Ginny says, but if he wears it over a shirt it fits great.

"Did you know he used to be an engineer?" she asks brightly.

Chhung? An engineer? Hattie says something about the pit, and Chhung's house plans.

"Oh," says Ginny. "You know, I asked someone about that nasty hole the other day. That's a drainage ditch."

A drainage ditch.

"He knows how to improve that lot," she goes on. "He's smart. He's just not accustomed to doing the work himself."

"I bet not," says Greta, her gray eyes gone dark. "The poor man!"

"The boy hates helping," Ginny goes on. "But at least they know where he is when he has a shovel in his hands."

"Do they worry about him?" Grace looks to have slept on her eyebrows funny; the hairs of one are headed up, of the other, down.

"Wouldn't you?" Ginny is poised and quick.

"A cute thing like that," agrees Beth.

"Though that hair," says Candy. "Don't you have to wonder if the Good Lord intended kids to have that color hair?"

Her own white roots are showing today, but never mind.

"Maybe he can go to school now," says Hattie.

"Wouldn't that be a happy outcome," says Greta.

In any case, Ginny digs into her meat loaf, smiling enigmatically as planning begins. Beth is thinking casserole; Ginny, chicken; Hattie, fish; Candy, quesadillas. Greta is going to bake them a raisin bread in her woodstove, and Grace is going to do a salad from the greenhouse. They know food doesn't solve anything, but they want the Chhungs to know people are thinking of them. And hasn't the group always reached out when there's reaching out to do? Aren't they the Pride of Riverlake, just as their Fourth of July banner proclaims?

"Though don't you wonder if there isn't something the matter with their karma?" says Candy. "I mean, if they are just not in a state of grace?"

Greta considers. "First Pol Pot and now this, you mean."

"It's their fate," says Beth, flatly.

But Hattie just as flatly disagrees. "It's their luck. It's their plain bad luck, that's all."

An unsupported assertion she would certainly have had to defend back in the lab. Here at the Come 'n' Eat, though, adamance is enough. Everyone eats peacefully. Then Beth looks back up.

"This may not be the moment to ask," she says, "but are we ready for a change of subject?"

"We are," says Ginny.

Beth looks shyly at Hattie. "If things are just not happening with you and Carter . . ." She plays with her toothpick, turning red.

"Maybe you're wondering, Is he fair game?" says Ginny, helpfully. "Maybe you're asking, What really is God's will here?"

No one says anything.

"It's a reasonable question, after all," she goes on. "It'd be plain unnatural not to wonder, What is He trying to tell us? Is He sending us a message?"

"Oh!" says Candy, finally.

Hattie considers her glazed chicken.

"You don't have to answer," says Greta.

"You don't have to agree," says Grace.

"I shouldn't have said anything," says Beth.

"I don't own him," says Hattie—casual enough, she thinks. Though what a blocked thing her energy is suddenly—her *qì*. A thing with a life of its own. Or, no—*a lifelessness of its own,* as Lee used to say, of her own flagging *qì*, toward the end. *It has a lifelessness of its own.*

I'm going to miss you, Hattie told her then. *I am. I'm going to miss you every single day.*

To which Lee fluttered her lashless eyelids and moved her lips behind her oxygen mask and said, *Swab.* Wanting her mouth swabbed.

Swab.

"You're a generous woman," concludes Ginny.

Hattie doesn't answer, but she does manage to meet Ginny's green eyes for a moment. *For thine is the power and the hogwash.*

Flora is wearing all white today, like a cloud or a nurse.

"Here," she says suddenly, sliding a cup of coffee in front of Hattie; her white shirt flashes bright in the sun. "It's on the house." And when Hattie looks up at her wonderingly, she just shrugs. "It's what I have to give," she says, then turns.

Sophy: How They Even Got Here

When Sophy's dad was happy, he would explain stuff like how a country needs two wheels. *"Can't you see how people have two eyes, two ears, two hands?"* he would say in Khmer, pointing to his own eyes and ears and hands. *"Our land needs two wheels. One is the wheel of the Dhamma—that is the Buddhist wheel, the Eightfold Path, the Way. The other is the wheel of law. If the wheel of law is not strong, the cart cannot go. If the wheel of the Dhamma is not strong, the cart cannot go, either. When Pol Pot came, the wheel of the Dhamma was okay, but the wheel of law was no good. Because of all the corruption,"* he would say. *"You probably don't know what that means, corruption. But one day you will know. One day."* And then he would go on to say how, like, in the olden days, Cambodians were lords of all their neighbors, and had reading and writing and poetry and irrigation, and, like, how everything would have been great except that the Thais came, and then the Cham, and then the Japanese—or maybe the Japanese were the Chinese? Anyway, it was hard for Sophy to understand. Like did they all just wake up one day and think, Let's invade Cambodia? Because it was wack, it really was, the way that, after that the French came and after that the Vietnamese and, like, no one thought, Man, that is so copycat. Like no one thought, That is a thousand-year-old idea, man. They just thought, Let's do it!

The point being that it wasn't just because of Pol Pot that Sophy's family was wack. It was also because the wheel of law was broken because of corruption and invasions, and because there wasn't enough money to send her dad and his brother and sister all to school, just one of them. Which was why Sophy's uncle went to public school for a couple of years, but then stayed in the village and had a vegetable farm like his sister who didn't get to go to school at all, while Sophy's dad got to go from the public school to a temple school with monks because he was the oldest. And then from the temple school he went to a school in the city, and then he got a big deal job as an engineer and grew a potbelly like a rich person and took a fancy name and started talking like somebody from Phnom Penh instead of from Battambang. Like he started doing the whole m' Penh clip 'n' dip thing. And he married a Chinese Cambodian because he was Chinese Cambodian, which was obvious. Like if you ever saw him sitting in front of the TV, you'd see how he has pale skin and Chinky eyes, and kind of an oval face like Sophy's sister Sophan's, it isn't round like Mum's and Sophy's, and her sister Sopheap's. That's because all four of his grandparents were from China, and if his brother or his sister or any of his cousins were alive they would all be, like, eating Chinese food. Of course, if you asked a lot of regular Cambodians what food is the best, they'd all say Chinese too, but they'd say it in kind of a different voice than Sophy's dad—like, not as though Chinese food was their food, but more like they had to admit it, even if they only liked Chinese Cambodians a little more than they liked the Vietnamese, who they hated. But anyway, because Sophy's dad was educated and Chinese Cambodian he married another Chinese Cambodian who was, like, rich and beautiful and tall. She had skin as white as cotton, and she didn't move all her parts at once, but would, like, turn her head, and then smile, and then pick up her teacup, and then nod. She drank café au lait like a foreigner, and not only could she read and write Khmer, she knew French too, and Chinese. Her French was so good that she didn't have to repeat things the way other people did when they were talking to French people, and that really impressed Sophy's dad. But what really really got him was her Chinese, because his grandparents spoke Teochew dialect and his parents knew a little, but he hardly knew any. And here she could not only speak Teochew dialect and

Cantonese, because her family were city people, but Mandarin too—
like, she even knew the characters, which if you think Khmer script is
bad, is even worse. Like practically nobody can read them besides
people in China. And that was why, when they got married, Sophy's
dad went and stood on the graves of his ancestors, and told them, and
why a flower opened up right near the graves that very moment. Like
he turned, and there was this blooming flower that had been closed
just a moment before, a white one. Of course, when Sophy and
Sopheap and Sophan heard that story later, they were, like, And the
flower just opened? Are you sure? Like what kind of flower was that?
Not that they would have said that out loud, because that would have
been, like, big time disrespectful. But anyway, their dad said that that
was one of the happiest moments of his life, and they did believe that,
because he never looked the way he looked telling that story at any
other time, ever.

And even now he talks about his first wife as if she is their real
mother, it's like Sophy's mom just somehow ended up giving birth to
them by mistake. Like he talks about how things would be different if
his first wife had lived—like how Sarun would not be involved with
gangs and how instead of asking why why why, Sophy and her sisters
would be asking stuff like how they could be more polite and how
they could show more respect. As if any kids in America ask that! But
that's what he thinks. He thinks that if his first wife had lived, everyone would be, like, looking at them and asking, Whose family do
those children belong to? Because they were so shy and perfect and
obeyed every single thing in the *Chbap Srey*, which is, like, this stupid
book of rules for girls. A lot of kids said their moms used to laugh at
the *Chbap Srey* back in Cambodia, but Sophy's dad's first wife must
not have laughed, because she was the book for real. Like she didn't
go from sweet and shy to loud and bossy as soon as she got married.
Instead she talked softly and walked softly and covered herself and
didn't show off, and sat the way you're supposed to sit, with her legs
to the side. She was so perfect that sometimes even Sophy thinks if she
were alive they would somehow all still be living in Phnom Penh, in
the fancy concrete house with two floors that Sophy's dad bought
himself. He still talks about it sometimes. Like about the roof garden,
and the garage for the car, and the big gate in the garden wall with a
guard to open and shut it. Which, like, Sophy and her sisters can't
really imagine, because their mom cleans houses and they are poor

and dark, even Sophan who looks like their dad is sort of dark. Not as dark as their mom, who is what they call *sra'aem,* but they don't have skin like cotton either, because their mom is pure Cambodian. Meaning brown skin and round eyes and curly hair, though people always said she was pretty, and pretty rich too, for someone who lived in the countryside. Which was why she was originally married to Sophy's dad's brother. Because her family had, like, a hut with a tile roof instead of straw, and a mango farm, besides; they weren't just, like, rice farmers. Of course, it's sort of wack to think about how Sophy's mom was married to Sophy's uncle before she was sort of married to Sophy's dad. Like Sophy's mom still remembers when Sophy's dad and his first wife and some other people came to live with them after everyone had to leave Phnom Penh, which was pretty rough for everyone but especially for the first wife. Because on the one hand it was pretty lucky that they could go live with Sophy's uncle, like if it weren't for him, Sophy's dad probably wouldn't be alive to remember how great his first wife was and everything. But on the other hand, they all had to sleep in one room and cook their food outside, and eat a lot of things you couldn't really call food while the soldiers threatened to send them to *Angka.* (*Angka* being what they called the people who were running the country, they were kind of like the government except that nobody voted for them, in fact everyone probably would have voted against them if they could have.) Do you want to go see *Angka?* the soldiers would say. I think it's time you went to go see *Angka.* The soldiers took Sophy's dad's first wife for one of the Khmer Rouge to marry even though she was already married, and when she refused to marry him, the Khmer Rouge buried her up to her neck and left her to die. Which she would have, except that Sophy's dad found her and dug her out, and that was so happy! Except that then she couldn't make herself eat, and died anyway. It was the sort of stuff a lot of kids wrote about in their old town, because the teachers wanted them to, all the stories. But if the teachers didn't ask, the kids never would. Because, like, who wanted to write about eating bugs and rats? And people not dying and then dying anyway, or disappearing. Like *Angka* would take people out for a walk and no one would ever see them again. Or sometimes they'd get killed right in front of your eyes, like a soldier would strangle someone with a plastic bag, or hit them on the back of the head like their dad does to Sarun, only not with a newspaper but with a shovel.

Right where the soul was, they would hit them, and then they would bury them even if they weren't dead yet. Like they would just shove them into a pit with, like, a bunch of other bodies and start shoveling.

Even with everything going wrong here, Sophy's glad she didn't live there. It was, like, too wack.

But anyway, after a while all that was left of the family were Sophy's mom and dad, and Sarun. Of course, her mom was not her mom yet. And she didn't know that Sophy's dad (who wasn't her dad yet) was still alive, and he didn't know she was alive either. So they were, like, so happy to find each other in the refugee camp! Because there they were, looking for the same people and crying over the same people. And because she was a woman she had a food ration she could share with him, and once he got stronger he could protect her from the Thai robbers and do a lot of other brave stuff besides. Like he would sneak out of the camp and go to the Thai villages and come back with rice, rolling it up into a piece of cloth so it was like a tube. And he would, like, tie that to his body and run run run past the Thai soldiers, and then he would sneak back into the camp and sell the rice so he was, like, a hero. And then he and Sophy's mom found Sarun, who had nobody left to take care of him—like there he was, all by himself, this baby toddling around with all the other orphans, Sophy's dad probably wouldn't have even realized the kid was his sister's son except that he had this scar on his cheek, like a bullet hole. And then even though Sophy's dad had barely seen his family for a long time, Sophy's dad remembered hearing about that scar, and how his sister had said her baby must have been a soldier in his last life. And then it turned out that Sophy's mom had heard about the scar too, though she had never seen the baby either, because he was born during the fighting. And she agreed that it was, like, their fate, to find the baby and save him. So she and Sophy's dad rescued Sarun, and fed him rice so he wasn't starving anymore, and got him medicine so he wasn't sick anymore, and after that they stuck together, the three of them. Because no one else was crying for their family members, and before they found each other they were completely alone in the world, and couldn't even cry. That's what Sophy's mom always says. She says she couldn't even cry until she saw Sophy's dad, a familiar face. And then when she finally cried, she cried so much that when she stopped crying she couldn't see for a long time. Until Sophy's dad told her he had found Sarun, and then she tried to see him, and then she did! And now they have to stick together because they're all that's left, and because it's too complicated to explain to people how Sophy's mom couldn't see for a while, or why she never really married Sophy's dad, or why Sophy and her sisters call Sarun their brother when he isn't their brother. Like who even knows if there are names for what they are, or for their kind of family?

Like what do you call a person who is, like, twins with someone who isn't there? Sophy doesn't think her dad will ever really accept that her mom lived instead of his first wife, it's like Sophy's mom lived by mistake. So that everywhere she goes is somewhere his real wife isn't going, and everything she does is something his real wife isn't doing. And Sophy's dad also lived by mistake, because he was the educated one *Angka* was trying to kill, the only reason he lived was that *Angka* messed up and killed the wrong brother. So that even though Sophy's dad didn't die, he sort of got reborn anyway as his brother, into his brother's life, and everything he does is something his brother isn't doing, except that he is sort of doing it, depending on how you look at it.

It's all, like, wack.

Now Sophy's dad is old and has diabetes, which isn't so bad yet, but is going to get worse unless he watches out. Like he should not eat so much white rice, as Sophy knows because she went with him to the health clinic in their old town, and the doctor said to tell him about white rice, it was really important. So she did, she told her dad how white rice will turn right into sugar, and how that's bad for diabetes. And she told him that he should eat brown rice instead, because brown rice does not turn into sugar right away and that's, like, good for diabetes. Of course, even though she was supposed to be translating the hard parts of what the doctor said, she said a lot of the words in English, because she speaks Khmer the way he speaks English, meaning barely, and anyway who even knows if they exist in Khmer, words like *simple carbohydrates* and *complex carbohydrates*. Like even if she knew those words in Khmer they would still be in English. And she told him that he should think about it for a while and then look in a mirror and then decide what to eat, because once he told Sophy that that was what it meant to be Cambodian. Like being Cambodian meant everyone living together, and not killing things, but it was also not reacting to things. Like if someone does something to them, he used to say, they should consider that thing. They should ask why did that person do this thing? And what did they do, that this person has done this thing? They should ask that, he used to say. And then they should look in a mirror, and only after thinking about it for a long time, should they decide if they should do something. He used to lean forward with his legs apart and shake his finger in the air at them as he said that, and then sort of swoop his finger quick to the side, as if he was lopping off the head of somebody saying the wrong answer. *You shouldn't just react!* he would say. Lop! *You should think!* Lop! *You should think!* So now she asked him if he would please think about what he eats the way he thinks about what to do. Like she asked him if he would please ask himself why the doctor said those words. *Simple carbohydrates. Complex carbohydrates.* And, like, she asked him in the very most polite way, with her head down, and in a soft voice, using sweet words, she was, like, all *piek p'aem, piek pi'rouah.* And she, like, used the respectful form for "eat," and did not call him *Ouv* but *Pa.* But he just said he did not like brown rice.

"*It's expensive,*" he explained.

She nodded.

"*It doesn't taste like rice,*" he explained.

She nodded.

"*Cambodians,*" he said, "*eat white rice.*"

And that was that. Lop! He kept on eating white rice, two bowls with every meal, because he doesn't believe in diabetes, though he does worry about his heart. Like he thinks his heart goes too fast, he's afraid the arteries of his neck are going to explode from blood overload. Or else his chest. He's afraid his chest is going to explode from blood overload. The doctors say chests don't just, like, explode like a bomb, no matter how overloaded they are, but her dad used to so insist and insist his was going to anyway, that in the clinic in their old town Sophy would sometimes just stop translating what he was saying. Like sometimes after a while she would just say, He feels dizzy a lot, and can't breathe. And Dr. Blitzman would nod sympathetically and readjust the end of his tie so it lay flat on his stomach. He wore these special ties with funny things on them like rubber ducks and basketballs, but when he looked down he mostly just frowned and said things like sure, her dad could certainly take herbal medicine from the *kru* if he wanted to. Two visits later, though, he would not be surprised to hear it didn't work. He was always telling her dad not to smoke. Like if he wanted to feel better, Dr. Blitzman would say, he should stop. Because that, he said, would work. But then he would just go on to the next patient, because what else could he do? Once he asked Sophy if she knew what *burnout* was. He wasn't talking about himself, he said. He was talking about the other people in the clinic, and why there weren't enough of them—why the clinic was *under-staffed*. But she still thinks of *burnout* whenever she thinks of him. She remembers him saying, "Do you know what burnout is?" And then laughing a little laugh. "It's what can come of inspiration, if you're not careful."

It's what can come of inspiration, if you're not careful.

Most days Sophy's dad puts on the big TV and watches sports, yelling and cheering if things are going good and slumping down if things aren't. Like if his team loses he'll turn off the TV and go get himself another beer, and then sometimes he'll sit back down in front of the screen as if he has something to ask it. Of course, the TV does sort of look like a temple altar, Sophy's mom having covered the whole entertainment table with, like, figurines and plastic flowers and incense holders and Buddhas. There's doilies and little bowls of candy too, and some Marys and Josephs and baby Christs someone gave her, and a picture of Sarun in a baseball uniform, so it's not as weird as it sounds that her dad will sometimes just sit there and sit there with his eyes moving around, looking as though he's expecting Buddha to come talk to him out of the screen. Because the whole thing is like something between an altar and a computer that went down, it looks like any second it could *ding* and come back up, first with a blank screen, and then with that noise that means the computer is thinking. So that if you're patient, there it'll be, pretty soon, the answer.

Why why why why why.

Other times her dad'll play with his slide rule or his drafting tools—like he'll draw a little bridge while he's sitting there, just make up a river and put this bridge over it for fun. Or else he'll sit there and smoke and ask, like, how did he get to be the educated one who moved to the city and had a fancy house and a car? Where did his good karma come from? And then what happened to it? And was there something the matter with the karma of the whole country, that Pol Pot came? Did they do something wrong? That's when he isn't drunk. When he's drunk he'll say mad stuff, like that he ate the livers of his enemies during Pol Pot time just like the Khmer Rouge (which Sopheap says the Khmer Rouge really did, though she sort of doubts that their dad did too). Or else he'll wave a kitchen knife in the air and tell Sophy and her sisters that they're going to be hookers and that if he ever hears they are going around with boys he is going to kill them. Lop! Which is, like, one reason why Sophy didn't exactly run and tell him about Ronnie the minute she started seeing him.

Now Sophy's dad and mom have Sarun and three girls and a baby too, he is so cute! But Sophy's dad is, like, ashamed he had children with Sophy's mom, and that's why he's so strict, besides the fact that Cambodians are just strict. So that if anyone does anything wrong, he doesn't just say you were wrong. Instead he says, *You should be ashamed to have been born. You should be ashamed. Why were you born? Why?* And then they'll say it too. *We're sorry we were born. There's no reason for us to live. We're sorry we were born. We're sorry.* Especially Sarun will say it, but Sophy will say it too sometimes, and Sopheap, and Sophan. *We're sorry. There is no reason for us to live. We're sorry.* And mostly that's that, though every once in a while he'll look at them and say, *To destroy you is no loss,* the way they did in Pol Pot time. Because that's the way he talks when he's drunk. It's, like, *destroy* this and *destroy* that. Like if he wanted to kill somebody, he wouldn't say that, he wouldn't say, I want to kill you. He'd say, *I want to destroy you,* and he'd mean it.

Which sounds pretty bad but the funny thing is that, back in their old town, Sophy's sisters and her were happy. Like they all slept together, the three of them in two beds pushed together, and even though there was a crack in the middle, they didn't care. They had an agreement that whoever slept on the crack could have the biggest poster to put up, and so it was always Sophan who slept there, because she just loved that *Titanic* movie! Sophy liked Britney Spears and Sopheap liked Tiffani-Amber Thiessen, but Sophan's thing for Leonardo DiCaprio and Kate Winslet was different, because she thought Jack and Rose were, like, perfect! And Sophy knew what she meant in a way, because Sophy could hear their voices too sometimes. Like she could hear Jack say, *Never let go,* and she could hear Rose say, *Put your hands on me, Jack,* and she could hear him say, *Make every day count.* She could. She wasn't as bad as Sophan, though, who so wanted Jack and Rose to get together in their next life that she was, like, burning incense for them all the time. She didn't care that she had to do it at home, on their chest of drawers, because of the monks all fighting at the temple, some of them controlling the upstairs and some of them controlling the downstairs, you couldn't walk in the door without being on one side or the other. Pretty soon the whole top of the bureau was basically an altar to Jack and Rose, with oranges and incense and plastic flowers and swans and stuff, sort of like what their mom liked to put all over the TV, only with this giant *Titanic* poster above it. Sophy had just this little Britney Spears poster and Sopheap's poster of Tiffani-Amber Thiessen was even smaller, but that was okay. They actually all liked the Jack and Rose altar, arranged so neat and beautiful, not like their room in general, which was a mess! It really was. Not that they cared, in fact they loved the whole mixed-up scene, and would take pictures of themselves wearing their own clothes and each other's clothes and write down what people said about their outfits and how much it messed them up, though even without the clothes people would probably have mixed them up anyway. Because all three of them had, like, long hair, and they were almost the same height and almost the same age and their names were so much the same too. Like Sophy's name is Sophy, and her younger sister is Sopheap, and of course, the youngest is Sophan the *Titanic* fan. It's hard to explain to people, but that's just what Cambodian families do, and their names all have meanings like "hardworking" and "polite" and "beautiful," but that's even harder to explain. Like your name means "beautiful"? Sophan always used to imitate the look on the black girls' faces when she told them that. They were, like, "Whoa! Put down yo' cell phone, and listen to this!" A lot of Cambodian kids have English names now like Linda and May, but their dad is old-fashioned because he wasn't young when he came, he wasn't like some kids' parents, who were, like, twenty. He was, like, fifty or something and a lot more Cambodian. So Sophy and Sopheap and Sophan use their Khmer names unless somebody makes a mistake. Like if someone calls Sophy "Sophie" or "Sophia" instead of So-PEE, she just lets them, so what. She figures a lot of Cambodians don't speak Khmer, why should they?

Anyway, the beds took up the whole room. You could not get into bed except by climbing in at the foot, and Sophy remembers how one day their social worker Carla said something about that to, like, this visitor. "They're used to it," she said, and Sophy remembers that because she had never heard Carla call them *they* before. And *used to* was what they were supposed to say about America and American food even though they were born here, the beds didn't seem like a thing they were used to or not. It wasn't until a lot later that she realized that what Carla meant was that it was something her friend would have to get used to, if she were to end up in their lives, somehow. That it was, like, Cambodian. But so what, Carla was still all right. Like when she called, she'd say, "Hey, my love," like she was a kid instead of a grown-up, and she took them shopping and ate with them and corrected their grammar, and back when they were listening to all that hip-hop and rap, Carla was the one who told them it was bad to be ghetto and hooked them on TV shows like *Dawson's Creek* and *Beverly Hills 90210* instead. Like she made them change their style. And the sad fact is, if Carla hadn't gotten sick, they would probably still be in their bedroom singing "Wannabe." If Carla hadn't gotten sick, they would probably never have gotten in trouble the way they did. If Carla hadn't gotten sick, they would probably still be doing the moves like Britney Spears and talking about how Sopheap could be a TV star like Tiffani-Amber Thiessen!

Even Sarun said it was too bad when Carla got sick, and Ronnie said it too. Like it was just some bad shit, he said.

Back when Sophy's dad became a big deal engineer, he changed his name to Ratanak, which was fancier than his old name, which was Souen. He kept his family name, which of course in Cambodia goes first instead of last. That was Chhung. But he needed a first name that went with living in the city, and so he changed it, and only went back to being Souen when he went to go live in the village with his brother after the Khmer Rouge came and made everyone leave Phnom Penh. And then it was lucky he had changed his name and changed it back, because it helped hide him. But even now Sophy's mom calls him Souen instead of Ratanak sometimes, and that makes him mad. She doesn't want to make him mad, but she can't make city names come out of her mouth—they're, like, too long. Country names are easier to say, like her own name, Mum.

Sophy's mom wasn't good with her mouth, but she was good with her hands. Like in Cambodia, she was good at everything from planting seedlings to scraping off leeches to picking out head lice to sewing, and here she was good too, no one could put eyes on a stuffed animal faster than she could. But she wasn't loud like some of the other women, full of talk and opinions. She was quiet even in Khmer, and could not learn English, because that was something you did with your mouth. Or that's what she said. Sophy's dad said she just liked to act *ting moung*, like she did during Pol Pot time, like she couldn't hear or think anything, like she was some kind of dummy. He would sing her this song they used to sing in Cambodia that went *"You know you must plant trees / To do well you must plant l'ngo and kor,"* which was kind of a trick song because *l'ngo* means "sesame" but sounds like "stupid," and *kor* means "kapok tree" but sounds like "mute," so that the song used to mean you'd better be stupid and mute if you want to keep out of trouble with *Angka*. Now it was just a way of making fun of Sophy's mom.

But back in their old town, her mom said if she was *ting moung* it was thanks to that woman living next door who went around with barely any clothes on, because guess who looked. And that was bad. But the funny thing was that the lace bra didn't even bother Sophy's mom as much as the fact that that woman could read and write and speak English. She had a job in the high school that kept her away some of the time, but she had all these holidays Sophy's mom didn't have, and when her mom was away, the woman was busy not only making eyes at Sophy's dad but trying to steal Gift. Like she was always giving him sweets and stuff.

"She thinks Gift recognizes her," Sophy's mom said. *"And she thinks she knows him, too. She thinks she's his* m'day daem.*"*

M'day daem meant his former mother, from another life.

"Do you think she maybe is?" Sophy asked.

"No!" her mom said.

But she worried anyway. She worried the neighbor might get a *kru* to do voodoo on Gift, and she worried in general about losing her kids, because she'd lost her sons before, and because that was just what Sophy's mom worried about. Like she worried the kids would leave, like they weren't really hers, but just borrowed or something. Sophan always joked that there was no one with an easier life than the old women hanging around the temple, because people like their mom gave them so much food and money. *"I give because that woman has no one to take care of her,"* their mom would say. *"Look at her. All alone. No one to take care of her in her old age. No children. Look at her."*

And once Sophan said, *"Look at her. Look at her,"* too, imitating their mom.

But Sopheap who thought more about stuff, like she'd been a teacher in her former life or something, said, "It's the ghosts of our brothers that make her like that," and then Sophan stopped and felt bad.

Before the monks started fighting, Sophy's mom went to the temple all the time. And her mom is still Buddhist now, like she doesn't believe in killing bugs or going fishing or anything, Buddhism is very strict. But instead of giving oranges and rice and *amok* to the fighting monks, now she sends money to this other monk, who sends it to Cambodia, or at least that's what he says. Of course, being American, Sophy and her sisters don't care about karma that much, which their mom wishes they would but says is okay. Because while she thinks it is better to die than to give up the teachings of the Buddha, she also thinks kids don't have deep thoughts yet—like they don't know themselves yet. Knowing yourself—*dung khluon aeng*—being this big deal to her. She thinks that they'll turn more Buddhist when they are, like, thirty or fifty, and know what life is. And in the meantime she's trying to build up her own karma, because in her next life, she definitely does not want to live when pretty much everybody else in her family is dead, in her next life she wants to die with them or, better yet, be one of the first ones to go. Because how lucky her father was, that he got killed right away and didn't have to watch a single other person get killed or beaten or starved, while here she's still seeing it and hearing it in her dreams. Like it never ends. *"Kit ch'ran,"* Sophy's dad says—she thinks too much. As if he doesn't? In their old town, Sophie's mom went to the *kru* sometimes and got medicine, but it didn't help. She still dreamed about having to drink cow piss, or walk over dead bodies, or sleep with dead bodies. Or about being covered with flies, or suffocating in the mud, or about ghosts. *K'maoch* who promise her food to eat, when actually they're going to eat her. *K'maoch* who want to be buried, but then pull her into the grave with them. Or baby *k'maoch* who want her to feed them but then grow up into giants that crush her. She had three children before, in Cambodia, by Sophy's uncle, but they all starved.

That was bad.

Now Sophy's mom has a new baby she is so happy about. She named him Gift because he is like her boys come back to her, a gift. But she still sits up at night a lot, afraid to go to sleep, because of the *k'maoch* and because she thinks Gift's mother from his last life really might come get him, that's why she puts scissors under his pillow, to scare that other mother away. How does she know Gift's *m'day daem* is afraid of being cut, Sophy says, but her mom says she just knows. She tries to make sure he never cries, because that might worry his *m'day daem* and make her come, and she keeps a light on too, because his *m'day daem* doesn't like light. And who knows if she's right or wrong, all Sophy knows is, it's not like sleeping with her sisters. There are two bedrooms in the trailer, so Sarun and her dad sleep in one, and her mom and Gift and Sophy sleep in the other. And Sarun and her dad have their own mattresses, but her mom and Gift and Sophy have one big mattress that they use sideways, which is okay because they're all small and fit fine. Mostly, though, Sophy lies down while her mom sits propped up against her wall, holding Gift all night, which he really likes and is fine with Sophy, except when her mom does finally fall asleep herself. Because then Gift rolls off her lap and starts crying, and that wakes everyone up. Sophy tries to sleep facing her wall, because noise coming from in back of you isn't as loud as noise coming from in front, and she blindfolds her eyes with a knee sock to block out the light, but lets her mom put her feet under her, if she wants, because her mom's feet get so cold. Her mom's hands get cold too, if she's not holding Gift, and sometimes she sweats and shakes and gets dizzy or *pibak chet nah*—like, just gets really, deeply sad. Her sadness is hidden inside, so you can't really see it, except that it kind of shrinks her up and sucks her into it, kind of like a *k'maoch,* which is messed up, seeing as how she's so tiny and skinny to begin with, like the kids are all two sizes bigger than her at least. Not that they're so tall, but they're definitely full-size people, while their mom looks like maybe she is or maybe she isn't.

Anyway, Sophy is just hoping that one day her sisters will be living with her again, the three of them sharing one room the way they used to. She doesn't care if it's Cambodian or not, because it was just the best! It was, it was, like, love or happiness, or heaven, or something. She sees now that she was bad, and that that was why things happened the way they did. Because in Khmer there's an expression, *One bad fish spoils the whole basket,* and that's what people believe— that if a girl is bad, it shows that that whole line of the family is bad. So that what Sophy did made everyone look down on her sisters, until finally they couldn't take it. Like it shattered their face, which is why they went bad and got into trouble too.

But probably she should just say what happened, right?

Okay.

With Ronnie, it was a lot like being with her sisters. Like they shared stuff and hung out. The downtown being full of fancy stores, and the whole city being, like, this showcase, Cambodian kids were not supposed to hang around downtown—Latinos either. Because the merchants didn't like the way it looked. They didn't like all the black hair, and they thought everyone was, like, in a gang. So you could wait for your bus downtown, but if the bus came and you didn't get on it, you got arrested for loitering, or for disorderly conduct, something. Even if you weren't doing anything, the police would come and harass you until finally you gave them the finger and then they could arrest you for that. They were tough—Irish, mostly, or Greek. And in the evening there was a curfew to keep kids off the streets, eleven o'clock, which a lot of people said wasn't even legal. But the town had that curfew anyway, and that pissed Ronnie off. "What is this shit?" he'd say. "Are we second-class citizens or what?" He was short, but he had this big way of talking, and Sophy loved that, even Sophan said like Leonardo DiCaprio, and he was! Like he wouldn't have just stayed downstairs in the *Titanic* and shut up and gotten drowned, he would have broken through the gate and escaped. And he didn't care he was short. "You're Cambodian, you're short," he used to say, laughing at guys who wore elevator shoes and stuff. You could tell he was used to being on a stage, being the lead singer of his band, and the lead guitar too, because he'd, like, spread his arms so wide you could see the bony sides of his body through the droopy armholes of his basketball jersey, and he'd turn his head from side to side, looking everybody right in the eye and showing off his earring, which was real platinum. Ronnie had the only real platinum earring anybody'd ever seen, and it really was real, like he'd bought it off a rock star who was getting a new one, and that was, like, so Ronnie. He was ahead of everyone, and not just in his jewelry. His thinking was ahead too. Like he'd say, "Pretty soon there's going to be a poop scoop law, so if Cambodians shit on the streets we'll know we should clean it up ourselves," and he called the police *Angka.* "Watch out, here comes *Angka,*" he'd say. "Watch out. They're going to send you to see *Angka.*" The whole point of school was to keep Cambodians off the streets, he'd say, which was why he, for one, was not going to school. "Because what is this shit?" he'd say. "Aren't these our streets?" He liked to walk down the middle of them sometimes, which of course brought *Angka* running. Downtown, but also where they all lived, in the Yard, because that was the trouble area where shootings happened. And when the blues came running, Ronnie'd run too, ducking and feinting, and having a good laugh later. "*Angka* is like a pineapple," he'd say. "*Angka* has eyes everywhere, but we got by the bastard. Can you believe this shit?"

Ronnie used the same words for a lot of things, only changing his voice. Like he was into Cambodian culture. He was into playing *roam vong,* and *roam k'bach,* and *saravan,* and not just rock, and whenever he found some new way of mixing them with rock, he'd say, "Can you believe this shit?"—kind of pleased, like. And with Sophy too, he'd say it. Like if she said her mom and dad didn't want her to date until she was engaged, he would say, real gentle-like, "I don't believe this shit." And when they'd go sit down by one of the canals and make out, he'd put his hand up her shirt and say, "Now this is some shit," and she'd think that too. Like she'd say, "Put your hands on me, Jack," like Sophan did when she was imitating Rose in the movie, and he'd do that. And sometimes he'd put his whole head inside her shirt and pull it down like a tent, and like, nuzzle and touch her, and it'd be like she had a baby in there, something really hers. And they could do that for a long time in the beginning. But then she started nuzzling him back, and then they could not stand it, it was just some shit! And one day she had to have him not just in her shirt but in her, she didn't care they were outside, she didn't care what happened, she didn't care about anything. Or maybe she did, because she made him pull out in the beginning. But then he pulled out later and later, until finally he said, "Oh, what is this shit, my love, what is this shit," and even though they had been planning to get some rubbers that very day, she couldn't say anything except, "I'm flying!" like Rose in *Titanic.*

And he said, "This is some shit."

Then they did it again, and afterwards they watched the water go gold in the canal, even though they knew that meant it was way after school hours, probably supper time or something. She felt like that shit just didn't matter anymore because they were, like, a man and a woman. And they were starting a new life, they were. Like they were going to leave this place and forget about Cambodia. First they were going on a honeymoon with all their brothers and sisters on, like, an island where there were beaches and you could jump off rocks into the water and stuff. And then they were going to *make every day count.* They were. They were going to *make every day count.* Maybe she would have gone home, if it wasn't already so late she knew she was going to be beaten. But that late there was no hope, her dad was definitely going to beat her with a broom handle or get drunk and yell at her with a knife in his hand, and so she didn't go home. Instead she sat with Ronnie and watched the water, which was moving fast and kind of weaving around, the way it did when the locks were open, making all these complicated patterns that changed and changed. And then she hid at Ronnie's house. She hung out with him in the day-time and slept with his sisters at night and, like, nobody in his family really cared. Because his dad had, like, two jobs, and his mom had three, and they were too busy to notice. And his sisters liked her, and she liked them. And, like, Cambodian kids ran away all the time any-way, that was just a normal thing for them, it wasn't until Sophy got to the foster home that she found out other kids thought it was wack.

But so what. Ronnie and her just hung out and thought. He gave her his old guitar and taught her to play, and in between lessons they tried to figure out what to do with their lives. Like she thought he should do music at night and computers in the day, but he said that was because she was half Chinese. He thought that he should just be a rock star and that she should just be a model, that would be perfect. She hadn't even convinced him that becoming a model was not realis-tic for a Cambodian, which she was, actually, and anyway would be a lot of stress even if she was beautiful, which she wasn't, when the blues showed up. They'll never know who ratted on them, but Ronnie thought it was the Bloods pulling shit as usual. Like here he wasn't even a Crip, just a friend of the Crips, who played at their parties and that was all, and still the Bloods had to go showing disrespect. The last thing Sophy said to Ronnie as the officer was putting handcuffs on her was please, please, not to go looking for anyone, but she knew what he was going to do.

And meanwhile, there she was, a runaway and a "stubborn child," as the cops liked to say. And a shoplifter, because she didn't have any clothes when she moved in with Ronnie, and Ronnie's sisters were smaller than her, and she tried on this T-shirt that made Ronnie whistle. Probably if Ronnie hadn't said he took shit all the time, she wouldn't have. But he did, and nobody thought the store owner would prosecute, but he did, too. And for a while she thought she was going to have a baby besides, but in the end she didn't, and that was a good thing, since things were bad enough. Like she was not only in for shoplifting, she was in for resisting arrest, because she'd tried to keep Ronnie from punching the cop who arrested her, and when the cop looked like he was going to grab Ronnie anyway, she'd blocked him.

So there she was, all of a sudden, in this big room with everyone looking like they were on TV. Like even her dad and mom looked they were on TV, and when they told the judge she was no good, that was like TV too. She kind of liked the judge because he chewed gum in court, and because once he came down from the bench and sat with them, scaring her mom and dad so bad she almost thought they were going to change their minds about her. Like, her dad closed his eyes while the judge talked, as if he was really listening or meditating or something, and even afterwards he sat so still he looked like a statue, it was as if he had gone somewhere and just left his body to keep his place. And when he opened his eyes, you almost couldn't tell whether he was going to say anything or not, which made her feel proud of him in a way. Because it was like right then he wasn't the dad whose eyes moved around and who smoked cigarettes and drank, but somebody else—it was like right then he was the dad he would have been if he had never left Cambodia. A dad with answers inside him. Like looking at him sitting there, she remembered how he once said that if you put a bird in a cage, it wants to fly out. And she remembered how true she thought that was, and how she wondered then if deep down he understood her. But when he finally opened his eyes in the courtroom he didn't say anything about what happens when you put a bird in a cage or anything like that. Instead he said, "We don't want her.

She is not our daughter, she is no good." Just like that, in about the clearest English she'd ever heard him speak. And then her mom nodded too, as if she understood him perfectly even though he was speaking English, and as if she agreed. And even when the judge made everyone take a break and gave them both time to think about what they were saying, they came back to the courtroom and said the same thing. *We don't want her*—her dad, like, lopping the air with his finger as he talked. And then Sophy just wished her sisters were at least there to say they'd missed her when she ran away and would miss her now that she was going to a foster home. But they were in school.

So she went by herself with the lady from DYS, her name was Fatima, to a foster home behind this big wire fence with, like, plastic woven through it. And Sophy was sent to a new school, and given a probation officer and a thousand rules, rule number one being that she was completely forbidden to see Ronnie. Of course, Ronnie tried to visit her there anyway, and once she really did see him, like, right on the other side of the fence. Like she could see the top of his head pop up, she thought at first she was, like, seeing things. But then he sent a paper airplane note saying that really was him, on a pogo stick! Leave it to Ronnie to even know what a pogo stick was. And then she loved him even more, and tried to write and tell him that that was some shit he'd pulled. Like she sent a letter to his house, disguising her handwriting. But she never knew if he ever got that note or not, because just when she thought she was going to get to see him a lot like that, bouncing up and down, he fell off the pogo stick and broke his leg really bad, and had to have an operation. Everybody else at school, when they got hurt it was because of car accidents. Only Ronnie would get hurt on a pogo stick, he really was some shit. But then stuff started happening with the Bloods when they realized they had a sitting duck, people said because Ronnie had already wet someone, to retaliate for the ratting. And that made Sophy feel terrible, because Ronnie had never wet anyone before, and wasn't even a real member of the gang, he was just someone who played for them at their parties, it was only because of all this that he had to get jumped in. Anyway, she didn't get the whole story, but she did hear how the situation got so dangerous that when Ronnie finally got out of bed, he had to go straight back to school, for the protection.

Of course, everyone was surprised to see him back, like, all of a sudden in the middle of the year. Like there he was with his textbooks in a backpack hanging off his wheelchair and everything. Sophy told Sopheap to take a picture for her, and Sopheap did, and snuck it in when she came to visit. And Sophy did laugh every time she saw it, and hid the picture in the math section of her school notebook, where nobody ever found it. And that was, like, a miracle because her foster parents were the nosiest people alive.

She hated the foster home. The kids smelled like B.O., and the house smelled like B.O., and she didn't like Wayne and Jane, who instead of making people use deodorant, made them all go to church, like, three times a week. And you couldn't just say Praise the Lord quiet-like when you were there either, you had to say it in a big voice so that everyone could hear you. PRAISE THE LORD! Every time someone came to visit her she felt worse. Like when her sisters came and brought pictures of what they were wearing and everything, she couldn't believe that no one wrote even once how they remembered that that was Sophy's shirt and what a ten she looked in it. Not that people had forgotten about her completely. In fact, Sophan said people were talking so night and day that she and Sopheap couldn't get away from it, one time they even tried to hide in a stall in the girls' room, but people looked under the door and found them. Because they could see there were four legs in there, and because everyone knew everyone's shoes. Sophan said lunch was so terrible, she couldn't wait to get back to class. And all because of the talking! That was one thing Sophy did not miss. People say, "The Vietnamese have their tricks, the Thais have their schemes, and the Khmer have their gossip," and it's true. Like it just would not be possible to gossip more than Cambodians.

And then one day Sopheap told Sophy how Ronnie had a new hottie wheeling him all around. Like she was bringing him ice packs and rubbing his back with a coin when it got sore from the chair, Sopheap said, and Sophy didn't even need to hear the rest.

She just thought about it all for a long time afterwards. Like she thought about what people were saying and doing, and she thought about what she had said and done too, just like her dad used to tell her. She looked in her own heart and in Ronnie's heart, and she cried, and when finally she acted, it was just what her dad would have wanted, an action, not a reaction. Like she did not run away and make Ronnie tell her who this girl was and where she was coining him. She acted like Ronnie was dead, and ran away to her own home, to her own mom and dad, and to the bedroom she shared with her own sisters, so she could light some incense on the *Titanic* altar and be in the pictures wearing her own stuff sometimes and her sisters' stuff other times. And sure enough, Sophan and Sopheap were, like, so happy to see her! And if you don't know anything about law, you would probably think, Great. Like you would probably never believe it could be against the law to run away to your own home, but it is. Forget that you're with your mom and dad where you belong, the police will still issue a warrant for your arrest. And if you think that parents are parents and love their kids by instinct because of being mammals, well, Sophy's dad was still mad. Her mom was not as mad, but her dad was so mad she couldn't show how she felt. Like she ignored Sophy in front of him, Sophy only knew what her mom thought because she cooked sour soup, Sophy's favorite, for supper. And Sophy enjoyed it very much, because then she knew her mom's heart.

It was great to be home, but Sophy wasn't snuggled up happy with her sisters for two days before an officer turned up to get her. Because, like, her own dad had turned her in! Her mom cried, her sisters cried, her brother banged his fist on the wall, and still the officer just stood there like a statue. Threatening to bring down more men until finally Sophy let him put those handcuffs on her again. Of course, handcuffs are not as bad as almost anything that happened in Cambodia, but she did think then that they had to be close. She cried and cried and couldn't wipe her own eyes and couldn't wipe her own nose, her mom and sisters had to wipe them for her. And through the whole thing the officer just stood there with his big belly, drinking his coffee, if she could have she'd have thrown that pink cup right in his pink face.

Instead she got put in the kind of girls' group home that's like a training program for whores, the pimps just sign you up. She was glad she knew that thanks to Big Erica, who told her back at Wayne and Jane's, and she tried to tell some of the other girls, but they were too gone. Like they'd show her some necklace and say they were in love and feel sorry for her that she wasn't in love too, it got to be so bad that after a while she had to pretend Ronnie and her were still in love, so the other girls would leave her alone. But that was bad, because his picture just killed her.

And then before you could say wack, her sisters were getting in trouble too. Like kids at school were looking down on them to the point where they knew trouble was coming and that they needed protection, and so Sopheap starting seeing a Latino guy, which was bad, and Sophan started seeing a Vietnamese, which was worse. And pretty soon after that they both ended up running away too. Like Sopheap was with the Latino guy when he borrowed a car, which was wack, especially as it turned out he had a gun on him. And Sophan and the Vietnamese got involved in drug dealing and got caught with a piece too, right about the same time as they heard Sophan's best friend's big sister was going to be valedictorian of their class. Like there she was, Cambodian and everything, but she had beat out all the Indian kids, and now she was going to college on a scholarship and was going to be a nurse. And then Sophy thought that it probably really was true, there really was something the matter with her and her sisters and their whole line. And she thought that their dad should really beat them the way he beat Sarun, because none of them was ever going to be, like, straight A.

Sarun was the lucky one back then. Like most days he came home beat up or else got beat up by their dad, but that was at least that. Like at least their dad knew what Sarun's problem was, at least he knew that Sarun would be fine if he just had some monks and teachers to beat him. Because in Cambodia, that's how kids became civilized. People here think monks are so gentle and enlightened, but when people in Cambodia give their kids to the monks, they say, *Do what you want, just leave us his eyes.* Meaning that the monks can go ahead and whip the kids until they bleed, or put those prickly skins of durian fruit on the floor and make the kids kneel on them, or make them stand outside in the sun without water until they faint. Like the monks did those things to Sophy's dad all the time when he was little, and now he thought someone should do them to Sarun. He thought the teachers should do it. Because in Cambodia, it wasn't just the monks, the teachers did the same kinds of things, because they were all trained as monks to begin with, and because it worked—like Sophy's dad said if they ever went to Cambodia they would see how people are so respectful and polite, not like here. Here the teachers don't beat anyone, which is why the kids are wild and the parents have to beat them even if the police come. He said they have to do it because it's the parents' responsibility.

And all that was bad, but at least Sarun never got put in a foster home the way Sophy did and then her sisters too, which she didn't even know right away because, like, no one told her. Like Sophy didn't even know until she ran away a second time, just to visit home, she couldn't help it, she hadn't heard anything from anybody in such a long time. So that in she walked, and right there was, like, the most wack thing of all. Because Sopheap and Sophan were who knew where, and there were just her mom and dad by themselves, sitting real quiet-like on the couch. She had never seen them sit together like that, as if they actually liked each other. But there they were, and he was smoking and drinking but not drunk, and, like, the room didn't even smell like Hennessy or beer. And they didn't have a Thai soap opera on, or *The Killing Fields,* or a kung fu movie. Instead they were watching some shopping channel she had never seen them watch—one of those channels where you walk through this fancy house, starting with the big front door and the doorbell that plays music. And then, like, there's this curving staircase, and you hear how the floors are heated, and how the kitchen has two ovens and not just one, which her parents thought was amazing. But, like, how empty that house seemed, they were saying, and wouldn't burglars come and steal everything, when in walked Sophy. And this time they started crying—her dad even, like, put out his cigarette, they were so glad to see her again. Because their apartment was feeling so sad and empty without the girls, and the new thing was, they thought they might lose Gift. Because Gift was throwing a fit one day and Sophy's dad was so drunk that he held Gift out the window and threatened to drop him. So now that crazy neighbor who was always trying to steal Gift when she wasn't making eyes at Sophy's dad was going to report him—charge him with being an unfit parent, and maybe Sophy's mom too, or at least that's what they heard from another neighbor. Because their old town was like that, everybody reporting on each other as if they were still in Cambodia, and with the same wack results. Because even if the crazy neighbor was just mad that Sophy's dad wouldn't look back at her, if she filed a 51A and Sophy's mom and dad really did get called unfit, she just might find a way to get her hands on Gift after all. Like what if she registered as a foster parent, right? It was like voodoo, it really was. It was worse than voodoo.

"*We are losing them,*" cried Sophy's mom. "*The children. We are losing them.*"

Them, she said, not *you,* as if Sophy wasn't one of the children anymore. But Sophy knew what her mom meant and felt bad for her anyway.

"*Soon we are going to be all alone,*" cried her mom.

And her dad said, "*I made everyone disappear.*"

He was so upset he couldn't breathe. So Sophy sat with him while her mom made supper, and when he sat down to eat, he looked at his rice and said, "*This is my last bowl of white rice. After this, brown rice.*"

And Sophy said, in the politest way she could, "*We respect your wishes.*"

Then they talked about what to do, and it wasn't like any conversation Sophy had ever had with her parents before. Like she said she could see how she had brought shame to her whole line, and how she came from the bottom of the market, and how she must have been a whore in her last life, and how she should kill herself. But her dad said, "*Please don't kill yourself. Let's just think what we should do.*" And so they thought and thought instead, and finally decided that they should leave town before the 51A was filed. Because Sophy was pretty sure that once it got filed, they couldn't leave anymore—like once it got filed the police could come find them even if they left the state, because the police from different states worked together, and they had computers. And now that Sophy had run away again, there would be a warrant out for her arrest too, which sounded bad, but the kids in the group home talked about stuff all the time, and she was pretty sure the police wouldn't chase a kid across state lines just for shoplifting and running away. So that made two reasons for them to move, in a way it was sort of lucky. Because everything was clear, they just had to figure out where to go. Sophy talked and talked, and her mom and dad nodded and nodded like she was an expert or something.

"*This is our fate,*" her mom said.

Then in walked Sarun, and you could see he was, like, whoa! to find Sophy there and everything so different. He was so surprised he just sat down, and nobody even told him to get cleaned up or demanded to know where he'd been, especially since he wasn't high for a change—like you could see his pupils were normal. So their mom just put a plate of rice and chicken in front of him, and gave him a fork and spoon, and he just, like, started eating, agreeing between bites that it would be good to get out of this place. Because even if the gangs tried to stay out of trouble, they got talked about like trouble-makers, he said, and then they did end up in trouble. And to everyone's surprise, their dad agreed with him just like that. This was what happened when the older people all fought, he said.

"The older people set a bad example. And then things keep going, around and around in a circle. So now we have to break the circle," he said.

But how were they going to do that? Their dad said they could try using the church, which made Sarun groan because he really couldn't stand the whole path-to-Jesus thing. And here no one had ever even made him say Praise the Lord once. But he listened anyway because there had just been a shooting involving the kid brother of a friend of his, and, like, he had just found out. And while that kind of thing happened all the time, it was different when someone you knew pulled the trigger, especially since Boreth was, like, fourteen, and the kid he killed was sixteen. Of course, that kid was no good, but still. What was Boreth doing with a gun at all? That was an Asian Boyz thing, that wasn't Sarun's gang, and at least Boreth used a revolver, so he didn't leave shells. So maybe he wouldn't get caught. Still Sarun was realizing this town was ugly. And so he listened to what their dad had to say about how someone had said something about someone else a church agency was trying to help. He was just saying how the issue there too was a girl who had run away to her own home, when Mum suddenly looked up and said, *"I am going to learn to speak English."* And then Sophy started crying, and Sarun starting hooting, and their dad started smiling. No one had to say they'd made a decision, they all just knew. They were going to move somehow, and as soon as they could they were going to come back and get Sophan and Sopheap.

The bus ride was long, but they didn't care. It was their fate to be going, even the three transfers were their fate. And how lucky it all was! It was lucky that the church agency had arranged for this other family to move, and it was lucky that that family changed their minds at the last minute. Because of Cambodian New Year, and because of, like, the cold—like that other family was afraid their blood might freeze. But Sophy's family was not afraid of the cold, because Sarun had been north before with his friends and knew that everything was heated. And her dad wasn't worried either. *"Do you know what the monks say?"* he said. *"They say every thousand years we return to places we've lived before."* His finger moved back and forth, not violent-like, but more like a windshield wiper. *"We will be comfortable. We will be used to it. We have lived there before."* He said he didn't think the agency even realized they were a different family than the one they thought they were moving, like they were a Cambodian family with a girl who had run away to her own home, and that was enough. What kind of good karma was that? They brought their lunch and dinner to eat on the bus, and a deck of cards too, that was Sarun's great idea. Because besides the bus ride they did have a lot of sitting around bus stations to do. Sophy didn't even know her dad could play cards, but it turned out he'd learned in the refugee camp, and that Sarun could play too. So it didn't matter that her mom only knew how to play a little, her dad just taught her mom and Sophy some games, like gin and French-style blackjack. They gambled with pennies, with Sophy and Sarun leaning over the back of their seats, and for a while it looked like Sarun was going to clean up, but in the end it was their mom. No one could believe it, but there she was with over three dollars! While they played they took turns taking care of Gift, who just wanted to be carried up and down the aisle all the time. Up and down, up and down, up and down, sucking on his fist and grabbing his ears and wrinkling his nose. Of course, there was a lot of flirting with people, too. Like people would play peek-a-boo with him and he would make goo-goo eyes at them, if he had been running for president of the bus, he definitely would have won. As it was everybody searched in their pockets for candy and cookies to give him, so by the end he was almost as rich as their mom, only in goodies instead of money.

They could have stayed on that bus forever, and they weren't the only ones—like some people had their territory all staked out, and had made themselves these little nests. If there was someone who looked uncomfortable, it was Sarun, because even on the bus people could see he belonged to a gang. And they didn't like that, especially since he did stuff that made them look at him, like touch all the tops of the seats as he came down the aisle. His hands in general looked huge and sort of in the way, except when he was holding the cards. Then they looked at home, in fact expert-like. Sophy had never thought him anything like her mom before, but they did both have this beautiful way of holding things, and could do stuff like push one card apart from the others without using their other hand. It was interesting. Because she was not his real mother, and yet there was this thing they could both do, and Sophy was her real kid and couldn't do anything like that. Maybe it was just that Sarun had played a lot of cards, so he could do what their mom could do naturally because of having practiced.

Anyway, between games Sophy'd look out the window, look and look. Because her mom and dad and brother had been other places before, but she hadn't, and so she thought it was pretty interesting that the roads were full of people going places. Like where were they all going? In the beginning she thought they were going to work, but there were people driving around all day, not just in the morning. So what were they doing? Then the mountains started, and she was amazed. Like what exactly was a mountain? She liked the way you had to go around them, like they commanded so much respect. And they didn't get smaller the closer you got to them—like a lake will do that, sometimes you have to back up to realize how big a lake is. The mountains just got bigger. And they hid a lot. Not like they had something to hide, it was more like they had so much going on, you couldn't see it all. There were a lot of trees growing where you wouldn't think anything could grow, like right out of a rock cliff, and she liked all the ice falls too and lost a couple of hands of cards because of them. Because she knew water could do that and had seen that before in her old town, but had never really thought about it. And now that she thought about it, she almost couldn't believe pouring water could just get stopped right in the middle of pouring down like that. Like it was almost scary.

"Gin!" said her mom, and Sophy'd never seen her look so happy in her whole life. Her mom looked up and laughed, and her dad smiled as he checked her cards to see if she really did have what she thought she had. Her dad knew how to shuffle the cards by making this little bridge with them, then letting them fall down like they were in a factory, and of course Sophy's mom and Sophy wanted to learn to do that too, and by the end of the trip, he had taught them. But he started by teaching Sophy's mom first, and that made her beam like he had just brought her flowers or something.

One thing bad about the mountains was that it got dark early because of them, that was kind of a surprise. So that when they finally got out of the bus for the third time, at their stop, it seemed like it was the dead of night even though it was actually just supper time, and because of the dark, Sophy's dad was afraid of losing a bag. So they made the driver wait while they counted them twice. Thirteen bags. The driver wasn't too happy about it, but somebody else said they should ignore him. "People leave things on the bus all the time, it is just so easy to do," said the man. And later on that night, Sophy kept hearing the man's words. *People leave things on the bus all the time, it is just so easy to do. People leave things on the bus all the time, it is just so easy to do.* Like how confident the guy was, that he could say something so definite. She'd never heard anybody talk like that before.

People leave things on the bus all the time, it is just so easy to do.

Church people met them, and took them to a house where the people weren't home but had said Sophy's family could stay, so they had all three bedrooms to themselves, and could even use the kitchen if they wanted. The woman in charge of them was named Ruth. She had white hair like an old lady, but she braided it in two braids like a girl, and her face was like a girl's too, open and interested. She was very fat but got around okay, and everything she wore was fleece. Like she had a fleece hat and a fleece jacket and fleece mittens and fleece pants. And she had a cozy personality too. "Is there anything else I can get for you?" she kept saying. And "How can I help?" And "If you think of anything else, just tell me." She sang all the time, or at least hummed, because that was her job. She was a song evangelist, she said, whatever that was, Sophy would've asked except that she had so many questions already and didn't want to be asking something every minute. Like Ruth told them the church had other people coming too. "From Somalia," she said. "They're Bantus. Muslim." And Sophy would have asked about that, except she didn't have to, because Ruth had just figured out what *Bantu* meant herself, and told them. "I never knew that," she said a couple of times. But the way she said it still made Sophy think about the guy who said that about how easy it was to forget things on the bus.

The house was so comfortable and warm, they would not have minded moving in for keeps. Like there were soft beds and a soft carpet, and pretty curtains and all kinds of wicker furniture. There was heat you could turn up or down in every room. And hearts—there was kind of a heart theme, with heart-shaped candles and heart-shaped pillows, and hearts stenciled on the walls. And of course there were Bibles, a Bible in every room, though nobody told them they had to follow Jesus or asked them to say Praise the Lord! even once. Every day Ruth would come take them to church, and every now and then some lady would say how glad she was that they were being saved from temptation, but that was all. People were just really friendly. Like they made sure they were saying your name right and asked a lot of questions about Cambodia, and even sort of liked it that Sophy's mom didn't speak English and paid her extra attention because of it. And even Sarun liked hearing Ruth sing, he said she had such a great voice it was almost worth sitting through the religious shit to hear her, though he thought she should open her eyes when she sang. But Sophy thought she just did that because she didn't want people to watch her when they were supposed to be watching the screen with the words.

They stayed in the heart house for four great days. Playing cards and looking at the people's stuff, and walking around and telling riddles. Like it turned out Sophy's dad knew all these riddles that her mom did too. Like he would ask, *What has a stem like a candle but opens up like a cup?* And her mom would answer, *A lotus!* Or else he would ask, *What cup of water can the wind not find?* And her mom would answer, *The milk in a coconut!* And then they would laugh until they cried because of how much the riddles reminded them of Cambodia.

Meanwhile Ruth kept coming to visit, and every time they learned something new from her, like about maple trees, or about hypothermia, which was kind of scary, but they were glad she told them. The whole thing was like a family vacation, which they had heard of but never had before. Of course, it was cold. And it wasn't pretty, if you looked outside. Like there was still snow, but the snow was all dirty, and everywhere there wasn't snow, there was mud. Everything was a different shade of gray, it was like someone had forgot to flip on the color switch for this town. You especially noticed it after the church video, because the video was, like, so much more bright and real. But they were all happy anyway, talking to each other about the cold and staying in this warm place. They were even starting to like the services and the way everyone talked about love, even if it made them miss Sophy's sisters. Like there was this big mirror in the downstairs foyer, right inside the front door, and every time they passed it Sophy looked at them all together and thought how great it would be if Sophan and Sopheap were here too, planning and walking around, and eating and joking. But the rest of them were still happy. Once she even saw her mom and dad hold hands, and once her dad said Sophy was a very polite girl, something he had never said before. None of them missed home at all. It was like they were a regular family.

If only life in the trailer was like the heart house! It was going to be. But that first night in the trailer they realized, not right away. The trailer smelled. The trailer had mildew. The trailer was cold. They were excited to think that it was, like, theirs! But they couldn't sleep. First some kind of animal came right up to their window—like you could hear it outside, clawing around—and after that they kept hearing other sounds too. Like Mom kept hearing *k'maoch,* and Sophy kept dreaming her sisters had run away from their foster homes like she did, only to find out there was no one there. If she knew where there was a pen and some paper, she probably would have written them a letter right that very second. But instead she had to try to go back to sleep in this strange bed with, like, her mom sitting up, and the light on, and Gift fussing, and on top of it there was this big storm the next day, and the trailer turned out to leak like the *Titanic.* Sophy's dad said it could be fixed, and that getting used to the trailer was nothing compared to getting used to the Khmer Rouge or America. But still when they went outside and saw the mountains all around them like walls, they just came back in.

They had their cabinets to fix and a lot to mop up, and in the middle of it all, their new neighbor came over, and that was Hattie. And Sophy was glad because she thought the kitchen looked bad with one drawer missing, and the cookies were good. But her dad said they should not be too friendly because Hattie said she was half Chinese and grew up in China, but he thought maybe she was Vietnamese. And why would she bring them cookies unless she wanted something? he said.

Of course, that made Sarun laugh. "What could anyone be wanting from us?" he said. And behind their dad's back, he said, "He be dreaming, man. Dreaming."

But their dad kept insisting that they should be careful. That woman might not even be a human, he said. That woman might be a *k'maoch.*

Sarun laughed and laughed.

Anyway, pretty soon he and Sophy's dad were working on digging a drainage ditch because the ground was too wet to grow anything. And while you obviously couldn't grow mangos here, if the soil was drained they thought they could try to grow apples and pears, and if that didn't work Sophy's dad had heard you could grow Christmas trees. Of course, there were hardly any other black-hairs here, but they didn't care. They were all doing better. Sophy's dad even seemed to like her mom, now that she had these tapes and was really trying to learn English, and Sarun wasn't sending anyone IMs, because there was no cell service. And Sophy was perfect as an angel, so polite and hardworking, her dad looked at her one day and said, *"Now if you go to Cambodia, people will say, Yes, that is a Cambodian girl. So polite! Whose family does she belong to?"*

"I thought you told the judge you didn't want me," she said.

And her dad just laughed then like Sarun, and that was about the happiest moment of her life.

"Someone must have borrowed my mouth and made strange words come out," he said. And when he did that lopping thing with his finger then, it was like he was trying to lop his bad words out of her memory, so she wouldn't hear them anymore.

Life wasn't perfect. Like there were all these flies! And her mom missed her friends, and the temple too, messed up as it was. And when they got Sophy's sisters back, it wasn't going to be easy to convince them they were going to like it here, because there was, like, no movie theater or mall, or anything. And it was a lot easier to make money in their old town because everyone knew from everyone else where to find work. Like there were factories making medical supplies and airline seats and stuff, and at night you could always, like, make key chains, or bag up parts for a kit. Doctors were easier to find too, and food and medicine. And you could walk places. Here you needed rides for every single thing, which was hard because they weren't on, like, any kind of program. Like they were just this special case some pastor had thought should be part of his ministry but that other people wondered about, especially when they found out that Sophy's family wasn't even the Cambodian family they thought they were. Like the one time Ruth came to visit she said that the pastor in charge of them wasn't the church pastor anymore, and that some people were glad, but that she was so upset she was leaving too, which was why she came, to break the news. It made them feel so bad. And who was going to help them figure out what to do about school and stuff now? Because what a good student Sophy was going to be this time! *An A student,* she'd always liked how that sounded. *An A student, straight A's, all A's.* Ruth said they shouldn't worry and that someone would help. But in the end, she just disappeared like Carla and nobody else showed up, and the first thing that happened in school was that this boy offered to help Sophy figure out what was going on. Hershey, his name was, like Hershey chocolate, he said everyone called him that all the time. And she felt sorry for him because it wasn't his fault that he was named Hershey, and he felt sorry for her back, and wanted to show her stuff like how to sign up for free lunch and how to get her locker to stay shut. It was the kind of help she had to make sure her dad never knew about, but she didn't, like, know how to explain it, and before she could Hershey came by the trailer because she left her protractor at school and he knew she couldn't do her homework without it. And that was the end of school.

And that was too bad, because even going for a little while made Sophy realize that she actually missed school. Like she even missed their old school, with the wack teachers and the wack kids and the wack stories, it was lucky they had the whole summer to figure out what to do next.

Then Hattie came over with the wheelbarrow, and they all liked her more after that, Sophy especially. She liked Hattie's dogs and Hattie's cookies, and she liked the way Hattie said, *Ants do like peonies.* And then Sophy's dad changed his mind about Hattie and wanted her to teach Sophy Chinese, and maybe do home schooling, since Hattie used to be a teacher.

But then he hurt his back. And then he asked for white rice. Sophy said, *"You've stayed off white rice all this time. Do you really want to go back?"* Like so respectfully. But he said yes, just a couple of bowls until he felt better. Then he didn't get better and didn't get better, until he was not only eating white rice but drinking again too, and smoking weed. Which everyone smoked in Cambodia, or at least the men did, in fact Sophy's uncle used to grow it on his farm—pure stuff, not like the stuff Sarun used to bring home. Sophy's dad didn't smoke it in their old town because it was illegal in America and someone could report you, but here there was no one to report you anyway. So he was not only smoking it again now but making Sophy's mom put it in chicken soup, the way they used to in Cambodia.

"*We should move somewhere else,*" he said sometimes, when he was high.

"But, like, where? Where can we move?"asked Sophy.

"*What about Long Beach.*"

"Dad, there are, like, so many gangs in Long Beach."

"*Cambodia,*" her dad said after that. His eyes were even more jittery than usual when he was high, and huge-like. "*We should move back to Cambodia.*"

But how could they go back to Cambodia when all they had there was, like, an uncle who could get blown up by a land mine anytime? And what would the kids do? When they only half spoke Khmer if they spoke it at all, and couldn't read or write one word?

But that's how he would talk, and all Sophy could do was be really gentle and polite, hoping he would stop. And sometimes that worked, sometimes he stopped if she talked sweet enough, or if she prayed.

The praying was a new thing she knew her mom and dad wouldn't like. Because she wasn't praying to the Buddha, and she knew what they would say. They would say she was forgetting her culture. Never mind that she was half Chinese, actually, they would say to be Cambodian was to be Buddhist, and that, like, would be that. But the blue car was coming to their house all the time, and her mom would never get in it, and so sometimes Sophy did, because wasn't it rude to keep saying no to the driver when she was so nice? Sophy knew how the driver might feel because her mom was *ting moung* with everyone sometimes, even Gift. And hadn't the church been really nice to them too? Of course, it turned out later that this church was actually different from the other one, but Sophy didn't realize that in the beginning, like she thought they had to be the same because why else would the car be coming? And she really liked the driver, Lynn, who was short and, like, couldn't talk for some reason—like she could understand and she could write, but she couldn't talk, it was almost like she was from Cambodia or something. And she never looked offended when they said no, they weren't going anywhere, she always just shrugged and held up this piece of paper that said NO PROBLEM, and winked. She was so nice that one day when Sophy's mom was out housecleaning and Sophy was alone watching Gift, she decided to try going. Why not? She asked Lynn to wait a minute while she ran out to ask her dad if it was okay. And he was, like, drunk, and he and Sarun were digging, and the way she asked, so quiet-like, she wasn't sure he even heard her, exactly, or gave his permission. He just kind of moved his head then went on digging while she, quick, asked Lynn to wait just another minute while she put Gift's diapers and stuff into a grocery bag. And then they got in. The blue car had a carseat for Gift that you wouldn't think he'd like but that he actually loved because everything was so interesting, even she thought it was interesting. Not that the drive was so different from the drive to the grocery store, but somehow she was just more noticing. Like Sophy didn't see one other trailer with crates for stairs like her family had, she thought they should really get rid of theirs. And she saw that a lot of other people had whirly things or flags or little decks with planters on the railings, and of course that some people even had, like, real houses. Sophy didn't like the ones that were falling down with sinking porches and peeling paint, but some were neat. Like the car stopped at this blinking red light, and right there on the corner she saw this little white house with blue shutters and a flag with a flower on it hanging over the door, and a little walkway between two little squares of lawn. And the more she looked at it, the more her eyes filled up with tears, it kind of reminded her of the heart house. She even tried to show it to Gift, but he was too busy playing with his feet to care.

The church center was two towns over, and in a white house too, only bigger and older, and with a giant cross that took up pretty much a whole wall. The entrance had a half-moon window, and a big curving staircase with a little door under it, and a lot of old wood paneling, but there was also a new wall of hooks and cubbies for the kids' stuff. A short lady with frizzy hair welcomed them right as they walked in and asked, "First time?" And when Sophy said yes, she said, "Wonderful!" as if Sophy had just said the best thing ever. Then she showed Sophy where to put her stuff, and the funny thing was that she seemed just the right height person to be doing that. Like she was the perfect height for the hooks and cubbies, and hardly had to bend down to show them. And the other funny thing was that Gift got it right away that this was a place for him. Like he looked at all the shoes lined up in the other cubbies, and when Sophy took his shoes off and put them in his cubby, he crawled over and patted them. They were the only ones who brought their stuff in a grocery bag, but the lady didn't seem to care, and Sophy at least put the bag in the cubby neatly, so it wouldn't mess up the whole thing.

In their old town there were all these youth centers where you could hang out and get free food, but it never occurred to anybody to see if there was a center where you could bring babies, since between Sophy and her sisters and their dad, there was always somebody who could watch Gift while their mom worked. But now that Gift could crawl so fast and was pulling himself up and cruising, this was so great. Like they had this play space in the basement with carpet, and there were blocks and balls, and a little picnic table with paper and markers, and even, like, a little playhouse with a little play kitchen. And a corner that was all trucks! Gift practically jumped out of Sophy's arms when he saw the trucks, and when Sophy had to change his diaper, she could only get him to lie down by letting him play with a truck at the same time.

There were other babies there too, and other people taking care of them, which was the part Sophy liked. Like it was great when the short lady introduced her to brown-haired Renee, and black-haired Simone, and blond-haired Kate, who were, like, from all over! Like Renee was from Detroit, and Simone was from Vietnam, and Kate was from a farm pretty close by, but they all helped take care of a baby, like Sophy. Or babies, in Kate's case. She had twins to watch after! Which was why she came as often as she could. Because how could she even let them out of the house back at the farm, when one could go one way and the other another and there was, like, dangerous equipment and pitchforks and fertilizer everywhere? Simone had two kids to watch too, but hers were one older and one younger, and that was easier in some ways, but harder in others. Like the older one was old enough to know she should not just run off, but the younger one would pull the older one's hair, and then the older one would get really mad. So Simone had to kind of keep them apart, which wasn't so easy at home because they lived in a trailer, like Sophy's family. And so she came as often as she could too. Lucky Renee was like Sophy, with just one kid to take care of, she said she hadn't even realized before coming that she was so lucky, and that was how Sophy felt too, like she hadn't even realized. "We are so blessed," Renee said, cooing at Gift and trying to teach him to give a high-five, and when she said that, Sophy felt like she knew just what Renee meant. *We are so blessed.*

None of them could believe Sophy had never been to a Bible study class before, or that she hadn't even realized that that was where she was going, really. But they were excited she was going to be in their group! They got her a pamphlet about their church that said "Where friends become family" on it, and they got her a Bible to keep too, and made her put her name in it. Then they showed her how it had two halves, the Old Testament and the New, and explained how even though the pages looked really thin, they didn't tear as easy as you'd think. Class didn't start for another half hour, so they just hung out for a while, and that was fun, because the three of them were already, like, a team and did what Kate called zone defense. That meant that you didn't follow your kid around, but just kept an eye on any kid that was near you. Like you tried to notice if someone had a smelly diaper or was acting funny—like if they were taking a nap under the picnic table or something, the way one of Kate's twins was one day. That turned out to be a virus, but there were all these other things it could have been, Renee said, like a staph infection, or meningitis, stuff Sophy had never even heard of. And that alone was probably a reason to come back to the center, to find out about viruses, and how it was bad to put soda in Gift's bottle. Like Renee said that right away, that juice was one thing but soda was bad, and that Gift shouldn't be eating so much candy either. And Simone said that if he was a boy he should probably wear boys' clothes, and not just any clothes because that was confusing for Americans. And Sophy figured that Simone could probably say that about what was confusing for Americans because she was Vietnamese and had been through it herself. Of course, Sophy wasn't going to go telling her parents she'd learned anything from a Vietnamese! Though now that she was talking to Simone, she could see that every Vietnamese was different, the same as Cambodians. Like wasn't Sophy different from her mother and father and brothers and sisters even though they were a family? She was, she was different.

   And it was a good thing she liked Simone, because people put them together right away. Like when the short lady came down, she said, "I see you've found Simone"—because somehow Sophy was meeting Kate and Renee, but was finding Simone. And they really did have a lot in common, because they both had black hair and so on, but Simone was actually a lot older than everyone else. Like she was nineteen. She looked sort of like Sophy and Kate and Renee, but they were all fifteen or sixteen, and Simone was hipper, that was the other thing. She did her nails, and her hair was feathered, and she carried these cool silk bags in beautiful colors that her aunt sent her from Vietnam, Sophy could never look at those bags without thinking what it would be like to have an aunt back home who sent you things, and to get little silk bags in the mail. Like that just seemed so great.

She was lost in that first class, and a little worried whether the short lady could really watch Gift and all the other kids by herself even for just an hour, but she liked it. Like she liked the room, which was originally the dining room of the house, they even sat around the original dining room table, like a family. The leader was this woman named Ginny, who had blond hair and wore a chain with a cross draped over the collar of her turtleneck like a lot of the girls did. And everyone was really nice, but especially Ginny. Like she would always make sure Sophy was on the right page, and she would look at her special a lot, so that Sophy would know if she had any questions, she could just ask. Sophy didn't ask any, though, because the whole thing was, like, so surprising. Like she thought it surprising that someone who looked like Simone would hunch over a book like that, so studious. And that the class would spend so much time talking about just, like, a couple of sentences—that was surprising too. And that they talked about all these people—like Paul and Peter and Jesus—like they knew them, even though they were all dead. Or at least she thought they were dead. Anyway, the time went by fast, because the story was interesting. Like they were talking about some king named David, who promised a cripple he was going to give him back all the land he had lost, and told him he'd be welcome at his table forever, only to have the cripple say, "What is thy servant, that thou shouldst look upon such a dead dog as I am?" And the group all agreed that that was probably how they would feel if someone said that to them. Like dead dogs, and like they just couldn't believe it.

"Except that you can believe it," said Ginny, looking at everyone with her green eyes. "You can. Believe it. You don't feel worthy, but you are. In God's eyes you are worthy."

After class, the center had a singing group back in the basement, where the kids played in the middle and their caretakers sang songs about lambs. It wasn't as interesting as the Bible study class, and Sophy could hear what Sarun would have to say about that kind of song almost more than she could hear the song itself. Like she knew how he'd sing the words his own way and roll his eyes and say, They are, like, on something. And she felt funny because she didn't know the words, and Gift wouldn't stay in the middle the way he was supposed to either. But still they stayed the whole session because Lynn was expecting them to stay, and because the room was so much nicer than the trailer, and because of the doughnuts and the soda and the cookies. The cookies weren't as good as Hattie's, but they were good enough that Sophy started going twice a week after that, on Mondays and Thursdays. And she really looked forward to it, and found that even when she went home she could still see the center in her mind—like she could still see that arched window, with this little crystal ball that threw rainbows all over, and she could still see the neat little entrance area where people stashed their stuff. On rainy days all the kids' rain jackets would be hanging there, and that just amazed her, because some of the kids had such beautiful little jackets, with lady-bugs and cats on them. She tried not to stare at them, the same way she tried not to stare at the special bags people had for their baby stuff. But after a class where they talked about prayer and the part of the Bible where it says, "Ye ask, and receive not, because ye ask amiss," she tried praying, not with evil, selfish motives, but with right purpose, the good purpose that Ginny talked about. And right the next day, the most amazing thing happened. Like Sophy came into the center and this lady just walked right up to her and said, "Would you like a jacket for your baby?" And even though Sophy said he's not my baby, the lady reached in her bag and said, "Please take this. I was about to give it to the church to give away." And it was this yellow jacket with a patch pocket like a bumblebee, just the right size for Gift. Sophy was so amazed, she couldn't even say thank you. It was just, like, so wack! But the lady didn't seem to mind, she just smiled and left.

And then Sophy found out that her Bible study group leader was not just any Ginny, but Hattie's friend Ginny! Not that Sophy guessed, Ginny was the one who asked, quiet-like, "Aren't you Hattie's new neighbor?" And when Sophy said yes, Ginny said she had kind of thought so, and that she had been sending a car for her for some time, and had been filled with gladness when she heard that Sophy had finally started to use it.

"You sent the car?" said Sophy.

And Ginny said yes, and smiled, and said, "Of course, you didn't have to use it. But I knew you would someday."

And when Sophy asked how she knew, Ginny said she just knew. "Don't you ever have things you just know?" she asked. And when Sophy said she couldn't think of one, Ginny said that if Sophy ever did, she should write it down and tell her. And Sophy laughed and said okay, she would write it down. And Ginny said if it wasn't a Bible study day, she could still find her in church. "Do you know where the church is?" she asked. And when Sophy said, "In the living room?" Ginny laughed as if Sophy had said something funny. "Yes," she said. "It used to be down in the basement, but we've grown so big, we had to put an addition onto the living room. Now it's right down the hall. Have you been there?" And when Sophy said no, because she thought it was for Sundays, Ginny said, "Well, I go there pretty much every day just to sit and pray. It's been the saving of me. So when you think of something you just know, you can come have a look there." And Sophy said, "Okay."

It's been the saving of me.

Sophy didn't go right away. Like she couldn't think of something she just knew. But then one day she went to take a look, and as soon as she walked in, she did know something. Like as soon as she walked in she knew she just wanted to sit there and look up at the windows so bad, and maybe Gift knew she wanted that too, because he was quiet for a change. So quiet, that she could actually sit down with him in her lap for a few minutes, and let him play with her buttons and put his fingers in her mouth while she looked around. Probably if any-one had asked her before that whether she cared about rooms and whether they could change her being, she would have said no, espe-cially since she had never even thought before about whether she had a being. But sitting there, she suddenly knew that she did, she had one, and that it was being changed. It was. The church wasn't fancy. But she loved the windows all around, and she loved the mural up front with, like, these purple-blue mountains dipping down to a bright bright river that wound around to a big glowing cross. She loved the airiness of the space too, and she loved it that it wasn't crammed full of gold statues. Like she loved it that there wasn't incense burning and making her cough, and that it wasn't full of Cambodian women afraid of *k'maoch* either. It was different here. Like everyone at the temple in her old town was suffering so bad inside, but couldn't do anything but suffer and be good and wait for their next life, while here, people were being reborn, like, right away! In this life! They didn't have to build up their good karma little by lit-tle, never knowing if they'd built up enough. They could be saved today, all they had to do was accept that Christ had died for their sins. And that was it! In fact, there wasn't anything else a person could do, really—they couldn't save themselves, no matter what they did.

Because that's what it said in Ephesians, that no amount of good deeds would help, that people are saved by faith, and faith alone. So that, like, the only thing that would work was accepting Christ's sacrifice and love. Which was hard for Sophy to really get, in the beginning. Like it almost seemed like cheating.

But that's why the Bible was called Good News! And it wasn't even in, like, one passage in the Bible, it was in a million of them. How the Lord knew everything about you, like your downsitting and your uprising and all your thoughts and ways to begin with, and how He didn't look on outward appearances, but on the heart. So that you didn't have to undo anything bad you'd done, you just had to be truly sorry. Like King David had an affair with Bathsheba, and before he repented, all he could do was groan and lose weight. But once he repented, God forgave him just like that! Just like that, his transgression was removed as far as the east is from the west, and he wasn't the only one who started all over. Paul did too, and a lot of other people. They were all reborn in Christ, Ginny said, as they had to be, because new wine needs new bottles. Then she asked if people knew other people who had been born again, and they all did, except Sophy. And that was embarrassing until she remembered that her dad had been reborn, in a way—not into a brand-new life, but into his brother's life—and that his first wife had sort of been reborn out of the mud, but then died. She didn't really expect them to care, but they listened like it was the most interesting thing they'd ever heard, and finally someone asked if she wanted to be reborn like them, or in a different way. And when she said in a different way, they cheered, and when Ginny said, "It says in John 3:3, 'Except a man be born again, he cannot see the kingdom of God,' " Sophy started crying. Because she did so want to be reborn. She wanted to be reborn into the right life, her real life. Her old life was just so wrong.

"I don't know why I was born," she said. "I am so ashamed. Sometimes I think I should kill myself."

She couldn't believe those words came out of her, but they did, and what happened next was, like, even more unbelievable. Because right then and there Ginny made everyone bow their head and pray for Sophy.

"She is crying out like Jonah, Lord, she is crying out of the belly of hell!" said Ginny. "Hear her! Hear her!"

And they all held hands and prayed that God would hear her, and when Ginny asked Sophy if she felt the power of that, she said yes, because she had. It was like having her sisters back, she wasn't alone anymore.

A couple of weeks later, the church had this special camp meeting like they did every year. They got together with two other independent churches, and rented a campground, and organized all kinds of special things. Like they had activities and food, and were giving out devotional books for free. Sophy couldn't go for the whole time, but she came for some of it, and brought Gift, who loved the children's group. And she loved everything!—starting with how you crossed this little bridge over a stream to get to the campground, and how the first thing you heard was the ringing of a bell to call people to service. She loved the Ping-Pong tables and the dining room and the first-aid building, and she loved the smell of the barbecues and the pines. The pines were these big round trunks rising right up out of the ground, with nothing else growing around them—like the floor of the forest was all just clear and open and bouncy with pine needles. And the meeting hall was cool too, this big huge building, with enormous flap doors on three sides of it. The doors were propped open on poles, so that they made these covered entrances that made you feel like you were going inside, except that inside still felt like outside because there were so many doors, and what walls there were had these big windows. There was a pop-up in the middle of the roof too, with windows all around it, so that the light just poured in, and you could feel Jesus looking down. And everything was, like, old. Like the wood and the windows with their little panes were old, and the organ and piano up front on kind of this open stage were old too. There was a big plain cross just standing up there by itself, and a long long altar, kind of like an eternal bench, along the whole front of the hall. And there were these huge hangings with quotations from Galatians and Hebrews that looked like they had been there for even longer than the pine trees outside, and were going to be there until the end of the earth. Of course, there were some new things too, like a projection screen and a computer, and a tilted table with buttons and lights for the sound system. But everything else was old, even the hymnbooks piled up at the end of the pews were old. It was cool.

Sophy loved it that there were all these strangers mixed up with people she knew, because somehow that made it even more special to see Kate and Simone and Renee, like they were old friends. Renee was having trouble with her knee, like don't you know it would be God's plan for her to tear her meniscus, she said, complaining-like. But Kate and Simone and Sophy helped her around and brought her drinks and carried her backpack, and that made her feel better. And Sophy loved that as much as Kate, probably, she loved being able to help a friend. The four of them sat together through the songs and announcements, and through some sermonizing Sophy didn't understand but didn't mind listening to because it was nice to be sitting there in this big open space with the ceiling fans going, and because it was fun hearing other people sighing and saying Amen to things even if it wasn't their turn to talk, and because the preacher told a lot of funny stories about bad things he'd done, and what Jesus had said to him to straighten him out. The preacher wasn't from their church and didn't look like much, just a normal guy walking back and forth with brown hair and a mike in his hand like someone on TV. He had these big half-moons of sweat under his arms even though no one else was sweating, and that was weird, because it was warm out, but not really that hot, and that kind of made you want to laugh at him in a way. But no one did laugh at him, because they liked the stories, even though every one of them started with something like skipping Bible study because of the World Series, and every one of them led to "And Jesus said to me, Bill . . ." They were all the same, but you really did get the feeling that Jesus talked right to him like that, and that maybe you could get Jesus to talk to you like that too. And that kept you interested, like his sermon, which started out pretty bleak with Job 18, but went on to talk about different kinds of hope and how hope was usually a good thing, but could be a bad thing if it made us blind, like if it blinded us to the difference between a trial and a chastisement, for example. Like if it meant we just started blindly hoping God was going to work everything out for us, and if as a result we failed to change when God was telling us to change. And he talked about how we should welcome chastisement, painful as it was, because it was God's message to us, and because it was a form of love.

"For as the Bible says in Hebrews 12:7, 'What son is he whom the father chastiseth not?' " he said. "The Lord only chastises those He sees as His children. The Lord only chastises those who are His chosen. But you know, the chastisement is lost unless we learn from it—unless we learn the lesson He is trying, in His great love, to teach us. The chastisement is lost unless we try to understand what we need to do to get right with God. And that is why I ask you now to look in your hearts, and to think whether God has chastised you in any way. I ask you to look in your hearts and ask if He's been trying to tell you something, if He's been trying to teach you. And if He has, I ask you to embrace that, and to turn to the Lord our God now—to embrace the only hope which is true hope, namely the hope in God. In Hebrews 12:1, Paul tells us, 'seeing . . . we are compassed about with so great a cloud of witnesses, let us lay aside every weight'—and so let us do that—let us now lay aside every weight. Compassed about with our own great cloud of witnesses, let us now accept the Lord's chastisement and lay our weight aside."

And then this music started and the preacher started calling people up to the altar in the front of the hall, and for a moment nobody went. And that was embarrassing because who would, like, just walk up there in front of everybody? But first a few people started going up, and then a lot of people, and pretty soon it seemed just, like, normal for Sophy to help Renee get up there, and then to stay herself, even though she'd never done it before. Because there were all kinds of people up there, men and women, young and old, a lot of them with their heads buried in their hands, and the preacher wasn't telling funny stories anymore.

"Are you carrying a weight just like Paul was talking about?" he was saying, his voice all, like, big and rolling and coming from all around you. "Are you carrying a weight you would like to set down? Can you feel it there on your shoulders, if you reach back can you feel it in the muscles of your neck, do you just know it's there, all the time, something you're so used to you don't even think about it as a weight, something you might even forget about during the day, but that rises up to torment you the minute the busyness lets up? It's something that haunts you, something you can't escape. You turn a corner, and there it is, and you turn another corner, and there it is again. Your torment. Your chastisement. It's something you've tried to hide, something you've tried to deny, but that weighs you down and weighs you down, that causes you more pain than you think you can bear but that is just the Lord preparing you, really—preparing you for this moment, now, in this tent—helping you understand that this is what He wants from you, to come up here and lay your burden down. He wants you to lay it down so that you can feel hope again, the only true hope, which is hope in Jesus Christ. He wants you to lay it down so you can get right with the Lord. It's what He wants, it's what He's trying to get you to do. So if you feel Jesus is speaking to you now, if you feel called to the altar, come up. Let the Lord enter you, come up. Come up."

Sophy didn't even realize until she got to the altar with Renee that she'd been carrying a weight around. And the first minute she was kneeling down, she didn't realize it either. But once she kneeled a little longer, she suddenly realized that the preacher was talking to her special, inviting her special because he knew, he knew. "You've sinned," he said. "And it weighs on you, doesn't it. The knowledge. It weighs you down and sets you apart from others," he said—and when he said that, she suddenly remembered what she did with Ronnie, and how she'd gotten pregnant, and how terrible that was, and how she didn't have one person in the world she could tell, not even her sisters because she was so bad and it was so terrible. So that pretty soon she was crying like everyone else, remembering and crying, and just so glad when Ginny suddenly showed up and knelt down beside her, and put her hand on her back, and asked if she could pray alongside her. Because that was the first time she told anyone how her breasts had hurt so bad and how she had thrown up and thrown up, and how it was like she was possessed by the devil, how it was like the devil had entered her body, so that it wasn't even hers anymore, it was the devil's. She told Ginny how she got to be so tired she couldn't keep her eyes open in school. And she told Ginny how on her second day in the foster home she woke up in a circle of blood—how everywhere there was just blood and blood and blood, and how she hoped it wasn't going to, like, stain the sheets and how she was trying to figure out what to do except that she was cramping and cramping so she couldn't think and couldn't stand up, and how she wanted to call for help but didn't want to call Wayne or Jane or Big Erica who she barely knew, and so how she just struggled to the bathroom alone and was just lucky it was empty, because it wasn't always. And she told Ginny how she sat on the toilet then, while people came and knocked on the door and yelled but thank God went away to the other bathroom so she could at least sit there sweating and cramping by herself while these, like, huge bloody clumps came out of her, they were so big they kind of slid down to the bottom of the toilet bowl and piled up, she just hoped she didn't see a baby down there. Which she definitely could, because it had been in her for, like, three months, she thought, or maybe longer, every day she had been trying to figure out how to get rid of it but didn't know how, she just wished she would die. Like she wished her sisters or her parents or Ronnie or someone would come in and find her all by herself and dead, but not, like, with her pants down and her underwear dirty, and the linoleum floor all a mess. It was a long time. But after a while she finally got herself into the bathtub, and turned on the hot water, and closed her eyes so she couldn't see the water all, like, red all around her, and her bloated body floating in the middle of it like one of the dead people in the water after the *Titanic* sank. Even now it makes her want to kill herself to think about sometimes, though sometimes it makes her take extra good care of Gift too.

In a way she still can't believe she told Ginny.

But Ginny just nodded and nodded and listened and nodded and said that life was sacred, and that she, Sophy, was God's child, and was born to reflect His glory, but that people have sinful natures. All around them people were crying, but Ginny wasn't crying. "Romans 3:23," she said in this gentle voice. " 'For all have sinned, and come short of the glory of God.' The Bible doesn't say some have sinned. It says all. All have sinned. You're not alone, child. You're not alone. And you're right to be upset. 'For to be carnally minded is death'—that's what it says in Romans. To be spiritually minded is life and peace, but to be carnally minded is death. As you know. Because you've felt it, haven't you—that it was death. How lucky you didn't have to have that baby cut out—you could have gotten so lost that you had it cut out. But the Lord spared you that, didn't He. He said, Sophy, you have sinned, but I am going to have mercy on you. And He did. He chastised you in the most helpful way—bringing you here to us, to your salvation. So that it was an act of love! An act of love! We have to give thanks for that." And Ginny hugged her and handed Sophy tissues from one of the boxes along the altar while Sophy said how she hadn't thought of that. She hadn't thought of how things could've been even worse, though she was still sorry she had ever slept with Ronnie. Because that was so wrong, she said. And she was glad she got punished, she really was, and sometimes when she looked at other girls now and saw how they were dressed, like, in the summer especially, she just knew where they were headed, she said. And she wanted to tell them, but knew that they'd just laugh and so she hated them, she said. She did. She hated them. Then she cried and cried and cried some more. She cried so much that she was afraid when she stopped, she might not be able to see anymore, like her mom in the refugee camp. She was afraid when she stopped, her eyes might not work. But when finally she did open her eyes, she saw the most beautiful thing instead. It was this bird flying across the meeting hall, this white bird. Taking off from a support pole and flying right away. "Did you see that bird?" she asked, though she was almost afraid to ask. Like she thought Ginny was going to roll her eyes the way her sisters and her had rolled their eyes back when their dad told them that story about the white flower opening beside his parents' grave. But Ginny didn't roll her eyes. Instead Ginny looked at her hard and said, "Maybe it wasn't just a bird. Maybe it was a dove." And when Sophy suddenly remembered, Renee!—how was Renee going to get back from the altar?—it turned out that someone else had already helped her. "Don't worry," Ginny said. "You are walking with God now. God is showing you the way." Then she said, real quiet-like, "Isaiah 54:4: 'Fear not; for thou shalt not be ashamed: neither be thou confounded, for thou shalt forget the shame of thy youth. . . .' And not only will you forget; in His great mercy, God will forget, too. God will forget, too. Do you know what He told Jeremiah? He told Jeremiah that there would be a new covenant with the people of Israel, and that He would 'remember their sin no more.' And the way He forgot their sins, He'll forget yours, too, child. He'll forget yours, too." Sophy thought it was funny how Ginny repeated herself, and how she called Sophy "child." Like no one had ever called Sophy "child" before. But she didn't mind. The strangeness was, like, so strange it wasn't strange. And when Ginny asked her, "Do you accept Christ's sacrifice for you?" she said yes. And when Ginny asked, "Do you call upon the name of the Lord?" she said yes. And the next day Ginny brought Sophy this real silver cross on a chain, and said it was hers for keeps. And Sophy said she would wear it always, and never take it off.

> *Change my heart O God; make it ever true.*
> *Change my heart O God; may it be like you.*

When back in her old town, Sophy's probation officer used to say, "Think how bright your future could be," Sophy never knew what he was talking about. Like it was just another thing he liked to say besides "You have a choice" and "You make your own fate." Because, like, what was a "bright future," anyway? She always wanted to ask him that. But now that she was leaving the desert of her past, now that she was headed for the Promised Land, she felt like she finally understood the words. Her future was going to be bright.

But first God must have wanted her to cry, because she cried at just about every Bible study group meeting, for weeks. And that was okay because there was always someone there with a tissue for her, and a hug. So that more and more, she found that she could not wait to get back to the Bible study group. More and more, she found that as soon as they opened their Bibles, she felt this peace come into her. And more and more, she found that the words sank in deeper, and that the lessons seemed harder and wiser. Like when they read that passage about how God gave the Israelites manna in the desert, and told them not to save it, only to have some of them try anyway, so that it bred worms and stank, Ginny talked about how hard it was to put your whole faith in God, and that was so true! It was hard not to try to take care of things yourself. Like could you really just let the Lord sit on the throne of your life? Could you really just leave it all to Him, just like that? Sophy found that a lot to think about. And the time they talked about Paul, and how he failed to practice the good deeds he desired to do, and instead did the evil deeds he did not desire to do, that was a lot to think about too—like how we could be strangers to ourselves like that, even enemies. Like that was so true and so sad.

And it was sad too, when they talked about what it meant to belong to the family of God, and how that could be at odds with your family of origin, because it was like the Bible knew her whole life then. It was like God knew how hard it was going to be for Sophy to choose Him first, like He knew how hard it was going to be for her to think about leaving her family even if it was so she could be adopted into a better family. It was as if He knew that she was going to be an enemy to herself in this way. "In Ephesians 1:5, the Bible says, He 'predestinated us unto the adoption of children by Jesus Christ to himself, according to the good pleasure of his will,' " Ginny said. "Do we all understand what it means that He *predestinated* us? It means He foresaw our struggle. He did. He foresaw it. But He foresaw, too, that we would give ourselves to our new family." She looked at Sophy then with her green eyes, and they were, like, a special effect—like they had this special power. "He had that faith," Ginny went on, and it was as if she knew that Jesus Christ had faith in even Sophy. She knew.

He had that faith.

Sophy couldn't always come to services on Sunday, but that week she did, and as soon as she sat down she could see that God meant for her to be there, because Pastor Blake was talking about her, and her struggle. "Think about what Jesus tells the apostles in Luke 18," he said. "In Luke 18:29–30, He says, 'Verily I say unto you, There is no man that hath left house, or parents, or brethren, or wife, or children, for the kingdom of God's sake, who shall not receive manifold more in this present time, and in the world to come life everlasting.' There is no man who shall not receive manifold more. There is no man who shall not receive life everlasting. It's a great deal, isn't it? It's the deal of a lifetime, a deal you wouldn't want to pass up, a deal you couldn't pass up. Eternal life! Eternal happiness! Naturally you want to take God up on this special offer. And yet maybe your family of origin is against it. Maybe they're threatened by the idea that you're about to win the lottery. Maybe it makes them feel their own poverty. Or maybe they're Christians themselves, and are mostly happy for you, except for a particular family member who cannot welcome the Good News. Not that he or she is a bad person. They're not. They're good people, who love you. But they're like people who just have to have their coffee in the morning. You know how some people just have to have their coffee in the morning? Because they've been having coffee in the morning their whole lives, and just can't imagine starting their day with tea? They can't change, can they? Of course, if they really wanted to, they could. And maybe there are good reasons why they should. But no matter how good the reasons are, they are going to resist, aren't they? They are going to insist on their coffee, and that you have coffee too. You can tell them, Well, tea has antioxidants. You can tell them, Tea has less caffeine. You can offer them tea every day, just in case they'd like to try it. But in the meanwhile, you've got to drink what's right for you. You can't drink coffee because they can't handle change, even if that's a challenge. Matthew 18:17 tells us that if a brother refuses to listen to the Word, you should tell it to the church, and if he refuses to listen to the church, you should 'let him be unto thee as an heathen man and a publican.' In other words, a pagan and a tax collector. You should make him as welcome as a pagan and a tax collector. But it isn't so easy, is it? It isn't easy, and yet we need to understand that this is exactly what Jesus Christ our Savior asks of us. Isaiah 30:13 tells us how important it is to keep a wall around our belief. It tells us how the devil goes looking for weak spots, and how fast the wall can fall, and how important it is to know where the broken-down spots are. And so often we find that it is just one or two people that make up our gap, don't we? It's not everyone. It's just one or two people. And so often we find that if we think about it for a moment, we know who those one or two people are. So let's take a moment today, and look in our hearts, and maybe we can share the names of our greatest challenge with others later, so we can begin to think how to deal with them. So we can begin to think how to close up our gaps and take advantage of the Lord's good deal. Because we wouldn't miss out on the deal of our lives, would we? We wouldn't want to miss out."

And the next Bible study class, that's what they did. They went around the table, naming their persons of challenge. And when they got to Sophy, she surprised herself with her answer.

"Sarun," she said. "My brother Sarun."

Because when she thought about telling her family the Good News, when she thought about telling them about the love and peace she'd found in the Lord, Sarun's voice was the voice she heard the loudest. Like she could hear her mom and dad, but she'd been telling them her whole life about how she didn't know if she really believed in *kam* and *k'maoch* anyway. And her sisters were just, like, whatever. Sarun was something else.

"Can you hear him?" asked Ginny. "Can you hear his voice if you try?"

And sure enough Sophy could, easy. It was easy to hear him laughing and laughing.

"Let's see if you can hear what he would say," said Ginny. "What would he say when he was done laughing?"

"You got to be shitting me," he said. "You been listening to that superstitious bullshit? That gang be shooting up something serious. That gang be ripping you off."

But what? What were they trying to rip off?

"They're the Khmer Rouge all over again," he said. "They want to control you. Control your mind." He tapped his head. "You know those remote control cars, you push the stick left and the thing goes left? You push the stick right, and the thing goes right?"

"Has he ever even been in a church?" asked Ginny. "Ask him. Has he ever been in a church and really listened, with an open heart?"

"Have you ever even been in a church and really listened, with an open heart?"

"No, and I'm not going to listen to none of that shit."

"Because you'd rather hang out with your friends and break into video parlors and steal the computer chips out of the machines," Sophy said. "You'd rather steal them and fence them so you can buy cars to crack up."

"That's right, man. You got it." He laughed. "I've already got an old man who wants to tell me what to do fucking twenty-four hours a day. I don't need two."

"That is so sad," said Ginny, and the look on her face was truly mournful and sorry—like her eyes were far away, and her mouth was soft, and she held her cross in her hand like it was someone's heart. "I'm sure it hurts you to know how he thinks. To hear how angry he is. How bitter. How he can't let go of his bitterness and how he doesn't want you to, either. How he doesn't want you to move on. Because you love him, don't you?"

"I do."

"Matthew 18:9 says, 'If thine eye offend thee, pluck it out, and cast it from thee.' But that's not so easy with someone you love, is it."

"No," Sophy said. "It isn't."

"It isn't so easy to let him be unto you as a pagan and a tax collector, like Pastor Blake said Sunday."

"No." Sophy bent her head then, and probably would have cried, except that Ginny looked at her with such kindness.

"Just know we're here to help," she said.

Reading the Bible by herself was hard and weird. Like Sophy wasn't much of a reader to begin with, and it sounded so strange, with all the *thous* and *shalts* and *saiths* and *begats*. She didn't like the cover of the Bible either, with, like, that goth writing. And she didn't like those thin pages, and that tiny print with no pictures. The only thing she did like was the material of the cover, and the way you could kind of bend it in your hand. Like it was so soft, and nice to hold. And she liked the gilt at the edges of the pages, and how it made the edges of the pages soft too, and she liked the way the bookmark hung back behind the book when you were reading—how it was right there to mark your place when you stopped, it was almost like it knew you were going to need it, like it knew you, and was sort of waiting for you. It was, like, the exact opposite of the words, which she could never have read without the Bible study group. But now she read the way they read in class, just a little at a time, like it was this million-piece puzzle you worked on bit by bit, or like she was learning a secret code. She marked her Bible up the way other people did, too, with, like, this special highlighter that didn't go through the page. And she prayed all day, the way Ginny said she should, practicing her faith, and increasing her belief. Because she did have doubts, she couldn't help it. Like did she really believe Mark when he said that if you tell a mountain, "Be thou removed, and be thou cast into the sea," it would move? She didn't think that would work, she really didn't. Even if you said that without doubt in your heart, she didn't think it would work. But she thought she might conquer her doubt one day if she tried, and in the meanwhile she thought she should not pray instead of reading, but should, like, both pray and read. Because Ginny said that prayer was like a house she was building, but that the Bible was the rock she was building her house on. So she wrote on a piece of paper, "And ye shall know the truth, and the truth shall make you free," and put that in the beginning of the book, to help her get started on days when it was hard. And that helped, she thought, it really did.

And ye shall know the truth, and the truth shall make you free.
It did.

Hattie II: Rising to Fight Again

There's a strange van in town—a white van, with more panels than windows. It's the kind of under-detailed vehicle that puts Hattie in mind of fetal pigs—that looks as if it got pulled off the line before it reached full van-dom. A thing designed for equipment, really, not passengers. And what a strange way of driving it has, going up and down the road the way it does. Hattie can't help but notice as she crosses the room to wash out her brush: up and down, up and down, until finally it stops at the top of the Chhungs' driveway. Sarun lopes up the hill as the kid in the passenger seat jumps out to open the tailgate. Maybe four or five kids in there? All black-hairs, and presumably Cambodian, though who knows. Gangs, Hattie knows, can be pan-Asian, mixed-race, anything; even thuggery's multicultural these days. Sarun climbs in; the back doors close; the door-closer hops back into the passenger seat up front. The van speeds off with a roar. Hattie sits down with a frown.

Did anyone get out?" Sophy asks later. She's brought an old tennis ball for Annie, and is playing fetch in the house—something Hattie would not normally encourage. But how amazed Sophy is to find that dogs will chase things! And what an interesting way of throwing she has—her hand springing open as if she's setting a bird free. She opens her mouth, too, the way Gift would, as if that will help somehow.

"More wrist," says Hattie, gently.

Sophy adds more wrist. Still, Cato and Reveille barely look up. Only Annie, foolish Annie, scrambles madly after every ball, dribbling or not, her back paws slipping out from under her.

"Did anyone get out?" Sophy asks again.

"No," says Hattie. "No one got out. That is, except to let Sarun in." She thumbs through their textbook, undoing some dog-ears. She irons out the creases with her thumbnail.

"Sarun got in?"

"He did."

Annie catches a ball on the fly, leaping up gracefully into the air, but Sophy doesn't notice. Neither does she see how though Annie lands ker-plop on her hip, the ball's still in her mouth; her tail's going wild.

"His friends from the city?" asks Hattie.

Sophy nods, trying to wrest the ball out from between Annie's teeth. "We were doing so good," she says. And though as she speaks, Sophy does manage to pry open Annie's mouth, reclaim the ball, bop Annie on the nose with it, and send it back across the room, the bounce is entirely in the ball. Her voice has none.

"You're still doing good," says Hattie. "Your family's going to be okay."

But Sophy's forehead crumples anyway—despite the dogs, despite Annie, despite the soft light and soft air that they seem to pull in around them. Such happy animal innocence! And should not innocence touch innocence?

Sadness, though, will stake itself off. "You don't understand."

"He said he would quit that gang," says Hattie.

Sophy nods.

"Your father's going to be upset."

Sophy nods.

"And just when you were starting over." Starting over being the town pastime, it does seem.

Sophy nods again, her long lashes shining.

.   .   .

Chhung has set up a guard station by the pit, with a blue web folding chair and a plastic-crate coffee table. What with his brace, he has to grip both arms of the chair to settle himself down—it's an ordeal. And yet once he gets there, he doesn't stay put. Instead he sits for a while, then gets up. Then walks a bit. Then goes lowering himself all over again as if he can't help it. Of course, there's something in a person that loves a chair. Hattie'd be the first to admit it—all those months she spent in Joe's reclin-o-matic, after all. Still, how sad to behold that something in action, and then in action again.

Back when Chhung and Sarun dug together, they took breaks all the time. They stepped back, took stock of things. Had themselves some water, or a cigarette—swatted flies. Treated themselves to new Band-Aids. Sarun, like Chhung, was wearing a straw hat sometimes—hanging Band-Aids around the brim so that they hung down in a fringe. A little Carmen Miranda, Cambodian-style. But now Chhung smokes and drinks while Sarun works like a machine. Sarun does eat with Chhung when Sophy or Mum brings lunch out; but other than that, he just digs and digs. With more efficiency than show now—as if *he's come to see what true labor is,* Joe would say, *namely invisible.* As he's wearing cut-off sweats and no shirt, his tattoos show today instead—a writhing blue-black mass with a dragon theme. Monsters breathe fire over his sweaty back.

The acrimony doesn't begin until late, when Chhung hits a certain high. Once the light turns thick, though, his voice, likewise, turns viscous. The pitch of his Khmer is the same, the *trrip* and *ay* and *ai* of it, but add urgency and volume, and it all seems to embody more than the words can possibly say—bearing something fierce from another realm into this one. The strength and pain of it roll right on in through Hattie's windows, open as they are, now, most days; she's begun closing them when Chhung starts and Sarun, in turn, begins to answer, but there's no blocking their awful duet. What with her storm windows off, she has just the single pane of glass to pull down—a skinny thing that keeps the rain out, but that is finally more poncho than barrier—and that window frame's not so tight, either. By dinnertime, Hattie has to turn on the radio if she wants peace, and loud, never mind that the result is not peace.

"Is Sarun all right?" Hattie asks Sophy.

Sophy tucks Annie's head between her knees. "Yes."

"Are you sure?" says Hattie. "Because sometimes . . ."

"Yes!"

Annie licks and licks Sophy as if after some essential canine nutrient.

"Okay, fly-swatter game," Hattie says, producing a plastic fly swatter—this being one of Sophy's favorite games, usually. Hattie pronounces a word; Sophy swats the character for it. Today, though, Sophy twirls the swatter between swats, and when Annie wants to chew on the swatter, lets her. She slumps down in her chair, the soles of her feet turning in.

If Sarun has to walk by his dad now, he scuttles—head down, arms at his sides in a fashion Hattie hasn't seen since she was a child. It's a posture that used to infuriate Hattie's mother. *Stand up!* she'd insist. *Straighter! Straighter!* Terrifying the person, of course. Sarun does not appear too terrified. But when Chhung orders Sarun to kneel, as he likes to, Sarun does just kneel. Then Chhung struggles to his feet and, as best he can, hits Sarun at the back of the head. Aiming, it seems, for somewhere between the primary visual cortex and the cerebellum: a potentially devastating place to strike. It's just lucky he's using a rolled-up newspaper so that, all in all, the striking seems to hurt Chhung more than it does Sarun. Who could defend himself easily enough if he wanted to, anyway. He doesn't even try, though. Quite the contrary, he moves in closer if his father is having to reach too far—helping Chhung out. Making sure he doesn't aggravate his back.

A filial son.

Hattie cannot stop watching. She tries to paint but—talk about compulsion—lets her brush go dry as she sits, binoculars raised, wishing she did not see, could somehow not see how, even with Sarun kneeling and holding dead still, Chhung misses his son's head every now and then; he has to step forward to catch himself if he's not going to pitch forward into the pit. A saving movement that so clearly pains Chhung, Sarun finally picks a spot smack in front of his father one day, kneeling in the most convenient place possible. He holds his hands behind his tattooed back. No hat. His earrings gleam, as does his light-colored ponytail—the ponytail riding up as he bends his neck forward.

Thwhap. Hattie knows she is imagining the sound—that she cannot possibly be hearing the sound. And yet as Chhung's arm drops through the air, she could swear she is hearing it anyway. *Hearing it with your heart's ear,* her mother used to say. *Your heart's ear being better than your two ears put together.*

Your heart's ear being your true ear.

A chipmunk stops right next to the Chhungs, jerking its head up with interest. Then it lowers it as if in imitation of Sarun.

Thwhap.

Sarun has to help Chhung back into his chair, too. He does this gently, leaning over his father, but looking off at the same time. Not as though he is looking for something—just looking. Away. As if something has caught his attention and, foveal creature that he is, he has to turn his head to look at it—though there's nothing out there to look at, of course.

As if, if he moves his head, maybe there will be.

Hattie washes her brushes out. Rolls them up in a bamboo mat, ties the mat up with string, then rinses out her inkstone. *One must always start with fresh ink,* her father used to say, *if the results are to be fresh.* She watches the water run black and black and black.

Is the beating because of the van?" she asks Sophy.

Sophy does not answer at first. But when Annie brings her the tennis ball, she suddenly allows, "Yeah."

"Sarun's friends from the city? The troublemakers?"

Sophy nods, throwing. Her brain having worked out its motor program, her motion is smoothing out with every toss now. She doesn't have to think about what she's doing; she can leave things up to her cerebellum.

Her lovely, undamaged cerebellum.

"What do they want?" asks Hattie.

"I don't know. Maybe they want the TV back." Sophy throws the ball once more, but this time Annie keeps it to chew on instead of bringing it back. Sophy wags her finger, laughing.

"Is it theirs?" asks Hattie.

"They sold it to us cheap."

"Friends' price?"

Sophy nods.

(*Discounts!* Joe used to say. *How is it possible for so many to be in love with discounts?*)

"Did your dad know?" Hattie can guess the answer but asks anyway.

Sophy pretzels up her body in answer; she sips some coffee. Two teaspoons of sugar, a ton of milk.

"He must have known," says Hattie.

And sure enough, Sophy splays her toes like a cat.

"So now Sarun should go with his friends."

Sophy nods into her mug.

"Can you give the TV back?"

"He would go anyway."

"Because?"

"Because in his last life he was a soldier. Traveling everywhere. Fighting. That's why he was born with that scar on his cheek." Sophy drills at her own cheek with a pointed finger. "You know, like from a bullet." She holds out her hand. Annie's been ignoring it and mostly just wants to chew but Sophy holds it out anyway, like a parent dangling a toy her child used to just love.

"And that's why he is the way he is?" Hattie asks.

Sophy nods.

"Do you really believe that?" Hattie is a little amazed—such a web of significance! Though no more extraordinary than any other, she supposes.

"I know it's not something you can prove." Sophy lowers her hand, giving up. "Anyway, we need the money."

"You know, there are other ways of supporting your family," says Hattie, helpfully.

But Sophy's hands are wound tight around her cup, her fingers laced up.

Judy Tell-All stops by with news: Carter, it seems, is seeing Jill Jenkins. Who's not that much younger than him, really—"I mean what's sixty-seven minus fifty-two, twelve?"

"Fifteen."

Et cetera.

"I don't know why you're telling me this." Hattie adjusts her reading glasses; she stares at her page. She'd been trying to add a rock to her bamboo, just to mix things up. Add some enlivening contrast.

Judy shrugs as if to say, *I just wanted you to know that I knew.*

And maybe: *I will always know things you don't. Watching the way I do.*

How does a person turn into Judy Tell-All?

Hattie picks up an old copy of *Science* as the screen door bangs shut. There's no point in trying to paint; her concentration's shot. And now poor Cato cries out as he slowly stands. *A puppy today but one day he'll be as inflexible as his namesake,* Joe predicted.

Poor Cato.

"Courage," she says. If only she could stop him from standing before his warm compress! Instead, she can only stand, too, lending moral support. "Come, my friend." What was it Lee used to recite? *Come my friend, 'tis not too late to seek a newer world.*

Come my friend, 'tis not too late to seek a newer girl.

Back when he was sixteen, Carter had arms that swung like pendula, as if they were weighted at their ends by his hands. Which did just hang there sometimes, awkward and large, like a gorilla's, but were more often reaching up to some wall or ceiling; he was always trying to see how much more he'd grown and how his range had expanded. Including, it seemed, his range of females, many of whom he'd talk over with Hattie, if only to show how little they meant to him. And she—playing older sister—would consider them in turn, if only to show how little they meant to her, either.

"Kind of serious," he said of one. "We talk and talk."

"What do you talk about?"

"Oh, what it means to be alive. Things like that."

"Hmm," she said. "That sounds interesting."

Another was consumed with shopping.

"I'm fascinated," he said. "I mean, it has got to be an act, right?"

"Hmm," she said.

"Come on, Miss Confucius, tell me. Is she pulling my leg?"

"Pulling your leg?"

"Now you're pulling my leg! You know precisely what that means—don't pretend that you don't!"

How much they laughed back then!—laughed and laughed until Carter met Meredith, the provost's daughter.

"Courage," she tells Cato again. And there—he's a bit better now that he's standing; it's not as bad as getting up and down, or stairs. She puts some music on. Sweeps the cabin, licks a finger, rubs a window pane to see if the grime is on the inside or out, then gets out a bucket and brush and tackles the spider webs on the outside of the house. Her lights are so encased in filaments, they seem like giant egg sacs themselves, evolved to be not only extra-large but extra-sticky. Her hands are soon webbed with goo.

She has only just scrubbed off her hands and sat down to ink-making when another visitor arrives.

"Sophy?"

Sophy stands stiff as a porch post. Hattie tells her to come in, but she won't; Hattie has to put down her ink stick to go open the slider.

"I brought you your newspaper," says Sophy.

And so she has—grasping it so hard, she has given the thing a waist.

"Sarun's run away," she says, petting Annie.

"Did he go in the van?"

"We're not sure." Sophy picks Annie up by the shoulders. "My dad's flipping out."

"Let's go look for him."

"Look for him?" Annie, hind legs up, is craning forward to lick Sophy's face.

"Where are my keys?"

On their red hook.

Chhung declines to come, but Mum sits, small and tense, in the front seat next to Hattie. She has a handkerchief knotted tight around her fingers; she worries the cloth. Sophy holds Gift in the back. As Hattie doesn't have a carseat, they do have to keep their fingers crossed that a cop doesn't catch them, but never mind. They circle the lake. Then it's up into the hills on the east side—rising so high on the inclines that Hattie all but forgets their errand from time to time. They're so high, they seem to be crossing the sky—the clouds just ahead, immense and otherworldly; the mountains down below, pid-dling and inconsequential. The trees on the mountains are not trees but tree moss. The roads are like insect trails.

At lower elevations, though, the roads are normal enough again, and finally dry, with cars sending up plumes of dust—the terrors of early spring having given way to something more bucolic. Some of the farms have developments "eating up their fenders," as people say, but look how they buzz now with plowing and planting. The air smells of grass and manure; the lambs and kids are filling out; and, most spectacularly of all, the dandelions are blooming. The car passes field after field of the most joyous, feckless yellow; it should really be named the state weed. Isn't Ginny's old farm around here? Rex's place, as people still call it—next door to the commune? Hattie reseats her glasses, squinting at a three-story barn with a broken-down sugarhouse; she fiddles with her radio. Tuning into a Christian music station at Sophy's request. Though what in heaven's name are they talking about? How men are absent from family life, and women becoming wild, and here it comes, of course, Ephesians 5:22–23: *Wives, submit yourselves unto your own husbands, as unto the Lord. For the husband is the head of the wife, even as Christ is the head of the church. . . .* Paul seeing eye to eye with Confucius on this one. Can Sophy really be interested in this? But there she is, leaning forward, listening, her broad forehead gleaming like a polished rock. Hattie tries to tune the show out and mostly succeeds, but is thankful when Gift begins to fuss so that Sophy finally has no choice but to sit back and play with him. She bounces him, kisses him, tickles him; she claps his feet and plays peek-a-boo and lets him chew on her knuckle, then bounces him some more until finally Hattie asks, Does he like music? And sure enough, a tape of Greta's calms him down. Some kind of Social Club—a Cuban thing—maybe it's just the novelty that does it. Anyway, his eyes widen, and his fists bang; he suddenly shrieks and suddenly quiets. He looks more like Mum every day— Sophy, too—that same broad forehead. Now Sophy wipes his drool with her fingers as the car makes its way from one town to the next— down the wooded lanes, across the open fields. They enter a green valley.

Mum is quiet and unmoving. Her shoulder strap crosses her too high for comfort; another person would draw it down into her lap, or slip it behind her. But Mum just leans back. Never mind that the strap still crosses her chin and part of her cheek; she is holding her handkerchief more loosely now, and watching the road with such interest that Hattie wonders how many times she's sat in the front seat of a car. Many times, surely, back when Sarun had wheels? Sarun, Sarun. They check out the town centers especially, though a lot of them aren't much more than a gas pump that works or doesn't. A Chinese restaurant or a tattoo parlor or a video store; a general store with sagging steps and a live-bait sign. Everything needs paint.

At least the apple trees are blooming.

How can they find a boy who could be anywhere?

Sarun, Sarun, Sarun.

The city is just outcroppings of signage at first. A pizza place. A car wash. But then, suddenly: storefronts, sidewalks, parking meters, sewer grates. Streetlights and traffic lights; dogs on leashes, the poor things. How are Hattie and company going to search a whole city? Anyway, there's Gift's diaper to take care of, first; and wouldn't it be nice to find him a place to toddle around? Hattie is in truth keeping an eye out as much for a park as for Sarun, when they spot—yo!—a familiar blond ponytail sauntering toward the bus station, alone. He's wearing a black-and-silver sweatshirt Hattie doesn't recognize, and swaggering as if he is not coming down a sidewalk exactly, but something with more roll.

"Sarun!" Sophy sweeps her hair back like a girl in one of their Asian romance tapes. "Sarun!"

He startles; stops; does a theatrical double-take.

"Yo! Sarun!"

He hesitates, glancing over his shoulder, but then turns smartly on his heel, strides over and salutes. His hands are clean for a change and, though scarred and scratched up, Band-Aid-free.

"What are you doing here?" says Sophy. "We've been worried about you."

"Had to get out of there."

"We've been driving all over, looking for you!"

"Yeah? Well, you found me." He reaches in to cuff Gift; he ruffles his hair.

"You hungry?" Sophy's tone is nothing Hattie's ever heard from her before—wheedling and appeasing, girly. "Want to get something to eat?"

"You going for pizza? Burgers? What?" He glances across the street at a Mexican restaurant; his pupils are the dark bright of sunglasses. "I'll pass on the tacos. No burritos today, nope. *Gracias.*"

"Don't be actin', *Bong*!" Now it's Sophy who looks away.

Mum says something in Khmer from behind her seat belt. Her tone is mild, her manner is mild; she does not say more than ten words in all. Though her window's half up, she doesn't roll it down; neither does she turn her head. Still, Sarun heeds her in a way that he didn't his sister. Not answering, exactly—he doesn't answer. But he does straighten up, stretching. He looks off at the bus station. Then finally, hunched over, elbows on the car door, he thrusts his face in the half-open window and talks, looks off, talks some more, looks off.

Riding a donkey, looking for a horse, Hattie's father would say, but if you saw him from a distance you might almost think him flirting.

Mum blinks, her handkerchief in her lap.

"All right," he says. "I hear you."

And with that he climbs into the backseat of the car, next to Gift, asking would Hattie shut that noise. "That Goya shit," he calls it.

A kind of talk Hattie doesn't like, but all right. For today, a house special: no lecture, she just turns off the music. Gift, happily, doesn't seem to mind. Sarun's doing gymnastics with him—launching him from his knees to the ceiling, flying him around like an airplane. Gift squeals and squeals. It's the kind of overexcited vocalizing that used to end, with Josh, in a tantrum. But Gift doesn't go over the edge. It's Sarun who tuckers out—still playing, but more and more mechanically, until finally, when they stop for pizza, Sophy takes over. She touches Gift's nose, blows on his face, lets him play with her shirt strap. He climbs in under her shirt, making noises. Everyone else is silent, though the atmosphere once they're back in the car is growing lighter; maybe it's just that as Hattie drives faster, everyone's hair is whipping and blowing. In any case, something feels to be streaming away. Mum puts her hand up, keeping her hair from her face, and yet no one moves to close a window. *Yī xīn yī yì,* Hattie's father would have said—one heart, one will.

A moment of grace, Hattie's mother would have said.

Sophy brings a plateful of food over to Hattie the next day, to say thanks. Everyone, she reports, is fine. Her mother in particular is happy.

"Sarun knows her heart," Sophy says. "She doesn't have to say anything. He knows her heart."

Then she nods to herself and smiles a private smile—her own gaze inward, as if on her own known heart.

Hattie hums and goes looking for her wetsuit. Time to see if the lake's warm enough for a swim.

No need to go looking for Everett; this problem male hulks at the corner like a trading-post bear. He's wearing an unfrayed sweatshirt and a buoyant blue feed hat but his jeans are all grease and wrinkles, his bootlaces all knots and creativity; and there's something unsettled and unsettling in his normally mild glance.

"Mind if I walk, too," he says.

To which the walking group replies, No, no, of course, though—a man in their midst! And a man who wants something. They maintain an unaccustomed silence as they head down the main road and over the culvert. They pass the big field. They pass the four corners. They pass the new speed-limit sign that had to be put up after the other one got run over. They wave hi to Judy Tell-All driving by in her exhaust-spewing pickup; and is that Jill Jenkins out in a car with Neddy Needham? Who's a lot less of a puffball since he started his crash fitness course; and what a nice sport wagon he drives, with a bike rack and a sunroof. And now look.

"Two-timing Carter?" asks Beth, quietly. "Having a side dish?"

Hattie shrugs.

"Because isn't Carter seeing Jill? That's what I heard."

Dá guān—detachment. "I'm trying not to know," says Hattie.

"You're what?" says Beth.

Above them, the clouds darken, then lighten, then darken, then lighten. *There's no one more bipolar than Mother Nature,* Lee would say. But never mind—Everett is still keeping pace with them. Not hurrying them. Just kind of keeping them company, though their pace can't be his pace. There's a grace to the man, thinks Hattie. If only all men knew what he knows. Though maybe that's his trouble, or related to it—his obligingness. A willingness that can turn mulish. Hattie minds him less with every step, in any case, and can almost believe the group could walk the rest of the walk the way they're walking now, preoccupied.

But finally Greta asks, "Is there something on your mind?"—tilting her head in her Greta-like way. Lee's first lines showed up around her mouth—all those faces she made. Greta's, in contrast, are forming zip across her forehead, and what surprise is that? When she spends every day lifting her eyebrows, as now, with interest.

Everett straightens his hat. "Ginny kicked me out."

"No kidding." Beth slows up. "Did she really?"

"I am so sorry to hear that," says Hattie.

Greta throws her braid behind her back, a sign of concern. "So where are you living now?"

"In a tent. Here I built that house with my own two hands, with my own two hands." Everett holds them up. "And what did it get me?" His normally shaven face is unshaven. "A tent," he says. "I'm neighbors with a rosebush."

Beth stops dead. "A rosebush!" she exclaims. "We're going to have to do something about that!"

"A hydrangea'd be great," Everett says drily.

"She means about the tent," says Greta. "Is there something we can do about the tent?"

"Nothing wrong with a tent," he says.

They walk a bit more, their eight arms swinging. The mist shines brilliant; the sky is like a light box. Then it blinks off.

"You're upset," says Hattie, finally.

"She changed the locks on me, Hattie," says Everett. "She changed the locks."

"That's outrageous!" says Beth. "What gives her the right?"

"She says the house is hers. Says the money came from her farm so it's hers."

"When you've been married for thirty-seven years?" says Hattie.

"You remembered."

"That is not right," says Greta.

" 'Course, she's said stuff like that before," says Everett. "It didn't just start. But the locks, now." He shakes his head. "The locks're a development, see. They're a development."

"You're going to have to fight that," says Greta, firmly.

"Am I," he says. "Take her to court, right?"

"Exactly."

"Well, guess I'm going to need a phone line, then—what do you think? And maybe a lawyer. Think I'll need a lawyer?" He winks.

"You will," says Greta.

"A lawyer need payment?" he says—his mock earnestness a little like Sarun's, thinks Hattie, only with a different laugh.

"We can help you with the fees," says Greta.

"You can use my phone," says Hattie.

But Everett gives a sideways jerk of his head, as if trying to get a fly off his neck. "Guess what I'm going to do to thank her," he goes on.

Hattie pictures his clothes hung up all over, like last time.

"Kill myself," he says instead. Calmly—with an air of satisfaction, even. A kind of grin cuts across his face.

Still, Beth looks him in the eye. Long way up as it is, she telescopes herself skyward, like a mother talking to a grown son, and says, "You are not."

And Everett, sure enough, takes a more or less immediate interest in his shoelace knots. "Might as well, now," he says and starts walking on. "Wouldn't you say? Might as well. I gave her my life. Gave her everything I had. Don't you think if she was going to dump me at the end she should've warned me?"

"You're saying you gave her your love and it wasn't returned," says Beth. "You're saying you were—" Her face goes blank.

"Used," he says, helpfully. "I was used."

It's drizzling out. *Mizzling,* Lee would say.

"Though maybe things just changed?" tries Greta. "Because things do change. Like didn't she find Jesus? Isn't that at least part of what happened?"

"And maybe she did love you," agrees Hattie, supportively. "Maybe she loves you still." She pauses. "I mean, I know it's hard to tell."

"She used me up," he insists.

"Or maybe she didn't love you but didn't know that she didn't?" says Greta.

"She knew," he says. "She knew. But she was just obeying the will of God, see. Following orders. She was just following orders."

It starts to shower. Hattie can feel the damp in her joints, and water is organizing itself into beadlets on Greta's fleece jacket. Only Everett's sweatshirt is getting soaked through, though, the water capping his shoulders and belly.

"That is just crazy!" says Beth. "That is just nuts!"

"It's horrifying," agrees Greta, quietly. Rain or no rain, she looks up, her eyes shining gray like the sky but with fine streaks of gold. "Horrifying."

"I am just so sorry," says Hattie.

They all walk on, their hands in their pockets, as if wet hands are a particular concern. Cars *shhush* past.

"I wasted my life," says Everett.

"The whole thing?" Beth's nose drips. "You can't have wasted the whole thing."

"Thirty-seven years anyway," he says—water dripping off the bill of his hat, too. "So what would you call that—most of it? Could you say I wasted most of it?" His voice is calm enough.

Still, Hattie remembers how suddenly he went stomping off at Millie's and is careful.

"That's a long time," she says. "And maybe you did waste your life—who knows. Because people do, it's true. Make mistakes. Marry wrong."

The downpour lets up as suddenly as it started; and out comes the sun then, like a strange, late guest—half pleats of light, half swords.

"See things too late," Hattie goes on, squinting. "Waste their short time on earth. And who even cares, right? Who realizes?"

"Who gives a rat turd." Everett shades his eyes. And he's right—who's ever going to know his heart? Or Hattie's, either, for that matter? Mum—unlucky as she's been in so many ways—is lucky in this one.

Sarun knows her heart. She doesn't have to say anything. He knows her heart.

Greta and Beth are quiet.

"Of course, you did raise those great kids," says Hattie.

Everett nods.

"But think Ginny'll ever see?" she asks. "Think she'll see how she kept you around when it was convenient but kicked you out when it wasn't?"

Everett laughs a bleak laugh. "Cows'll fly before she sees. But I want you to tell her anyway."

"What she's done."

He nods. "I want you to tell her."

"You want her to see."

He hesitates. "Cows'll fly before she sees," he says again.

"I'll tell her anyway," says Hattie. Remembering how she hesitated last time—*you're hedging!*—but determined to do better this round.

"Much obliged, Hattie," he says. "I'm much obliged."

And that, it seems, is what he came for, because at the next corner, he disappears into the strange light.

He said he's going to kill himself over you," says Beth at the Come 'n' Eat. "Or not over you. To get back at you. He said he's going to kill himself to get back at you."

Ginny works on her peach pie. She's wearing a bright pink T-shirt and looks to have just had her hair done, but her face is tired and slack, and her ears, which she usually keeps covered up, are showing. She has big ears—Buddha ears.

"He said he spent his whole life loving you, and that if you weren't going to love him back, you should've told him. Instead of keeping him around. Letting him waste his life. Or if not the whole thing, most of it." Beth can bike sixty miles a day but confronting a friend is something else. Her voice trails off.

"He said you locked him out," says Greta, taking over. Her back's straight, and her head's up; her braid falls like a cataract. "He said he's living in a tent."

"In a tent?" Grace's eyes are so round with amazement, she looks almost bewildered or pained.

"He said you said the house was yours, even if he built it." Hattie looks straight into Ginny's green eyes. "He said you used him. Used him up."

"Is that right." There's a white stripe across Ginny's ring finger where her wedding band used to be.

"He said he gave his life to your marriage, and that if you were going to dump him at the end, you should've said so. That you shouldn't have let him waste his whole life. We said that maybe you loved him, or that maybe things changed. Or that maybe you didn't love him but didn't know you didn't love him." Hattie tries to maintain a certain tone—not accusing Ginny of anything, but not groping like Beth, either. "But he said you said you did. You did know."

"Well, maybe I did and maybe I didn't." Ginny sets her mug down, speaking calmly—adopting Hattie's tone as if borrowing a cookie recipe. "But, you know, I was only doing the will of the Lord."

"That's what he said."

"Then we agree. And if Everett had been with Jesus, he'd have known what there was to know himself, wouldn't he? It's been his choice, to remain in ignorance and darkness. It's been his choice." She leans forward and sighs. "He's an obstinate man, that Everett. I know the Lord's given him to me for a reason. I know he's my trial. But honestly"—she bows her head—"that man's made me suffer."

"He's made *you* suffer!" Greta bangs her cup down.

And Hattie almost laughs. *Hogwash!* But instead she says, "You wronged him and now you refuse to see how. You refuse to see *him,* you refuse to see that you don't see"—trying to say what Everett wanted her to say, trying to remember what that was, though the trying's tripping her up. *Hattie gone batty* just when she would *rise and fight again*! She is more frustrated than she's been in a long time.

A sign of life, probably. Still, there's Ginny draining down her cup. Pushing back her chair. Reaching for her walker. *For mine is the Power and the Glory.* She no longer looks tired as she puts a couple of worn-out dollar bills on the table; quite the contrary, she appears quite revived, giving a gay toodle-doo as she leaves, which several people can't help but return out of habit.

"*He's* made *her* suffer!" explodes Greta again, brandishing the end of her braid.

"And hasn't it been his choice to remain in ignorance and darkness," fumes Hattie. "Hasn't he brought this all on himself."

Grace sneezes. "Sometimes I don't know about that church of hers," she agrees, pulling out a shamrock-print handkerchief.

"You mean, why don't they get up a mission to Africa, right? Or start an environmental ministry or something." Candy rucks up her chin. "When, I mean, will you look at the earth."

"That is just a fact," declares Beth.

"Because they believe in salvation through faith," honks Grace. "They don't believe deeds matter."

"But where Paul told us to spread the Good News, shouldn't we do that whether we're getting credit or not?" Candy's red hair is shining. "And why do they keep to themselves the way they do?" She's upset about a recent ecumenical powwow, which the pastor of the Heritage Bible Church refused to attend. "Opening up their own school as if everyone else has cooties. And people mix us evangelicals up with them—that's what gets me! As if we're all the same, because we don't want our kids watching porn. Because we don't want to see babies getting killed. Because we honor God's plan and believe in the family. When, I mean, they are just fanatic!"

Silence.

"That is just a fact," says Beth, finally.

Flora, all in green, appears with a coffeepot in each hand. Her flat, smooth nose is shining with sun and her earrings flicker, too—a little fish hanging in each lobe. Thanks, they all say. Caf. Decaf. Thanks.

Greta looks at Hattie. "Do I hear your friend the Cambodian girl's involved with this church?"

"I don't know the extent of it," answers Hattie, slowly. "But this blue car does come to pick her up and bring her to some center."

"You have got to stop that." Beth jabs at the air with a toothpick. "You have got to nip that in the bud."

Hattie nods.

"Maybe get her involved in something else?" says Greta.

A great suggestion, but when Hattie asks for ideas, only Candy has an action item for her, namely to pray on it. Because in her experience, she says, God can be a genius at this sort of thing.

The cell tower has somehow passed after all.

"How could anyone do this?" demands Hattie. "With all of town so against it? Who?"

But *it is just a fact,* as Beth would say. Jim Wright has not only gone and allowed an appeal of the cell tower case but, confoundingly, approved a permit. As long as he's lived in town! explodes Greta. Owing as much as he does to his neighbors and teachers! Everyone who's ever lent him a can of motor oil is irate. But, well, he's taken his money, and two other zoning board members besides—both of whom have already skipped town with their families.

Good riddance! says everyone.

And when it turns out that plywood is being stolen from the cell tower building site, well, no one is exactly distraught. People don't like it that crime is going up in general—new folks, they say. New folks bringing problems in their pockets. But in this case they just shrug. Someone building himself a deer camp, they joke. Cash 'n' carry, only without the cash.

Now the plywood on site's been stamped with the cell tower company's name, and there are NO TRESPASSING signs posted, too. As for where the plywood's gone to, though, who knows?

"Somebody must know," insists Hattie.

Because in a town this size, people do generally know who's behind things. And this is Riverlake, after all. A good town, a town that prides itself on having everyone in its picture.

But no one, in this case, has seen anything.

It rains so hard on the Fourth of July, the Pride of Riverlake doesn't even march this year.

Sophy pokes at her cheek with an eraser. "I wish they'd stop."

"Of course you do," says Hattie.

"I wish they'd kill each other already."

"Oh—don't say that." Hattie pushes a plate of Russian teacakes toward her, and Sophy does take one. Instead of eating it, though, she nudges it from one spot on the table to another, like a chess piece. "Is your dad still hitting Sarun with newspaper?"

Sophy goes on nudging but nods.

"Then it isn't likely to happen soon, thank goodness. It's hard to kill someone with newspaper."

Sophy looks up. "I guess that's good."

"Yes, it is," agrees Hattie. "It is good." She sees Joe, emaciated and yellow, his eyes stuck open and his chin fallen back; she hears Lee's long, loud silence.

But no more thinking of these things. There's a lesson to teach; and so, though it is *bǎ miào zhù zhǎng*—like pulling at seedlings to make them grow—Hattie teaches. And at the end, has an idea.

"*Qǐng wèn,*" she says, as they put away their books. "I've seen you playing the guitar."

"My old boyfriend gave it to me. I'm teaching myself." Sophy looks proud of herself. "I have this book."

"*Qǐng nǐ shuō Hànyǔ,*" says Hattie. "Do you remember how to say 'I have a book'?"

"*Wǒ yǒu yī shū*. I mean, *Yí gè.*"

"*Yī běn.*"

"*Yī běn.*"

"Good. The whole sentence, please."

Sophy rolls her eyes but says, "*Wǒ yǒu yī běn shū,*" and stands up.

"*Hén hǎo*. Well, here's my question, then"—is this impulsive? Never mind—"would you like guitar lessons? If I am able to arrange them?" It's Hattie's attempt to get Sophy *involved in something else*.

Sophy sits back down.

"I can't promise," Hattie warns.

But Sophy does not hear her. "Yes!" she blurts. "Yes! I'd love that! Yes! I would! Yes!" Her lips are parted and her eyes brimming; she looks as though she might cry.

"I can try but—really—I can't promise," Hattie warns her again—encouraged by Sophy's response but *hedging*, as Everett would say. She has to.

Still, Sophy keeps exclaiming and when Annie comes to visit, throws the poor dog right up in the air. Annie's face is as shocked as a dog's face gets; Hattie laughs.

.   .   .

And at yoga the next day, she ignores the way Carter circles Jill Jenkins. She ignores Jill's tossing of her shiny black hair; she even ignores Jill's backbend demonstration, though how truly remarkable that, with just the lightest support of Carter's well-placed hand, Jill can still do a backward bend right straight into a bridge. *Well, if it ain't a tendered loin!* Lee would say. But Hattie ignores even Lee. *Dá guān*—she simply watches, at headstand time, for Carter's return to the world of the right-side-up. He is the last of the headstanders to come back; but here come his feet, finally, lightly touching down. One and then the other. And there—he's levered his long body upright, moving with such grace that Hattie half forgets her mission for a moment: It is as if some invisible agency has judiciously supplied a bar, at just the right moment, at his hips. And here, now, he stands, before her—a barefoot man with a magenta-colored face. A zinnia.

He untucks his T-shirt.

"Guitar lessons? I am rusty as the Tin Man," he begins—taken aback but relieved, too, she can see, to be having a normal-ish conversation with her. "Moreover, I am in danger of turning into a one-man rec center," he says.

Still, come Saturday afternoon, Hattie is introducing Carter to the Chhungs. She doesn't stick around. But from back in her house, she can see Carter produce his guitar with a flourish; Sophy, she can see, too, is already enthralled. The dogs need their teeth brushed; every shirt Hattie owns has a spot on it; and for once she has a clear idea what she's going to focus on if she ever makes it back to her bamboo—a more natural splay of the leaves. Like the fingers of a hand, she thinks. She wants them to fall like the fingers of a hand.

But out come her binoculars instead. For there sits Carter, laughing up a storm, joking and whistling. He produces a harmonica and another guitar—or, no—what is that? A banjo. Hattie didn't even know he played the banjo. But there he sits, strumming the thing and howling and generally showing off. And there's the whole family, come out to watch him—Sarun and Mum tilting their heads back and forth while Chhung taps his foot and slaps his knee. He's still wearing his brace, but can sit all afternoon in his guard chair now; it's an encouraging sight. How much more cheering yet, though, to see him like this—imitating someone in a Western, it seems. Hattie can't hear much over the banjo, of course, but her mind supplies a soundtrack easy enough: *Tap, slap, tap, slap.* Is this the demonic man of the afternoons and evenings?

Tap, slap, tap, slap.
Tap, thwap, tap, thwap.

Carter switches back to his guitar, waving his audience good-bye; and now the lesson begins. Sophy plays; he points something out. She plays a little more; he nods—better. They both bend over their instruments; you can almost see the learning move between them, like a ball. What a good teacher he's always been! Learning is a dance, he used to say, and even from a distance Hattie can see how their rhythms are firmly in synch. He imitates that little waggle she makes with her head; she laughs; they try different picks. He presents a book to her. Then for stretches of time that grow longer as the lesson goes on, they drape their arms over their respective instruments and talk; the symmetry ends. For he is mostly talking and gesturing now, while she is mostly holding still, rapt.

Hattie can remember holding still, rapt, once upon a time, herself.

Carter's ways of moving have not changed, Hattie sees. The motion of that stick, for example, as he draws something on the ground; the moment of pondering that comes next. He ponders with his elbows on his knees, his wrists loose, his hands dangling like fruit—hmm. An exaggerated pondering this is, more about modeling pondering than about pondering plain and simple. And now come the retreat of the hands, the advance of a foot. His back straightens as he corrects a line with his heel, making an elaborate scuffing motion. He rolls his eyes as if to suggest just how mistake-prone he is, how very like a normal Joe—a little corny self deprecation, designed to put you at your ease. Which Hattie always did love him for—the out-and-out graciousness of it. Never mind what he's explaining, which, if Hattie knows Carter, may or may not have anything to do with the guitar at all. The handedness of nature, the location of the fertile crescent, the miracle of gastrulation—Carter could be talking about anything, believing as he does both that one thing should be allowed to lead to another and that you should never cordon off certain topics as too technical or too abstruse. Or too sensitive: Hattie does hope he and Sophy will get to talking about the Bible one day—Sophy going off in the blue car more and more, Hattie notices. To that center. That church.

Ginny's church.

In Chinese, Hattie would say Carter *huì zuò rén*—that he has a way with people. Which is not so much a matter of skill, maybe, as of humility. *I never go walking with three people,* Confucius said, *but that one of them proves a teacher.* Now she watches as he lays down his stick and, with a rueful smile, looks at his watch. How genuinely he would love to stay, his body says. What a marvelous time he has had. But, well, next week. He stands and stretches. Mum appears, then disappears, then appears again; so that when Carter leaves, it is with three paper plates of food, in a stack. His shadow against the trailer as he thanks her is enormous. Hattie watches as he turns his car around—watches Sophy watching him turn around, too. Standing there on the crate by the front door, waving, her head tilted to the side. One hand plays with her hair.

A fifteen-year-old girl! A sixty-seven-year-old man!

But, well, a father figure.

Mum appears behind her; Carter waves to them both in his rearview as he heads up the drive. Did he notice Sarun digging? Did he register the pit? What with all his waving, he could well have missed it, Hattie sees.

Well, maybe she'll point it out next time. For now, she puts on some music—first, some Brahms four-handed piano music. Then a Brahms clarinet thing Carter's mother used to love. *Proof,* she liked to say, *that some blooms come late.*

Joe, of course, used to have a different reaction to it—to Hatch music, as he called it.

Carter Hatch, Carter Hatch, he used to say. *Why didn't you marry that Carter Hatch?*

And when Hattie said it was him, Joe, she loved, he laughed.

*H*ow *easily she could never have met this Carter Hatch! But one day back in Qingdao they began to talk about the Communists the way they used to talk about the Japanese. The People's Liberation Army, they said. The fighting. The fighting. The fighting was every- where; the fighting was coming. It was coming here. And then where would they go? Everywhere else in China people moved inland. But how could they move inland, with the Communists inland of them? They had best learn to swim, said Hattie's father.*

Hattie's mother begged a favor of one of the missionary couples with whom she'd originally come to China. Of course it was a tragic story, a terrible story, that the Wilders' daughter had been killed in an anti-foreigner uprising—the sort of story that tested a person's faith in

God to the utmost. But it did mean they had an extra set of papers with which to leave the country. And so Hattie's mother wrote them: Please. If you would please at least take my daughter. How she wished she had made the kids citizens! Everything would work out eventually, she was sure. But if the Wilders would first take this daughter, well, how grateful she would be.

The Wilders' daughter having been adopted and, it so happened, a half-half like Hattie. A hùn xúe'er.

"It's God's will," said Reverend Wilder.

Molly Wilder's hair had been lighter than Hattie's, but with some hydrogen peroxide Hattie's was made to match; a doctor carved a small cut into Hattie's right cheek, too, where Molly Wilder had once been hit by a windmilling ski. Of course, Hattie was amazed, as she sat for her surgery, to think of this Molly, skiing. And what exactly was a windmilling ski?

Never mind. Her mother found some eye shadow like Molly Wilder's—green stuff, the color of inchworms. She curled Hattie's eyelashes with a scissor-handled clamp, and applied mascara; the mascara came in a cake, like a slice of ink stick. And when she was done, Hattie's brothers gaped. A foreigner! Even Mrs. Wilder, when she saw Hattie, was amazed. "Molly!" she cried, and swooned. She was wearing a cross heavy as a pickax; it lodged itself in her armpit.

And the next thing Hattie knew, she was having supper with her mother's family in Iowa. The food was strange, and the forks and knives, but she had expected that. The slabs of meat, the blood on the plate—she had been warned. And hadn't she grown up in Qingdao, after all, with an American mother? She had eaten all sorts of things. The silence, though—she had never in all her life sat at a silent table.

"Days don't get more glorious than this," Grandpa Amos would say eventually, with a flare of his enormous nostrils. He raised his jutting eyebrows, as if to counter some shrinking force centered in between his eyes. "And to have our grandchild returned to the bosom of the family. Well, we have to thank the Good Lord for that."

"Pa," one of Hattie's uncles would say then. "You have been saying that every night for a week."

"Well, it's still true." Grandpa Amos smoothed out his napkin as if, like his face, squares of cloth wanted attention if they were to maintain their rightful expanse. "And isn't she a joy."

Grandma Caroline shook. Though she had Hattie's mother's

*name, and Hattie's mother's ways, she was, awfully, nothing like Hat-
tie's mother at all. Instead, she was thin and nervous, with hands that
trembled so bad she sat on them. And, as if to go with her darting way
of talking, she had a stinging way of thinking.*

*"I suppose her stature is her father's," she said now. "Doesn't it
seem her father's?"*

Hattie tried not to cry.

*"How about if you tell us something about China," said Grandpa
Amos, consolingly. "How about if you tell us what it's like there?"*

*And, staring at the sprigs on the plate ware, Hattie tried to think
what to say. Farmers that they mainly were, her aunts and uncles were
disappointed that she knew nothing about soy—what they grew—
though she was at least able to explain that farmers did not use com-
bines in China, preferring, as they did, water buffalo. And of course,
Hattie did like soy sauce, and soy milk. More than that she really
couldn't supply; but happily, Uncle Jeremy insisted that that was
enough—maybe because he, unlike the others, had nothing to do with
the growing of anything. He was an anthropologist—a kind of spy, he
explained, if you can imagine a spy looking, not for secrets, but for
understanding.*

*"It's good to have you home," he said, adjusting his glasses. And,
"You have your mother's spirit, may we see her again one day."*

*That made Hattie want to cry, too, as did the ongoing efforts to
save her heathen soul. "Eternal life," Grandpa Amos would say, over
ice cream. "Maybe you're not ready to accept Christ's sacrifice. I can
understand that. But eternal life." He'd shake his head. "That's a lot
to give up." Grandma Caroline sat her down on a hard bench. "'The
unbelieving shall have their part in the lake which burneth with fire
and brimstone,'" she said. "That's what the Good Book tells us. Fire
and brimstone. Do you know what brimstone is?"*

"Sulfur," said Hattie.

"So your mother did teach you something."

"She told me to look it up myself."

*For all the tension, they certainly would have held on to Hattie,
had that seemed the Lord's plan. But, well, Grandpa Amos's prostate;
and Grandma Caroline's thyroid, besides. The Good Lord did not
seem to be equipping them for a young girl's care. Plus how much
sense did the country make for Hattie, anyway? A place she would
probably be treated like a freak, said Uncle Jeremy. No, the answer
was for the family city folk to take her—if only he and Susan weren't*

headed to Tanzania! But, well, Susan's research. Uncle Jeremy did have some Christian friends, though, also living in the city, with a big house. What if Hattie were sent to live with them until her parents got themselves out of China? Picture her a kind of exchange student, he said. Though, of course, if she were to teach the other kids a little Chinese, well, wouldn't that be nice?

How many musical instruments the Hatch family had! Their music room housing not only several violins, but a viola, and a cello, and a harp, and several wind instruments, besides. The piano was Mrs. Hatch's baby Bechstein; Dr. Hatch's Steinway console sat closed up in a corner. Maybe with its big name and small sound, it really would be relegated to the basement someday. In the meanwhile, the piano in the basement was Carter's no-name spinet.

"To each his own ears," Mrs. Hatch would say gently. "If you would please just close the basement door."

Carter being a fan of country music, of all things, who, besides the piano, played the harmonica and guitar.

Hattie had just turned seventeen when she came. Carter was fifteen—blue-eyed like his father, and still growing but huge already, people said. Taller than his father, and gangly, with a way of twisting himself up that was almost girlish. No one would listen to him play except Mrs. Hatch, when she wasn't fund-raising for her symphony, and Hattie—which Carter said didn't bother him. Still, he would always tell Hattie when he had learned a new song, and play it for her first chance he got.

"Is it insipid?" he would ask.

"Insipid?" She would frown. "I don't know. What does that mean?"

That made him laugh. "Insipid is what it is. Like it never read any books. Like it never met a sarcastic person. Like life is a field full of daisies."

"But you like it?"

"I don't know. I guess. I mean, it's not a Brahms quintet." He strummed a little.

"What's a quintet?"

People called him a sweet boy, almost as brilliant as his older brother Anderson. He was the charming one, the sensitive one, the one who would play four-handed piano with his mother. Reedie was *the baby. Hattie liked them all, and tutored them as best she could, though they were not too keen on learning an extra language. Weren't Latin and French enough? Dr. Hatch wanted them to be Renaissance men, but even Renaissance men, they complained, did not speak Chinese. The only reason they paid any attention whatsoever to their tones or characters was because they knew how stranded poor Hattie was. Dr. and Mrs. Hatch talked about it—the Revolution, the chaos. It was in the newspaper.*

"Do you think you'll ever see your real family again?" Reedie would ask at dinner, playing with his food. "I mean, your Chinese family?" And, "Is it true Jeremy told your American family we were Christian?" And, once, "Are you going to stay long?"

Mrs. Hatch shushed him.

They were as interested in Confucius as her mother's family had been in soy. She tried to explain that her family was only pángzhī—a side branch of the family tree, or not even that. A twig. She tried to explain that her parents were from Qingdao—a big city, a port city. The Germans, she tried to say, the Japanese. Occupation. The Communists. The Hatches listened. But things Confucian had a special handle for them—Miss Confucius, they called her. "What would Confucius think of Kerouac?" they liked to ask. "What would Confucius think of Brylcreem?" It was just how American families were, she thought, full of banter; and how much better to be bantered about than not, especially since, as the reality of her situation began to dawn on her, she could not always leave her room. Then what a blessing it was that one of the boys would eventually knock on her door— dispatched, of course, by Mrs. Hatch—and demand a Chinese lesson.

"Miss Confucius!" Reedie or Carter would cry—it was never Anderson, always Reedie or Carter. "I've forgotten how to write my name again!" And with increasingly outlandish pleas of ignorance, they would slowly coax her out.

Why did she really try to teach them something? Anyway, she did, though how strange to break down her native tongue into something foreign to herself. Sounds, tones, vocabulary. Was this how her mother had felt, teaching English in China? It was like performing a dissection on herself, and not even for herself; it was like performing a dissection on herself for a bored and antsy class. Thank goodness for her English! People said she spoke so well, they forgot she was Chinese, or half Chinese, or whatever it was she was. Yet even as they forgot, she remembered that she was whatever it was she was. A person away from herself. With what she guessed must be Chinese ideas and what she guessed must be Chinese feelings. She was pretty sure she dreamed in Chinese. And she craved Chinese food, of course. Mántóu. She craved mántóu. Lǎocù huāshēng—peanuts generally. Cù—American vinegar was not vinegar. She missed sea cucumbers, squid. Spicy clams. Before this she had known that her mother was American, but not that her father was Chinese, really.

Now, every day, she knew: Her father was Chinese. She was raised in China.

And yet she was not her old self, translated. Neither was she a Chinese in America. She was just foreign—wàiláide.

What she had always been—wàiláide.

From elsewhere. A stranger.

She wrote things in Chinese, just to see things in Chinese.

Mostly, though, she tutored the boys, who tutored her in return. Reedie taught her about baseball—RBIs, MVPs, the seventh-inning stretch. This involved watching TV, and eating cotton candy. Anderson did famous presidents: George Washington. Abraham Lincoln. FDR.

Carter's program, meanwhile, began as a great-experiments course but turned into a kind of experiment of its own, in which he would look at her and tell her what she made him think. For example, when he found Hattie in the library one day, examining some horn-handled knives, he asked her why she was frowning. And when she asked if the knives were a wedding present, then observed that giving knives was bad luck, he laughed.

"B. F. Skinner," he began, and went on to describe an experiment Skinner had performed with pigeons. "He gave the birds treats every now and then," he said. "A click and a food pellet, on a completely random program. There was absolutely no rhyme or reason to it. But here's the interesting thing: The birds developed funny little bobs and dances, as if they were trying to repeat whatever it was that brought the food—as if they were trying to figure it out. Was it looking up? Looking down? Clawing the ground?"

"The birds danced?"

"Yes!" Carter gestured as if amazed himself. "Can you believe it? Even pigeons try to connect what they do with what happens to them. Really, they have no control. But they're wired to try anyway. They

have a connection bias, just like people—a tendency to look for cause and effect, whether it's there or not."

"Really." Hattie eyed some of the other objects on the library table—a geode, a geodesic dome, a wooden pyramid puzzle.

"It's called the superstition effect," he went on. "Jerry told me about it."

Jerry was one of Dr. Hatch's grad students.

"Am I superstitious, do you think?" Hattie picked up the puzzle, which immediately broke apart. "Is that what you mean? Like a pigeon?"

"Do you really think giving knives is bad luck?"

"Yes."

"QED," he said.

She thought about that.

"Aren't you going to ask what that means?"

"No," she said.

"Because you know I'll tell you."

"Yes."

They were quiet.

"You think I'm like a pigeon? As ignorant as that?"

"No!" he said. "Very definitely not." But after a moment he added, "I can see that you're from a long way away, that's all."

"An ignorant place. A backward, superstitious place."

"I didn't say that."

"An unscientific place."

"Oh, Hattie." He flushed in a way people in China mostly didn't, though she did a little, like her mother. His eyes shone blue and clear. "Are you going to go hole up in your room now?"

How much Carter taught her! That "The Star-Spangled Banner" was based on an English drinking song. That moss has leaves you can't see. That Houdini had a tool pocket in the lining of his mouth.

"Do you know how you can tell a coyote's tracks from a dog's?" he asked her once. Hattie had been living in America for six years by then and had finally not so much started to get used to it, as started to accept that she had ended up in a place she would never get used to— that she was like Lin Daiyu in Dream of the Red Chamber, *trying to make herself at home in a home not hers. But there she was, in the meanwhile, with Carter, at his parents' summer house in Riverlake, looking at some tracks in the snow. They were on winter break from their respective colleges.*

"No," she said.

"Look."

And though they were mostly similar, Hattie immediately saw how directed the coyote's tracks were, compared to the dog's—how the dog's went every which way.

"A dog plays," he said. "A coyote is always looking for dinner."

"They have to," she said, after a moment. "Coyotes are on their own."

"Jerry says we've neotenized dogs. Domesticated them so that they never learn to stare down a rival the way a wolf does—any of that. They're playful, but they remain children all their lives. They never grow up."

"Well, maybe coyotes wouldn't mind not having to grow up," she said.

It was cold out—windy. The snow was blowing across the lake in diagonals, like a series of sailboat-less sails. Carter cleared his throat.

"Let me ask you, then. Do coyotes allow themselves to have feelings that go nowhere?"

Even her eyelashes were icing up. Still, she gave her heart's warm answer.

"No," she said. "They're coyotes. They know how to take care of themselves."

Then she let him take her arm and lead her in, and though they were just friends, they did warm up each other's digits and more that day. In the morning they agreed to forget what had happened. But forgetting how they'd laid their socks by the fire, and then their long johns, and then their red selves—forgetting how they'd touched each other's scars and more—was harder than somehow ending up on opposite coasts after college. Hattie couldn't say he wasn't honest. And probably she should have told him she was a virgin, just as he probably should have asked. (His own status could be surmised.) Anyway, they both saw what a mistake it was, to have given in to the moment like that. They agreed.

Still, she was relieved when at Christmas, Carter came down with the flu. The following Easter and summer, Carter was in Kenya; and the following Thanksgiving, Hattie really did strain her ankle too badly to travel.

And had she not gone back into biology, that probably would have been that.

. . .

Jed Jamison and Everett are talking so loud on the checkout line, Hattie can't help but hear them, and she's not the only one. The whole store can hear them, and the whole store's listening—the whole town, it seems.

"Heard you're building yourself a pole barn," says Jed.

"It ain't a pole barn," says Everett. He has three loaves of bread under his arm and a jar of peanut butter. "It's a home for me to live in."

"Heard it's on Ginny's property. Ain't it on Ginny's property?" When Jed steps toward the register with his wagon, Everett, right behind him, and Hattie, at the end of the line, move up, too.

"Our property," says Everett, taking his step. "Seeing as we are not divorced. It's our property."

"Heard it was the farm that got sold to pay for the property," says Jed. "Heard the money came from Rex's place. Making the new property Rex's place, too, right? In a way it's Rex's new place."

"Interesting," says Everett. "Here Rex is stone dead but he has himself a new place. And here Ginny and me've been married thirty-seven years but our place is still her pa's. How do you like that."

"Hear you're not real married at the moment," says Jed.

"Did you. Well, we're still involved, see," says Everett. He nods. "We're involved."

"Heard you're putting up your pole barn right in the middle of her view," says Jed.

"It ain't a pole barn," says Everett.

"Your structure, then. Heard you're putting up your structure right in the middle of her view." Standing almost as tall as Everett, Jed has to lean way down to unload his groceries from his wagon.

"Had to be located somewhere, Jed. And where'm I going to sleep? Tell me. Seeing as how I'm so welcome in my own home. You going to put me up?"

"Not tonight."

"There you go. Where'm I going to sleep if I don't build? She mention who put up the house she's so kindly hogging, by the way? Who figured out where to put the sunroom, so as to take in the view?"

"Don't think she did." Jed moves down the counter to be checked out. "Not that I recall."

"She'll see better when she can't see," says Everett. "Mark my words, now. She'll see better when she can't see."

"Heard it's a thing of beauty."

"It's tall, Jed. I'm not going to tell you different. I'm building tall."

"Heard you're ruining her garden with deer." Jed's helping bag up his groceries himself.

"Deer do roam these parts, Jed. I didn't invent 'em."

"Heard you're sprinkling your lot with apple scent so they'll come eat up her garden," says Jed. "Heard you're wrecking the whole thing."

"There a law says a man can't sprinkle apple scent in his own yard?" says Everett.

"No, sir, there is not," says Jed.

Everett sets down his econo-sized peanut butter. "Well, then, how do you like that. This here's still a free country, it turns out. A free country."

Jed laughs and, when he yawns, puts a hand up to his mouth, egg carton and all. "Guess it is."

Then Everett yawns, too, and, back behind them, Hattie. She turns her face, hoping they won't see her—*Hattie nose full of beeswax!*—and happily, they don't seem to. Still, she's glad to see them leave the store.

Thank you so much!" says Sophy. She's had two guitar lessons from Carter and already she's, like, a lot better! So much so, that she's brought her guitar over to show Hattie. She's even begun writing songs, she says, and as Annie noses open the guitar case, jumps back, then creeps forward again to investigate, Sophy plays one. No sneakers today. She's wearing silver flip-flops Hattie's never seen before, and her toenails are pink and purple, alternating—another new thing and nothing you'd call shy. Yet she sings so quietly Hattie has to strain to hear. It's only on the last time around that she catches the chorus:

> O, believe us when we say
> We'll keep the gard'n snake away
> And choose you, Lord, choose you.
> We'll take you in,
> We'll take you in,

Into the deepest part
Of our soul and heart
We will,
We'll take you in.

Hattie claps. Of course, *In the deepest part / Of her soul and heart / she does / does want to laugh!* But she does not. Instead, she asks, Do you believe in Satan? And when Sophy says yes, Hattie asks what he looks like.

"He's like a *k'maoch*," says Sophy.

"So there are ghosts in both Christianity and Buddhism?"

"It's all, like, the same thing." Sophy makes a face Hattie's never seen before—*two commas and, between them, a sea change,* Lee would say.

Hattie is careful.

"So you're liking going up to the center?" she asks.

"I'm trying to drag my mom to, like, an ice cream social," answers Sophy. "They have a guy who plays the accordion—I know she'd just love it. This guy playing and everyone, like, laughing and joking."

"Like your sisters have come back. Or like life in Cambodia, before Pol Pot."

"I guess." Sophy retunes one of her strings, turning the peg, listening, turning it some more. She tucks a stray hair behind her ear as if to help her hear better.

"A warm place," says Hattie. "With people you can turn to."

"Yeah. Except people don't even care who your family is or anything." Sophy runs a thumb down the strings, listening as each one sounds. "It's hard to explain."

"I think I understand—we had all that face stuff in China, too," says Hattie. "Everyone focused on who your family was. The church was a lot more welcoming."

"They are!" Sophy stills the strings with a flat hand. "You're right! A lot more! Like they gave me this pamphlet that says 'Where friends become family' and it really is true. It really is like that."

"And doesn't that make a difference if your own family isn't doing so hot," says Hattie.

Sophy scrutinizes her nails, which are short on one hand and long on the other. "I just wish they'd kill each other already," she says.

"Is your dad still hitting Sarun with the newspaper?"

"You asked me the same exact thing before. In those exact same words."

"Did I?" *Hattie gone batty!* Though didn't Sophy just say something she'd said before, too? "Just checking, Sophy."

"Checking up on us."

Checking *in* on you, Hattie would have said. But, well, never mind. With teacherly patience, she says, "Does it bother you?"

Sophy considers, strumming. "I probably shouldn't say that anyway."

"No," says Hattie. "You shouldn't."

"So why didn't you say so?"

"Would you have wanted me to?"

"I don't know. I guess. If you're going to think things. Yeah, I would."

"Well, all right then. Next time, I will. I won't hold back." Should she be promising this? Too late. "Next time I'll say, 'Don't say that, Sophy! That's terrible!' "

Sophy laughs so hard she has to cover her mouth. "Where's Annie?" she asks. "Aren't we going to have cookies?"

Yet more e-mails about money, and then this one:

Dear Aunt Hattie,

I don't know how to write this, but my son Alexander has died. It is a terrible story. He was, as you know, fifteen, and friends with his cousin, a year older. Of course that cousin had been having problems, as we all knew. But he'd been living in Australia. We did not see him so often, anyway. We knew he would not come back from Australia even for his father's funeral. But we did not know he was so-called paranoid schizophrenic until he came to a family reunion and beat my son to death. But that is what happened. While they were playing horseshoes, apparently they had some fight

Hattie reads this e-mail again.

Can this really be because of the graves?

She begins to write, *I cannot begin to say what sorrow,* but then stops. What can she say, really? That will help. What can she say that will help?

You'll but lie and bleed awhile. . . .

No.

At the end of the e-mail Hattie wants to say, *For all of the horror of this, I just do not believe that moving my parents' graves will make a difference,* but does not. What use can it be, parrying belief with belief? And what can the grieving hear anyhow? What with the sound of their own hearts so loud.

Hattie understands.

Still: How many more of these appeals can she read? *Dá guān*— she sets up a file, so that when the next e-mail comes, she can simply click on it and drag it over. Then she gets out her inkstone and brushes. Though how heavy the inkstone today! And does it not seem that she is going to be working on the knots between her bamboo segments forever? Like the character for heart, *xīn,* only without the dots, she thinks; but somehow they hook back wrong and seem to connect nothing.

She goes for a swim.

*H*attie *had majored in biology in college. After graduation, though, she had gotten a job teaching Chinese at a private school, where she probably would have stayed except that one hot Fourth of July, Dr. Hatch asked her how she liked it. And when she said that she liked some things but had maybe had enough of pattern drills, he said she should go back into science.*

"Science?"

"You know. The systematic interrogation of the natural world." He speared some figs on the grill; his bald head shone.

By then Hattie was no longer avoiding Carter, but when he drove up the driveway, she did still take note.

"I hadn't thought of it," she told Dr. Hatch—noticing, as she spoke, that Carter had gotten himself a new VW convertible just like his old one, only blue. He had the top down and his radio on—bluegrass—and got out of the car alone.

"Well, perhaps you should think about it," said Dr. Hatch. "You were good at it."

"Was I?"

"You can't really be surprised to hear this."

"Oh, no, Dr. Hatch. I am. I am." A hot dog rolled off her paper plate; Dr. Hatch eyed her as she rescued it, grass clippings and all.

"You like to shake things, I've noticed," he went on. "Give things a shake and see what's what."

"Do I?" And was he giving things a shake himself? He did like to get things going, she knew. "I don't know that I shake anything on purpose. But there's a lot I don't know about the world. So maybe that's, I don't know." She hesitated. "A disturbance."

Carter winked at her as he entered the yard but then went to stand as far away from her as possible—a game they used to play. But was it a game now? She tried to focus on her conversation with Dr. Hatch.

". . . though there's more to your avowed ignorance, isn't there? he was saying. "Than simple ignorance. You're interested in reality. The ding an sich, as they say. The noumenon." (This was Dr. Hatch as Renaissance man.) "In knowing where it lies, what it is—never mind that it always lies just beyond us, somehow. That we are like blind men groping an elephant. Even the nature of the blindness interests you. The limits of our senses, of our processing apparatus. Am I right?"

What blind men? What elephant?

"I guess I'm interested in how differently people think, if that's what you mean. How differently people see." She hesitated. "And what we can't see, because of how we see."

"The blindness that goes with vision. That vision depends on, in fact."

"Yes. Or—not even interested. Aware of it, I guess."

"Thanks to Carter's work with the Nerve-Muscle Program. That huge quantity of information that comes into the eye but is filtered out by the brain representing the proverbial tip of the iceberg."

"What's filtered out." She nodded.

"You are aware of people's arrogance."

"Their certainty."

"Their mistaken, arrogant certainty."

With what arrogant certainty he said that!

"My mother used to say, 'We must see that we don't see,'" she said.

"A point that's been made since Plato," Dr. Hatch went on. "But

*that in your case, stems, no doubt, from growing up in another cul-
ture. So that you're aware of other ways of seeing. Other lenses."*

"No doubt."

*He gave her a hard look; he had Carter's eyes. (Or, she supposed,
Carter had his.)*

She hung her head.

*He softened. "As people realize and don't, I imagine," he went on.
"It's hard to explain."*

*He looked at her. "Don't accept not fitting in," he said then. "No
one fits in."*

"I see."

*"Be a part of the picture," he said. "Make yourself a part.
Remake the picture if need be."*

*Her grass-flecked hot dog rocked a bit on her plate. "I'll try. I
mean, I'll do that."*

*"Don't be a gadfly. The sort who brings disorder instead of per-
spective. Who dismantles but doesn't rebuild. Who fails to understand what it means to build to begin with, really. What force and
imagination it takes to get the simplest thing done. Gadflies are a nui-
sance and a distraction.*

"I won't become a gadfly," she promised.

*He gave her a sympathetic look. "I'm sure it's hard to be adven-
tive. Temporarily naturalized, that is."*

She didn't know what he meant, and yet did. "It is."

*"My mother was in your situation once upon a time," he said.
But he did not go on and, whatever he meant, she did not ask, for
Carter had snuck up behind her with a clean hot dog for her plate. He
then disappeared once again.*

*She ate the hot dog but refused to look and see where he had
gone. As Carter did or didn't notice, but as his father did, of course.*

*He said nothing, though, apparently having other things on his
mind.*

*Dr. Hatch was a clean-cut man, with a neat head, of course, and
neat ears. His crisp shirt had not softened in the humidity; his Swiss
watch gave off a silvery cool. And yet he was triumphing, at that
moment, over more than the weather. For having experienced a salad
with grilled figs in California, he was now conducting an experiment
himself—wanting to see, he said, whether embers too spent for fish or
meat weren't just right for figs. Which would certainly have been fine*

with Mrs. Hatch had he not bought bags and bags full of subjects for his experiment; figs were expensive in their neck of the woods. Moreover, she had never known anyone in the family, she said, to care for figs in any form. Still, he maintained that he had not overbought; and now his grad students agreed he should have bought many more.

"Have a fig," offered Dr. Hatch in closing—insisting that Hattie take a whole half-fig, even if it was the last one. "Take it! Take it!" he urged. And finally, she did take it, even as Dr. Hatch turned to Mrs. Hatch and said, still smiling, "You might put some work into your battle-picking." To which Mrs. Hatch drew up her egret neck and raised her fine chin—a patrician affair that had something to do with who her family was before it went to seed. It was Carter who, suddenly reappearing, stared at the ground, looking as though he was going to bawl. He sat on a lawn chair, his feet turned out like a duck's; the back of his neck stretched on and on, sunburned and knobby.

Hattie did not sit down with him.

She was twenty-four then and had not heard from her parents in years. Of course, she and her Iowa family were still writing letters; though working from Tanzania wasn't easy, Uncle Jeremy and Susan were particularly dogged about "trying other channels," as they put it. And yet even so there were days when Hattie probably would have drowned herself, except that she didn't want to drown herself in an American lake. She wanted to drown herself in a Chinese lake, where people would find her and think of the poet Qu Yuan. She didn't want people just to think she was nuts.

So she wrote down Dr. Hatch's words and tucked them into her wallet. She replayed the moment he said them, leaving out the swipe at Mrs. Hatch and the awkwardness with Carter. And she went back to school for her doctorate—taking some courses, then starting work on synaptic transmission in Guy LaPoint's lab. That was before Guy's lab got folded, over his protests, into Carter's—a brand-new proposition and, seeing as Carter was in his twenties, a small coup. Of course, people got their careers started earlier back then; they got their Ph.D.'s faster, and Carter was Dr. Hatch's son, after all. Not the very most brilliant son, but still a wunderkind, working in a new field. And what interesting stuff he was working on—Dr. Hatch wasn't the only one who thought so—the connection between cortical interneurons and the firing of a simple cortical cell. The very process, in short, through which data from the outside world registered, or failed to register, as something "seen"—the place where the objective world was filtered, and perception made.

You mean, *Lee would say later*, where we all go a little haywire.

By the time Hattie ended up working on her dissertation with Carter, she was no longer uncomfortable with him. And yet theirs was hardly a normal advising relationship. They avoided personal subjects, and they certainly did not share food or clothes. Every now and then, though, Carter would look up and say, "Miss Confucius. You will understand this."

And then, while Hattie's lab mates looked on with envy, Carter would work out some point with her as if there were no other living being in the room. Everyone knew that Hattie could get through to Carter if he was tied up, or draft a letter in a pinch, and he never rewrote her papers. What's more, they spoke, sometimes, in a kind of code.

"A mollusc?" she might ask as he looked over a paper from a rival lab, for example. (Lowly molluscs, lucky creatures, having no blind spots, thanks to the superior design of their optic nerves.)

"No," he would answer. "I see a blind spot here." Or else, with grudging respect: "Well, yes. You'd have to call it a squid."

Certain committees were the Sudd—impossibly clogged with vegetative matter, like their namesake, an un-navigable section of the Nile. And certain members of certain committees were epiphytes, bombillators, Ignoriahs. Their own lab, of course, was the Hatchery.

Or maybe the Junior Hatchery: There was, it seemed, no escaping Carter's father—El Honcho Hatch, as people called him. When Carter grew a beard, for example, people said it was to bug El Honcho Hatch. And was Carter not just like El Honcho in his impatience? The time that he said that people who could not get to the point should go into psychoanalysis instead of science, for example—did he not sound like El Honcho then? It was the El Honcho in him, too, they said, who told a certain dean to stick to fund-raising. They called him, what else, El Hatchette or—more and more—El Hatchet.

Carter, luckily, was used to this sort of thing, he said.

Hattie was seeing Joe at the time—a colleague from back when she taught Chinese. Carter was married to Meredith, the provost's daughter, a lawyer. Whom Hattie didn't dislike, exactly, though she did think Meredith's living room a lot of hooey, what with its sunken conversation pit and its coffee table full of crystal balls. The fawn-

arium, Hattie called it; *and it always seemed to her a kind of extension of the living room that Carter was not allowed to eat dinner at
the lab, or to do lab work at night. A matter of taste more than of out-
and-out jealousy. So that if something had to be run, Hattie would do
it herself or with a lab mate; Carter would have to call on the sly, to
check in. Whispering, so that Meredith couldn't hear them, even
though it was really all just shop talk. Spurious data. Lab dynamics.
What went wrong, what they should try differently. New directions,
new projects. He was good at conceptualizing things; she, at design-
ing experiments; and neither of them was ever so happy as when they
were getting results. Results! She remembered how slowly he would
speak when they had a finding—how excitedly he would ask her to
describe exactly what she'd seen, and how carefully she would
respond. And what an extraordinary thing it really was, to see truths
emerge. To know that the work would be cited and built on—to
know that for all time, for any researcher who cared to try it, that
truth would hold. It was as if Hattie had finally set foot on solid
ground—as if she had arrived in a country that would not vanish.
And to share such an arrival with someone else—well, was not
"home" a feeling of sharing the same reality?*

*She was careful around Carter, though, and he around her. They'd
learned their lesson; they put their prefrontal cortexes to work. The
most they ever allowed themselves in the way of anything personal
was a reference, every now and then, to possibilities not bestowed
upon them by evolution. For while life was, of course, brilliantly
adaptable—no one denied that—they shared an appreciation for how
many genetic accidents became fixed over time. What it meant to
have been shaped by particular circumstances and narrow goals, for
millennia—what it meant to have had our structures adapted and
readapted, but never fundamentally redesigned.*

*"Why don't we have three eyes?" Carter would wonder, some-
times, on the phone. "Why should we be bilateral because our ancestors were bilateral?"*

Or, "Why can't we see behind us?"

Or, "Why can't we see infrared?"

Or, "Why can't we echolocate?"

To which she would reply, "Some things are not given to us."

*Then he would pause; and, well, Hattie would have to admit that
there were whole years where she more or less lived for those*

moments of saying nothing. Even after she married Joe and had Josh, she still heard them—as Joe knew, of course. She had no secrets from Joe. And mostly, he would just hold her tighter then—wrapping her in his long arms, and kissing her face in a circle. Sometimes, though, he would go out for a walk with the dogs; and once when he asked her what she heard when they made love, and she didn't answer, he went on to ask her what she saw, and who. Who? And when she didn't answer that, either, he went and slept on the couch for a week. Even when he was sick, he would ask her. Groggy, his voice raspy from his breathing tube, he would ask, Are you going to look up Carter Hatch when I'm dead? Never mind that she hadn't seen Carter for decades by then. The sicker Joe got, the angrier he got—not unlike a child separating from his parents, Hattie thought. She understood. And yet still, it was hard to hear. Be kind, she would tell him as he slept. Please. Give me your kindness to remember, not this.

But he could only give what he had. You should have married Carter, he'd say. Why didn't you marry Carter?

As if she could have married Carter! When Hattie was too old for Carter. When Hattie was too short for Carter. When Hattie had no taste. When they were too like brother and sister, when Hattie was impossible. When she didn't see where he was coming from; when she didn't see where others were coming from. When she didn't see how things worked. What the world was.

"Don't you see?" Carter would say. "Don't you see?"

There was a Nobel laureate next door to the Hatchery; Hattie was not nice to him because of his prize. Neither was she nice to his minions when they treated students the way they had been treated.

"You forget that you yourself will only be a minion, as you put it, for a while," Carter said. "Do not overinvest in this cause."

And: "Not every grievance is founded, you know. What's your evidence?"

And: "You identify too much with the trod-upon. It's an outsider's outlook."

But she could not help seeing what she saw—people treated as expendable. "They make themselves part of the picture, then just get airbrushed out," she said.

Carter shrugged. "This is a lab, not an experiment in living."

"You sound like El Honcho."

"I don't care who I sound like, and may you learn not to care, either."

They had different ideas about integrity. She believed it something in the person; he thought it something in the work. Not that there weren't lines you couldn't cross—there were, absolutely. Still, he thought it important to understand where you had leeway; he thought it better to be effective than noble.

"You're like Meredith," he said once. "More interested in how the world judges you than in what it becomes."

And: "It's a kind of vanity."

And: "There's no doing right without doing wrong."

And, once: "You're not on trial."

"Interesting," she said.

"It's important to know your position from yourself," he said.

"Is it."

"Miss Confucius, enough."

She was in training in his lab for now, he would say. When the day came for her to go, she should go. And, they hoped, if they played their cards right, maybe come back as an equal, someday. If not to the university, then at least to the region.

"We have to be able to have lunch," he said, several times. "You must agree to be sure of that."

And of course, she would promise, though she would not have taken either his word or hers too seriously had he not hesitated over his hummus and pita one day and added, thoughtfully and deliberately, "I'll help you."

"If you remember, you mean," she laughed.

But he didn't reach for a carrot stick as she thought that he would. Instead, he looked her square in the eyes and said gently, "I'm going to do everything I can."

And when she laughed again, he said, "Hattie." And, "Don't laugh."

To which she replied, "I'm just trying not to cry, Carter."

And when he put his sandwich down, and wiped his hand, and took her hand for a moment, she accepted it. And when she got an offer at a far-off lab, she accepted that, too. And when a job opened up in his department, he let her know right away.

"This is just right," he said. "You go away and then you come back. Perfect."

Hattie made the shortlist; her job talk was a hit. But then Guy LaPoint began to call Hattie Carter's mistress; and when the department chair sought out people's opinions, as he liked to, Carter did not speak up for her.

The job went, in the end, to Guy's protégé.

"I thought you were going to help me." By special dispensation, Carter and Hattie were actually talking, for once, out loud on the phone.

"People thought it was true," said Carter.

"But it wasn't." Hattie fingered the nubs of her bedspread.

"People see what they see, Hattie. You know that. What they're primed to see."

"But I'm not your mistress."

"There was no use insisting."

"Because we are construing creatures, you mean?" she said.

"Hattie."

"Because our brains can't be stopped from editing out the ambiguous and unexpected in favor of the 'predicted' and 'coherent'?"

"Insisting would have only further reinforced what they thought, Hattie. Moved it into their cortical storage. You know that. Once there's an established mental framework . . ."

"Don't people ever change their mind?"

"Hattie."

"What would it have cost you to say something, Carter? You have tenure."

"Hattie."

"Did you really just not want to piss Guy off? Is he that dangerous?"

"Hattie, stop."

"I know. I never have understood these things."

"No, you haven't."

"And why shouldn't you see by the light of your interests, right? It's how we're made. As the Chinese say, 'If it has milk, it's the mother.' "

"Miss Confucius. Stop." He sounded as though he were sixteen again, and upset over his guitar. "Stop."

"You said you would do everything you could," she said.

"I did," he said. "Stop. I did. I promised."

She stopped.

"El Honcho thinks I'm in love with you," he said.

"Does he." She closed her eyes.

"I don't see what more I could have done," he said.

.   .   .

The blue car bumps down the driveway; Sarun and Sophy emerge from the trailer to greet the driver, a buxom woman in a flippy red dress. She looks like a magician's assistant, but no—she's the magician: From her trunk she produces a computer monitor and a keyboard. A printer, a hard drive. Cables. Everyone is smiling.

"A present!" says Sophy later. "Can you believe it? Someone was giving the whole setup to the church, and they, like, thought of me right away!"

She and Sarun have used computers before, as some of their friends in their old town had them, and the library did, too. But to have their own!

"We're going to have e-mail!" Sophy twirls and dances, her face turned like a daisy to the sky.

She is especially excited about hearing from her sisters. Not that Sophan and Sopheap haven't been writing letters, they have. However, the letters have been short and not very interesting. Their e-mails, Sophy hopes, will say a lot more.

And sure enough, when she reports back in a few days, it is to say that her sisters are writing about all kinds of stuff—what they're wearing, and what their foster parents are like, and what they think of the other kids. And how much they wish they could IM but how that's not allowed. They can't even do that much e-mail, really, because they're limited to ten minutes per kid per day, and though the foster parents don't read every single thing, they can.

"So there's a lot they can't write," concludes Sophy, sitting in Hattie's kitchen. "Like how much they want to get out of there. They can't write that."

Still, her eyes shine. No smirky commas today; Hattie feels her own spirits soften and lift.

"You can't believe what Sopheap is eating," Sophy goes on. "They have, like, eggs every single day. Like boiled eggs and scrambled eggs and egg salad. For a change they have peanut butter—she says she's just waiting to get a peanut butter omelet for breakfast."

Sophan, meanwhile, is living in a pasta palace—meaning, like, spaghetti, tortellini, fettuccini, ravioli! She signs her name Sophani! As for Sophy, she, in turn, tells them about Annie, and about Sarun, and about the trailer, and about how cold people say it gets up here in the winter, though it might not anymore because of global warming. That's if it doesn't get colder instead, which it could also, people say, she's not exactly sure how, but it could. Also she tells them what happened with their dad's back, and how much she misses them, and how much she likes the church. Because the church up here is not like the church down where they are.

"Like I told them how there's all this great food," she says. "Not just pasta and peanut butter. And great stuff to do." And what she's learning in Bible class—she writes about that, too. The Good News. "It's hard to get by e-mail, I think," she goes on. "But maybe they will one day. Like all of a sudden it'll just click. That's what Ginny says."

Hattie stands to make coffee—setting the kettle on the stove and turning the gas to high, but then lowering it so flames don't start lapping up campfire-style; some adjustment's off.

"Do you mind if I pray before my cookie?" Sophy asks Hattie's back. "Because we were just talking about that at church—how some of us are shy about praying in public. I know this isn't public, really. But I'm trying to practice."

"Of course, you can pray," says Hattie. "Did I ever tell you my mother was a missionary? We prayed before every meal."

"In China?"

Hattie nods.

"Except she was American, right?"

"Yes."

"So you prayed in English?"

"Yes."

"Cool." Sophy slips off her flip-flops so she can knead Annie's tummy with her feet; her toenails are all purple now. "I mean it would have been okay if you prayed in Chinese, too. Either way. I'm just glad."

"Because you've been worried, haven't you? That maybe I'm not with Christ." Hattie starts to pour hot water over the grounds in the paper cones, only to run out. She refills the kettle partway and sets it back on the stove.

Sophy nods. "We were talking in Bible class about how important it is to keep a wall around our belief. Like how the devil goes looking for weak spots, and how fast the wall can fall, and how important it is to know, like, where our gaps are."

Gaps. Walls.

"Well, I'm Christian," Hattie says, still standing. "And my mother's family are as God-fearing as they come. Lots of ministers and deacons. The women all sing in the choir."

"Do you go to church?"

"I do. I go to the Unitarian church every Sunday, just about."

"What about your mother?"

"Was she with Christ, you mean?"

Sophy nods.

"Yes. But, you know, my mother eventually found that she could not go on converting people. And I guess I inherited some of her feeling that we could not rightly go on thinking that my father's whole family and most everyone else we knew were going to hell as they deserved because they refused to accept God's pardoning grace—that baptism was the only door to a sanctified life. It was just so hard to believe God could really have set things up that way. As if all that mattered was whether or not they were with Christ—as if that were more important than the people themselves, and if they were good."

Sophy's face is blank, as if stuck between thoughts; the kettle whistles.

"Does your church teach that, too?" asks Hattie, turning. "That your mom and dad and brothers and sisters are all damned?"

Sophy bestirs herself enough to scratch Annie around her ears. "Ginny says that we can forgive and turn the other cheek and stuff, but that we can't be soft on salvation."

"And that you need to steer clear of your family?" Hattie pours. "That they're gaps?"

"Yes."

Hattie pours a bit more.

"So did she stay a Christian?" asks Sophy.

"My mother?"

Sophy moves Annie's head up and down.

"She did." Hattie places the mugs on the table, sits, then thinks ice—it's warm out, after all—and stands again.

"Did she believe in God and pray?"

"She did."

Hattie puts the ice in a bowl; it shines invitingly. Still, Hattie is surprised that Sophy immediately accepts some. Maybe her parents drank iced coffee in Cambodia? Or is her acquaintance through Dunkin' Donuts? Who knows where she's learned what she's learned.

"Did she believe in Satan, and in heaven and hell, and in the second coming?" Sophy goes on.

"She believed in them as allegories. Do you know what that means?" Hattie sits.

"It means she didn't really believe."

"She did, Sophy." Hattie's voice rises like a gym teacher's, more emphatic than she would have anticipated. "She did believe. She was a good woman. God-fearing."

"Did she make you pray?"

"No. She believed it was our choice." Hattie's own ice cracks loudly.

"And if you made the wrong choice?"

"She believed in universal salvation. Do you know what that means?"

"It means she didn't believe in salvation by faith through grace."

How hard Ginny's been working! A certified teacher, who never could find herself a job, people say. But now here she was, it seems, teaching with a vengeance.

"She did believe in salvation by faith through grace," Hattie says. "She just didn't believe that that was the only path to salvation. She believed God's pardoning love extended to everyone."

"What about 'I am the way and the life'?"

"You mean John 14:6. 'I am the way, the truth, and the life: no man cometh unto the Father, but by Me'?"

Sophy nods.

"I don't know, but I am going to guess that she would argue that 'by Me' God doesn't mean by way of Christian faith, but by way of Christ's sacrifice—that it is as a result of his sacrifice that everyone 'cometh unto the Father.' "

Sophy is quiet.

"You know, churches are smart," Hattie goes on. "They know their parishioners. A good pastor listens carefully, and then works hard at giving his flock what it needs. And don't you find that? That the church gives you something you need?"

Sophy nods.

"They understand you and serve you. Include you. But let me ask you. Do you actually believe in God, or do you just like the church?"

Sophy waggles her head. "I try to believe."

"What about karma and reincarnation? Do you believe in any of that Buddhist stuff anymore?"

"Sort of. Reincarnation for sure. And grace is kind of like good karma."

"Except that one you earn and the other is a gift from God."

"I guess." Sophy hugs herself, crossing her arms under her breasts.

Has Hattie pushed too hard? She drinks a little.

"Oh, but I forgot." *Hattie gone batty!* "Do you still want to pray? Because I'll pray with you. It's okay. We can say grace."

But Sophy does not want to pray anymore. Neither does she want a cookie when Hattie pushes the plate toward her.

" 'Daniel purposed in his heart that he would not defile himself with the portion of the king's meat, nor with the wine which he drank,' " Hattie recites softly.

Sophy uncurls.

"I'm not a gap in your wall," says Hattie. "Do you remember how Daniel kept his window open? Keeping his own faith? I'm just keeping my window open, like Daniel."

Sophy has her silver flip-flops on. "God has a plan for me," she says. "I believe that."

"Is that what Ginny told you?"

Sophy heads straight to the slider. Her flip-flops make no noise as they hit the floor but they do *smack smack smack* as they hit her feet. She leaves the screen door half open behind her.

First the cell tower and now Value-Mart! A Value-Mart rep's been invited to a select board meeting, but it is not clear what for; the town has no leverage over their project. Still, on Value-Mart Day, as they call it, people jam Town Hall. The floor fans roar as if with the outrage of the people in front of them; the people themselves, though, sit stony and stunned.

"All the zoning ordinance says is that 'any prospective enterprise must be adjacent to and contiguous with existing town businesses,' " says Greta, grim. "It says nothing about the size of the enterprise or its nature."

Her mouth is tight, as is Hattie's; four or five rows behind them, Carter, too, Hattie can't help but notice, is all but lipless. Who can believe Value-Mart could have gotten this far? When there'd been so much controversy over even an inn that it had had to close its doors? And who would have dreamed that the inn's owner would go offering the thing to Value-Mart, much less that Value-Mart would want it? But open a new exit off the interstate, and what do you know—

the world's rolling in. Everyone's seen the renderings: a concrete box taking up an entire acre, it seems, and many more acres paved over for parking. Hattie pictures the cars in their spaces—a very different lineup from the one before her now: so many concerned citizens, sitting, in the heat and humidity, with their thighs V'ed—their legs making for a kind of zigzag if you look down a row at lap level. Everyone is sweating, Hattie included; she cools her fingers on the metal struts of her chair.

Road Budget. A review of the town library hours. Discussion of a proposed new stop sign at the corner of Cat and Dog Streets. As Jim Wright's left town, Judge Lukens is subbing in until they can name a replacement chair; he moves through the agenda with dispatch, his reading glasses a small glinty interruption of his large, focused face.

"Next—Introduction of Value-Mart," he says.

The Value-Mart rep stands. An older man with a close-cropped beard, he talks so glowingly of the jobs Value-Mart can bring Riverlake that though most people remain cross-armed, Beth, Hattie sees, tilts her head one way then the other; and she's not the only one wavering. Why doesn't Neddy Needham stand up the way he did at the cell tower meeting? *Whose town is this?* he should be demanding, with dignified passion. Answering, with heat, *Not yours, sir. Not yours!*

So far, though, this meeting is more desperation than glory.

"This a done deal?" asks Jed Jamison.

The rep smiles. "Well, we do, of course, require a number of permits from the state," he says. "Environmental, septic, traffic, and so on."

"Have you filed for them?" asks Hattie.

"We have."

Silence.

"You need any permits from town?" Judy Tell-All's eyelashes are spiky as ever, but her manner is not.

"We need a conditional-use permit," the rep concedes. He has the app right in front of him. "So far as I know, though, we are in compliance with the ordinance as written."

Murmurs. Can an interim zoning ordinance be passed? Greta sits forward. No urging Hattie to talk today; Greta simply throws her braid back and raises her own hand high.

"I'm wondering if you know anything about a lawsuit going on north of here," she says—standing, uncharacteristically, almost before she is called on. "As I understand it, the town tried to rework their zoning ordinance against Value-Mart, only to find the legality of the entire state statute from which their power derives being challenged."

Now it's Judge Lukens sitting forward; he cups his good ear.

"Ah, yes, I have heard about that, ah, lawsuit," says the rep.

"Is it not true that regardless of how the ruling goes, our neighbor is in trouble? Is it not true that even if the court rules in its favor, the legal fees stand to bankrupt the town, and that Value-Mart is banking on that? That they know they can force the town into mediation, and into making concessions that way?" Greta does not sit immediately the way she normally does, but stands swaying an extra moment instead, like a bull that could charge.

"Well, I don't know that we're banking on anything, as you put it." The rep shuffles a little to the side, as if to stay clear of trouble. "For that you'd have to talk to the legal department."

"But you did take the town to court," puts in Neddy Needham at last. He does not raise his hand, but simply stands as Greta sits, as if taking her place. Jill Jenkins, next to him, looks up admiringly; and indeed, it is hard not to notice, not only how much weight he's lost, but how his voice has deepened, and his air of command. Some people are calling him "Ned" now, instead of "Neddy," and it isn't just Jill Jenkins, it seems, who's registered the change: For there sits Carter in a hot square of window light, studiously immersing himself in the intricacies of the agenda. Never mind that it is only six lines long; he scowls at it as if at a federal science budget.

"I, myself, did not personally do anything," says the rep.

"You took the town to court," repeats Neddy. "With a willingness to bring down the whole zoning ordinance if you had to."

People look up hopefully, but Neddy stalls out, failing to attain any great oratorical height. It is Jill Jenkins who leaps to her feet like a madwoman.

"I find that outrageous!" she cries.

Chaos erupts. Lukens calls for order; Greta elbows Hattie. Before she can figure out what she might usefully interject, though, Carter raises his elegant hand.

"I see that there is one more item on the agenda," he says coolly. "A review of the policies of the Riverlake waste management district."

The crowd settles down, respectful but puzzled.

"But perhaps there are other questions regarding Value-Mart?"

Judge Lukens speaks quietly—addressing Carter publicly and yet privately, it seems. "This is a signal matter we have before us."

"I move that we simply move on," says Carter.

He looks at Hattie then as he used to so often in lab meetings—with a glance she used to call *code blue*. And immediately—not holding back—she says, "I second."

Judge Lukens frowns. "Well, then. Will all those in favor . . ."

The motion is carried narrowly, but is carried.

Carter looks at Hattie again and winks. Then comes an all-in-one preparation to speak she knows so well, it brings a lump to her throat: the way he clears his throat with a rumble. The way he pushes off the arm of his chair. The way his mother's chin comes up first and then, after it, like a piece of artillery, his father's gaze.

"This item concerns the question of waste," he begins. "As some of you know, Greta Rodriguez here has been agitating for some time for an increase in our trash fees. Her idea, if I may attempt to summarize it, is to reduce the waste generated by Riverlake by accepting all recycling for free, but charging money for the disposal of trash. Is that not correct, Greta?"

Greta half stands. "Yes. I propose we charge five dollars a bag." She sits down wondering, Hattie knows, why they are even talking about this. A matter important to her, yes, but—! Her braid bulges out over the back of her chair.

"A fine idea," continues Carter, "but let me verify, if I may, Mr. Chairman, that our town has the capacity to change its disposal laws. That is—if I may ask a question for the clarification of the public: Is this town, as it appears from the by-laws, an independent waste management district?"

"To the best of my knowledge." Judge Lukens looks to Rhonda, the town clerk, for confirmation.

Rhonda nods.

"Then it is in a position to set its own disposal fees?"

Judge Lukens looks to Rhonda again. She stands in a manner befitting a town official.

"Yes," she says. She sits.

"Wonderful!" says Carter, with a strange burst of energy. "Then let us discuss Greta's proposal. Though I'd like to ask, if I may, one more question before we do. In going through the by-laws the other day, I noticed that Riverlake has not changed its tipping fees in some time. In fact, the last time they were adjusted was, it appears, in 1922. Is that correct?"

Judge Lukens looks to Rhonda a third time. She takes off her reading glasses and stands up tall again.

"That's true." She exchanges looks with Lukens as she sits.

"I pause here to note also," says Carter, "for the illumination of the public and for the record, that tipping fees are the fees we charge dump trucks for emptying their trash."

Rhonda stands yet again; Hattie looks down. She hadn't seen it, not having wanted to see it, but the truth is inescapable now: The love of her youth—of her life, even, maybe—her own Mr. Combustible—has become a parody of himself. *Slipping,* just as he feared. Digressing. Wandering after *the wraith of an idea.* It is too awful to watch. She presses her fingers to her eyelids; if only she could block her ears, too.

"So it would not be strange to suggest," continues Carter, "that perhaps some sort of fee adjustment is overdue on that front, too?"

"Professor Hatch. Carter," says Judge Lukens. More irritated than indulgent, anyway; Hattie is glad for that. He does not raise his voice, but does give all to understand, much as Hattie's mother used to, that he is exercising restraint. "Do you have an update to propose?"

"I do." Carter passes a scrap of paper up to the front of the room. "And while we are waiting," he goes on, "I have a question for the representative from Value-Mart about your trash. Mr.—I'm sorry."

"Toutmange. Giles Toutmange."

"Nice to meet you, Mr. Toutmange. Do you have any idea how much trash you'll be generating a day?"

"I do not have that figure."

"But it would be in the tons, no doubt, per month?" Carter raises his eyebrows—his *pup tents.*

Hattie wants to cry.

"That would be my guesstimate. Yes."

"Thank you, Mr. Toutmange." Carter sits the same way he stood, only in reverse. He takes his time, like an old man.

Carter, an old man.

Judge Lukens, meanwhile, is grinning.

"Proposed," he begins. He stops, adjusts his reading glasses, and starts again, reading as slowly and clearly as if he had just concluded an experiment and had a finding to report. "Proposed: That the

Riverlake waste management district set its tipping fee at ten thousand dollars per load."

There is a moment of silence; then suddenly the hall explodes in clapping and hooting and stamping and cheering. The select board approves the proposal on the spot; Carter winks again at Hattie. Her eyes fill with tears. The measure, says Judge Lukens, will take effect in sixty days.

Professor Hero! People leave flowers on his doorstep. Blueberries. Blackberries. Someone washes Carter's car for him, leaving a soapy THANKS on the windshield; people reminisce about his father and grandfather. What leaders the Hatches have always been, they say. We always knew they'd come back.

"Good work." Hattie holds a hand out at Millie's. "Well done."

"You were a fine second," he says, accepting her shake. His grasp is warm and firm; their hands make a lovely foursquare.

"I had faith in you," she says. She does not volunteer how her faith wavered, much less how happy she was to have it restored.

He winks. "I'm sure it was a leap," he says. "That Toutmange was an Ignoriah par excellence, wouldn't you say?"

"A regular bombillator," she agrees, smiling.

"What a team we've always been." He laughs an appreciative laugh. But then he looks away. He is wearing some sort of silver amulet on a leather string; who knows what it means.

Outside, though a hazy stillness lingers, the summer people are leaving. How fast the summers go around here! It does seem that the days have only just warmed up. But already the nights are earlier and cooler, and the fruit trees heavy. Hitherto outdoor mice are starting to move in; the goldenrod is up; Millie's is closing earlier, having lost its summer help. School is set to start.

Still, though they've missed all the deadlines and done none of the forms, the Chhungs are talking home schooling. The first day of school comes and goes; the Chhung kids are still at home. The second day, Sophy appears at Hattie's door, shorn; she's wearing a small silver cross on a chain.

All these new pendants!

"It's good to see you again," says Hattie, carefully. *Dá guān*—with as much detachment as she can muster.

Sophy picks Annie up roughly. "I cut my hair."

"I see," says Hattie.

"It's crooked."

It looks as if she cut it blindfolded.

Still, Hattie insists, "It's cute. Fetching." Diplomatic in a way she can only hope Sophy will forgive—trying to pretend she isn't *thinking things,* though: Her Sophy! Her beautiful Sophy.

"It's not supposed to be fetching. It's supposed to keep me from temptation." Sophy cradles Annie, who licks and licks her face; she wrinkles her nose, drying it with a raised shoulder. "It's crooked," she says again.

"Well," allows Hattie, "it could use"—she thinks—"adjustment."

"I was hoping you'd make it even. Our scissors suck."

"You can't do much with dull blades," says Hattie.

"That's what I told Sarun." Sophy lets Annie spill out of her arms. "I told him you can't do much with dull blades."

"Well, sit down. I do have a better pair."

Scissors, comb, towel. Sophy dunks her head in the kitchen sink then perches on a stool, an old beach towel draped over her strong shoulders. A seaside-like sun bathes her striped back.

"Should I take off my cross?"

"If you want to."

She leaves it on. Hattie squeegees a section of hair with two fingers, cuts, squeegees again; the excess water beads into her hand. She consults the dogs. What do they think? They sweep the floor with their tails. Hattie did use to cut both Joe's and Josh's hair, once upon a time, but she's rusty; she hopes Sophy doesn't end up with a crew cut.

"There." Hattie directs Sophy to a door mirror at last; Sophy reappears with a shy smile. A satisfied customer, though, if anything, her beauty bursts forth more lusciously than ever. Her eyes have more lilt, her lips more pout; her cheekbones could be Sophia Loren's. The short roundness of her new do seems to change even her proportions: Her neck seems longer, and her breasts so full that the cross above them just seems a tease.

Ooh, la-la! Lee would have said. *Get that girl a diaphragm!*

But luckily, she is dead and not here, thinks Hattie—even as she thinks, how could she have thought that? How could she?

"So will that do it?" Hattie asks, sweeping.

Sophy nods, trying to tuck her hair behind her ears; it doesn't stay. "It's so I can go to school."

"Did your dad change his mind?"

Sophy nods; her hair sweeps teasingly into her eyes. "After I cut it. Plus I prayed."

"Well, wonderful." Hattie gets out her dustpan.

"So no more Chinese lessons," Sophy says. "Now that I'm starting school again."

"Ah," says Hattie. "Are you excited?"

"It's better than being stuck in the trailer all day."

"I bet."

Sophy plays with Annie. "Sit," she says, and is delighted when Annie obeys, even if she immediately stands back up. "You're getting big!" she tells Annie.

Annie sits again.

"I wonder if you're going to have time for your Bible study class," says Hattie. "What with homework and all." She raises the subject casually, trying not to upset Sophy again. And Sophy, happily, does not seem upset.

"No," she says. "But it's okay, because I'm going to the church school. So I'll have Bible study every day anyway."

Church school?

"You know. The one down the street from church."

And then Hattie remembers: the school Candy complained about. The one the church put straight across from the public school on purpose, people say, to draw kids away.

"How are you going to get there?" asks Hattie, carefully.

"The blue car."

"Ah. Well, good luck and come poke your head in every now and then. Annie's going to miss you."

Sophy kneels to give Annie a hug. "Do you think she'll know I've left her?"

"Are you leaving her?"

Sophy touches noses with Annie. "Eskimo kiss," she says. Annie's tail thumps.

"Would you like her?" asks Hattie, after a moment. "You can have her if you'd like."

"Can I really?" Sophy's on all fours, now, like Annie.

"Of course."

"Though would my dad let me keep her? That's the problem, isn't it."

"Good point."

Sophy sits back on her heels. "Maybe I could keep her here?"

"Sure. If you'd like. This can be your kennel."

Sophy plays with Annie some more, considering.

"You could walk her. Teach her tricks. Feed her ice cream."

Sophy waggles her head; she chews on a hangnail, her lips drawn back. "But to do that I'd have to come back all the time, wouldn't I?"

"It wouldn't be so bad. You could have a cookie while you were here. Review your Chinese." The more Hattie thinks about this, the more she likes the idea. She smiles.

But Sophy doesn't smile. "Like who even speaks Chinese anyway," she says, suddenly. "This place is full of dog beds and dog dishes. It smells like dogs. You can hardly breathe in here."

Is that true? When the windows have been open all summer? Hattie is stung, though of course people do get used to smells, and what was it that Lee once said? *I, personally, have always loved your kennel—I mean, living room. It just reminds me of—oh, I don't know. Dogs.*

"It's a trap," says Sophy.

A trap?

"Oh, Sophy. It might smell like the dogs, but it's not a trap."

But already she is escaping out the door.

Chhung is unhappy about Sophy quitting Chinese, but cheers up when Hattie offers to tutor Mum in English instead. Your trailer seems a little quiet, she says, what with Sophy at school during the day. And he agrees: Mum could use both the company and the practice. Thanks to the English program on TV, Mum understands more and more. And thanks to *Sesame Street*—Big Bird. She's learned a lot from Big Bird. But her pronunciation—he shakes his head. Not clear. Hard to understand. Hattie suggests they ask Mum what she thinks of the idea, but Chhung insists he knows.

"She like it." He raps on his brace with his knuckles for emphasis. "I know."

The air smells so strongly of cigarettes that Hattie asks if she can open a window.

"Would you like lessons, too?" she goes on.

"No, no," he says. "I don't need."

But late the next day, when Hattie sits down with Mum at the kitchen table—an L in the counter, really—he pulls his easy chair in extra close. The TV is, what's more, off—a surprise to Hattie on more than one count. Hasn't he heard?

"America has been attacked by terrorists," she says.

Chhung blinks even as his eyes shoot back and forth. "Wha?"

"Terrorists," she says, slowly. A new word for her, too, and how to explain? The World Trade Center—big buildings—New York. New York City. Mum and Chhung nod. Hattie finds a pencil and draws the two towers. Didn't they see it on TV? The plane, the fire, the people jumping out the windows? Desperate, she says, they were desperate—the easiest part of the story for them to understand. People jumping rather than burning, people having no choice—of course. Not owning a TV herself, Hattie watched as much as she could stand at Greta's—the events repeating again and again on the screen and then again and again, all night, in her head; only to be recounted so often on the radio today that it seemed that history could just get stuck; no one was ever going to move past this. And what a different America they live in now, with such a different idea of what's possible—a world so different from the one Lee and Joe knew, she could never explain it to them. It's a cockamamie way to see things, Hattie knows—plain nuts. And yet she feels it—how Lee and Joe have retreated to the back side of a divide. How she's gone on. And how she's left them behind now—she who was once left behind herself. She feels that. She's gone on.

Chhung, meanwhile, thought it was all a movie.

"I don't like." He waves his hand. "Watch DVD instead," he says. *"Killing Fields."*

"It wasn't a movie," says Hattie. "It was real. Terrible. Many people died. Many, many people."

She knows, of course, that it will not seem like so many people to the Chhungs; that like her parents, they counted hardship by the millions. The millions wounded, the millions dead. Still, she is annoyed when Chhung shakes his head. He translates for Mum, who likewise shakes her head and frowns matter-of-factly. Her hair bun bristles with pins and looks about as likely to unravel as a polyp, but still she pats it, as if to keep it under control.

"Not so serious," says Chhung. And, with confidence: "He cannot win. American destroy him right away." He taps on his back
brace. "American verry srrong."

It was what Hattie's father used to say about America way back
when: America is strong. America is not weak like China. Hattie
understands, but knows herself on the other side of a divide here, too.
Is there any point in going on?

"Lesson time," she says finally.

She turns her attention around like a cart.

Officially, Chhung has left Sarun to dig on his own because of
Gift; Chhung is supposed to babysit so that Mum can concentrate.
Right now, though, Gift is napping on the couch, his bare tummy rising and falling. His legs turn out like a ballet dancer's; his short arms
lie along the sides of his head as if that is as comfortable a position as
any. He looks to have no shoulders.

"Tie?" asks Mum.

"Tea," says Hattie. "Yes, I would love some tea."

Mum fills a white enamel saucepan with water and offers Hattie
some dried anchovies.

"Thank you. Delicious." Hattie has always loved little fish—
salty sweet things, too. "Thank you," she says again, her irritation
subsiding.

Mum's head bobs.

"You should say, 'You're welcome.' "

Mum tries. Hattie takes notes: stresses all three syllables, and the
syllables are very short.

"You're welcome," Hattie says again.

"Yor wel-cum."

Hattie's mother may have been a heretic, but when Hattie was a
girl, her English lessons were based on the Bible. She can still see her
old green primer with the cross on its cover; all those bearded foreign
devils with helmets on, too. Still, it was a textbook. Mum should
probably have a textbook. For now Hattie simply runs through the
vowels, noting problems.

"Can you say bait?"

"Baay," says Mum.

A bit of twang there; trouble with the ending consonant. Hattie
goes on. "Can you say bat?"

"Bat."

Good. A bit short, but good. *"Beet?"*

"Beee."

Hattie makes a note. *"Bet?"*

The next lesson, Hattie works on pronunciation again, but adds some phrases: *Thank you, Thanks, You're welcome, How are you.* The sounds are hard for Mum, but she smiles the whole time, tentative but eager. Learning English at her age is not easy; she might as well be trying to *tuck Mount Tai under her arm and jump over the North Sea,* as Hattie's father used to say. Still, she reminds Hattie of how students make the teacher. Mum is such a different student from Sophy, but then her students were all different, she remembers. And how each one gave her a bit of herself—she remembers that, too. She looks forward to coming again.

The third lesson, Gift is awake and hurling things. Having just dis- covered that he can walk and throw things at the same time, he picks up the remote control and throws it. Next, a bottle opener. Next, a bunch of keys. *A-meh!* he shouts, *Ma! A-meh-meh-mam- mam-mam.* His chest is streaked with drool, his face bright with naughty delight. Still, Mum calmly opens the kitchen window and sets out a dish of dried mango, leaving it to Chhung to make loud scary noises—*hecq! hecq!* He leans forward, raising a threatening hand when Gift tries to touch one of the figures on the TV stand. But Gift just laughs and reaches for a porcelain basket instead.

Mum frowns.

"Do you want to meet another time?" Hattie asks.

Chhung shouts. Gift goes running out of the room, his diaper hanging half off. *Meh-meh-ma-maa!* Chhung glowers. Mum leans forward—to comment on all this, Hattie thinks. But, no.

"Why," she says, instead "Caa."

Hattie thinks. "The white car? Is it back?"

"Frren," Mum says. She closes her eyes, shaking her head.

"You are worried about Sarun. His friends."

"Wor-ree," she says clearly. A word she knows.

"He's upsetting your husband."

Mum nods, pensive. She presses hard between her eyes with her thumbs, her other fingers spread-eagled, then lets her hands fall to the table. "Chiouw?"

"Child? Me? Yes. I have a son."

"He-ahr?"

"Here? No," says Hattie. "He lives far away. Far far away."

"Gone?"

"Gone? Yes. He's gone."

Mum takes this in. Her face is smooth as a girl's, but her glance is a mother's gaze, appraising and thoughtful. She has brilliant dark eyes, with wonderfully clear whites.

"Chiouw gone," she says. "No . . ." She hesitates.

"Stay?"

"Staay," says Mum. "No staay."

"Do children stay in Cambodia?"

Mum nods.

"It's hard here, you're right. The children don't stay."

"Mo-der, fa-der . . ." Mum stops.

"Yes. Mother, father are alone here. The children don't stay. The children go." Hattie speaks clearly and slowly. "The children go."

"You, sef?"

"Do I live by myself? Yes."

Mum shakes her head. "Hahd."

"Yes, it's hard. Quiet." Hattie continues to speak clearly. Slowly. "You do everything yourself. Decide everything yourself. Eat by yourself." She smiles a little, though she can see it would be all right if she didn't—that it would be all right with Mum. "Some people like it but I find it hard."

"Hahd," Mum says again, sympathetically. "Sarun."

"Sarun."

"Why. Caa."

"Sarun is getting in the white car."

"Sophy."

"Sophy, yes."

"Brew. Caa."

"Sophy is getting in the blue car."

Mum shakes her head.

"It's hard." Hattie doesn't know what else to say. "I'm sorry."

They should really work some more before Gift comes back. And Hattie has a lesson book for Mum in her bag; she should get it out.

But instead they just sit a moment, two women at the same table. It's quiet.

N ow Mum huddles with Gift. Chhung drinks. The TV is loud.
      "Are we having a lesson today?" asks Hattie.

No one answers. The kitchen window is closed; the air is full of smoke.

"Sarun?" asks Hattie.

Mum nods, stroking Gift's hair; he gnaws on her shoulder.

"Do you want to go look for him?"

Sophy bursts into the trailer with her backpack. She glances over at Hattie as she heads to her room—not intending to say hello, apparently—but then stops, realizing that Mum has started to cry. Chhung says something in Khmer; his finger slices the air.

"I don't care what happens to him," Sophy says.

Still, they all pile into Hattie's car—even Sophy, and even Chhung, who seats himself in the front passenger seat. He rolls his window down, sticks his elbow out, and lights a cigarette. No back brace today; he could reach for his shoulder belt easily enough. Hattie does not dare ask him to buckle up, though. Neither would she say no to Sophy, probably, if Sophy asked for a Christian radio station, but happily she does not ask. Instead, they listen to a talk show: It's the cities everyone's worried about—all those subways that can be bombed, all those communications that can be jammed, all those reservoirs that can be poisoned. Will people be moving out of the cities with time? Will they be moving to towns like Riverlake, seeking haven? Hattie can only hope not as she makes a quick round of the Come 'n' Eat, the skate park, the lot with the hoop back behind Town Hall. The library. The town beach. Millie's. It's a gray fall day, with mist that hangs like something in a Chinese landscape painting—the sort of shifting, breathing layer you get with wet paper and a soft brush. A loose wrist, a little luck.

No luck.

"Maybe we should call the police?" says Hattie.

No answer.

"Maybe we should call the police?" she says again.

Stonewalling.

"You know," says Hattie, "if you people don't want to help yourselves—"

"We can't call anyone because the police in our old town could come after us," says Sophy, finally. "After me, because I ran away and after them because of the 51A." She explains.

"But if they left before it was filed?" asks Hattie.

"In case it got filed, I guess." Sophy shrugs. "It's not, I don't know—"

"Rational?"

Sophy is quiet again but then asks, "Is that like 'sensible'?"

"Sort of. It's more like 'reasonable.' "

Sophy thinks. "It's not, like, *rational.*"

And though Hattie is the enemy, Sophy does meet her eye in the rearview; and in that glance, Hattie at least recognizes, for a moment, the Sophy she knows.

She takes a good look.

They head back home to a terrible wait. Happily, they are in a wet spell—the first one after a dry summer. There is wind and rain to distract them, the pounding relentless at night, and the morning a distraction, too, what with its fast-moving clouds and its sense of letup and change.

Only fools hope things last, Joe used to say.

Hattie hasn't been painting much, but now to kill time she starts working on some bamboo in snow—trying to convey the weight of the snow. Of course, the snow is just the white page, actually—a judicious absence of ink. The weight of it's all suggestion—a matter of bending stalks and burdened leaves, and of using these things to trick the eye into "seeing." It's the sort of trickery they were always interested in at the lab for what it said about how people saw—for what it told them about how the brain put things together. But her interest is different now; she thinks and works, trying to forget about the Chhungs. Why should she care about the Chhungs? When, look! What a good heavy load she's evoked—wet snow, it seems. Spring snow, such as would have represented the spiritual hardships of the literati, in her father's view. The burdens borne by scholars like himself who "retired" rather than collaborate with a foreign invader—*yǐn shì,* who were strangers, in many ways, in their own land.

If only the Chhungs would call the police.

Dá guān. She paints.

It is a full week before, finally, on a day of real sun, with bright, leaf-littered roads and dark, newly nude trees—hallelujah!—Sarun reappears.

"Where was he?" asks Hattie, over tea and candy.

"Can-a-da." Mum's face is so girlish with relief, she looks like Sophy.

"Canada? What was he doing in Canada?"

"Eat frut," she says.

"Frroot." Chhung, behind them, enunciates carefully.

"Eat fruit?" guesses Hattie. "Like pears and apples?"

Mum nods, smiling. The window is open; she lifts her face as if smelling a breeze.

"Have a lot fruit up there," explains Chhung. "More fresh."

"The fruit is fresher."

"Cambodian like to go there eat. America fruit no good. No tay."

"No taste."

He gestures at his nose, his eyes jumping excitedly. "No smell." He grins his lopsided grin. "Like baiseball."

Baseball.

Hattie laughs at this rare joke as Mum produces a durian, which to Hattie smells as rotten as the durians in the United States—like something you wouldn't want to step in, much less bring home special. Still, Mum slices it open with pride. Six quick slices, top to bottom, with their big kitchen knife, and there: the fruit opens like a petaled flower. There is a fingered mass in the middle, which proves delicious; Hattie smiles her approval as Mum shows off a big bowl of other fruit, some of which Hattie recognizes: Tamarind. Pomelo. Dragon fruit, lychees, jackfruit. Things Hattie hasn't seen in decades, and is excited to see again.

"Like it?" asks Chhung, his eyes going.

"Yes," says Hattie. "I like it very much."

Over Hattie's objections, Mum slices open a green mango, too, offering this to Hattie along with an orange-colored salt; Hattie dips.

"Delicious," she says.

Chhung beams. "Cambodian like fruit."

"Of course they do." Hattie eats. "Chinese people, too."

Chhung's eyes crinkle with pleasure.

"The kids bring the fruit back?"

Chhung nods.

Is that legal? Never mind. "So at least you know what he's doing and where he's going," she says.

Mum nods, too, then, real relief on her face. Chhung, though, suddenly laughs, his shirt pocket heavy and swinging; he puts a hand up to steady it.

Carter and Sophy are laughing, too, as Hattie walks by with Reveille. She tries to hum. The last time she went Cato-hunting, he was stuck in a closed-up basement; she found him with a dead bat in his mouth and perfectly fine. This time, though—well, how much more likely that he's collapsed of old age or been nabbed by a fisher. Those fisher being fast and vicious, after all; they can flip a porcupine and gash its stomach in a wink. A thirteen-year-old dog with arthritis wouldn't stand a chance against one. And if Cato has indeed been nabbed, well, he wouldn't be the first of her dogs to go over the years. Hattie's prepared.

Still, she's finding this a grim walk from which she'd love distraction. The fields are certainly a help, with their great weaves of white and purple asters—the wild apple trees, too, with their rings of fruit at their bases, like Christmas tree skirts. Hattie breathes deep as she passes them. The air smells like cider. And the mountainsides! Those leaves could break a stone with their brilliance. All those red maples.

But to drop in on the musicians—impossible.

And yet there goes Reveille, anyway, bounding down the driveway to Sophy, who laughs and lets him put his muddy paws on her lap; he dots her sweatshirt with paw prints. Hattie follows hesitantly. But then—lo!—just like that they are pitched into the kind of accidental peace that makes you realize how easily people could stop being themselves if they could.

"I want you to listen," says Carter. "Come on, now, Sophy, let's hear it nice and loud. The way you just played it."

"Okay. This is 'Turn, Turn, Turn,'" she says. "The words are from Ecclesiastes, I think."

Is it a coincidence that she's singing a song based on the Bible? Hattie looks at Carter, but his focus is on Sophy.

"You think?" reproves Carter. "You *know.*"

Sophy laughs, her cheeks dimpling. "I guess." She looks at Hattie, who smiles to hear how much louder she's singing now, her voice so rich and strong—molten—that even Reveille's ears prick up. Who would have imagined Sophy would have that voice in her? A contralto. And as the last note sounds, Sophy freezes her strumming hand in a surprising new fashion, too—midair—bowing her head dramatically. Her hair falls forward, curtaining all but her shiny nose.

"Bravo! Bravo!"

Reveille's ears swing outward like automatic doors; Carter and Hattie stand side by side, clapping.

"Play another one," says Carter. "Play 'The Sounds of Silence.' "

Sophy makes a face.

"None of that," he says. "Come on."

"Come on," Hattie echoes.

And again Sophy plays, and again they clap, solid with joy. Hattie and Carter are both in jeans and fleece; Hattie can feel her skin flush. Probably she glows, like Carter. His eyes laugh. *If we make our own realities,* Lee used to say, *why don't we make ones we'd choose?* But somehow they cannot ask Sophy to play a third song. Some moment has passed; it's time for Carter and Sophy to settle back down to their lesson.

"Back to the search," says Hattie. She zips up her vest as if she's cold, though she's not.

"Good luck." Carter gives a kindly grin. "Cato's a special dog to you, isn't he? Kind of your main man."

She laughs. "I guess. Four legs and he sheds, but at least you can count on him to wag his tail like he knows you."

It's just a joke. Still, Carter bristles.

"Well, and who might that be directed at," he says—neutrally enough, but he's digging his hands in his pockets and looking down.

As if she is El Hatchet now!

"I hope you find him," says Sophy. "I do. I really do."

"Thanks," says Hattie, calling Reveille. Who is more than ready to leave now, as is she.

And yet when, exhausted and dispirited, she finally finds Cato back at the house, how she'd love to run down through the ferns to tell Sophy and Carter! For, behold—it is, it really is Cato. Bloody and bedraggled, as if he's been in a tangle—at his age! He should know better. It doesn't seem possible that he would survive any sort of contest, but somehow he has. Imagine. There's blood all through his gray muzzle, though; he struggles to his feet even more slowly than usual when he sees her—one leg at a time, whimpering. And even on all fours, his back legs remain half bent under his body—his back will not straighten. Poor Cato! *Come, my friend.* Of course, even curled into his backside, his tail goes full speed; his heart works just fine. Though is that a chunk taken out of his back leg? Oh, Cato, Hattie says. Thanks to yoga she can still make it down to hug and pet him; he smells dank, as if he's been through some standing water. Who knows where he's been? Anyhow, he licks and licks her—her *main man*, indeed—warm and alive, thankfully, whole and home. Her Cato, come back! She sees to his wound.

Everett's new home is nothing like a pole barn. It is more like a fire warden's tower, with a cockamamie truss system leading up to a platform, on which sits a hut. The hut can't be too comfortable but appears to serve its purpose: What with its main window facing Ginny's bedroom, the thing is driving her nuts. She pulls down the shades, but even so can feel him watching her, she says. She can't sleep. She can't eat. She can't pray. As for whether he really is watching, Judy Tell-All says, Of course he is. He's like the terrorists, she says. Watching us and watching us all these years. Watching us, still.

Thinking things, Sophy would say.

Everett nose full of beeswax!

But others say, Where would he get the time? Now that Value-Mart's up and left, and the inn's been sold again, there's a mini-mall going up on the site; and guess who's the general contractor on it. Everett's a busy man. Plus you'd have to be pretty crazy to sit watching a pulled-down shade, they say. And sure, Everett's mad, but crazy is something else.

"Sounds like someone has a guilty conscience to me," says Carter in yoga class. "Sounds like someone's projecting."

And after that people talk differently. "She's projecting," they say. "She is. She's projecting."

The sort of people who, *when they see a wall falling, come to help push,* Hattie's father would say.

Jill Jenkins, though, is an exception.

"It's not her fault the cell tower passed," she says, loudly. "It's our own fault for not going to every darn meeting. For relaxing our vigilance. We're just like the government sitting on all that intelligence and doing nothing. Did we not know this was coming? We did. We knew."

Carter shoots Hattie a questioning look; and indeed, Jill's comment seems both wholly accurate and oddly heated to Hattie, too. Why should she help him out, though? Confirming and conjecturing, playing big sister the way she once did. *Dá guān*—she focuses out the window instead. The yoga class has an edgewise view of Everett's tower; what an experience it's going to be to watch its nightmare double, the cell tower, growing, too, across the lake.

And didn't you always help when you could.

Twins.

Sarun used to slink around his father; now he saunters around him, brazen. Mum watches him with dismay, but still he goes on looking his father in the eye instead of training his gaze on the ground. And when Chhung speaks, Sarun sometimes listens, but sometimes doesn't. He's wearing an MP3 player in a red armband; the black wires loop up his back to his ears. His head bops. Which might be why Chhung is now throwing things—a little like Sophy playing with Annie, or like Gift. One morning there's a lamp out front. Another, a basketball jersey. Yet another, Sarun's armband. And in the evenings, Hattie hears yelling—mostly in Khmer, although Sarun sometimes yells back in English.

Drinking. Drinking is at least part of the problem.

One night Hattie sees Sarun being beaten. Or thinks she does—where are her distance glasses? They should be on her head; why are they not on her head? She is about to get out her binoculars when suddenly her glasses appear on the kitchen table; and so it is that she sees that Sarun is tied up, or at least that his hands appear fastened behind his back. How did Chhung manage that? And though it's a little hard to make out exactly what's happening, she does see violent up-and-down movements: Chhung's arm, Chhung's torso. Chhung's arm. Is that a belt in his hand?

She calls Greta. No answer. What with Cato still weak, Reveille stands beside Hattie, his ears and tail up—taking Cato's place, it seems. She pets him reassuringly—he's bigger than Cato, and easier to reach, anyway—as she tries Grace next. By which time—thank heaven—the beating has stopped. Sophy is bringing her father a drink; she offers it to him with two hands. May it be something nonalcoholic. Chhung drinks, taking a break. It's hard to see where Sarun is.

Still no answer.

"It's okay," Hattie tells Reveille. "It's okay."

Reveille's ears relax; his head drops; his tail wags. He's ready to play.

"Go find Annie," she says.

She is about to make herself some *mántóu*—a lot of work but worth it—when she sees that the beating has resumed, only with—what is that? Hattie pulls down her distance glasses.

The kitchen knife.

She calls 911, gives the address, then hurries next door. The dogs know it's something serious. Too serious for Reveille; it's Cato who, rising to the occasion, follows her. One of her walking shoes comes untied; she doesn't want to stop to tie it, but finally does—a moment Cato takes to pee against a tree. He can only raise his leg to half-mast, but does so with surprising ease, or so it seems by moonlight. It's windy out; the cedars are whipping and rocking—rioting. And the ferns—by day all yellow and brown, headed toward dormancy—are glinting a bright steel gray now, rippling, an eerily live sea. She hurries on.

Yelling, crying, banging. Smashing. Hattie knocks and knocks—pounds—until finally Sophy cracks open the door.

"Is everything all right?"

Cato, front paws up on the crate beside Hattie, wags his tail as if echoing her concern, but Sophy stands stone-faced. The door is barely open; she's backlit by the TV; it's hard to see the expression on her face. The whites of her eyes catch a bit of the moonlight, though, and gleam, unlike her pupils, which keep their flat black.

Her choroid coat, absorbing the stray light.

"I was just wondering," says Hattie.

"You are a nosy old busybody!"

"Because I saw . . ."

"What can you even see? At your age?"

"I . . ."

"You're imagining things! There's nothing to see!"

Sophy slams the door so hard, Cato barks.

"The police are on their way," Hattie calls. She thinks the Chhungs would want to know; she'd love to explain. But the door stays shut. It's everything she can do to step down from the crate without reinjuring her ankle; and back at her house, she does not watch the police arrive—she's too tired. Was she seeing things? Anyway, she's stiff and heavy, leaden; her limbs have *a lifelessness of their own*. It's the way they felt for a good year after Joe and Lee died—so heavy, she didn't think that they would ever really lighten again—or, if they did, that they would lighten for good. And sure enough, she sleeps now like a dead person.

It is two days before she can think about dropping back in on the Chhungs. Finally, though, she wakes in a courageous frame of mind.

Come, my friend, 'tis not too hard to go and knock next door.

Robe. Bathroom. Breakfast. For the dogs, for herself. Coffee.

Annie catches a mouse but lets it escape; Hattie sighs.

Then finally she is knocking, a bag of cookies in hand. Chhung appears with a closed face; it's day one all over again. His eyes go and go. The sun behind him is bright; the cartilage of his ears glows pink.

"English lesson?" she says.

No answer.

"Conversation class?"

He steps back—fades back, it seems, leaving the door ajar. Hattie climbs into the trailer after him, though he's disappeared—into his room, maybe? She waits in the living room for a minute; the TV's on mute. She goes to knock on Mum's door. No Mum, but Sophy is sitting on the mattress, her back propped against the wall. Her Bible lies facedown on the bed, which is a jumble of bedding and pillows; the room is otherwise spic 'n' span. Mum's folded clothes are in one pile, Sophy's in another, Gift's in a third, and in the far corner, there is a small altar with a statue of the Buddha, some plastic flowers, and an incense holder. Sophy's face is in her hands, her fingers tucked as if for safety under a blue stretch hair band.

"Sophy," says Hattie, quietly. "Are you okay?"

Sophy's fingers venture out. Though the air is cool, she's wearing shorts. Her elbows rest on bare knees; her silver flip-flops sit to the sides of bare feet.

"Listen. If ever you want to talk, I'm here."

The curtain wafts.

"A busybody neighbor is sometimes a helpful thing."

Sophy wraps her arms back around her knees, burying her head. Only a sliver of forehead shows; her hair fans wide. She says nothing. Still, Hattie can hear her voice: *So why didn't you say so? If you're going to think things?*

"I'm worried about you," Hattie offers. "About your family."

"Well, don't be." Sophy's voice, coming from behind her arms and knees, is muffled. "It's God's plan."

"What does that mean?"

"It means my dad is right—Sarun has to stop."

"You mean Sarun is the gap the devil is looking for."

The curtain lifts and collapses.

"Speaking of whom"—Hattie almost says "of the devil"—"Is he okay?"

"Why shouldn't he be okay?"

"Well . . ."

"You're crazy." Sophy looks up, her eyes rimmed with makeup. "You're old. You're seeing things."

Seeing things.

A *lifelessness of its own*—that leadenness—Hattie feels it return, then, even as she hears, *Don't you just want to slap that girl?*

Is that Lee's voice?

"Like what do you want from us anyway?" Sophy goes on. "Like who asked you to ask questions? Ginny says I've got to ask myself what you want from us, bringing us cookies and giving me free lessons, and now, like, to my mom, too. Getting yourself in the trailer. Like what's that about?"

"Is that what she says." Hattie lifts her chin. "Well, and what about the church? Do you ever ask yourself why they give you things, and send a car for you? Do you ever ask yourself that?"

"They want to save me."

"Ah. So they don't pretend to do it out of the goodness of their souls."

"They do it because Mark told them to spread the Good News. It's not creepy."

"I see. Well, let me ask you this. Did people ever do things for each other in Cambodia? Because they were living in the same village?"

"How would I know? I never lived in Cambodia."

"In your old town, then. Did people ever do things because they were all in the same boat, and because it made them feel part of a community?"

"Ginny says you need us," says Sophy. "She says you need us more than we need you."

"I'm sure that's true."

There's a noise in the next room—Sarun. Talking in what seems to be a perfectly normal voice to Chhung.

"Ginny says you're desperate. She says you spy on us, the same as Everett spies on her. It's not checking up, it's spying, and you do it because you're a, a . . ."

"A lesbian?"

"Ginny says you're the one who called the police on us."

"Not *on* you," Hattie says, but Sophy, starting to stand, isn't listening.

"It's true, isn't it," says Sophy. "You did—you called the police on us." One foot gets caught in some bedding, but she kicks it away savagely even as, with a familiar gesture, she tucks her hair behind her ear.

Hattie answers slowly, plainly—as if talking to Mum. "Sophy. Listen to me. Your dad had a knife in his hand."

Sophy throws a sandal at her but misses, of course. It hits a wall and falls to the floor as Hattie leaves.

Did you have your driving glasses on?" asks Grace, squinting. Beth wants to know if they have a social worker. Because they should have one! she says. That is just a fact! Greta is going to call as soon as she gets home to see why they don't, though the state—she gestures at the eternal nature of the state with a dinner roll. And Candy nods to that—budget cuts, she says. As for what they common citizens can do in the meanwhile, there is much concerned discussion, especially about the van. What is the role of that white van? Hattie tries not to look at Ginny—*When is a snake not a snake?*—as she reports that it stops in Riverlake on its way to Canada. "Where the boys go to eat fruit," she says. "Cambodians like fruit."

"And supermarket fruit can be awful, it's true," says Grace.

But Beth shakes her head, skeptical. Besides growing out her hair, she's been trying flowered skirts lately, and Mary Janes—a softer look. Yet still she wields her fork and tomato wedge like a hammer. "I vote we open up that van and see what's really in there," she says.

How can they go breaking into the van, though, when they're not the police and don't have a warrant, either? Never mind if it's drugs, as Candy fears. "Fourth Amendment," says Greta, who before she was a librarian, taught civics; and people do see this. Just as they seem about to move on to another topic, however, Ginny says thoughtfully,

"People say there might be terrorists coming in from Canada now," and all stops.

Terrorists!

People at a far table sing "Happy Birthday"; Ginny sops up what's left of her soup with some bread.

"We have to do something," says Beth. "That is just a fact."

They think.

"Maybe someone should talk to Sophy?" Greta looks at Hattie. "See what she knows?"

"You mean, maybe this is all about fruit," says Hattie. "The rest being so much groundless speculation."

"Exactly."

"She's pretty mad I called 911."

"But of course you called 911," says Beth. "I would have called 911. Anyone would have called 911."

"I don't think she's speaking to me," says Hattie.

"Oh, no." Greta touches Hattie's arm. "That's not fair."

Hattie shrugs, thinks for a moment, then turns calmly to Ginny. "Maybe you can try?"

It's what they would do in the lab sometimes—give things rein, and see what happened. Not that she suspects anything in particular. But to suggest that there might be terrorists in the white van—how odd.

Ginny is pleasant. "I'd be happy to ask," she says.

And her report the next meeting is all sunshine and equanimity: The van is bringing fruit on the way down, she says, and on the way up, plywood.

But of course! —Beth's tomato pitches forward. They're the plywood thieves!

Others, though, are slower to relax. No chemicals? No fertilizer?

Ginny shakes her head bemusedly, like a teacher with her innocently mistaken class. As for how Sophy knows, well, how many secrets can really be kept in a trailer that size? "If you ask her, I'm sure she'll tell you the same thing herself," she finishes.

Greta presses her fingers to her lips; she looks as if she is about to eat them.

"Ask her." Ginny turns to Hattie. "Please, be my guest. Honestly, I think it's God's plan for you to ask." Ginny's green eyes are round and misty. "Honestly, I think she's ready."

Ready.

In what you are proud of, Lee used to say, *you can see in what way you are nuts.*

"Ask," urges Ginny. She pulls her hair down over her ears. "Ask."

B ut what, pray tell, should I talk to Sophy about?"
     If Carter is surprised to see Hattie at his front door, he doesn't show it. Neither is he surprised she will not come in. He simply steps forward onto the porch, folds his arms, and listens. A sounding board. He has bags under his eyes, but his nod is crisp; he's taking things in. Of course, she's worried about Sarun, he says. And it is indeed high time someone looked into their social worker situation. As for the kitchen knife—while he believes that Hattie saw what she saw—well, what we see . . . As he knows she knows. He, too, is glad—very—that no one has been hurt. Though what's this about Ginny? Hattie elaborates: Sophy's coolness. Her involvement with the church. Her belief in Sarun's evil. Ginny's confidence.

"She knows what Sophy will say," Hattie finishes.

"And don't we know that sometimes? What people will say?"

Hattie rubs her arms. It's cool out, drizzly—*plotting weather,* Joe used to say. "Carter. Come on." She tries again. "It's the way she said it. As if Sophy were in the bag in some way. 'Ready,' as she said."

Carter's eyebrows lift as if in concert with invisibly rising antennae. "And this, you believe, is related to the beatings."

"I'm not sure why Ginny's interested in the van. But she is, and the van is related to the beatings."

"So getting Sophy away from Ginny would stop them."

"I don't know. But Sophy is mixed up in this somehow and needs help, Carter. Not just Sarun. Sophy, too."

"Because?" Carter turns a hand up.

"Because she's on the wrong path."

"Ah." His arm swings back in like something on a hinge. He leans against his doorway; Hattie leans against a post. (*Taking your post,* Lee would have said.) Moisture soaks through her flannel shirt; there's an instant stripe of cold down the back of her shoulder.

"You believe she's being influenced by Ginny," he says.

She nods, folding her arms, too; the flannel between her fingers is dry.

"Ginny is at war with Everett, and like combatants the world over displays gracelessness under pressure. That doesn't make her a danger to Sophy," he goes on.

"She's a fundamentalist, Carter."

"And?"

"Do you really want Sophy growing up questioning evolution?"

"Questioning is fine."

"Denying, then."

In the dim light his face is coarse-grained, his features fuzzy and grayed. His eyes, though, drill into her all the same, his pupils huge. "Is Ginny a creationist?"

Hattie hesitates. "She must be."

"You don't actually know."

"No."

"Has she said anything to suggest that this particular tenet of faith is important to her?"

"No."

"So it may be critical to public discourse, but less critical to her."

"She believes in the inerrancy of the Bible, Carter."

"But you've never heard her argue the point."

"No."

"Has Sophy said anything to suggest she is becoming a creationist?"

"She may well with time, Carter."

"With time she may become a Communist. The salient question, it seems to me, is why did you reach for that? You're not here because of creationism. That was just pressing my buttons, as Maisy used to say."

The famous Maisy.

"Will you talk to her about creationism if it comes up?" asks Hattie.

"Of course."

"What about homosexuality?"

"Has she said something homophobic?"

"No, but you know it's coming. Romans I."

"If it comes up, I will see what she has to say about it."

It's Carter the train—making his stops and moving right on. She is irritated but reassured, too. Reassuringly irritated.

"And what about Ginny? Will you talk to her about Ginny? Tell her to be careful?"

"I cannot tell her with whom to be friends, Hattie. I tried that with my own children and, believe me, it backfired completely." He grimaces.

"Sophy worships you, Carter. You're in a position to help."

"And don't I always help when I can."

"I didn't say it, Carter."

He takes in the darkening sky. "Let's say, for the sake of argument, that that's even true about my position vis-à-vis Sophy. What do you care? Why are you here?"

"Some of us can't watch, Carter. Some of us can't watch people get pushed halfway around the globe only to get plowed under once they get here."

"Airbrushed out, like you."

"I didn't say that, either."

"You're holding back."

"If you're asking do they matter to me? Yes. Are they part of my picture? Yes."

"You have come out of retirement to advocate for the vulnerable once more."

"I suppose I have. Yes. 'I have risen to fight again.' " She rotates her ankle a little, shifting her weight.

"Is that a quote?"

"It is."

He doesn't ask from whom or where.

"And what's this 'plowed under'? Is Sophy being plowed under? And why weren't you friends with Meredith? I always wondered that, you know. You two had so much more in common with each other than you ever did with me."

"Meredith was about justice, capital *J*, Carter. I'm just a person who can't watch things sometimes."

"I see. And now Ginny is going to plow Sophy under? Religion is?"

"Sophy's going to the church school, Carter, not the public school. Do you realize that?"

"Many fine minds have come out of religious schools, Hattie. Think of the Jesuits. That whole line of thinking that believes all truth is God's truth. Belief in God doesn't preclude the study of biology or philosophy."

"Belief in God's truth is one thing, and belief that He's acting through you, another. And she's not being educated, she's being indoctrinated. She's being taught who to trust and who not."

"And let me guess: You are not to be trusted."

"It's not right, Carter, and you know it."

It's getting colder. The rain is picking up, the wind—all of nature's gusting. Only they remain locked solid in argument.

"Cutting her off from your fine person is a shame, Hattie, but it's not a crime."

"Ginny is teaching her groupthink."

"She is imparting a culture."

"A culture that makes its own truths."

"All cultures make their own truths, Hattie. The question is, Does their world work? Is it adaptive? Does it help us procreate? Or does it obscure so much fact as to be maladaptive?"

He tells a story then about Cotton Mather. A Puritan, he says, who half believed in science but half, still, in witchcraft. "When his newborn child died, he had reason to believe it was due to a curse on his wife. And yet he did an autopsy anyway. Cut up his own dead child, looking for a cause."

Hattie shudders. "And?"

"He found that his baby had blocked bowels. Can you imagine? What a moment that must have been? To have made such a discovery! And yet his baby is dead all the same. And not even because he mattered to someone—to die of a curse is still to matter to someone, right? To die of blocked bowels is plain arbitrary bad luck."

"How sad," says Hattie. "Though couldn't the block have been an act of God and in that way a sign of mattering, still, to the Almighty?"

"Very good. Either way, though, my point holds: Cause and effect is a story, but it's not necessarily a story about you. And one way or another, we seem to want stories in which we figure."

"People, too," she says, after a moment. Trying not to *combust*, trying to play along—to see where he's going. "People in whose pictures and stories we appear. Or better yet, gods. A community, imagined or real."

He nods. "The question being, of course, why."

The racket of the rain on the porch roof has gotten loud, but Hattie takes up the thread of Carter's thought as if they're back in the lab. "And the answer, maybe, that such inclusion fosters cooperation and social cohesion. Which contributes in turn to the survival of the gene pool—that is, to the genes of the individual and of his or her kin."

An obvious answer to an obvious question; they're rusty. Still, Carter smiles. "Go on."

"That is, if the belief in one's inclusion isn't in itself sustaining, in some way, to the individual. Enabling one to survive extreme challenge, for example."

"Good."

"And/or else a by-product of other cognitive biases that were once useful—and maybe still are. The connection bias, for example." Carter grins broadly at this—remembering their youthful conversations, maybe—but Hattie pauses midthought—surprised and pleased that she can still speak labspeak (*Hattie not so batty!*) but bored by it now. It doesn't speak of what she wants spoken of. "So you won't talk to her," she finishes.

"To Sophy?"

The rain.

"To Sophy."

"When the church is providing her with the very stories we're discussing?" he says. "A context? A community? A feeling that she figures?"

Where friends become family.

"You are willfully refusing to know what I know you must about some of these groups, Carter. What they are."

"And how do you know what they are, pray tell?"

"I know by the lengths to which they will go to reel the kids in. Sending cars. Opening a school right across from the public school. They are like glial cells. Astrocytes telling a girl what kind of neuron to be. Assigning her to a certain layer of the cortex."

"Neurons may differentiate once and for all, Hattie, but people do not. And what if Sophy needs a reason to wake up in the morning? A web of significance?" He stretches as if waking up to a fine new day, though the pouring rain is like a wall of water now. In the small room that is the porch he all but brushes her with his arms. His rib cage rises; his untucked shirt lifts high. Triangles of goose-pimpled flesh flash at his sides. "Honestly, I think if I could get religion, I would." He relaxes.

"This kind, Carter? Would you really get this kind, when freedom of thought is so important to you?"

"It's a marketplace of ideas, Hattie. We can't tell Sophy what to choose. It's up to her to decide what works for her."

"Ginny thinks she knows God's will, not just for herself but for Sophy. She thinks she can see God's plan for Sophy."

"Which you imagine dangerous."

"Of course it's dangerous, Carter. Look at this Osama bin Laden."

"It depends on what she sees." A slight retrenching there, such as one rarely saw in the old days—as he seems to notice, too: He twists his body self-consciously, stretching again.

"Now you're the one who's reaching, Carter. Or have you simply avoided involvements for so long that by now it's just habit?"

"When God sends her to flight school we will worry."

"Even if there's no Guy LaPoint, you hold back. Even if there's no one making hay with your every mistake."

He stops. "That's not fair."

"You stonewall even if there's no El Honcho watching. You play smart."

"Hattie."

"How can you pretend to care about Sophy and stand by while this happens?"

"Hattie."

"How can you refuse to see what's going on?—to see her?"

"Hattie, stop."

"You know what people used to say about you in the lab? They used to say you knew everything except what you'd go to bat for."

"Excuse me." His look is dark. "Did I not go to bat for this town?"

"You took a stand against Value-Mart. That's principle." Hattie is no longer cold. "Meredith was right about you: You know all kinds of things, and you can play all kinds of things. Instruments, games, anything. But you've never learned to care about anything, really. Anything or anyone." She glares at him now—fixing him in the hard pour of her anger. "You refused to see even your own brother."

A pause. He raises his head slowly; and when his eyes meet hers now, they are a storm of their own.

"And what about you, Miss See-It-All?" he says, finally. "What about you? Are you sure you're not just upset that you need Sophy more than Sophy needs you? Are you sure you're not just upset that that's been the story of your life?" His face is purple, his mouth low and tight, and his shirt suddenly loose—having failed, it seems, to contract with the rest of him. "And when you say I've never learned to care for anything or anyone, don't you mean I never came to care for you?"

Hattie tries to focus on the talk at the Come 'n' Eat: plywood, the cell-tower site. Plywood disappearing from the mini-mall site now, too. People's voices, though, seem thin and far away, as if they're coming over the sort of vinegar-and-wire-with-stretched-parchment affair she used to make with her students in her hearing unit—working models of Alexander Bell's liquid transmitter. *Mr. Watson, come here!* the kids would say, when they were done. *I want to see you! Mr. Watson! I want to see you!*

Mr. Combustible.

Don't you mean I never came to care for you?

Candy is speaking: "It's been disappearing in batches." And: "Who can watch all night?"

"That is just a fact": Beth.

Disagreement: Should they tell the police about the van? What do they really know?

Agreement: It's finally Everett's job to secure the site. As Everett has said himself. How plain unfortunate, though, that the price of half-inch has gone through the roof lately.

"That wood was worth five thousand dollars, easy," says Candy.

Five thousand dollars!

"Everett's extreme but you have to say, he's honest," says Grace. Her own honest face is shiny, like some sort of solar shield.

No one looks at Ginny.

As for whether the owner should have insisted on someone with builder's insurance, well, people around here can't afford that sort of thing, says Candy; and seeing as how her husband was in the building trades before he died, her word is considered definitive.

Are you sure you're not just upset that you need Sophy more than Sophy needs you?

Are you sure you're not just upset that that's been the story of your life?

On her way home, Hattie sees, out in front of the Chhungs', a pile of plastic and glass. She squints.

The computer, its screen smashed in, thrown out onto the ground.

Should she tell someone? She is trying to decide when she finds

Cato lying just inside her door, his big head on his paws. He seems to be waiting for her, except that when she comes in, he does not work his way to his feet. Neither does he open his eyes. And already there are flies. Reveille stands uncertainly behind Cato's body—lifting his head, barking, then ducking his head. Then lifting it and barking again. Trying to convey the news. Hattie pets him. He licks and licks her hand. Annie jumps frantically, confused.

"Cato," says Hattie, kneeling down. "Cato."

How strange to feel his fur as thick as ever, but cold. His body inert, like his collar—all the miraculous processes and exchanges of life she used to describe with such alacrity to her students—his cell divisions, his transcriptions, his Krebs cycles—shut down.

Oh, where are Lee and Joe now? *Come back! Come back!* Because she would not at all mind having someone to pet cold Cato one more time with her now; or to help her take off his collar; or to help her lug him out to the yard. Probably she should wait for help with the lugging. But a dead dog in her house. And the flies—the damned flies. Plus she knows from experience what the smell from even a dead mouse can be. And so she drags him out by the paws, on his back; his legs having gone all stiff already—calcium ions having flooded his poor muscles. He is heavier than she realized; his tail goes on forever. She keeps stopping to cry. But then she drags some more, cradling the rough pads of his paws in the palms of her hands. His toenails claw her, his familiar overgrown toenails—the same, though everything else has changed. She wants to do something about them—trim them so they'll look nice in dog heaven. How dry the pads of his paws. Dead dry. Oh, to have somebody to help her now! Somebody to sit with her in a little sendoff at the pet cemetery, tomorrow, too—maybe she'll call Greta. Though why does she bury her animals and cremate her humans? Never mind. Tomorrow she will bury Cato, back in their old town, alongside all the other dogs Joe and she had. But, well, cover him with a blanket in the meanwhile. Lock him in the shed, so the fisher won't get him. Those damned fisher.

Your main man.

Sweet Cato, who was there when Joe died, and Lee, too. Sweet Cato, whose ears would have pricked right up if he'd ever heard either of them laugh again. Who will remember them now? And who will remember Cato? Will Reveille remember? Will Annie? What do dogs remember?

She wants to know, though what can it matter? When time, that great fisher, will nab them all in the end. What can it possibly matter?

Josh has met Serena's parents.

"And?"

"I didn't drool."

"Her parents don't mind you're American?"

"They say journalists aren't really American. They say journalists are like nomads—our own tribe, really, wandering all over. And anyway, I'm a quarter Chinese, right?"

"Something like that. But what do you think?"

"I think she's a great cook. And that our kids, if we have kids, will be—what. To an identity crisis born. Maybe they'll get religion. Like everyone else, once globalization has made mincemeat of the nation-state. It'll be their identity-in-a-pocket, a little affiliation-to-go."

Hattie doesn't laugh. "Does marriage come before kids?"

"Maybe."

"Does Serena believe in marriage?"

"No, now that you mention it. But her parents do, so. And you're going to love her. She likes to swim."

"Wonderful."

"She's very warm. You know—Chinese. Speaks Chinese, by the way, as well as Russian and Portuguese and English. Her parents are very Chinese, too. Especially her mother."

"What's her name?"

"Lola."

"A nice Chinese name."

"Isn't it? Just like Hattie. I keep telling them how Chinese you are."

"And?"

"Lola says aren't you lucky to have the skin—it's such a savings. She says she only spends half as much as everyone else on her face."

Hattie laughs and hangs up cheered, though was it *holding back* not to have told Josh about Cato?

Your dog has died, you mean.

She'll write him an e-mail. Grace and Greta, meanwhile, have left flowers for her, a bag of biscuits for Annie and Reveille, and a condolence note. Cato, they said, was a good dog.

. . .

There's been a fire at the mini-mall site. Some wires got crossed; someone was in a hurry. Something sparked. It happens, say some. Only Ginny is suspicious.

"Oh, I don't know," she says. "I mean, who can even say how much plywood was stolen now, right?"

The thieves probably stole some more, then set the fire to cover their tracks, agrees Beth. Greta is more skeptical. What kind of a way is that to get away with something? Even she concedes, though, that it is strange that there'd be trouble with the electrical when Everett's dad was an electrician—wasn't he an electrician?

"He was," says Grace. "And Everett grew up helping him."

"So he must have known his safe practices," says Hattie. "On the other hand, people do make mistakes. It could still be an accident."

"It was a coverup!" insists Beth, who, having suddenly cut her hair again and given up on skirts, seems more pugnacious than ever. "It was!"

Candy hesitates but finally nods. Beth's right, it was a coverup. Their connection biases at work.

"So then," says Ginny, "should we turn the boys in?"

When they don't know that the fire had anything to do with the plywood, or that the plywood has anything to do with the van?

"No, we should not turn them in," says Hattie. "There is just no proof."

"They are innocent," agrees Greta, "until proven guilty."

Ginny folds her napkin perfectly in half.

Deer bound across Ginny's lawn, eating things up; her ornamentals are no longer ornamental. And seeing as how Everett's gone and taken her chicken wire down, her whole vegetable garden's gone, too—her last tomatoes, her leafies, her squash. You can see how Ginny might be upset. But should she be letting hunters come hunt in retaliation? Usually she posts her NO HUNTING signs all over. This year, everyone's invited instead, and not just for deer. Ginny's letting the bear hunters come, too, starting immediately.

All of which so disgusts Jill Jenkins that—never mind that for many, lying around opening their hearts is the best part of yoga—she cannot wait until after her headstand to explode. Her chest heaves with outrage, her arms flail around; she seems wholly unacquainted with yogic serenity.

"Do you know what these guys do? They put radio collars on their hounds, and train them to tree bears," she informs anyone who doesn't know. "When the radio signal goes off, they go driving over. Then they put down their beers, get out of their trucks, stand there at the base of the tree, and shoot."

Silence. This is not a hunting crowd, of course—and they're outraged, too—but still.

"Think we'll be able to meditate?" says Hattie, finally.

People laugh. Carter smiles.

Hattie straightens out her mat.

A lot of the hunters are neighbors—some of them rough customers, but not all of them as bad as Jill paints them. And it's only every now and then, really, that you see a flatbed with a bear, though Hattie did see a cub on its back the other day, its narrow snout reminding her, disconcertingly, of Annie's.

I'll but lie and bleed awhile.

It's hard to feel that Ginny's got the right idea, especially as poor Everett hardly seems worth harassing. He does not go out and, what with the mini-mall trouble, isn't building anymore, either. The fire wasn't much, really, as fires go, but coming on top of the plywood, people say, it could ruin him. He can't pay his subcontractors; he can't pay the lumberyard. All he can do is drink, it seems, knowing that there are hunters all around him—knowing that he's treed. Hattie and others have started leaving food at the base of his tower, but what else can they do? Besides shake their heads—that tower—all that scrap wood hammered on every which way. It's pretty crackpot. Hattie shouts up to him one day, standing in the goldenrod. The sun is bright in her face as she fashions a crude megaphone out of some cardboard, then shouts and shouts into the clear fall air. Sounding a little crackpot herself—she almost can't blame him for not answering. And what would she say if he did? That she talked to Ginny? That she could try talking to Ginny again? When she can see how much good it did the first time, and when Ginny is conveniently out of town, anyway? Visiting friends, people say.

At least the food's disappearing. What's more, he's been spotted twice in town.

"He's alive," says Beth. "I'm not worried."

And should they suspend yoga? That's another question. There are DO NOT TRESPASS signs up all along the boundary between this property and Ginny's; bullets are not going to whiz past them as they cross the field to class. Still, the studio stands all of fifteen feet in from the property line, and some of the hunters are kids—twelve, thirteen, fourteen years old. There is reason for concern.

"I do not want to suspend," says Jill Jenkins—at least waiting to speak until after class this time. "As it is, life revolves around hunting. Do you realize there are whole weeks we can't teach a thing? The kids plain don't show up. Do you realize? Our culture is as screwed up as anything in the Middle East. They're not the only ones who can't seem to do anything about their extremes. It's us, too. It's us."

And in truth there is a kind of magnificence to her wide-flung arms. Probably she'd have confronted Guy LaPoint, too, once upon a time.

As Joe used to say, *A good indignation brings out all one's powers.*

Still, the class sighs; and Carter is not inclined to continue, he says—his gaze fixed, as if he's only just noticed them, on the covered forms at the back of the room. He pulls down the sleeves of his long-sleeved T-shirt; and people, of course, take their cue from him. They are not going to be able to concentrate, they say. Because shots are disturbing. They're just a disturbing sound.

Jill strides out, her yoga mat rolled tight; Carter, head down, ties his red laces. Who knows what's going on? Well, never mind. Hattie's had enough of dog pose for the season.

You can't see hunters from the trailer. The noise is hard to miss, though, as the mountain cul-de-sac gathers noise up; things resound, especially sounds like this—a perforating sound, like something a paper punch might make, if it had a setting for punching air. It's disturbing, just as the yoga class said. A disturbing sound. Reveille and Annie have their neon orange bandannas on, to be sure they can be seen if they go out, and Hattie is keeping an eye on Chhung— watching him over there by the pit. He's wearing his brace again, she sees, and though he still shouts most toward sundown, he's shouting a lot in the daytime, too, now. PTSD, Greta says. He's bound to have PTSD.

Post-Traumatic Stress Disorder.

Hattie is keeping an eye out.

And so it is that she sees a cop show up at the trailer one morning.

It's just one cop, and a fairly small one, at that—a kid, really, a lot like the kids Hattie used to teach. A pointy-headed skinny thing, more like an asparagus than an agent of the law. No one would ever listen to him if he weren't wearing a uniform. Is he there to question Sarun? Sarun is outside, digging, but no problem. He and Chhung come in. The cop sits with Sarun on the couch awhile. One on one end, the other on the other, as if on a first date. Sarun nods. Answers questions. Chhung watches. After all of five minutes, the cop stands and pulls his belt up. Tucks his shirt in. Mum offers him a snack, but he declines, shaking Mum's hand instead. Chhung's, too—insisting, you can see, that Chhung not get up out of his chair. He shakes Sarun's hand last. Sarun bows a little, his arms at his sides.

Down the two crates, across the packed dirt. The cop starts his car, backs up, turns around, and heads up toward the road. The Chhungs watch from the doorway as if they've never seen anything like it—an asparagus with a car. Then the door closes. Sarun throws himself back on the couch—half sitting, half lying down in the eternal way of teenagers, as if the one thing they do not want to do is bend at the hips. He's propped up on his elbows, remote control in hand, but Chhung has other plans. They head back outside. It is a breezy day, sunny, full of blowing leaves and wild turkeys. Hattie watches a flock cross her yard—jakes, she knows, by their size and by the way their mature middle tailfeathers jut out, longer than the rest. The turkeys step warily, young but canny—aware, it seems, there is danger everywhere. Hunters. Who knows what. Reasons to fly off.

B anging. "Hattie!" In the middle of the night, banging. "Hattie!" Hattie comes up slowly, trying to kick off her covers, only to find that they include a lead apron. Which for a moment she almost can't throw off, though it's blocking her $q\bar{\imath}$.

Someone banging at the slider.

"Hattie!"

"Sophy?" Suddenly Hattie's up, the dogs are up, they're all hurrying to the slider. "What's the matter?"

"You have to come! Quick! Hurry!"

Sophy runs off, a dark figure in white T-shirt; Hattie grabs a flashlight. The dogs want to follow, but she says, Sit. Stay. Reveille obeys; Annie sits but does not stay. Both watch—alert as turkeys and missing Cato, Hattie knows. Cato! If Cato were still alive, she'd bring him for sure. Cato, Cato. Cato the Wise. Where is her robe? Why is she out without her robe? And why is she out in her slippers—she is slipping in her slippers—and what is that sound? Mum crying—wailing. Something Hattie's never heard before. Mum wails in high-pitched waves—keening. That must be keening. The sound of a grief beyond grief. Does Hattie really want to know what caused it? Down through the ferns, half withered now. The trailer door is open. She climbs in carefully, not wanting to trip—why is she out in her slippers—but, there. She's in. Alone. How bright it is. The living room is empty.

"Sophy?"

The wailing.

"Mum?"

The kitchen is empty. Sophy and Mum's room is empty. But then there they are. Mum and Gift huddling in the corner of Chhung and Sarun's dark room; and before them, huge Sarun, sprawling. He's on his back, his arms and legs akimbo, taking up the whole carpet—a giant with giant amounts of blood. Hattie puts a hand to her mouth and nose; she can feel the rise of retch. The stench of blood is everywhere, that metallic smell, mixed in with the cigarette smoke—what happened? There's so much blood it is hard to know what happened, where the wounds are. Hard, in the low light, to see—how slow her retinas are to adjust. Slow. Don't they have another lamp? But no. There is just this one lamp, a desk lamp, really, on a low table. Hattie draws her nightgown in, kneeling—thank goodness she can still kneel—because, well, first Cato, and now this. This. She tries to breathe. To think. Not to retch. A gash in the arm—the head, too. A gash in the back of his head. A pool of dark blood. His hair is matted.

"Sarun?" She slaps his face a little. Gently. His cheek cool and wet, his skin soft and smooth, like Joe's when he died. Though warm, still—at least his skin is still warm. He's not cold like Joe and Cato; he's warm. Warm.

"Sarun."

He's breathing, but his breaths are shallow and his eyes half shut. Mum wails. Gift, too, is crying and hitting his mother.

The smell.

Hattie nods at Mum reassuringly, then turns, relieved; Sophy's appeared. "Call 911," Hattie tells her.

"Will the police come?"

"You have to call, Sophy. Your brother's unconscious."

Sophy looks at Sarun, then at Mum.

"My dad will kill me."

"Now. You have to call now. Now." Hattie speaks slowly and clearly, as if they're having a lesson; Mum, though still crying, looks up and nods. Sophy goes. Is their phone working? Hattie tries to listen; Sophy is talking, good.

Good. Head injury, better not to move him. Hattie checks his pulse. Okay. His heart is working. Okay. But how to stop the bleeding? Should she press something to his head? To stop the bleeding? Or not? Infection, the blood-brain barrier.

"Sarun?"

Bleeding to death. He's bleeding to death.

She presses a corner of the sheet to his skull, but where there should be bone there is mush; she can't press.

I'll but lie and bleed awhile.

Mum is wailing again. Wailing, wailing. Stop, Hattie wants to say. Just stop! Gift, too, is still whimpering, his arms around Mum's neck, but his body craned around. He's chewing on a plastic figure—blue and red, a superhero. She's holding him with her knees and arms. His diaper is turgid.

"Sophy!" calls Hattie. "Ask if we should try to stop the bleeding! Tell them his skull is smashed!"

But Sophy is talking to an operator, not a doctor.

Germs.

"Sophy! Put some water on to boil!"

What if there's an unstable piece of something? A piece of skull. She doesn't want to dislodge anything. But bleed to death—he could bleed to death. And so she finally just grabs the sheet again, and moves his wet hair out of the way. Then, there. She presses gently. The blood soaks through to her fingertips, warm and sticky. She should really press harder, but it's squishy—the spot's squishy. Harder. She stares at the gold earring there by her thumb; it's mottled with blood. A lacy pattern like a cell structure revealed by a Golgi stain. The links of his necklace, too, are all caked. But his scar, the round one Sophy said was made by a bullet in his last life, is here, now, in this life, blood-free.

"Sarun? Sarun?" Still nothing. Pale—even in the low light, she can see that he's pale.

Pale as Lee, when she was dying. But not raving, as she was. Lee raved and raved before she stopped.

"Do you need a whole pot?" yells Sophy.

"No. Just be quick."

Press harder.

"A half-pot okay?" calls Sophy.

"Do two half-pots. Use two burners. Hurry up."

Bleeding. Blood in his ear but not coming out of it, she doesn't think.

A car motor. Doors. EMTs. Thank god! Hattie hesitates to let go of the sticky sheet, but here comes a purple-gloved hand holding a surreally white pad. She almost falls as she stands—suddenly lightheaded—but is caught by other hands, three large bodies taking up the airspace now. Thank god, thank god. Mum abruptly stops crying—Gift, too—as if they don't want to cry in front of strangers, or as if they are just plain shocked: What beings are these, in fluorescent yellow vests? They have walkie-talkies in their pockets; they're wearing purple gloves. The woman's hair is clamped up. No one blanches. They simply press, replace, wrap. Remove his earrings, hand them to Hattie. The gauze goes over his forehead to the back of his head; around his chin, too; he looks like a mummy. They cut and tape even as they check his temperature, his blood pressure, his pulse, his breathing rate. His pupil size, but not to see if he is high—to see if he is reacting. Shining their light in his eyes. What's his name? asks the woman. Sarun, says Sophy. His name is Sarun. She doesn't roll the r—making it easier for the EMTs to pronounce. How're you doing, Saroon, says the woman loudly. Can you hear me, Saroon? How're you doing? Can you hear me? Sarun's eyes flutter. Good boy! says the woman. Now we're going to put this collar on you. We're going to lift up your head and slide it right under you. Ready? There you go. Now we're strapping it up. That's going to stabilize your neck. Now we are going to move you—ready? She looks at her partners. One-two-three! Sarun groans as they lift him in one sure movement onto a blue trauma board. They strap him down with straps. He stops groaning. Saroon! Are you there? Saroon! Saroon! Ah, there you are. Good boy! says the woman again. What happened? An attacker, says Hattie instantly. Exhausted but not batty. A stranger. Just walked on in. No one they know, they don't think. Any sign of the attack weapon? No. And no one saw anyone? A rise of suspicion just as Sophy appears—do they still need the water? Hattie speaks clearly, not looking at Sophy but aiming her story toward her. They just came home and found him like that. Hattie shakes her head. Terrible. Has she volunteered too much? Should she say something about Chhung? Give him an alibi? Never mind. Suspicious or not, the EMTs are moving Sarun and the board—one-two-three!—onto the stretcher; they're covering him with a sheet. A blanket. Strapping him down again with what look to be seat belts from an airplane. When did all these things become blue?—the stretcher, the sheet, the blanket. Didn't they all use to be white? Never mind. What do you think? asks Hattie—almost asking, Is it serious? *Hattie gone batty!* Well, they'll do a scan at the hospital, says the woman, but she's guessing depressed occipital skull fracture. Is he going to die? asks Sophy. And the woman looks at her then with her kindly eyes; she has eyes like Cato's, a little rheumy, with a dip to their lower edge. We're doing our level best, she says. But if you want to do something, you could say a prayer. He could probably use some prayers.

And so Sophy prays, her eyes closed and her lips moving; Mum prays, too. And Hattie prays as well, though she does not believe in instrumental prayer. Her prayer is more like meditation, usually, a way of expressing wonder. Gratitude. Perplexity. Grief. She does not expect results, especially as she is not even sure who she's addressing. But today, she just puts in her wish list. Please, dear God. Please. A few last flies buzz around—flies, this time of year!—a few survivors. May Sarun survive, too, she prays. May Sarun survive, too. And as she prays, it suddenly comes to her; as she prays, she suddenly knows—the shovel. Not the knife, in the end. It was the shovel.

The shovel.

Hattie blind as a batty.

Her nightgown is heavy and soaked—the lead apron of her dreams.

The EMTs are moving Sarun out of the trailer. Out through the living room, out through the front door. Down the crate steps. Can Mum and Sophy and Gift and Hattie all ride in the ambulance, too? Debbie—the woman's name is Debbie—shakes her head no as the men pop the stretcher wheels down. No. Hattie gestures then at Mum. Go, she says. Take Gift. Go. We'll follow. Mum nods, understanding. Hattie smiles. The EMTs align the stretcher with the ambulance. Then, there: Up go the wheels and in slides Sarun like a baguette. Sophy helps Mum in next, then starts to hand Gift up but Debbie says sorry, no babies. We'll follow you, says Hattie again. Mum nods. She says something to Sophy in Khmer, her voice urgent and alive. Her face, though, is like plastic. A green dolphin air freshener dangles from a grab bar in the ceiling.

Back up to Hattie's house. How can she still be holding Sarun's earrings? Anyway, out of that nightgown, where are her shoes? If only they had a diaper for Gift; they take off his dirty one and hold him over the toilet. Where, to their surprise, he pees. Good boy! Though what diaper rash—the poor thing. It's raised and patchy, a yeast rash. They dab him with Vaseline and wrap him in a towel; the hospital will have diapers. Her keys on the red hook. Sophy kisses Annie's nose through the screen Hattie should really have replaced with a storm door by now—Sophy pinning her hair back with both hands. She looks to be putting her ears on. Then the engine, the headlights. Hattie's distance glasses. And there, as she turns the car around: Chhung, sitting in the guard chair in the moonlight. The trees behind him glint as if with frost; his white brace, too, glows dully. His cigarette flares orange. He himself is more shadow than substance, though, like the shovel Hattie can barely make out. It grows out of the dirt beside him like a plant. He is going to go to hell! says Sophy, beside her. He is! He is going to go to hell!

Mam-mam-lehla-la! agrees Gift.

Ratanak Chhung, the lucky one.

The one who got sent to the temple school; the one who lived.

Hattie turns her headlights back off as they roll by.

The coming of Sophy's sisters, three days later, is not subdued. What with the blue car in the shop, Sophy asks if Hattie will pick them up at the bus station; and so it is that Hattie gets to behold Sophan and Sopheap teetering down the bus steps. Shouting, Mum! Sophy! Gift! Sophy! as they try not to trip in their high heels. Their knees are too high, their thighs are too short. The railing's in the wrong place. They are carrying too many bags—some three or four bright bags each. Which mostly have shoulder straps, a sign of some sense, except that several of the straps have slipped off the girls' shoulders and are fanning out midair. Sophy and Hattie try to help take the bags, Sophy shouting, Sophan! Sopheap! at the same time—making enough of a commotion that people stop to watch. But of course, the girls would be a sight anyway—three Sophys, it does seem—the three of them almost exactly the same height, as if that were the fashion, with the same flat behinds and the same narrow waists. And the same shy energy—as if they could either bubble up or disappear, depending. They are smooth-skinned, bright-eyed, live-bodied; their hands seem to be everywhere. Sophan looks more like Chhung, and Sopheap and Sophy more like Mum, but Sophan and Sopheap look like each other, too, with chipmunk-red hair they've had straightened; it falls silken and perfect, awaiting a ruffling wind. Sophy's hair, in comparison, is bedlam. And yet anyone would know the three of them to be sisters by their happiness. Sophan and Sopheap play with Sophy's short hair, amazed; and when she cries, they wipe her eyes for her, crying, too, then cup her radiant face in their hands—their fingers on her cheeks, in her hair. They fondle her earringless ears. No hoops! Sophy shrugs and laughs through her tears. And look—Mum is crying, too. The girls hug their mother gingerly. With Sophy they are babble and arms. With Mum they seem worried they could squeeze her into another shape by mistake. They move their warmth out of their limbs, into their faces; it's what hippies say energy workers do. Move their energy. Still their bodies. The sisters' eyes get large and liquid; they tilt their heads. Nod. Say something in Khmer, consult with Sophy, say something else. Their smiles grow and grow—their mouths widening, their cheeks lifting, their eyes crinkling. Then they nod again, lowering their gaze, until time itself seems to be blossoming with joy. For there is Mum, looking for once unbuffeted by the world. No larger than she was, but more firmly here somehow. Not a half-being whose other half may still be hiding out from the war; not a half-ghost undecided about her commitment to this moment and place. Instead, she is the slightly undersized, perfectly whole being on whom the natural order of things lightly rests—reserved, as always, except for her face, which has something of the look of an extra bus headlight.

Now Gift is threatening to cry, excited to be held by Sopheap and Sophan, but scared of them, too. You don't remember us! they say. You've forgotten us! Sophy tries to take him back, but Sophan and Sopheap will not let him go until he starts out-and-out wailing. Then back he goes to Mum, his crying stopping so abruptly that everyone laughs, even Gift himself, after a moment. And who's this? Ginny? ask the sisters. *Ginny.* No, Hattie, says Sophy. This is Hattie. So nice to meet you, say Sophan and Sopheap then. So nice, Hattie!—never mind that a bus station official is telling them to move out of the way, please, no one can get by. Sophan and Sopheap and Sophy come together for a moment. Then Sophy is hoisting Gift onto her hip, and

Sophan and Sopheap are flanking their mother, each insisting on taking an arm even as they refuse to let Hattie help with the bags. The group keeps having to rest, rehoist, rearrange, reseat. Rest again. Yet still they refuse Hattie's help—half shuffling, half tottering through the bus station like some newfangled pushmi-pullyu. They rest. Then it is across the parking lot to the car, where Sophan and Sopheap can finally quiz Sophy some more. Why'd you do that to your hair? I told you. No, you didn't. And you didn't tell me, either! I did! You didn't! They pull and tease until Sophy finally swats their hands away. Happy to be annoyed, happy to be swatted back, happy to return the return swat. A sister, still, though wisps of hair play about Sophan's and Sopheap's eyes and necks—a sister, though they are wearing makeup and chains and hoops, and cute tops with tight jeans. Sopheap's hoodie is red with AMOUR printed across the front; inside she is wearing a white top with red trim. Sophan's top is sparkly—midnight blue with metallic trim. Only Sophy, the country mouse, is wearing a plain blue sweater and plain blue sweatpants. Still, she swats at them, a sister. Who does still wear a necklace, at least—her sisters play with the cross—and though she never takes it off, she takes it off now and lets them try it on. First Sophan, then Sopheap, who wants to wear it awhile. She wants to see if it makes her feel anything, she says, and so Sophy lets her borrow it for the whole drive back to the trailer.

It's a squeeze, getting the three girls and Gift into the backseat of what is, after all, a subcompact car, but they don't mind. They insist that Sophy sit in the middle, Gift on her lap. Everything is in English. In the front seat Mum faces forward, but with her chin lifted high and her head tipped back.

"Can you understand them?" asks Hattie.

Mum moves her head in something like a nod, though not a nod, either—picking up words, Hattie guesses, a phrase here and there. Every now and then the girls say something in Khmer, but Sopheap and Sophan do not speak as much Khmer as Sophy; mostly it is English, English, English. What is there to do around here? they want to know. They don't like Sophy's Christian radio station; Hattie happily shuts it off. Wow, cows, they say then. Why do they have those yellow things in their ears? And what's that smell? They roll their windows up; they hold their noses and point. What's that? They are impressed that Sophy knows what a pony is. A llama.

"They have mad ears," says Sophan. She asks if dogs pull people on sleds around here.

Sopheap and Sophy laugh. "No, no," they say. "That's Alaska!"

Sophan, though, is still curious. "Do people here burn wood to keep warm?"

It is a few minutes before Sopheap finally says, "So, like, Sarun is in the hospital?"

Sophy nods.

"And, like, what happened? Dad beat Sarun up and somebody called the police?" Sopheap asks lightly, in a just-wondering voice.

"Yeah, except it wasn't somebody." Sophy noses Gift's back. "It was me."

"You?" says Sophan.

Silence.

"Because there was blood everywhere, you should have seen," says Sophy, finally. "And, anyway, I didn't call the police. I called 911."

More silence. The windshield darkens, then brightens—the car passing through the shadow of a cloud.

"Wow," says Sopheap.

"Those are cool cows," says Sophan.

The cows are black except for what look like huge white cummerbunds fitted around their bellies.

"They're called Dutch belted cows," says Sophy. "Because of, like, their belt." She lays Gift down flat across her knees, so that his head is on Sophan's lap and his feet on Sopheap's.

"You shouldn't feel bad that you called," says Sopheap.

"He was going to die," says Sophy.

"It was a good choice," says Sophan, playing with Gift's hands; he grabs her earrings anyway. "Ow."

"Definitely," says Sopheap.

Sophy, in the rearview mirror, is blinking hard, her nostrils red; she looks as though she might cry.

"Actually I made a lot of bad choices," she says. "Like a lot of them."

"Still," says Sophan. "That one was good." She nods supportively.

"And then what happened?" Sopheap pulls Gift's feet up to her cheeks; she kisses his toes.

"He got to the hospital and was bad but then he woke up and was talking. And everything was good until he had this big drop in blood pressure. Because of the bleeding in his head, I think it was called 'subdural.' Because it was, like, under his skull, and I guess *sub* means, like, 'under.' And that's why you guys were allowed to come visit. Because he was unconscious again and they thought he might die."

Sopheap stops playing.

"We were, like, mad scared," says Sophan. "When we were, like, informed."

"I guess it was pretty serious." Sophy jostles Gift on her knees. "But now he's okay, except that they had to drill these holes in his head."

Gift chortles.

"Holes?" says Sophan, finally. "In his head?"

"To drain the blood out."

"That is so wack," says Sopheap.

"It was," says Sophy. "It was wack. Anyway, it's still great you came. Because he has to stay flat on his back now and can't even, like, sit up to eat, and his head is half shaved and half regular. And he has this huge bandage and these things that, like, squeeze his legs all day. Wait till you see. And his roommate cuts these farts you will not believe."

The girls giggle. Sophy sits Gift back up straight.

"So Dad went wild?" says Sopheap.

"Because of the *puak maak*?" says Sophan.

"Yeah," says Sophy, handing Gift up to Mum for a visit. "Because, like, Sarun was supposed to stop seeing them when he came here, but he didn't. Like first they got us this TV and then they were e-mailing all the time and then Sarun was taking off with them in this van and doing shit. And that made Dad mad. Sarun gave him money, but he was still mad. And then the police came just to talk, but Dad, like, went wild. Because they came."

"Wow." Sophan folds her arms.

"Was he like an animal?" says Sopheap.

"I guess. I mean, that's what he said. That he was like an animal." Sophy stops. "It was actually really complicated, I wish I could explain it."

"You explained it." Sopheap's arms are folded, too.

"I don't know." Sophy's arms are jammed between her knees and her shoulders scrunched up. "Anyway, it made a big mess. Like there was blood everywhere. I thought we'd be cleaning forever, but Hattie hired somebody to come clean it for us. Like even though Mum does cleaning she hired someone anyway. So we could use that room when you came, and because it took, like, special carpet cleaner."

"That was so nice of you." Sophan leans forward, grasping the headrest.

"It was nothing," says Hattie.

"She saw everything." Sophy looks straight at Hattie in the rearview mirror.

Hattie feels herself flush.

"That's so great," says Sopheap.

"When can we go see him?" asks Sophan.

"Tomorrow," says Sophy. "If anyone asks, you're supposed to say it was break and entry. Like it was a stranger, we don't know why."

"We don't know nothing," says Sopheap.

"*Nada,*" says Sophan.

"Zip," says Sopheap.

"He couldn't remember anything when he first started talking, and that was lucky, because that way we got to tell him what he should say. Of course, he said he wouldn't have told the blues nothing anyway. He said even if he had no brain left, he'd know better than to talk."

"*Meh-meh-a-lala!*" says Gift, standing up in Mum's lap. He bends and straightens his legs; they really need to get him a carseat. "*Beh-bahb-ba!*"

"And one good thing is that the hospital saw him for free," Sophy goes on. "I mean, they knew he didn't have insurance but they saw him anyway. Free care, they call it."

"Cool," says Sopheap.

"*Bababababehbehbeh,*" says Gift.

Hattie makes Sophy take Gift back to the relative safety of the backseat.

"So how do you like school here?" asks Sophan.

"Are you really going to a church school?" asks Sopheap.

Hattie helps them bring their stuff in but does not see them again until they are gathered outside a little later, around Sophy and her guitar. Sophy plays "I Surrender All"; Sophan and Sopheap listen with their arms folded, then start doing dance routines. *Flaunting their fertility,* Lee would say. *Grinding their gynecologicals.* Sophy focuses for a while on her playing, her eyes on her fingers as she reaches for certain tough chords. In the end, though, she breaks into a tune Hattie thinks she recognizes from the radio but can't quite place—the theme to that *Titanic* movie, maybe?

The blue car does the driving the next couple of days. By the time it breaks down again, Sophy's sisters, to Hattie's surprise, have already gone back to their foster homes. Her lone passenger is Sophy, who sports Sopheap's sparkly hoodie and big hoop earrings. It's misty out; corkscrews of steam rise from the engine hood like genies.

"I'll have to give you Sarun's earrings," says Hattie. "The wires are a little bent, but we can fix them easy enough."

"You can give them back yourself if you want," says Sophy. "I mean, like, Sarun's been asking, when are you coming, anyway? Like yesterday he said, 'Where's the Vietnamese lady? Isn't she going to come spy?'"

Hattie laughs. "Tell him the Vietnamese lady will come in with you soon."

"He says he wants cookies."

"Will do," says Hattie.

Sophy cracks open the window. Cool air charges in but their feet stay warm, thanks to the heat—the blower blowing on them like a mini-desert wind.

"How's he doing?" asks Hattie.

"He hates that neck thing."

"The collar, you mean."

"He says it's like Dad's brace came off and got wrapped around his neck instead. But anyway, his hair's growing in already, and they're taking the bandage off pretty soon, and the stitches are supposed to, like, melt by themselves."

"And what's the prognosis?"

"Is that, like, prediction?"

"Exactly."

Sophy tucks her hair behind her ear; the earring catches in it. "His *prognosis* is great. Like he can see okay and his memory is fine and he talks as terrible as ever—I guess he talked ghetto to the doctors and scared them, but then he switched to normal and they laughed."

Hattie smiles. "And his vision?"

"Fine."

"How very very lucky." That shattered occipital bone, after all,

with his occipital lobe just below it—his primary visual cortex—
Hattie shudders.

"The surgeon said time will tell but that he has good karma. He
said my mom must've built it up for him." Sophy turns the radio
on herself, surprising Hattie; maybe it's something she does in the
blue car?

"Is the doctor Buddhist?"

"Jewish, I think. But he knew a lot about it. Like he was asking
what Theravada Buddhism meant. I guess he only knew about
Mahayana, because it's, like, more popular."

"It must be hard that your sisters went back."

"I wish they could have stayed."

"Your mom, too, I bet."

"My mom?" Sophy loosens her seat belt, freeing her kangaroo
pocket.

"Wishes they could've stayed, I mean."

The children don't stay.

"Yeah, well, Sophan's home was cool about her staying longer,
but Sopheap's home wanted her back, like, immediately, I guess
because they were traveling unsupervised, and once this other girl
went home and got in trouble. And Sophan and Sopheap wanted to
go back if they were supposed to, so they could get out of there on
time. Like they were trying to make the right choice for a change."

"That's great."

"I guess." Sophy moves her hands around in the pocket. "Anyway, it was a lot of godless chatter with them around."

"That may be," says Hattie carefully, "but wasn't it great?"

"I don't know." Out pops a hand; Sophy plays with an earring.
"It was complicated."

"I bet."

"But it was great, too, I guess." She gives a lopsided smile. "They
liked you."

"I liked them."

"Really." Sophy leans over, inspecting herself in the side-view
mirror—something else she's never done before. "They think you're
all right."

"Do they?"

"It's true. They liked you a lot more than they liked Ginny."

"Did they really?" Hattie tries not to smile too broadly, though she can feel the dopamine levels rise in her brain; it is a wonderful drive.

Of course, they've driven together, just the two of them, before. As Joe used to say, though, *Contraries are known by contraries;* what with Sophy's sisters gone, the car seems far quieter to Hattie than it used to. And maybe to Sophy, too, because she seems to be trying to fill up the air.

"I don't think they really even understood what happened until they saw Sarun in the hospital," she says chattily.

"Do you understand what happened?"

"I think my dad has PTSD. You turn left here."

"Sarun's not in the main building?"

"He's in the new one."

"Ah. I bet you're right about the PTSD. Do you know what that is, exactly?"

Hattie expects her to say yes or no, but instead Sophy says, "Ginny said you wanted something from us, but I never could figure out what it was."

"Really." Hattie turns on the wipers; Sophy closes her window.

"She said that one day I'd know and that it would be like a rock rolled back."

"Did she." Hattie musters up her courage. "I guess I'd have to say," she says, "that I'm just a lonely old bat." The windshield wipers go.

"You go right at the light."

Hattie puts on her turn signal. "I'm an old retired lady with a dead husband and a faraway son and no sisters. I've got Reveille and Annie, as you know. And I've got friends. But first Joe died two years ago and then my best friend went, right after him. Her name was Lee." She stops. "And now Cato."

"That sounds hard." Sophy hits an adult note even as she flicks her zipper toggle up and down.

"It is. Joe was a good man. And Lee was wonderful. Funny." Hattie makes her turn. "For a long time, I wished that I'd died, too."

"You should go to church more."

"I go every week, just about," says Hattie. "And I go to the library. There are always warm bodies there. And my walking group is great."

"Except for Ginny."

"She's not my favorite," admits Hattie. "And you know, there's no getting around the fact that I need other people more than they need me. I'm just not an integral part of anyone's picture, if you know what I mean."

She makes her turn, expecting Sophy to ask her what "integral" means, but instead Sophy says, "You mean you're old."

"Yes. In a way." Hattie nods. "Though you'd have to say I was always old, then. Or that I've been old longer than most people. Or that coming to America made me old."

Sophy doesn't ask Hattie what she means by any of that, either. Instead, she plays with her cross. "Sarun didn't steal any plywood, you know," she says suddenly.

And Hattie is just as suddenly grateful that she is in such a concertedly even frame of mind. "That was Ginny's idea, wasn't it?" she asks, coolly. "To blame him."

"It was. But he didn't do it."

"Don't I turn left up here?"

"At the light."

The wipers squeak on their downward stroke.

"She wanted to blame him because whoever got blamed for the plywood might just get blamed for the fire, too," guesses Hattie. "And she wanted to burn down the mini-mall to get Everett. Is that it?"

Sophy nods, more open now than Hattie has ever seen her. "How do you know everything? I told Sopheap and Sophan that, and they said you were just smart."

Hattie shakes her head. "I don't think so." She frowns.

"You keep going straight."

"Are you sure?"

"Oh, wait, you see? You know everything. Go right, kind of around that island."

Hattie steers. "I have a question about all that, though."

"You mean about the fire and everything?"

"Yes." Hattie glances sideways; Sophy's face is open and friendly. "Did you really think that would work—that people would link the fire and the stealing in the end? Without evidence? Did you really think Sarun and his friends would be convicted when they were innocent? Just because they were strangers and made people nervous?"

Sophy slumps a little, her hands back in her hoodie pocket. "I don't know. I mean, sure. I mean it was, like, Jesus's plan, so . . ." She shrugs. "Ginny said we were like Esther, put where we were put for a reason, we just had to look at what we were given and, like, try to figure out what it was. Like it was a puzzle."

"And you let her try to pin it on Sarun because he was ruining things for your family. Is that it?"

"I guess. Straight."

"Because here your family was, starting over, and he was driving your dad crazy. Messing things up with his gang. Disturbing things."

"He was no good."

"And this was a chance to stop him."

"The Lord gave us this chance—I believe that. I mean, why else would He have sent the white van, right? Why else would He drive it right up to our trailer and put it right under our noses? Why else would He have terrorists attack America so people would believe anything?"

Why else would He have terrorists attack America.

"You mean, spooking people so they would believe almost anything about that scary van," says Hattie, slowly.

Sophy nods. "I mean, the terrorists were probably sent to help a lot of people with a lot of things, not just us," she says.

"The Lord God acting with divine efficiency."

Sophy nods again.

"His plan," says Hattie, "just happening to accord with your hopes."

Sophy nods a third time.

"Because your father didn't want Sarun anymore, and you didn't, either."

"I told my sisters the whole thing was my fault, but they said I was too sensitive. Like how could it be my fault, they said, just like they didn't think they ended up in foster homes because of me, they said they just did stupid things themselves. Like the time Sopheap stole that car with her boyfriend. She said that was her own stupid decision, she just wishes somebody had told her she'd end up in a foster home for it. And Sophan said she was stupid to break into people's houses and, like, try on their clothes and listen to their stereos and shit. She didn't even steal stuff, but it was break and entry anyway, and they definitely should not have snorted any of the people's coke. Like that was just so stupid. And when I said didn't they feel that people looked down on them because of me, they said that was no excuse. They said they made bad choices and didn't think about the consequences. And now they're making, like, different choices. Like Sopheap says she's going to be an independent woman and not get married or have children or anything. She says in ancient Cambodia women were more powerful than men, and that she's going to go back to that and be like a she-man." She makes a muscle.

Hattie laughs. "Wonderful. But this thing with Sarun really is your fault, you're saying."

"It is." Sophy's eyes suddenly fill. "I'm no good, Hattie. I'm not even a real older sister. Like when I was talking to my sisters, they sounded so much smarter than me—like they sounded older than me, instead of my being older than them. And look at the mess I made. I should never have been born."

"Oh, Sophy." Hattie pulls into a parking spot and turns her engine off. "You know, part of this may be your fault, but what about Ginny?" She digs some tissues out from the between-seat storage compartment. "Hasn't Ginny sinned, too? I mean, who set the fire, right?"

"I set it." Sophy blows her nose.

Hattie shuts the compartment lid.

"I did. I set it," Sophy says again. "Do you see what I mean? How wack I am? Do you see?"

"Did Ginny help?"

"She showed me how to strike a match."

"Was she there when you did it?"

"No."

"Did she drive you there?"

"No."

"Sophy." Hattie speaks slowly, clearly, as if she is talking to Mum. "Did you know what you were doing? Did you know it was wrong?"

"I thought it was Christ's plan."

"You were like Esther, and Sarun was like Haman."

"He was, he was like Haman—like he didn't like anyone doing things different than him, or following different laws. He couldn't tolerate difference."

He couldn't tolerate difference.

"He couldn't tolerate holiness," Sophy goes on. "He wanted to kill it because he knew he was doing bad things."

"Was it drugs?"

"Bear stuff. Bear paws and bear—what do you call it—gallbladders. You know, like people use for traditional medicine. I guess the paws are for soup or something. The gang got them from the hunters and brought them up to some guy in Canada—it was all Sarun's idea. I mean, some of the *puak maak* knew guys who did it in Cambodia, I guess in Cambodia there were guys who, like, sold stuff to Hong Kong and Korea, places like that. But it was Sarun who realized they could do the same thing here." Sophy blows her nose again.

"He was the mastermind."

Sophy nods with energy—as if despite herself she's a little proud of Sarun. "The *puak maak* liked it because it was a new gig. Like they didn't have to compete with a zillion other gangs, it was theirs."

"Is it illegal?"

"I don't know. Probably."

"So why didn't you turn him in for that? Why try to get him for plywood the gang didn't even steal? Or did they."

Sophy folds up her tissue so she can wipe her nose on a fresh part. "I don't think so."

"Was it because you'd have to act by yourself on the bear parts? Whereas this way you had company?"

"I don't know." Sophy looks genuinely confused. "I mean, it just didn't seem like that was what Jesus wanted, I guess. Like Jesus sent me Ginny, and that wasn't what Ginny wanted, so it didn't seem like that's what He wanted. It didn't seem like the reason we were given what we were given."

"I see. But let me ask you—did Ginny make you help her? This is important, Sophy. Did she make you?"

"No." Another flash of pride. "I wanted to, I wanted to be like Esther. I knew Jesus would give us victory, I knew that He'd protect us." Sophy's face is blank, but her voice is strong. "I knew He'd be with us when we passed through the water and the fire. I knew He'd make sure we wouldn't get, like, drowned or burned."

"Or caught?"

Sophy slumps. "Anyway, that guy was building on the wrong foundation."

"You mean Everett?"

Sophy nods.

" 'For other foundation can no man lay than that is laid, which is Jesus Christ,' " quotes Hattie. "Is that it?"

Sophy unfastens her seat belt.

"How does it go after that?" Hattie looks up, undoing her belt, too. " 'Every man's work shall be made manifest; for it shall be revealed by fire.' Something like that. First Corinthians."

"You know a lot of scripture."

"I can't always remember what happened yesterday, but I remember my scripture from when I was a girl. Oh, wait, I'm missing part of it. 'For the day shall declare it, because it shall be revealed by fire; and the fire shall try every man's work of what sort it is.' "

"I'll never be as good as you."

"Of course you will, if you want to be. But tell me—you've heard that verse before?"

Sophy hesitates but then nods.

"From Ginny," guesses Hattie.

"She said Everett was meddling with God and should know better!" Sophy says. "Like he should know that verse 'Forbear thee from meddling with God' something something—"

" 'Forbear thee from meddling with God, who is with me, that He destroy thee not.' "

Sophy plays with her toggle. "I just wish someone would destroy me," she says, in a small voice. "I do. I wish someone would put me in jail."

"What about a foster home again? Or a girls' group home? I don't think they're going to put you in jail, Sophy."

Sophy presses her tissue to her eyes. "I made a bad choice," she cries. "I made a bad choice." Her earrings swing.

Hattie puts a hand on her hoodied back; Sophy's whole body is shaking.

"I should have listened to you. Why didn't I listen to you? I loved Annie so much!"

"Annie loved you, too," says Hattie. "And still does, you know."

But Sophy does not hear her. "I am ashamed to have been born," she sobs. "I am. There's no reason for me to live. I'm sorry I was ever born."

"Don't say that," says Hattie, but there's no stopping Sophy. She cries even as the clouds start to part and thin and lift; she cries even as visiting hours end and Hattie starts up the car. There is nothing to do but fill up the gas tank and head home.

. . .

Hattie might as well have told the walking group that Town Hall had fallen down. People seem to have turned into salt or stone or bronze—so resembling a life-size sculpture of themselves that Hattie can picture a little plaque next to them, with a title: THE NEWS.

"These are serious charges," says Greta.

"Thank goodness Ginny is out of town," says Candy. "Thank goodness the Lord spared her this."

"I think I'm going to have a brownie with ice cream," says Grace.

"Grace!" says Beth. "You are not!"

"With hot fudge sauce," continues Grace. "And whipped cream and nuts. Anyone who wants a bite is welcome to it."

Flora brings them five spoons; and within minutes only the cherry sits unclaimed, its fluorescent red bleeding into a last bit of whipped cream. They order a second sundae.

"Is everything all right?" asks Flora.

Yes, they say, but when her back is turned, they go back to morosely sharing their dessert. The table wobbles; no one fixes it. Neither does anyone comment on the new bear-shaped honey dispensers that now grace every table. This is just so disturbing, says Greta instead. If it's even true, says Candy. Beth's gut says Ginny's innocent.

"A flip-flopper," she says, her voice too loud. "The girl's a flip-flopper."

Greta objects. How can they call Sophy a flip-flopper when they never even asked her themselves about Sarun's gang?

"It was Ginny who said they were the plywood thieves. Sophy never said that," she reminds everyone.

Beth sets her elbows on the table just the same. "Before it was plywood; now it's bear parts," she says. "Before she hanged her brother; now she's hanging Ginny. That is just a fact."

Hattie looks at her. On the one hand, you couldn't say Carter broke Beth's heart. On the other, how hard it must be that, even with things so rocky with Jill, Carter never seems to have given Beth a thought. *Nothing's harder than nothing,* Uncle Jeremy used to say, back when Hattie was awaiting word about her family in China. Now Beth's not only cutting her hair short-short, but growing more no-nonsense, too—not to say less inclined, it does seem, to indulge pretty young girls in whom people take an interest.

"If Sophy were trying to hang Ginny," says Greta, "why would she insist that she herself was guilty?"

"Because Ginny didn't do anything and she knows it," says Beth.

"Beth," says Hattie, gently. "That doesn't make sense."

Reaching for the great gavel of logic. And of course, catching someone in a contradiction would have stopped everything at the lab. Here, though, it stops nothing.

"If even Sophy thinks she's guilty, why shouldn't we turn her in?" asks Candy.

"Because she's Cambodian?" says Beth. "Because she's an immigrant?"

"She's fifteen," says Greta.

"Her brain's not fully developed," says Hattie. "Her dorsolateral prefrontal cortex isn't in."

"Does that mean she didn't know what she was doing?" asks Beth.

"Consequences," says Candy. "It's really important that kids get taught consequences."

"Tell me you honestly think she had no idea what she was doing," says Beth.

"She thought she was doing the will of God," says Hattie. "She thought the whole thing was God's plan. She even thought the bombing of the World Trade Center was His plan—making people so nervous, they would believe anything, she said."

How sorry she is that she told the group anything! Why did she tell them? What was she thinking?

Now Candy at least hesitates. "The will of God." She rucks up her mouth.

"She thought she was doing the will of God but said later it was a bad choice," says Hattie.

"So she knew she had a choice." Beth gestures with a french fry.

"Later. She knew later," says Hattie. "I don't know how she could have thought she had a choice if it was the will of God. And I don't know that she wasn't manipulated into believing that to begin with."

"Of course, she was manipulated," says Greta.

"And of course she would be vulnerable to that," puts in Grace. "Think of her background."

"Because she's Cambodian!" says Beth again. "Because she's an immigrant!"

Candy makes up her mind. "If you want to know what's wrong with this country, I can tell you," she says—her left cortex resolving things willy-nilly, Hattie knows. Producing "coherence" at any cost. It's anything but rational. And yet, Candy's conviction is palpable: Her small eyes blaze; she looks about to burst out of herself. "What's happened to us that we are so afraid to say what's right and what's wrong?" she demands. "What's happened?"

"Nothing's happened," says Grace.

But Candy is on a tear. "This is what's the matter with us," she says. "This is why other people hate us."

"Why, because we think?" says Greta. "Why, because we are honest about the complexities of things?"

"Are you trying to say the terrorists are right?" says Grace.

"She's saying," says Beth, "that she can see their point of view."

And Candy agrees. "I can. I can see their point of view. We have gone wrong!" Her thin voice hammers.

Silence.

"Maybe it's you who have gone wrong," says Hattie, finally.

Flora slips them the check.

Everett: What Went Wrong, Now

In an ideal world, this shack would be out on the ice instead of in the air—a fishing shanty instead of a tree house. In an ideal world, he'd be pulling up the smelt instead of hanging out with the birds, wishing the wind would not howl so loud. Wishing he'd put in a stovepipe that vented right no matter which way the wind was blowing instead of only some ways. And maybe wishing some other things while he was at it, what the heck. And that that Cambodian kid'd get out of the hospital all right. That'd be one. That Ginny'd turn back into the girl he married. That'd be another. What the heck. 'Cause used to be, she was this sweet gal. Used to be, she was a gal no one would ever imagine getting mixed up with the Cambodian girl the way she did. Pursuing her. And causing his trouble, too, he's going to guess. The fire, everything, somehow. Causing it.

Causing it somehow.

What went wrong, now. He's talking about what went wrong. How a sweet gal got to be so angry the way she did.

What went wrong.

When she was born again, Ginny used to draw these pictures showing her life before and after. Two little circles, she'd draw, with a throne in the middle of each one. The before circle'd be her life, with an *E* in the throne, standing for herself. For her ego, she'd say—the part of her that was self-centered. The part that was all about me. Christ would be there in the circle, too, but He'd be kind of floating around along with other things she was doing. Cooking, working, driving the kids to baseball. They'd all be these dots floating all over. Until she took Jesus Christ for her Lord and asked Him to rule her life, she'd say. And then there'd be the after circle, see, with Christ on the throne. Her ego'd be off to the side, and everything she did would be arranged in a circle, like they were minute dots on a clock. Organized, so you could draw a line from them to Christ in the middle. And that'd be her new life, now. Organized.

That was the story she told.

But the way he saw it, her before life wasn't any near so disorganized as that. Or maybe it was sometimes. But other times it was organized around the farm. The farm was on the throne. And whether or not his life used to be disorganized, it's organized, too, now, see. Around telling why.

What happened. What went wrong. Why. It's on his throne, now, right smack in the middle of the picture. 'Course, there's folks would say that ain't grand enough for a throne. Folks who'd say that ain't like the Lord. Just like there's folks who only want to go forward. They don't ever want to go back. Look back. Understanding—they don't care about understanding.

Well, he's past caring now. He is. Everyone's got to pick what sits on his throne, and he's picked the truth. How it started with the farm, and with Ginny's pa. Rex the Farmer King, they called him. And he's going to tell it now, the whole darned thing. How Ginny got to be what she was. What happened. It ain't all straightforward, but what the heck. He's going to tell it anyway. He is.

Let's just say it's his idea of heaven.

It is.

In an ideal world, Ginny's pa's barn would be full of hay and that'd be a lot of hay, now. Rex once figured his barn could hold fifteen thousand bales. Think on it. Fifteen thousand bales. That did seem a big number even before he, Everett, ever came to help load an entire barn himself. And since he's had that honor, well, it's just gotten bigger. Heavier. Even for a big guy like him, it was a job. See, you're tired already from all the cutting and the tedding. The raking. The baling. You're tired. Then it's load, load, load. Theirs was the old-fashioned bale you get with an old-fashioned baler. The kind of baler that rams the hay into bricks, and then ties 'em up with twine. The kind where you can still see the hay. Lot of farmers did go with the new balers some time back—thought they were quicker. More modern. Nowadays you see those round plastic bales all over. But come to find out lately, critters get in there and putrefy. How do you like that. Seeing as they're all sealed up with no air, they putrefy. And from that you get disease. Botulism. They say you can't give that hay to horses. Horses're too sensitive. But the fact is, it'll kill a cow, too. It will. So folks are backing off those new balers. Coming back to the old-fashioned bales, where if a critter gets in, it'll mummify. Where it'll dry up and get crunchy, maybe, but that's all. It'll mummify.

Folks are coming back.

Old Rex'd have had a good laugh over that one.

'Course, old style or new, loading was work. But at the end you'd look up and see all that hay. And that was something, all right. Stacks and stacks, it'd be, stacks and stacks. Stepped up, so's you could climb on up to the top if you were inclined and have a look right out one of those little high windows, assuming it wasn't too cobwebbed. And you would have yourself quite a view, now. Quite a view. But Everett's always thought, even better's looking down. 'Cause it's a vast amount of hay, see. A vast amount. And ain't that the difference between people and cows, that people'd see winter coming and load up, where's all cows know is the hay's here or it ain't, it's fermented or it ain't. That's the older ones who'd know that. The older ones who get the sweet-smelling fermented on account of it's easier on their systems. The young'uns, now, they'd know something different. There's grain, too, or there ain't. That'd be what they know. Something different. 'Cause that's what they'd get, some grain with their hay on account of they were growing. Probably the cows know there's timothy in the hay or there ain't, now, too. Clover. A little mummy. They know. But people are the thinkers that would ever get the notion of building this vast thing to store hay in, see. The cows'd never have any such idea. They would not.

They're escape artists, though, those cows. You wouldn't think so to look at them. 'Cause they're big. Big as cows, Rex used to say. But big as they are, they can get through the fence in a wink. Big as they are, they know every hole in the fence, those cows. They know every hole that ain't even a hole but a hole coming up eventually. Potential. They understand potential. Smart as they are, though, a man like Rex was smarter. Rex could tell you where they escaped to, see. 'Cause they did not escape to the same place every time, now. Nope. That would make things too easy, if they escaped to the same place every time. Nope, some liked certain places and some liked others, and some liked certain places depending on something, and other places depending on something else. Say it just cleared. They might like a certain corner then, but if there was a bunch of them and not just one, they might like another corner. Or if it was cloudy. Cows don't like to go from light to dark, see. So they might avoid a certain dell on a sunny day, but head straight on over there if it was cloudy. Those cows could send you tramping around until you were plain worn out, they could. They could send you to the nuthouse. But Rex, now, Rex never would have to tramp around. 'Cause Rex could think like a cow, see. He could. He could think like a cow. Even after he got sick, he'd just sort of wake up sometimes and say, What about by the ditch? Or else, Them puddles. They're not going to like them puddles. One time he asked if Everett was wearing a yellow raincoat. Told him to leave it home. And Everett did, see. Didn't ask why, he just did it. 'Cause he knew Rex.

He knew him.

Folks said Rex's pa had the ability, too. Said his pa knew where a cow would go before the cow knew it itself. Said his pa could intercept it on the way. And, who knows, probably Rex's boys had it, too. That knack. Probably they had it, too. They just didn't know 'cause they moved to the city first thing. First chance they got, they moved. And maybe they knew where the cabs were going to go, or where the traffic jams were going to be. The breakdowns. Maybe they knew. But if they did, no one knew it, see. No one said it. Two boys, Rex had, Jarvis and Bob. Good kids. They never did talk about it, though. Cows and whether they could think like them. They just kind of stayed off the subject. Stayed off the subject of the farm in general. What was going to happen to the farm. They stayed off it.

No one would've guessed it'd be Ginny who'd come back in the end. The girl. But in the end it was, now, see.

The girl. A farmerette.

No one would've guessed it.

. . .

Everett was not a city boy, like Jarvis and Bob got to be. He grew up in the country. A country boy. But him and his dad were jacks-of-all-trades, see. Handymen. They'd fix your car if it broke down, get it out of a ditch if it fell in one. Fix your glasses, too, if in the course of taking care of the automobile you sat on 'em. Anything. Mostly, though, they did electric work. Wiring. 'Cause a lot of places had these bad wires, see. Mice'd eat 'em. Water'd corrode 'em. And guys'd try and fix 'em even if they had no earthly idea what was positive and what was negative. The old-timers, especially. The old-timers liked to hook things up and tape 'em. Kind of a Sunday-afternoon thing. Everett and his pa'd have to go straighten things out before their places burnt down. 'Course, his pa never would say much, on account of his accent. But folks appreciated that, now, see. They appreciated it that he'd just fix what was wrong and not say what they did stupid. And they appreciated it that he'd do other stuff while he was out there, too, if they asked him. Get out the patch kit if they had a cracked tub. Do their sash cords if their sash cords were snapped. It was all stuff they could do if they got around to it, was how they thought of it. If they had the time. Busy, they always said how busy they were. Implying they had more important affairs going than his pa. But his pa didn't care. He wasn't proud. He was from Hungary, see. He knew what hard times were. Communism. War. Never mind that back in the old country his family were teachers. Lawyers. He wasn't proud. Food before pride, he'd say. Food before pride.

That's why their family ate. As much as they wanted, every day.

Ginny was the first kind of hungry Everett ever knew.

He was proud of her from the first. Proud that folks knew her family. Knew their farm. That eighty acres they had—fields, mostly. It was good land. Level enough for around here. But now even with that good land they couldn't make a living off just farming it, see. Too cold up here. Season's too short. And the taxes just keep going up and up. Price of grain, price of equipment, everything. Up and up. That's why you see more and more of the great old farms with little developments at their edge, chewing up their fenders. They're getting nibbled up, see. Nibbled up. First the barn roofs get rusty. Then there's a spell of bad weather. Then comes some other country messing up the market. Mexico. Argentina. Places you never thought of. But next thing you know folks're forced to sell off land to pay their taxes, see. It's happened to most everybody, just about. Excepting Ginny's family. Ginny's family was the exception that never did have to do that. 'Cause Rex always found another way now. Or a lot of ways—he had a lot of ways. Kept some sugar bush so he could sugar in the springtime, for instance. He'd sell off his softwood for pulp, too, when the opportunity came up. Sell off his spruce and fir. And he did some real estate in addition. Had him a little business. Rex Realty. For a long time, just about all the farmers used him. Time to see the king, they'd say when they were in trouble. Time to see His Highness.

He was something in his time, Old Rex. He was something.

Everyone said it.

The real estate was a natural for him, seeing as he knew everyone and they knew him. No one ever had to tell him there was land coming up. He knew it like he knew the cows. Who was going to be selling. How many acres. He could see it before they saw it themselves. What they were going to have to get for it. 'Course, things changed once he got sick. But before he got sick he knew, and because he knew, he never did have to sell off land himself. Lost his pigs, once. Bank came and took 'em away. But he never had to sell off land. Other folks ran day and night and still could not hold on to their land. And, Rex, now, Rex ran day and night, too. Even with some good moves he ran. Day and night. But his moves were good. Effective. They were effective.

And back when they were in high school, Ginny was queen of all that, see. She dressed like everyone. Ate like everyone. You couldn't have called her uppity. But you could feel it, that she was what you call a have. Everett's pa said yes to everything. Other folks said no. Ginny said yes or no, depending. She could help with the car wash or she could not. She could help with homecoming or she could not. A compact girl, she was, back then, solid but light, with bean-green eyes and dirty-blond hair. Folks said she looked like her mother. A Frenchie. Died when Ginny was eight of something, Everett never did know what. All he knew was that Ginny smiled or not depending on whether she felt a smile coming on, and when it first began to seem that he was the boy who made those smiles come on, well, now, he was happy as Christmas Day.

Their very first date they danced all night with each other and no one else down at the Grange Hall. Right with Judy Perry and Randy

Little and Sue Ann Horn all looking, they danced. Belle Tollman. 'Course, back then the Grange had no electric. All they had was them gas lamps with them net hearts. You ever see how they breathe? How they pulse, like they're on fire and not on fire? Well, him and Ginny were like that. Burning and burning and yet not burning up, somehow, just like he was himself and not himself. Everything was strange. He danced just fine even though nobody would have called him a dancer before that, and his palms did not sweat even though they always did. Guess she was such a light-footed thing, she just pulled him along somehow. And when they left the Grange Hall, they just started out strolling, hand in hand—hand in hand, just like that. As if that was their habit. As if they didn't have to decide it. Though, well, her hand was so soft and dry, he could not pretend that that was ordinary. Because in fact, he thought it wondrous. A wondrous hand. Warm. He would not have believed you could feel a person's heart in their hand, but it turned out, you could. Made him want to live forever, now. He wanted to live forever, holding her hand.

They walked down through downtown and then up toward the farms. Not heading anywhere. Just walking. But knowing it was pitch black, too. Knowing it. 'Course those country roads were good necking—you didn't exactly have to go find yourselves a spot. For miles it was just the stars and the tall moving trees and the two of you, finding your way, you hoped, down your own road. Doing stuff you'd heard plenty about, but not enough, it turned out, when the time came. Well, he was nervous about that part. He was nervous. But before he stopped, and turned, before he pulled her arm along his side and her hand to his back, he told her he was hers and always would be, and was not nervous about saying it at all. He was just stating the obvious. That she was his world. That he'd lay down his life for her. He didn't know where he got such ideas. But if she was surprised to hear it, she didn't let on, now. In fact, she didn't say anything right back at all. She just kissed him as if she couldn't help it. Not as if it was something she could do or not do, depending. She kissed him as if it was something she was born to do, and then she said it. That it was something she was born to do. That she had no doubt. It was good, it was right. She knew. Then they kissed again, and it was the easiest thing, see. Nobody tells you how the dark helps, or how bodies seek each other. What seekers they are. Her mouth was warm, what with the night cold all around them. And her body was warm, too, so warm he got tight in the groin right off. It was like they were being joined by a third party right off. Eager to get in on things. And what a time he was having trying not to breathe so loud. What a time. He was greatly hoping she would not notice, and she didn't seem to, but after a while, she did pull lightly away. A piece of tact that just made him love her even more. That made him dead grateful, in fact, as they started a bit haltingly home. 'Cause his condition would only have gotten worse. Mortifying—it would've gotten mortifying. As it was, every tree seemed to be mocking him as they walked, poking straight up like it did. The trees were mocking him. Still him and Ginny made it, holding hands, all the way to her pa's farm. Then he kissed her good night and waited at the bottom of the hill to see she got in safe. 'Course, he was hoping she'd turn and blow a kiss. He was hoping. She did not. But she did stand a bit in the door glass once she was in. Pulled back the curtain, knowing he'd be looking, now, and waved. Her shape outlined clear by the light, and he could have sworn she was pressing her body into the glass, too, like in a movie. Remembering.

Pressing.

Those were happy times, all right. They were happy times.

They got hitched when they got out of high school. Then he got drafted, right off the bat, and all of a sudden it was, Good-bye, young wife. All of a sudden it was, Hope I don't come back in a body bag.

Ginny cried till she couldn't see.

'Course, those were hard months in 'Nam, watching people get blown up. Sickening, now, the whole thing was sickening. He'd never smelled blood before, death. He'd never seen any of it. Wounds. Guts. Things hanging. And everything happening sudden—you never knew what was coming. Startling. It was startling. Hot. He could see why his pa never did talk about such things. His first assignment was to help flush out the Cu Chi tunnels outside Saigon. 'Cause the gooks had them these tunnels outside Saigon, these miles and miles of tunnels. Lived down there like worms, then popped up out of nowhere— gave 'em an advantage, see. A big advantage. They were tricky to catch. He had him a good dog to help sniff 'em out, though. Virgil. A German shepherd, smarter than most people. A sweet dog. Smart. But one patrol Virgil stepped on a mine and blew up right as Everett hit a booby trap himself. Took a wall of nails in his chest and had to be shipped home on a stretcher, now, see. Took 'em a year to get his insides put back. A year and ten kinds of docs.

And well, now, those were bad times, all right. Dispiriting times.
The kind of times that made you think about human nature, and animals. Beasts. Evil. Things you were better off not thinking about, to
be frank. Ginny nursed him like a baby, though. And come one day,
he was free to start life all over again in a city a little south. Ginny had
read about it in a magazine, see. Described it just about every day
while he was lying there in the hospital. What a cute place it was. Big
enough to have a movie house, but small enough to be livable, she
said. She liked that word, "livable." Neither one of them wanted to
live the way her brothers did, with no trees. But a movie house—well,
that did sound pretty good. Cafés. Less snow. They found themselves
an apartment to rent. Bought themselves a couch with their wedding
money, but made good use of cardboard boxes for most things until
such time as he could replace them. And that was a busy time, all
right, fashioning tables and chairs. A four-poster bed. Ginny liked all
kinds of turnings and carvings, and those things took time. Equipment. They took equipment. That was a hurdle right there. But
Everett got himself a job at an outfit called J. H. Moses, and at J. H.
Moses he got to be pals with a guy with a shop, see. Norbert. Thanks
to Norbert, Everett was able to turn and plane and hammer while
Ginny pinned and sewed and stuffed. And what do you know, in a
couple of years they had them as pretty a place as you could wish for.
Queen Anne chairs with needlepoint seats. A mahogany table with
ball-and-claw feet. That four-poster bed Ginny hung with real lace.
They even talked now and then about a rolltop desk. A rolltop desk's
quite an enterprise, now, but they did talk about it. Cubbies. How it'd
have all these cubbies.

And those were happy times, all right. Healing times. Look forward, Ginny'd say. You got to look forward. And, Try not to dream.
That was a good one. Try not to dream.

He was all right, now. He was. He was all right. Prickly. He was
prickly. He wasn't so great at relaxing, neither. But what the heck. He
was all right.

He was all right.

In his first job, besides the carpentry he'd done wiring. Some
tiling, too. Plumbing. He'd even rocked a bit, painted. He was a good
painter. A jack-of-all-trades, like his pa. Willing. His new job was just
carpentry. And that was all right, too, see. That was all right. He
didn't much like the sites they got put on, though. In his old job they'd
done in-law apartments and shed dormers. Kitchens. Family stuff.

But, now, J. H. Moses was different. J. H. Moses was more oriented toward the boss's house. Three-car garages. Jacuzzis. One lady had her a toilet that would spray your bottom when you were done with your business—had it shipped all the way from Japan. Guess they were pretty popular over there. In all his years, he'd never seen anything like it, and most of the guys felt similar. They had to try it out, they said. They did. But when he said that back where he came from, rich people had three-story barns, they hooted, too. Called him Farmer Everett. Even Norbert called him Farmer Everett. Asked if all that furniture he was making was what rich people liked back home. 'Cause it was very traditional, he said. Old-fashioned. He said his own wife liked contemporary.

Contemporary. All that equipment, and his wife liked contemporary.

Ginny got herself hired as a teacher's assistant, and when that went great, signed up for a college degree. 'Course, the degree took years and years. Books. It took books. Cost them half a barn, too. But come one day she marched right up on a stage in her cap and her gown, and didn't they all bust with pride then to have a college grad in the family. She got herself a job right off, now, too. Second grade. And what do you know, the kids loved her. The parents loved her. The other teachers loved her. They did.

But the principal had it out for her, see. A mean old bat she was, a shrunken-up skunk a pig wouldn't poke. She didn't like Ginny's lesson plans. She didn't like Ginny's bulletin boards. She didn't like Ginny's bicycle safety unit. 'Course, old Gertie was fired at the end of the year, but not before she fired Ginny first. Left a record so full of black marks, Ginny cried for months. Cried and cried. Everett tried to help keep her chin up, now. Pointed out there were other jobs in the world. Other schools. Helped her get herself out to those interviews at other schools with her chin up.

Nobody ever did hire her, though, see. So she went and tried to get pregnant instead. How'd you like a little baby, she'd say. How'd you like a baby Everett. She was ogling babies in the grocery store. Looking at all the cute baby things. But after all those years of being careful, they couldn't be careless enough, now, somehow. It was strange. She prayed on it. Went to church and asked for God's help. And a couple of times there she was late with her monthly, see. She was. But she was never late more than a couple of weeks, now. The thing just kept coming back. Coming back and coming back.

And those were discouraging times, see, no question. They were just discouraging.

Especially as back home in Riverlake, her pa was doing even worse than she was—had been for a while. 'Course, Old Rex never would have suggested it. He never would have. But the farm was too much for any man to keep running on his own, and the fact was, he was getting older. Or maybe his angina started up earlier than they knew. It was hard to say. But one way or another, he was losing heart, now. He was losing heart. Every time Ginny talked to him, it was something else broke. The tractor was broke. The deep freeze was broke. The mower. 'Course, that mower was no good from the start. It was just the sort of thing you pick up at auction and curse every day afterward. A foretaste of damnation if ever there was one. A preview of hell.

The whole place was going to hell.

By the time they got up for a visit, a fox had gotten in the chicken coop. In all the years the farm had been a farm, a fox had never gotten in the chicken coop. But that day they walked into a half-empty coop. And that was a sorry sight, all right. Even the racket was only half the racket. Something you might not think was sad, but come to hear it, it was. Especially as it meant Rex had left the coop door open. There was no other explanation, unless some fox had learned to work a coop latch. Rex must have left the coop door open. But, now, nobody said any such thing, see. Nope. Nobody said any such thing. Instead they stood there as if they were on a school field trip and had to pick out the roosters from the hens. Him and Ginny all zipped up against the cold, and with their hats on tight against the sleet. Only Rex had his torn-up barn jacket all open, what the heck, his shirt showing a good-size wet stripe down the middle, on account of he was a good-size man. The kind of man who looked cooped up in a coop. He always wore a hat, but for some reason he wasn't wearing a hat that day. Had to give his hair a flick as he came in, so as to keep it from dripping down his neck. But didn't it look right dapper, now, like he'd just come out of the shower. That salt and pepper all glistening, and his face not pale, as they'd been expecting, but pink. Pink and grizzled. Rex had these roam-y eyes, now, sand-colored. He never missed anything, and that day he glanced around like he always did. Inspecting. But afterward there was this little linger in his look, now, just this little linger—as if he was coming back to something instead of moving on. Guess it was the look of doubt. Then he turned away, a man who had never turned away from anything, and by that they knew he was shook up.

That was before they even saw the news around the corner— before they even saw how one of the sugarhouse roofs had caved in under the snow load. Just caved right in. To be frank, it was hard to believe, even looking right at it. To be frank, even looking right at the roof dipped down, even looking right at how it'd busted apart in the middle, where the seam was, it was hard to believe. 'Cause that sugarhouse had withstood some fifty winters easy. And now here it was. The sides not snapped and splintery but buckled like the whole thing had turned out not to be made out of wood and metal at all, but cardboard. A cardboard house. 'Course, Rex really ought to have gone up there and knocked the snow off back when the storm came, now. Even if he'd seen the roof hold snow that deep before, he should have done it. 'Cause you can't always tell what the snow is by looking at it. Some snow's heavy, and some snow's light. He knew that. And that roof being a shed roof, the pitch of it wasn't steep enough for the snow to slide off on its own, now, see. Who knew what the pitch of the thing was, but to be frank, in these parts, you should not put up a roof like that at all. To be frank, in these parts, you should put up a gable roof with a nine-over-twelve pitch at least. And knowing those old sugarhouses had those damned shed roofs, well, Rex ought to have got up there with a shovel, the way he always had. He let the sleet fall on him and flat said so himself. He ought to have. But he was too dead tired to do it, he said. Too dead tired. And where that was the first time anyone had ever heard him even use the word "tired" with regard to himself, Everett did expect Ginny to start crying right then and there. He did. He expected it. But she did not. Instead she just listened, calm as a doorstop. The sleet was building up like icing on their shoulders and heads, but Rex and Ginny and him just stood there anyway, as if it was this fine spring day, while Rex explained how he wasn't really tired. How it was just his heart making him feel as though he was tired. He wasn't really tired.

"Because you're not getting enough oxygen," Ginny said.

And Rex said that was right, now. His doctor had said the same thing. He wasn't getting enough oxygen.

"We better be getting back," he said finally. "That sky is out to get us and the Good Lord seems to have taken a powder."

So they tromped back up the hill, their hands in their pockets, thinking.

Ginny and Everett shoveled out the barn floor. That floor was so caked with cow shit, it looked like it been refloored shit brown. But what the heck. They cleaned it all out. They shoveled out some paths through the snow, too, so as to make it easier to haul water up to the hogs. And come the end of the day, they took Rex out for a prime rib down at the inn. Talked over the equipment. The tractor. The mower. Ordered up some strawberry shortcake for dessert. Rex complained about the new folks in town. They want to bake bread for a living, then complain when they have to drive all over tarnation delivering it, he said. Ginny and Everett laughed. They laughed when Rex complained about the commune next door, too. How they complained about him. Complained about his chemicals. Complained about how runoff from his fields was trickling down to theirs.

"So I told them, When you figure out how to fix gravity, let me know," he said. "So I told them, Go fuck your sheep."

Ginny and Everett laughed some more.

"Because that's what they do, them hippies, you know, when they're not fucking each other," said Rex, scratching his jaw. "The sheep or the cows, depending on their equipment."

Ginny and Everett laughed again. They did not point out that some of their classmates from high school were living on that commune now. They didn't think it was needed. They were just glad to hear Rex sounding like himself.

"A bunch of rich kids, that's what they are," he said. "Think any of them got drafted? Those kids got off, every one of them got off. Their daddies got them off."

That was one of his favorite topics of conversation, along with the government.

"Think they care about the family farms down there in Washington?" he said. "Or do you think they're too busy with their girlfriends to care? Giving it to them every which way."

They ordered up some more shortcake. To be frank, it wasn't as good as what they had in the city. To be frank, this time of year the strawberries were mushy on account of they were frozen instead of fresh. Pulpy. They were pulpy. Ginny and Everett ate it up anyway. And as soon as they got in the car to go home, Ginny said, So what if we went back to help? And way before they got to the apartment, their minds was made up. Jarvis wasn't going back. Bob wasn't going back, neither. But they were. 'Cause that farm had been in the family for a hundred years, easy. Ginny's ma was buried there. Ginny's grandma and grandpa, and her great-grandma and great-grandpa, too. It was bigger than anything in the city, a lot bigger. Come to think on it, in fact, it was everything. And here they'd left Rex to run it on his own for years. What was that all about? As if movie houses and cafés were more important than the farm! As if they were more important than Ginny's pa! Everett called up work first thing the next morning. And, well, now, it didn't pain him too much to say he wasn't going to be framing up that four-car garage with the automatic door opener, did it. Ginny borrowed them a van for the furniture. And that was it. They didn't have to weigh and consider, see. They didn't have to decide. They were just going.

They drove up without telling Rex. Surprised him, and well, he was surprised sure enough. In fact, his sand-colored eyes teared up before he could put a stop to it. And now, that wasn't something you saw every day. Ginny teared up, too, just to see it. Everett got to work. There wasn't room for all the furniture they'd made, but they did put some of it to use. Piled the rest on a pallet in the basement, then spruced up a mite. Not to set things straight, now. To set things straight they'd have had to open up the walls and insulate. They'd have had to replace the windows with double-pane. Replace the furnace. Have a look at the pipes and the wiring. The wiring was probably some kind of cobweb, if you looked. Creative—it was probably what his pa used to call creative. They didn't touch it, though, didn't touch the real stuff. They were just making the place livable. Putting down carpet. Putting up wallpaper. Hanging some curtains. They washed the windows and reduced the heaps. 'Course, the heaps were an enterprise, right there. Rex was no worse than other humans when it came to clutter, but if he needed a chair, everything went on the table. If he needed the table, everything went on the counter. And if he needed the counter, it all went back on the chair. Ginny found all kinds of things as she worked. Prescriptions. The phone number of some woman Rex said was after him. Unpaid bills. Certified-mail slips. She held one up.

"You ever pick this up?"

Rex made a face. "Don't believe I did."

"What about this?"

Clean-shaven as he was these days, he looked more like a schoolboy than you'd have thought possible. Stricken, even. He looked stricken. Except when he was really in trouble, see. Then he'd wink.

"Help me out, now," he'd say. "Womankind's got it out for me."

And before things got worse, him and Everett would put on their hats and head out to the field. 'Course, they had plenty of problems out there, now, too. Out there, they had problems galore. But out there, they were at least battling sick animals and broken equipment. Time. Nature. Enemies worth calling enemies. Whatever went wrong, no one was going to shake a finger at them.

They fixed the sugarhouse in time for the sugaring season, kept the lines clear and had a good year. Spring breeding went fine, too. Pretty soon a new herd of wobbly-legged calves were escaping out the fence just like their forebears. Escape artists. The lambs were bleating away, and the pullets were laying their first little long eggs, and those eggs were delicious indeed. Tender. Ginny and Everett were glad to be on the farm, and Rex was taking it easy the way he was supposed to. Slowing down if he felt anything at all. Ginny and Everett took CPR out at the high school while Rex got himself accustomed to the idea of surgery. A bypass. He was having him a bypass. 'Course, everyone had them these days. Medicaid would pay for it. It wasn't going to be bad.

Those were happy times, in a way. They were happy.

But Ginny had her an account book, and a box for the bank statements, and every night she stayed up later, like she was in some farm movie.

"Depends on what beef goes for this year," she'd say. "If it's better than last year, we'll be all right. If it's worse, we'll be in trouble."

'Course, the real problem wasn't the price of beef at all. The real problem was Rex's real estate 'cause he'd always made some extra introducing this one and that. Getting them to shake hands.

"But now people don't call—have you noticed?" said Ginny. "Because they know that he's sick. He doesn't look like someone who could get the best price. He doesn't look like he has the energy."

"Well, and he doesn't, now, does he?" Everett said.

Ginny was sore at him for that. Said people should stand by her pa when he was sick, instead of going out and finding someone else to replace him. Saying they wanted ads, when that wasn't the issue at all. Brochures. She said he should think so, too. And Everett could see her point in a way.

Still, he said, "Well, and what if I don't?"

'Cause, to be frank, he was getting as sick of her scolding as Rex. Sick of her lecturing. In the city, him and Ginny'd try to work things out. Talk things over. Go down to the café. Have them some coffee.

But here he mostly headed out to the field and let her cool down. Here they had kind of a different style.

Not that he didn't get Ginny's worry. He did. He did get it. He knew Rex was out taking walks at the north end of the property, and he knew what that was about. Knew Rex had a number of acres in mind and knew it made him sick to contemplate. Sick. It was years ago that the bank came and took Rex's pigs, now. Years. But he still talked about it—how they came and took his pigs while he just stood there. Ginny talked about it, too—how her pa didn't say a word for a month. And now this. Land. This was worse. Ginny was afraid it was going to kill him. Or the walks. She was afraid the walks were going to kill him, especially as north was the side that bordered the commune. North was the side that bordered the hippies.

The hippies and their sheep.

'Course, those hippies had been living there for ten years at least. They were not new. But somehow in all those years, Rex never had got used to them. He didn't like their ganged-up ways, see. He didn't like the way they'd put together a hundred acres for themselves just like that. Ganging up. None of them was half the farmer he was. It was hobby farming, that's what it was. Play farming. A lot of the money came from their daddies. But where the hippies had all that land they seemed to think pretty damned well of themselves, he said. They did. They thought pretty damned well of themselves.

"How do you know?" Ginny asked him sometimes. "How do you know what they think? Have you ever talked to them?"

"Pa, we've been visiting over there," she even said once. Felt she had to tell him.

Rex did not like to hear it. But lacking other company, and seeing as how Belle Tollman was living there now, Ginny and Everett had gone to visit a couple of times. Toting pies along with them, and staying for longer than they should have. Laughing in the sunroom part of the great room, over by the big red woodstove, though, to be frank, Belle had changed. Ginny and Everett were shocked when they saw how disheveled she'd got. How she wore torn-up clothes, and walked around with a parrot on her shoulder, and didn't ever wear socks, just put her feet in her sheepskin boots barefoot. And her thinking had changed, too. The word "organic" was holy to her now. Organic. Organic. Ginny and Everett looked at each other. But at the same time, Belle was the Belle Tollman they knew. She was still wearing the

necklace she'd worn in high school, a silver necklace with an ice skate
on it. She still had Belle's quick way of talking. And she still thought
Belle-like thoughts. Asking why chicken soup was soup made with
chicken, for instance. Why wasn't it soup made for chickens? Wasn't
chicken feed, feed for chickens? In high school, Ginny had thought
that type of question weird, but now she thought it funny. Familiar. A
dear, she called her. "Don't you think Belle is a dear?" she said. She
did think Belle's husband, Paxton, weird. "Are those what they call
dreadlocks?" she said. "I think he's the one pa told to, you know."
But Belle herself was a dear. And Ginny liked a lot of the other commune folks, too. She liked the way they dressed—more regular than
Belle, but original, still. She liked the way they ate. Said she was going
to get some tofu, when she got the chance. And she liked hearing
news. When Belle said Randy Little was away getting a divorce, for
instance, but that he was coming back with Sue Ann Horn, Ginny
liked hearing about it. Talking about it.

"I guess they ran into each other one day and realized they'd
never loved anyone the way they loved each other," Ginny said.
"Belle said they talk a lot about us. How there's something special
about those high school attachments."

"Think so?" said Everett.

"She said they feel like true love in a way other attachments
never do."

"Got you before you knew any better, I guess."

She smiled and said how she thought high school friendships were
different, too. "I don't know that we made any real friends in the city,
did we?" she said.

"We did not," he said.

"We have roots here," she said. "We go back. It makes a difference."

"Think Belle and Paxton'll want to come have supper on our
Queen Anne chairs?" he said.

Ginny gave him the eye. "In due time," she said, "I don't know
that they won't."

"What a nice talk they'll have with your pa over dessert. About
the runoff."

"I don't have a crystal ball," she said.

'Course, they sure could have used a crystal ball right about then.
'Cause Rex thought they were going to have to sell ten acres. He

could barely get the words out. Ten acres. And that wasn't even going to guarantee they could keep going forever. That would only keep them going for a while. And what if the hippies bought the land? Rex was worried the hippies would buy the land. Everett thought Rex was jumping the gun. He thought he should try moonlighting first, the way Rex used to. He could do just about anything, he said. Jack-of-all-trades that he was. He could. Or how about Ginny? Ginny could try for a job at the inn, he said. There was some competition for those jobs, and you had to defend your hours with a shotgun. Still, Ginny could try.

"Or I could look into teaching again," Ginny said.

Everyone agreed she could look. In the meantime, they kept their thinking caps on. Maybe they should take a hint from the hippies and start a bakery, Ginny said. Or what about a café? She liked that idea and tried to warm the men up to it.

"We could have it right here on the farm," she said. "Call it the Farm Café. Everything would be fresh, or fresh-baked."

She was practically writing the menu when the idea of a mower came up. 'Cause the tractor they'd gotten up and running like nothing, see. But the mower, now. The mower was something else. Rex and Everett had disassembled the mower. Adjusted stuff. Lubricated and sharpened. Fashioned replacements, seeing as how you couldn't even get parts for the thing. They'd argued. What they remembered, what was plain common sense. What any jackass could tell. The moment of truth had come a couple of times.

The thing did not move.

"Looks to me like we need a new mower," said Rex, readjusting his hat.

Everett laughed. "Well, why don't we go order us one," he said.

'Course, now, in an ideal world they could have rented a mower. In an ideal world, they could have called someone up and got put on a schedule. But in the real world, folks don't rent their mowers, because mowers are too hard to move, see. They break too easy. And they're finicky, now, just finicky. Persnickety.

Still Everett talked to the commune about renting theirs. Figuring that, neighbors being neighbors, the commune just might risk it. Neighbors being neighbors. But come to find out their mower was a troublesome thing, too.

"We call it the beast of beasts," said Paxton, over pie. He pushed his chair back as if he felt crowded. "Hell, if I may say so, is a first cut with a temperamental mower."

"We would die a thousand deaths to rent a mower ourselves," said Belle. Her shirt had these little holes in the shoulder from the parrot claws. "We would. We'd die a thousand deaths."

So what if they bought a mower and rented it out to the commune? Ginny and Everett had the same idea at the same time as they walked back. 'Course, they brought the matter up real careful with Rex. They brought it up expecting he might object. But he did not object. Instead he told them he had an old friend in farm equipment. Giles and him went way back, he said. Their wives used to be friends. He could give him a call.

Giles turned out to be a little guy with a beard like rat hair. He wolfed down some cookies, saying there was something about them that reminded him of Ginny's mother. And when Ginny said she used half milk chocolate and half semisweet, just like her mom, he clapped his hands.

"I knew it," he said. "I knew there was something."

And then because they were like family, he told them how they were on the right track. He told them how if they rented the mower, they could take out a loan but get the hippies to make the payments.

"The hippies'll make the payments, but they won't own the mower," he said. "You'll own it." Giles looked at Ginny. "You'll own it. As you probably figured out already, living with the King of Deals himself as you do. You know, your pa's had a hand in every deal that's gone down here for decades. He even made a dime on my divorce." He winked. "Remember, Rex? When Diane and me split up and had to sell. Remember?"

"I do," said Rex.

"Mind you, I'm not saying things have changed," Giles told Ginny. "No, I'm not saying that at all. But your pa has always been the King of Deals. That's why everyone called him Rex." He looked off. "That's why after a while no one but his ma called him Avery."

Avery. Everett didn't know until right then that Rex was not born Rex, but Avery.

What the heck.

Giles had been casual about the down payment, but Ginny and

Everett were less casual. 'Cause even that was a lot of money for them, more money than they had. They were going to have to borrow even that from the bank. They checked the numbers again. Checked and rechecked.

"Think the commune'll pay that?"

Ginny said she was happy to go ask Belle. Saw it as an excuse to go visiting, he guessed. And sure enough, she came back smiling.

"Belle says yes," she said.

"What does Paxton say?"

She did not like that question.

"Why do you ask?" she said. "Don't you think Belle knows?"

"I'm just asking."

"Well, I didn't ask and I'm not going to ask," she said. "If you want to know what Paxton thinks you can go ask him yourself."

And probably he should have, now. He should have. 'Cause when Belle told Paxton about the mower, he put two and two together, see, and called up Giles himself. And then Rex's old friend, bless him, explained everything to Paxton, including how Ginny and Everett probably could have taught him a thing or two. Seeing as how they lived with the King of Deals himself. And seeing as how Rex had made a deal out of other people's misery for about as long as anyone could remember.

Sue Ann Horn told them all of it later, see. When she and Randy Little were finally settled in, she told them. Back at the time, though, Belle did not exactly come running to report on what Paxton said. She did not let on that the commune'd gone and got a loan from their daddies and bought their own mower, either. Ginny and Everett knew nothing about nothing until their mower was signed for and sitting in their field. They knew nothing about nothing until there it was, all prepped and green and brandy-ass new.

Theirs.

The last days on the farm were sad. Rex's bypass was scheduled, but most days he didn't look as if he was going to make it to the operation. Ginny kept calling the doctor's office. Terrible, she kept saying. He looks terrible. But the answer kept coming back the same. His condition wasn't critical enough for him to jump the line. Sure he was tired. Sure he was keeping to bed. He had a bad heart, they said. That's why he was having the bypass.

'Course, the funny thing when you thought about it was how clear Everett's pa's pipes were, thanks to his barely ever getting a bite of those steaks Rex was so used to. But Everett didn't ever say that to Ginny, now. Nope. He didn't say it. They were too busy trying to decide what to do. Trying to get used to the idea of some stranger handling the deal. A stranger selling the farm.

Jarvis and Bob came up to help out but made the mistake of asking how this could have happened. And then, well, if they really wanted to know they probably could have heard the story just fine in the city, and without even using the phone. Where the hell were you? Ginny kept saying. Where the hell were you? And, Did you ever think about the farm? Did you ever think what it meant? And, Would you look at Pa, now? Look at him! Look at him! Blasting. She was blasting. She was so mad she banged the truck into a couple of trees. Burnt up just about everything she cooked. She even had trouble with her shoelaces. Couldn't calm down enough to tie them.

Rex took to praying. 'Course, he always was some kind of Christian. Congregationalist, maybe. Everett'd never seen him pick up a Bible before, though. Rex had never had time for that sort of thing. Wouldn't have had the interest, either, unless there were passages in Paul about what the weather was going to do. But now he read as if the Good Book might tell him something. As if the Good Book could tell him how his old friend Giles could do him in for the commission on two mowers, for instance. Or whether Satan had gotten to his friend. He thought the Good Book could tell him that. His friend was in trouble, he'd say. He had to pray for him. Pray for his salvation.

Rex playing savior. That was something to see, all right.

"We're going to have to start over," Everett said, one day. Ginny was standing there in the kitchen door, smoking and giving him her back. But he talked anyway, now, see. Talked to her back. "Listen. We won't move to the city, but how about we move across the lake? Into town. How about we move into town?"

A puff of smoke came out of her.

"Far enough to put this behind us but close enough we'll still have our roots. You'll see a doctor and have us some babies. I'll find some work. Rex'll live with us. What do you say?"

She smoked.

"Those cigarettes are going to kill you." He didn't dare bring up the eating. Figured he'd let her pants talk to her personal. But the smoking, now. He had to say something about the smoking. "You see what it says on the package? The surgeon general says so. Everyone says so. You're going to get cancer."

"Oh, yeah?" She lit up another cigarette.

They called the doctor's office again. Said they wanted Rex looked at. 'Cause he looks terrible, they said. 'Cause there's a lot of stress here. All they wanted was an appointment, they said. And they did get one in the end, see. They got one. It wasn't for two months, though.

Ginny smoked.

It was Rex who brought up the subject of graves. Said they could try to save the family plot, now. They could try. He didn't want to be buried there, though. Nope. Said if he was buried there he could not rest for missing his cows.

"I'd just be all the time thinking about them. What a herd we had. Escape artists." He laughed. "Escape artists."

Ginny swallowed.

"Remember when we sold the dairy herd? When your ma died?"

"I remember."

"Thought that was the end of the world. Remember?"

"I remember."

"Thought there could never be as hard a time as that." He laughed a kind of laugh. "Just goes to show what a man knows."

He wanted to be buried in the Christian cemetery.

"Could be a mite lonely at first, but maybe we can buy up a couple of plots around mine. What do you say? See if anybody wants to join me. You. The boys. Everett. Improves your chances of going to heaven, you know."

"Is that right?"

"Starts you out one step closer. And let's face it. Some of us need the boost."

"I hear you, Pa," Ginny said. "I don't think we'll be burying you anytime soon, but I hear you."

"Pre-need, isn't that what they say?" he said. "It's good to decide on things pre-need."

"I guess," said Ginny.

Seeing as they were on the subject, she asked if he wanted her mother moved over there, too, to join him. Keep him company. "Not that we're planning on burying you anytime soon," she said again.

"Nah. Let the dead rest," he said. "Though I will miss her. What a good woman she was, your mother. I never did think I could manage without her."

They listed the farm with a big-name agency. Folks with an office in the city and brochures. And they did talk great. They did. They talked great. But they sent morons to show the place. Showed it to morons, too. It was morons walking around with morons. Ginny kept the place perfect as a magazine, but that wasn't enough, now, see. That wasn't enough. The morons would stop and say, loud enough for Ginny and Everett to hear, They prettied it up, but did they insulate the place? They prettied it up, but did they update the wiring?

Everett would've freed the cows to get Ginny out of there. Spare her the ordeal. But once, just going out for a walk, they'd come back to dead quiet.

"Pa! Pa!" Steep as those old stairs was, Ginny ran up them by twos. "Pa!"

Rex was asleep. He had pulled down his window shade so as not to see any more morons. In fact, so as not to be looking at the farm at all.

"I always used to tell Celia," he said, "that a family farm is a soap opera. I just plain don't want to watch."

'Course, they had their hopes even then, but what a sorry lot of hopes they was. Everett hoped never to see Giles again, now. That was one hope. He hoped never to see Belle or Paxton either. That was another. And Paxton he never did see again, luckily. Giles, neither.

But one day he looked out the window and saw company, and it wasn't a moron bringing a moron. It was Belle with her bare feet and that torn-up clothes. Never mind it was fall. Warm for fall, but still fall. She was wearing cutoffs so you could see the hair on her legs. A T-shirt with no sleeves so you could see her underarm hair, too. Luckily, she kept her arms more or less by her sides as she swung them. Not swinging them one back and one forward, the way most folks did, but both forward and then both back, so you could see her tits squeeze. Squeeze and hang, squeeze and hang, like they were being milked.

He intercepted her on the walk. Asked what she'd come for.

"I came to say I'm sorry," she said. "I didn't realize, I guess. I mean, I just had no idea. That all this would happen. I had no idea."

She was still swinging her arms. When he didn't answer right off, though, she stopped.

"Well, that's fine," he said. "But I don't think you should go in there."

"Why not?"

" 'Cause you might get yourself killed," he said.

"Rex might kill me?"

"Ginny," he said. "Ginny might kill you."

"She's mad, huh." Belle cracked her knuckles.

"I'd say so. Yeah. She's mad, all right."

"This is so like high school," Belle said. "Except that it ain't."

He laughed then—the first laugh he'd laughed in a while. "Nope," he said. "You got that right, now. It ain't."

"Maybe I'll write a note," she said. "Get some nice stationery. You know, with flowers in it. Think so? Think I should write a note?"

"That'd be safer," he said.

And two days later, here comes Belle's note in the general delivery. It's on stationery with flower petals, sure enough. The address was in purple ink and all around it there were designs. Scrolls and leaves. A parrot. He handed the thing to Ginny.

"A note for you," he said. "I think it's from Belle."

He did think Ginny would at least read it, now. He thought she'd read it and go blasting. But she did not read it and she did not blast. Instead she stabbed it with a steak knife and held it up over the kitchen sink. Then she took a lighter and lit it. Held it careful so the ashes wouldn't mess up the magazine look.

"I saw Belle the other day," he said. "She told me to tell you she's sorry."

"Oh, yeah? Well, if you see her again, tell her I'm fixing to jab out her eyes with a pitchfork," Ginny said.

One night, Rex woke up shouting, "They're out! They're out!" and leapt out of bed to go rescue the cows—thought they'd broke out of the barn. Ginny took off after him only to hear him fall clear down the stairs.

"Pa!" she shouted. "Pa!"

Ginny and Everett shot down to the stairwell and then half stumbled, half fell down the stairs themselves. Those stairs being genuine old farmhouse stairs, and steep, see. They were steep. 'Course, in all their years on the farm, no one had ever fallen down them before. But in their panic and the pitch black, Ginny slipped and then Everett did, too. His heel slipped, then his tailbone hit. And next thing he knew, they were all in a pileup at the bottom.

"Pa! Pa!"

Rex was still alive by the time they got the light turned on. Sitting there holding his chest, but the calmest of the three of them. Kingly. He was kingly. His eyes glowing this weird color in the lamplight—like he wasn't a person anymore, but something else. A king.

"Now, I know you know CPR," he said. Clear and calm. "But I want you to let me die. Hear me? I want you to let me die."

"Pa," said Ginny.

"I can't," said Everett.

"You can," said Rex, his eyes glowing. "You can. You're a poor man's son who's made quite a mess here. But this much I think you can manage."

"Pa," said Ginny. "You can't mean that. Pa."

But his eyes had stopped glowing and he was going pale.

Excepting the commune members, the whole town turned up for the funeral. They had a beautiful day for it, too, cool. Autumnal. The leaves falling down like even the trees were crying. 'Course, the people cried louder. Said what a good man he was. Said how he'd be missed. Said how he was a style of farmer you didn't see much anymore. An old-timer. The real thing. Said how what happened was a crying shame. They were outraged that he died before a cancel came in. Outraged by medical care in general. How impersonal it was. They didn't say why they stopped coming to him for real estate, though, and that made Ginny mad, see. She did try not to show it. She tried. But in the end she started blasting about how they killed him. How they weren't good enough to lick the soles of his dead feet. What hypocrites they was.

Blasting. She was blasting.

She slept hard that night.

The farm didn't sell for anything like what it was worth. Time was, when Rex could have gotten a whole lot more. Time was, when they wouldn't have had to pay commission, either. Instead it was six percent to sell the farm to the commune. Belle and Paxton tried to get other folks to explain. How they wished they weren't buying the thing. How they didn't even want it. How they were just worried about the runoff. And folks did tell Ginny. How this move might even be dangerous for the commune. Risky. How it might be risky.

Ginny hoped it ruined them.

"How can they so much as step into that barn?" she said. "How can they step into the house? Where is their conscience?"

Ginny and Everett rented themselves a place to live in. Everett found himself a job.

Ginny smoked.

Who found what first? It was hard to say. But one spring day, Ginny came home a little lighter, and he did, too.

"I found this land," he said.

"I found this church."

Now, he knew she'd been looking for a church. Knew she'd been shopping around, looking for something closer in. But mostly she'd been fixed on what she didn't like. The prayer bands, for instance. She didn't like the prayer bands, didn't like the whole electronic thing. Whoring, she called it. Whoring after seekers. And she didn't like the preaching that went with it. That was whoring, too. The preachers being whorers, a lot of them. Sleazy, she said. Corporate.

He did think she was being picky. Persnickety, even. She was being persnickety. But well, now, finally she'd found one she liked. A welcoming church, she called it. Small. She liked it that someone greeted her as soon as she walked in. She liked it that someone helped her find a seat. She liked it that people remembered her name right off. Personal, it was. This church was personal. The preacher didn't just stand up front like a stiff. He came down and talked to folks. Gave his sermon with his knee up on a front-row chair. 'Course, he had to hold his hands on top of the chair for balance. But he was about reaching out, see. He was about reaching people where they lived, and she got that, she said. Spirit. He had spirit. And the congregation had spirit, too. They'd even built the church themselves. Made it out of a house. 'Course, it wasn't nothing fancy, now. Nothing like what J. H. Moses would've done. But it was real, she said. It was like their beliefs, which were about keeping to the real word of God. Honoring it. Preserving it. They were about the real Bible. That's why they were called the Heritage Bible Church. And that's why they weren't Lutheran or Presbyterian or anything like that. Why they were independent. An independent church. Everett'd never heard of an independent church. But what the heck. He was just glad she had someplace to go. People to talk to. Glad she'd be getting out of the house.

"Great," he said. "You're coming out of it. Feeling better. Great."

'Course, she wanted him to come with her. Keep her company, see. And he did, once. Promised her he'd come again, too.

"When you're ready?" she said.

"When I'm ready."

"Promise?"

"Promise."

"Because they understand," she said. "They understand."

"Understand what?"

"That an evil has been done to us."

"Great," he said.

Today she'd probably claim she felt the same about the land as he did about the church. Today she'd probably claim it was mostly something the other person was keen on. But he remembers different, now. He remembers she loved it. And, to be frank, it was some land. It wasn't big. Five acres. A hoofprint. It wasn't what they were used to, at all. But it was closer in to things. And high, it was high. Faced southeast. Had a drop-dead view. You could even see their old farm, if you looked. You had to squint, but you could see it. He thought the thing priced reasonable for what it was.

"We can put up a little house," he said. "Can't you just see your sunroom? I'm going to put it right facing the view. Glass it in so you can use it all year round, and you mark my words. All winter long, you're going to sit in there like a cat."

"Is the money really enough?" she asked. "For the land and a house, too?"

"If we build smart."

"Think my pa would approve? Of us building a house instead of starting a new farm?"

"You thinking about a farm?"

"No."

"Then I guess he'd approve."

They were starting over. Drawing plans. They were thinking through the kitchen. The bathrooms. The flow. That being what they used to talk about over at J. H. Moses, the flow. They weren't building fancy, now. But it was going to be homey, with a great big front porch. They were going to have the mudroom they'd needed so bad on the farm. And instead of a parlor, they were going to have a great room like the hippies had, only smaller, with a red woodstove. The woodstove was sort of like the hippies, too, but he didn't remind her of it.

'Course, the hard talk was the kids' rooms. Should they have kids' rooms at all. But finally they decided on two, with a bathroom in between. If nothing happened, they could adopt, they decided. In fact, they were more or less planning to adopt—what the heck. If nothing happened.

And now, wasn't it a happy day when she said that. Just a happy day. He took her out to the inn to celebrate. Walked home holding hands, as if they were in high school.

They were happy.

They shot their levels, got their septic in. Dug for the basement, got in their drainage. Their water lines, their electric.

Ginny quit smoking. She was wearing a patch and dieting and walking with the town walk group. Looking one last time for a teaching job, in case that was God's will. But if not, well, she was thinking to open a café, she said. She still liked that idea and was wondering if there might not be a reason she still liked it. If it was God's will.

"We could call it the Good News Café," she said. "It could be one part café, one part reading room." She'd heard of a place where they had a room in back for a prayer band, but she thought a reading room would be better.

"Reading room?"

"For Bible study."

"You mean, Watch out, Come 'n' Eat, here comes the Come 'n' Read?" he said.

"Christians like to get together with Christians," she said. "It's how we stir up love."

She was wearing a silver chain like Belle Tollman's now, except with a cross instead of a skate. And she was talking more and more about folks at church. About how they thought. 'Course, to Everett they sounded a lot like folks at the commune, only with a stress on the divine. The divine instead of the organic.

But what the heck. He tried to listen. He did. He tried.

"They understand me at church," Ginny said. "They get me. What the farm meant to me—they get that. That our family had lived on that land for centuries. That it was important. But that I was the only one who saw that. They get it that Jarvis didn't see it, and that Bob didn't, either. That I was the only one who saw, and that that was a burden in a way. A gift and a burden."

"It was tough."

"It was. It was a weight. But I took it up anyway, didn't I?"

"You did."

"That's what folks at church say. They say I didn't shirk away, or duck. And they respect that. They think that was a beautiful thing."

"That it was."

"Seeing," she said. "I was a seeing person."

"That you were."

"It was a lot like seeing the Truth about the Lord. That's why they understand. Why they get how hard it was to defend the farm against forces much stronger than me. How hard it was to defend my father."

"Harder'n hell."

"It was. Fighting godless people out for themselves. Greedy people out to destroy everything good. Everything decent."

"It was tough."

"They stole from us, Everett. They cheated us and caused us to lose the farm so that they could help themselves to it. They dispossessed us. And you know why? Because they couldn't stand our goodness, that's why."

"I dunno, Gin," he said then, slow. Careful. "Were we that good? Like angels? You and me?" He didn't bring up Rex.

"The Bible says that all who live godly in Jesus will meet with persecution," she said. "And that's what we met with. Persecution."

"Gin," he said then. Slow. "Gin. We made some bad moves. We shouldn't have trusted Giles. We shouldn't have trusted Belle."

"They were out to destroy us, Everett. They hated Pa. They hated our farm. Hated it that we stood on our own two feet. Hated it that we stood for something. They hated the whole world where people believe in honor and don't sleep with everything that walks."

"They hated your pa, Gin. I'm with you there. His chemicals. They hated his chemicals. But we made some bad moves. We should have opened a café. We should have sold off some land."

"We were up against evil," insisted Ginny. "Don't you see?"

"Guess I don't," he said then, shaking his head. "Guess I don't see." He wished he had a field he could head to, seeing as how she was about to start blasting. She was going to blast.

But, well, see, she didn't, now. She didn't.

"At least you're honest," she said. "The sad fact is that this is the story more and more, these days. More and more." Her voice was patient. The teacher voice she would have used every day, if she had ever gotten another teaching job. "You don't see the pattern because you haven't talked to enough people, or on a deep enough level. But folks at church've heard people's real stories. Not just the chitchat. The real stories. And they recognize the pattern because they've faced it, too."

"You sure, Ginny? You sure this is right?"

"Don't you ever have things you just know?" She looked serious. "I just know."

The house was framed up, but Ginny thought they could still work in a café. All it took was a deck, she said. She wanted a big deck facing the view, so they could put out some tables and chairs. And a second fridge, she said. She was going to need a second fridge.

"Let's check zoning," he said. " 'Cause, to be frank, I don't know if you can have a business like that in your house. To be frank."

But down at Town Hall, Rhonda the clerk said that they could. Said people around here've always had to find ways to get by. Taken in sewing. Had themselves a repair shop. Scrappy, she said. They've always been scrappy.

"I'm just not crazy about this plan," he had to say then. "I want my home to be a home, Gin. I don't want it to be a restaurant full of strangers."

"They would not be strangers," she said. "They would be Christians."

"I don't want it full of Christians, neither."

"What's the matter with Christians?"

"Nothing the matter with Christians. I just don't want 'em in my house, Gin. I want peace."

'Course, that made Ginny mad. You could feel the rise. But she didn't blast—she didn't blast. Instead she just said, "I'm going to pray for you. I'm going to shower you with Christian love and kindness and use the power of that."

And, well, those were uncomfortable days, but happy days, too, now. They were happy. 'Cause Ginny was getting out cookbooks and trying new things. Sprouts. Avocado. Tofu. She was putting out bouquets and candles. Dyeing her hair what she called "real blond," on account of she'd always felt like a real blonde. And losing weight— she lost weight. Had her a special prayer program just for that, and what do you know, it worked. She wore pink now and walked with her walking group. Even took a massage class. Said she could see how hard Everett worked, and got him this pillow set for Valentine's Day.

The pillow set had a place to put his face, and a wedge thing to lie on. A roll to put under his ankles. Went together with Velcro. He'd never seen anything like it and would not have recognized it as a path to heaven. But turned out, it was, now. It was. Led to activities they hoped would fill up those kids' bedrooms, too.

"You see?" Ginny would say later. "I knew but you didn't, did you?"

And, well, he'd have to admit, "Guess I didn't."

"You didn't see, did you?"

"Nope. I did not."

She wanted him reborn for two reasons. One was so they could be buried with Rex someday. 'Cause while Everett was Christian, he was Eastern Orthodox, on account of his pa. Hungarian Greek Catholic. And that didn't count at the cemetery, see. That wasn't the right kind. But the other reason was, she didn't want to be unequally yoked. Yoked like draft horses? he said. Yoked like mules? But that was how Paul put it, she said. Unequally yoked. She wanted to be married to a committed Christian. Someone who'd given up trying to do things by himself. Someone who'd realized what a lot of bad decisions he'd made. Someone who had put his trust in Jesus instead. She wanted him to put the Lord on the throne of his life.

And one night, well, what the heck, he did sort of say that he would, now. He did. He was firming up again like a youngster, see, and in what you might call an agreeable frame of mind.

"I said I'd give you my life, and it's yours," he said.

"You did, didn't you."

"I certainly did."

"Meaning you're going to listen?" she said, touching him. "Meaning you're going to put your trust in Jesus?"

"Don't I always listen?" he whispered. "Ain't I listening now?"

"I love you," she said. Then she took him in her mouth, a thing she'd never done before. Worked her tongue in ways he didn't know she could. And that was a revelation, all right. Made him wonder if there was more instruction in the Bible than he knew. He did think he'd gone to see the angels. And, well, when he came back to himself, he might as well have been born again.

It was a good time. They were seeing his ma and pa more, and Ginny wasn't complaining. In fact, she was bringing them pie. Fruit. Articles from the paper. She was having folks from church over, now, too. It was kind of a trade. And what the heck—he was almost getting used to the Was he with Jesus thing. Figured it was like looking past Belle Tollman's parrot. What the heck.

But, now, the café stayed a sticking point, see. It stayed a sticking point. He made him a list of the issues, starting with privacy. Would a café in the house make them feel like they'd lost their privacy. Then there was cost. Was a café going to be the mower all over again.

But Ginny just said, "This is about keeping Jesus out of the house, isn't it?"

They went on building. Punched through their punch list, and come one day, Ginny was spending hours in the sunroom, just as he'd predicted. Loving it. She was spending hours in there, curled up with her Bible.

'Course, he hadn't predicted that part.

Just as he failed to predict that come one day the commune would subdivide the land. Sell it for housing. But, well, they had no choice, see. They had no choice. A lot of people felt sorry for them, but Ginny was blasting mad. And that was even before the hippies put a standing-seam roof on the house. Silver. The thing shone like a pie plate. So that where before you had to squint to see the farm from the sunroom, now you could see it plain. Now you couldn't miss it.

"We have to have the deck," she said then. "We have to."

'Cause what with the farm sitting a little lower than the house, their view of it would be blocked by a deck, see. And that'd be a good thing, she said. Because she didn't want to spend her time on earth in hate. She really didn't.

And he got that, now. He did.

Still one day he loaded up the woodstove and said, "Ginny. Gin. We can have the deck, but I just don't want a café. You can say this is about Jesus, but it ain't. It's about a café. It's about hanging up a sign and having strangers come for coffee. I don't want it."

She fingered her cross.

"I made us a new list of things to think on," he said. "Starting with coffee. I don't want my house to smell like coffee."

"Your house," she said.

"Our house," he said. "I just said that because I was trying to get across that I live here, too. It ain't just your house. I live here, too."

Her look was rock ice.

"This house," she said, "is what's left of the farm. The farm my family had for over a hundred years. It's not your house. It's my house."

"Ain't we married?"

"The money came from the farm."

"I built this house with my own two hands, Gin. I made every stick of furniture in it."

"You're a poor man's son who's done good," she said. "But this is my inheritance."

'Course, he wanted to deck her, then. If she'd been a man he probably would have decked her. Instead, he laughed. "Glad to hear I done good," he said. And that helped him, see. Helped him stop himself. And it gave him his pride back, now, to know he stopped himself. It gave him his pride back. "You mean, it's your house," he went on.

"It's my inheritance."

"Even if I put my heart and soul in it, it's yours."

"If you want to put it that way."

Now they were just plain fighting again.

"I never asked whose it was going to be, now," he said. "I just gave it everything I had. Gave you everything. I never asked."

"Well, maybe you should have."

"I'm talking about our marriage, now," he said. "Should I have asked about that, too? Should I have asked you what you were going to give me before I gave you my life?"

He did think she was going to stop and remember the dance at the Grange Hall, then. He did think she was going to remember how they danced with everyone watching and went walking in the dark, and about the stars and the trees and their warm bodies and the cold air. But instead her eyes just stayed this ice-green.

He could barely go on. "If I was a fool, you ought to just tell me now, Gin. If I wasted my life. 'Cause my life ain't worth much, but if I've thrown it away, I'd still like to know. I would. What the heck. I'd still like to know."

"Every life is precious to the Lord," she said.

"I'm not talking about the Lord."

"Well, you ought to be," she said. "Because it's His will that brought you to me. It was His will that you gave what you gave."

"Is that right." He laughed again, if only to make her mad, what the heck.

And what do you know, she was mad.

To be frank, they ought to have broke up right then, see. To be frank, they ought not to have gone on. But somehow he thought it was like a war, or like a bad winter on the farm. Somehow he thought things would come round again. Peace. Spring.

Guess he just didn't want to see the obvious.

They ought to have broke up. But then Jarvis and his wife got hit by a tractor trailer and died, see. And seeing as how Ginny and Everett had the bedrooms, they got the kids. Brian and Betsy, ages four and six. Good kids, but sad. For a bunch of years no one could think of much else but what those kids needed. Love. Those kids needed love. Then his pa died, and his ma. One right after the other, like they'd got planted together and so got cut down together, too. And wasn't that a tough harvest, now. Hard to say what the yield was. He buried them in a Greek Orthodox cemetery right the same day as Ginny found a lump in her breast. 'Course, the doctors cut that lump out in the end, see. In the end, Ginny was just fine.

But before they cut it out, she started talking about the commune all over again. And when she had some church folks over for brunch one day, he was surprised to hear how big she sounded. Fervent. How fervent in spirit, as they liked to say. 'Cause it wasn't her story any-more, now, see. It was His story, God's story. She was only in it because He put her there. 'Cause He arranged for her to be persecuted by the commune. 'Cause He arranged for her to be dispossessed and defrauded as a way of helping her discover Him. And she did discover Him, she said—that was the Good News. She did. She did discover Him. It was such Good News that she was on fire with the desire to share it. She was on fire with the desire to say how she had conquered injustice and bitterness. How she'd come to see it was all a test. A trial. How she was filled with forgiveness for her enemies—thanks, even. How she was filled with thanks. Because without them she might never have gotten God's plan. Without them, she might never have surrendered to God's will. Without them, she might have gone on trying to find meaning in a farm. Looking at her life as if it was about her. About her fulfillment, instead of about the fulfillment of His will. Now she was righteous and happy. Peaceful. She was peace-ful. Because she'd surrendered, she said. Because she wasn't trying to direct her life anymore. Because she was putting her trust in Him. She was living her life in Christ.

'Course, all that made the church folk clap for joy to hear. And though Ginny had just said how she'd forgiven the commune, come to thank the commune, even, they said, "Behold, all they that were incensed against thee shall be as nothing and shall perish." Then they went on talking about how the whole country had gone wrong somehow. How it'd been founded a Christian nation, but how it had gotten lost, like Ginny. How it was following its own law instead of God's law. Trying to fulfill its own will instead of God's will. An abomination of desolation, they kept calling it. An abomination of desolation. A place with communes instead of families. A place with sex instead of love. A place where men became women and women became men. They told Ginny she was Lazarus—that she was wrapped up in bandages, with a stone at her door. She was going to have to roll back the stone, they said. She was going to have to roll back the stone, and then she was going to have to take off those bandages and walk. It was a mighty task, they said, as she had her a mighty stone. But with the Lord's help she could do it, they said. She could. With the Lord's help, she could roll back the stone and walk.

It took Everett a while to realize he was the stone, now. Took him a while.

Unequally yoked. Ginny didn't want to be unequally yoked. But she couldn't just up and leave Everett, now, 'cause of Paul. 'Cause Paul said that even if a woman had an unbelieving husband, she couldn't just leave him. She couldn't just go. But, now, Paul also said that if an unbelieving husband should leave a woman, she could let him go. And so that was Ginny's idea, see—to get Everett to leave her. To drive him out. Or not Ginny's idea. It was the Lord's idea. It was the Lord's plan.

It took Everett some time to get all that, now. It did. It took him some time. But he figured it out eventually. That in Ginny's view, the Lord sent her the Wrights on purpose. And the Cambodian girl, too— He sent her the Cambodian girl. That Sophy Chhung. What in 'Nam they called a gook but did seem like something else here—she was a piece of the plan, see.

The plan to drive him out.

The fire wasn't no accident, now. Nothing was an accident. It all went together, somehow.

He knew it.

He just didn't know how.

But what went wrong to begin with was Ginny. What went wrong to begin with was her. 'Cause she had her a blinding kind of vision, just like Hattie said. A blinding kind of vision that Ginny saw plain as day. How the Lord was on her side. How He had a plan. How one day she was going to push back her rock and walk out of her cave, just like the Lord wanted. And then she was going to set the world back right, see—her and her church. They were going to set the world back right.

They were. She saw it. They were.

It was going to take time. But one day, they were going to do it. And then they were going to see it again: the ideal world. The world the way it used to be. The world the way it used to be. They were going to have it all back: The world the way it was, back when she was queen.

Hattie III: The Pride of Riverlake

E-mails:

You don't face what we face.
You don't know desperation, you don't know despair.
You don't remember.

Well, maybe they're right, thinks Hattie. But the World Trade Center; and Sarun in the hospital, all in bandages; and Chhung—Chhung, who used to make it past the Thai soldiers, Sophy once told her, with a sling full of rice—just wanting now to kill himself. He sits outside with his brace on. The weather isn't as cold as it usually is, a mixed blessing; who knows how long Chhung will be able to sit out there.

The weather's late.

Still, he should come in. He should. Instead of smoking and drinking the way he is, quiet. His quiet, in truth, as disturbing as the weather.

As disturbing as his yelling used to be.

The weather is going to come, after all. Even with global warming it will come. Riverlake's northerly. There's not much more than a fence or two between town and the Arctic, as people like to say; they've always gotten ice and sleet and hail. Not to say torrents like the one that overflowed Brick Lake, way back when—turned it into a raging river such as took out whole mills and barns, and a number of cows, too. Of course, if people hadn't gone and cut down the forests for farms, well, there might have been more trees to drink up some of the water—that flood wasn't all Mother Nature. But never mind. You'd still have to say that Riverlake gets torrents. Dumps. Wind. Sudden weather. Plummets where everything goes dry, and sounds start to change—snaps where the sound waves hug the ground and bring far-off things in. There isn't a pastor in the county who hasn't cracked the God's frozen people joke and people do laugh. This is deep-freeze country.

Chhung should come in.

Mum wants to know where you can go where there are no gangs and no churches; she asks via Sophy, in Khmer, having given up on English. Hattie doesn't know what to say. Mum prays. There's a Buddhist temple a few towns over, but she doesn't want Hattie to bring her there. Because there are hippies, Sophy says, and because the chants sound strange. Like they don't do that Cambodian nasal thing, she says; they don't do *smout*. Mum would rather pray at home, in her bedroom, where nothing sounds strange; she'd rather pray at her shrine, where nothing has changed. She has a small shrine, with a gray-green carpet sample to sit on; it doesn't look a whole lot more comfortable than the floor. But still she sits on it, her legs to the side. Holding her hands the way people used to in yoga—in that prayer position, only not as though she's in *The King and I*. Instead she presses the length of her forefingers to her nose, hard; it's as if she is trying to affix the cartilage more firmly to her face. She closes her eyes, moving her lips. No one knows what she is saying exactly, but Sophy thinks it's something like

> *I go to the Buddha as my refuge*
> *I go to the Dhamma as my refuge*
> *I go to the Sangha as my refuge*
>
> *For the second time I go to the Buddha as my refuge*
> *For the second time I go to the Dhamma as my refuge*
> *For the second time I go to the Sangha as my refuge*

Nothing too interesting, but of course that's the point. The point is to have no point—to empty the mind. To free oneself of oneself, good riddance. To rise beyond want, to rise beyond pain. Detaching oneself, *dá guān*. One day Mum cuts her hair off short—even shorter than Sophy's, and using those same dull scissors. It's about as even as a pasture the sheep ate down. She doesn't care. She sports a white shawl, too, over her blouse, and the next day there it is again—a plain white swath that should show dirt like crazy but somehow doesn't— as if it's beyond dirt, somehow, as if it hails from a world beyond laundry. A better world, indeed. Sophy calls it the temple granny look, and Mum does look as if she belongs in a long line of women sitting on a floor somewhere. It's as if Chhung isn't the only one to have removed himself from the trailer; it's as if in her mind and spirit, Mum has, too.

A lot of the time she is too tired to clean, so Sophy cleans for her. She cleans though Hattie tells her she doesn't have to; she cleans though Hattie tells her she can find someone else to do it. Sophy cleans because she wants to clean, she says; she wants to clean and clean and clean. Plus, she doesn't want anyone to steal her mother's jobs. And so she cleans and cleans while Hattie cooks Chinese food for anyone who wants it. Pork with asparagus, shrimp with peas. Beef with broccoli. Simple things, home-style. They like them. Hattie tries to help with Gift, too—Gift, who likes it when Hattie brings Annie to play with him. And so she does, though it means protecting Annie from infant torture. For Gift will pull Annie's tail if Hattie lets him. He'll feed Annie candy. Hattie tells him how she once had a dog who ate a bag of chocolate and died; and though he's too young to understand, he does listen, wide-eyed. Barely blinking—children his age don't blink much. Hattie remembers from Josh what an event it was to behold his lashes lengthening, then retracting again. And now here are Gift's, an event, too. Gift has Sophy's lashes, and Sophy's eyes— bright eyes, with a tilt. Though how relaxed his face is; even his lips are relaxed. He breathes through his mouth, his wide chin shiny with dribble. *A-beh!* he says. *A-beh!* Putting the stress on the second syllable, she would swear, and looking at Hattie as if to see if she can say it, too. *A-beh!* she says finally. He stamps his feet, delighted. His cheeks jiggle; his pant legs pool by his feet. She rolls them up for him, feeling him pat her head as she does, his warm tummy pressing like a compress against her forehead. *A-beh!* His shirt is stained on the shelf of his belly, where food always lands—a problem she had when she was pregnant, a problem she understands. *A-beh!* she says again, and he answers again, *A-beh!* It's a conversation. He has a few words, now, some of them multipurpose: *A-da!* is dog, but also birds and maybe bugs, for example—creatures. As for what language he's speaking, that is not clear. Sophy thinks *Ba-ba-ba!* is "yes" in Khmer—doesn't it sound just like *Bhat-bhat-bhat?* she says. But now as he pats Annie with concern he says, *A-beh*—wanting to give her his bottle. *A-beh, A-beh.* No, Hattie says, No bottle. Bottle for Gift, not for Annie, no. Still he insists, *A-beh.* A generous soul, speaking his own language, maybe. His hair has never been cut, so it's downy up top and wispy at the bottom, the hair he was born with—hair from another world, it seems. Angel hair. Sophy says they should cut it, people think he's a girl, but what with everyone so scissor-happy these days, Hattie's hoping they'll leave his alone. He's too young to be shorn by these self-shearers, too young to be clipped.

Sophy wants to clean Hattie's house in return for her babysitting, but Hattie tells her she's been doing her own cleaning. Some things you've got to clean yourself, she says, and Sophy nods.

"I get that," she says.

The trailer is not so much about teaching Mum English now as it is about teaching Hattie Khmer. Of course, she will never learn to speak it properly. The Internet says Khmer has some twenty-three vowels and sixty vowel sounds; that's too many new sounds for an old lady like her. She sees how Mum must feel about learning English, how it's like standing at a doorway you just can't enter. Hattie's learning to recognize some words and phrases, though. *Sra'ngout sra'ngat,* for example, which means "sadness," and *ah songkhim,* "hopelessness." Those are for Mum. And for Chhung, *ch'kuot,* which means "crazy," and *samlap khluon,* "suicidal." Sophy and Mum show Hattie a children's book about the Khmer alphabet. Neither of them can decipher its little upright assemblies of spears and zigzags and hooks and teardrops, but Sophy does know how there are no spaces between words when they're written, and how a vowel can go beside a consonant, but above it or below it, too. Above a consonant? says Hattie. Below it? Or around it, says Sophy. And when Hattie asks, Around it? How can it go around it? Sophy writes a letter and draws a kind of C around it; it looks like a clamp from Carter's woodshop. Like this, she says. The C is the vowel? Hattie asks, and Sophy nods with a little pride. She knows because her dad used to try to teach her about it, she says. Because it's the kind of thing he knows, he knows a lot of things. She starts to cry.

They all cry and cry.

Sophy has not been in school since the accident, but the church is not worried, she says. She says they know she'll come back; they have confidence. They believe it's the Lord's plan—even the accident was His plan.

If only Hattie believed in a plan.

Yesterday there was a storm, with a big wind, and lines of white-caps that passed and passed; Hattie sat in her car at the town beach and watched them. One line, another, another. How do the loons stay put the way they do? This one loon calmly, magically, holding its place in the waves—a lone black periscope, under which the waves rolled and rolled. The loons are an ancient species—twenty-five million years old, people say, relatives of the dinosaurs. To hear their laugh, their yodel, their howl—their many unearthly warbles—is to be put in touch with the numinous. But how weird that they're still here. Thanks to the weather, they're still here, and not just the juveniles— the adults are here, too. And so many other birds, as well: What with the leaves down, Hattie can see not only all the birds' nests—all the secret birds' nests—but dozens of the nest-makers, perched like snipers at the very tippy-top of the trees. Watching. Chattering. Why are you here? Hattie wants to ask them. Go south! Go south!

They do not move.

Today it is warm again. Hattie has only to step in the shade to know it's not summer, because in the summer the shade's warm; this shade's cold. But the heat is building in a summerlike way, as if some-thing's stalled—building and building so it can break. How can the holidays lie right around the corner? Turkey! Lights! Santa!

They watch for winter the way they used to watch for spring.

At least the days are shortening; there's that much right with nature. At least the planets are still in gear. Hear tell, too, that there's a bear hibernating under Grace's front porch. Imagine. People are surprised—warm as it's been, after all. If they were bears, they say, they would keep on with their fat-building, why stop? But they're not bears, and that bear has always wintered on Grace's property—claws her trees up good every year. And maybe there was a shortage of beechnuts this year—something. Of course, there're people who think she should get it out of there. Think how lightly it sleeps, they say. And they're right. A bear can wake in a flash. You might even call them nappers; a female can give birth smack in the middle of the winter. But Grace would never think of disturbing a creature's sleep. That's when you can feel its spirit, she told Hattie once—what it is besides its instincts and ways, namely innocent. They sense her interest in them, Hattie thinks. A couple of years ago Grace had a moose in her swamp, and the only silver fox ever seen in this area dug its burrow in her yard—a beautiful animal. More dark gray than silver, actually, with silver-white paws and a huge silver tail.

Oh, lake: Hattie's waiting for your shore to hem up and your waters to still—for a chill to spread itself over you once again, in so quick a sweep that it seems a spell has been cast—that some magician has waved a great wand and sonorously pronounced, "Saran wrap!" For there it will be, then, suddenly, again: a thin, still covering, complete with minute glassine wrinkles, as if the magician somehow failed to quite pull the wrap tight. Not that the wrinkles will much matter, in the end. In the end, the ice will thicken just the same; in the end, it will blanket the life below and keep it all safe. (How lucky that ice floats! Hattie used to tell her students. How lucky that ice insulates!)

And then in the spring, will come the thaw: cracks and slush and bays of melt. Open water. At the edge of the water there will be weasels, hungrily pulling up fish.

More of the e-mail she's been ignoring.

Dear Aunt Hattie
Dear Aunt Hattie
Dear Aunt Hattie

She reads and rereads them all. Decisions and accidents, parents and children, and worry—such a lot of worry. Such a lot of want. Not want such as she sees in the malls, but the kind of want her mother used to talk about—the kind that affected a person's posture. *Do you not see,* her mother wrote to Grandpa Amos, *how people want? Do you not see how people hurt? Do you not see how you refuse to acknowledge them except as candidates for salvation?*

Now Reveille and Annie sniff and hang around. Reveille puts his head in her lap. Annie chases down a mouse and brings it to Hattie, but then drops it, her tail wagging; the mouse scoots away.

Hattie sighs.

And that night, in her sleep, she sees her parents. Hattie has not dreamed of her parents for years; but there they are, waving their arms, whether in warning or greeting is not clear. In the morning, Hattie goes about her day as usual, but at night, there are her parents again. And there, too, is Qufu—the ancient trees, the mounds, the dust. The airless air. Though this Qufu lies right on the beach, somehow, like Qingdao; some of the grave mounds are made of sand. Hattie does not put much stock in dreams. Still.

Dear Aunt Hattie
Dear Aunt Hattie
Dear Aunt Hattie

Chhung at his station. Sarun in the hospital. Mum by her altar. Sophy, cleaning and cleaning. Even the Come 'n' Eat is empty, as if the town's lost its appetite.

"I don't know what to do," says Hattie. "I don't know what to do."

The chairs all around them are neatly pushed in, like the chairs of a classroom. Grace looks at her.

"Time," she says. "Give it time." For some reason she is wearing a watch today.

Watch.

"I can't watch," says Hattie.

"Watch what?" says Greta.

"Watch their lives fall apart this way."

Grace hands Hattie a horseshoe-print handkerchief.

"I have to do something." Hattie accepts the handkerchief, then realizes she's crying.

"Aren't you bringing them dinner?" Greta is singing a lullaby. "Aren't you helping with child care?"

"You are. You're helping. You're helping." Grace's voice is a hymn. "You're helping."

But Hattie shakes her head. "They need more. New karma. New *fēngshŭi*. Something."

Fēngshŭi?

Hattie explains—the graves. The e-mails.

"You've started reading them again?"

Hattie shrugs. "I see them differently now. Before they were all about superstition."

"And now?" Grace tilts her head, her face soft and dimply.

"Now when I read them I just see Mum praying."

"You wouldn't try to convert her."

"No."

"But you don't believe what she believes, either."

"That life is suffering? That all we can do is build up our karma?" Hattie shakes her head. "No."

Greta orders some more tea.

Flora is not the only one with a color theme today. Greta's gold. Gold turtleneck, gold jumper—golden tea, and golden honey, too. And though Hattie knows Greta's hair, of course, to be silver, in the sun it is golden as well, like her barrette. A vision of her friend more than her friend herself.

"Did your parents want to be buried in Iowa?" she asks.

"I'm sure they didn't, though they didn't want to be buried in Qufu, either," answers Hattie.

"So what did they want?" Grace's hair, live with static, stands on end—a dandelion puff.

"Probably they would just as soon have been sprinkled in a garden," says Hattie. "I had a friend who did that—had us sprinkle her in a peony bed."

"Wasn't that your friend Lee?"

Hattie doesn't remember having told Greta and Grace about Lee, but of course she has, many times.

"Yes," she says.

"Some people are keeping their parents' ashes instead of burying them," says Greta. "I know someone who made a receptacle out of a prayer wheel. She put it in her kitchen, so she can give it a spin every now and then."

"Really," says Hattie, and wants to laugh—the first time in weeks she's wanted to laugh.

"Maybe graveyards are becoming obsolete," says Greta.

"We're so much less connected to the earth than we were," says Grace.

"Hmm," says Hattie. "Maybe." Though a prayer wheel! Goodness. She shakes her head.

. . .

She e-mails her niece Tina in Hong Kong.

I have reconsidered my decision re: the graves. I do not myself believe in this sort of superstitious nonsense, let me say. But as I have come to see that many are in distress, I would like to do what I can. And so, all right. If you can arrange for a bone picker, I'd like to meet with him or her this weekend.

Him or her—why did she write that when there are no female bone pickers? Death, in China, being *yin*, has always been handled by its opposite, *yang*. And a bone picker in Iowa! On five days' notice! She is wondering if she should add a P.S. when, to her surprise—already!—Tina writes back.

Dear Auntie,

I have found one. His family from Taiwan but actually he live Los Angeles, so very easy to meet you there, he can just take an airplane. Of course, there is a reason he is so willing to help. He used to buy bonds at the office—giving them 2 percent right there, he never even thought about it before, how he is give money away. Now I save him money every transaction; that can add up to thousands of dollars savings, depending on his volume. So he is always willing to help us. And you too, willing to help! I am very happy. I always say it to Johnson, how important that family should stick together, even we are all over the world. People say home is where the job is . . .

Home is where the job is.

but life is too hard for everyone just say I am by myself, I come from nowhere. I tell my girls all the time. New generation, you know, they do not even know what life is. They think life is easy. They do not realize how your house can fall down any moment. Anyway, we all thank you very much. I have always believed you are wise. Now I know what I believed is true. I will tell the other family members, they will be very glad, too. I know I myself am crying while I write. That is how grateful I am. The situation with my daughter has been so difficult, I cannot sleep. Johnson say I am become some kind of ghost. We thank you, just thank you.

Hattie writes back,

I am glad to help. But, tell me. Do you really believe this? Because I am modern, like my parents. Of a scientific disposition, as you know.

Answers Tina,

I know it sounds like crazy superstition, even I think that sometimes. But you know Chinese culture is last 5,000 years, some part must be something right. Wrong part cannot be so wrong, either. Johnson says anyway it is cheaper than go to psychiatrist, but actually even Johnson is not just try save money. Even Johnson believe something in his heart. He is talk to the fengshui master. He is arrange our house in some crazy way. In fact to get from the kitchen to the rest of the house you have to go outside now, the maid is complaining in the bad weather she has to use umbrella. And he goes to the temple to burn incense, too. Especially when big trouble come, he goes to ask his ancestors for help. Because what else can he do? So many times we do not know how we can go on. He say when he go there, he feel better. So maybe it is a kind of crazy, but it is a crazy that make you feel less crazy. And maybe that has some kind of effect. You can say, that does not mean it is not superstition. And maybe you are right. Maybe it is just hang a sheep head to sell the dog meat—kind of like trick people. But I think so many people believe something for thousands of years, how can be nothing inside? I think our ancestors look after us. Look after you, too—how else can you live in United States today, so comfortable, and not so many people. We have too many people. Even you are rich you know they are there, try to grab your money. You can never say now we have siesta. Always we worry, worry.

Hattie writes,

Actually, we worry here, too. Maybe not in quite the same way. But think about the World Trade Center. We're guarding our airports and our subways. Our reservoirs. Our schools. Everyone is on edge, and losing money, too. Usually people come to see the leaves turn, but they're not coming this year. And what if we lose our jobs? What if we break a tooth? What if we get cancer, or Alzheimer's? I lost my husband and best friend to cancer, you know. Both in one year. . . .

She stops

Probably you will say, You see? That just goes to show the graves should be moved. I do not believe so, but who knows, maybe you are right. Recently my neighbors, too, had a terrible thing happen. . . .

She stops again.

So I remember worry, yes, and heartache, too. People here move and move. We don't feel quite in control. And research has shown, I believe, that that correlates with, if not religion exactly, at least magical thinking.

Replies Tina,

Maybe it is not so polite to say so, but I do not think fengshui is just think something magic. It is believe in some right relationship with the world. It is try to think what that is, not just do any way you like. It is believe your life will be more smooth if you say OK, I am not such a big shot. Our relatives are bury in Qufu for 70 generations. 2000 years. How can we say we are now bury all over? Who are we? As if we know everything! Talk about crazy.

Writes Hattie,

Who are we, indeed. I cannot say you have convinced me, and if you will forgive me for putting on my scientist hat, I must point out that we humans are prone to superstition. We're wired to seek cause and effect whether it's there or not—to make "sense" of things even if the result is nonsense. But never mind. Insofar as your thinking appears to have little to

do with the less tenable tenets of Confucianism, and more to
do with tradition and hope and humility and coping . . .

—and where you do not, thank goodness, imagine your will to be
the will of God—

. . . I will meet the bone picker this weekend.

Tina replies,

Thank you, Auntie, thank you. Thank you. Johnson say to
tell you of course we are crazy, but at least we are not pray to
Jesus Christ! Talk about crazy!

Hattie sighs.

Qufu is not the only graveyard with a claim on Hattie's parents.
Back when her mother went native, Hattie's grandfather wrote a
letter about the graveyard in Iowa, which Hattie unfolds now, on her
tray table, on the plane. She only has this letter because her mother
sent it back unopened, she was so mad; Hattie can still see Grandpa
Amos's face as he passed it on to her, years later. "Whatever you do,
don't send it to me again," he said ruefully. "I've seen enough of this
particular missive." Why didn't she ask him then why he wrote clear
across the page, as if he did not believe in margins? Now she will
never know, though she guesses it was to save weight: for what lovely
thin sheets of onionskin she spreads out on her tray table. They are
translucent and crisp, and quite unlike his handwriting, which is
loopy and close-packed, and hard to decipher even with her reading
glasses.

Dear Caroline, I do fear you will be the death of your mother.
She has heard so many stories over the years, and while I can-
not say that she has not had her worries about the hazards of
missionary life—the stories of beheadings were particularly
hard to shake—she could always put them aside, as long as
you had the Good Lord over you. But now she fears for your
soul, as do we all. What do you mean you do not care to be

saved? And how can Christian compassion be expanded? The way to salvation is open to all, but John 3:3 says, Except a man be born again, he cannot see the kingdom of God. To claim that a just God would not demand that all accept their salvation! Daughter, we are justified by faith alone. You describe your hand shaking, on occasion, as you assist at a baptism. That is the devil shaking you, body and soul. It is blasphemy to question the ways of the Lord. He is Justice; His actions are Just. The Buddha is a fine example of living rectitude, but he is not Divine. He is not Absolute, and demands a different fealty. To think him an "alternative," as you say, is to have a false god before you. Heaven help you. You have mixed yourself among the people, like Ephraim. Strangers have devoured your strength.

I have never seen your mother pray so fiercely. She has lost weight. She cannot eat. She has even developed a tremor, in consequence of which she leaves the serving to me when we have company, and sits on her hands in general. It is making her self-conscious and unsociable. I myself went for a walk by the family cemetery today, as I do in times of trial. We are blessed to have it so nearby. And in such a splendid spot! Can you picture it still? The plains extending as far as the eye can see and, in the midst of that enormity, our little spot, with its fence. I don't think there is another place on earth with a sky of that size.

Daughter, I do have faith. The devil has done his best on many of us, but our last days have found every one of our family recounting the reasons of the hope that was in us. This is your trial. Remember that salvation is possible for all but certain for none. I pray that you will call out like David and have restored to you the joy of your salvation, that one day you too will lie at peace here, your struggles at an end. We have much for which to thank the good Lord, and call on Him to aid you now. May He bless you and guide you. Yrs in Christ, Father

Hattie folds the letter back up carefully. Would Grandpa Amos have forgiven her for doing this? He did write, many years later,

I am coming to wonder how a heaven that would not have your mother could be heaven.

But who knows. Bless him, in any case, she thinks, descending already—her ears popping, and the Great Plains spread out below her in all their eventless modesty. Hattie likes their nondescript brown-green, brushed here and there with white. And the general levelhead-edness that seems to have grown up out of the level land—she likes that, too. Though why did she not let anyone know she was coming? On the one hand, no one has the claim on her parents that she does, and everything was so last-minute. On the other, well, what would it have taken to drop people who had e-mail, an e-mail?

Greetings, all! Forgive the group missive, but I wanted to let you know . . .

The plane lands with a jolt and a bounce; Hattie gathers up her things. There's a jetway now—things have modernized. And what a cheery new lounge, with such cheery new carpet; it could be a chil-dren's playroom. She finds a pay phone.

Just tell them you're here to disinter some folks—Lee's voice.

Rings.

She holds on for twenty rings, checks her address book, dials again, and goes twenty rings more. No answer. No machine. Some years ago, there'd have been dozens of numbers to call. It was nothing to scrounge up a last-minute supper if you needed one, and no one ever had to buy sports equipment; there were always skates or nets or cleats around somewhere. But her mother's family is all over now, just like her father's. Only the youngest of the uncles is still bravely hold-ing out in Grandpa Amos's house—Uncle Samuel. Living alone, though he's in his nineties now. Who knows if he can even hear the phone.

She dials a cousin—no answer there, either.

Were the handsets of these public phones always so heavy? And that coil it's attached to—was it always so stiff and wayward? *So wound up,* Lee would have said.

She'd forgotten.

An athletic Asian man with porcupine hair approaches her out by the baggage claim. "Mrs. Kong?"

Somehow Hattie had not imagined that the bone picker would be dressed all in black. But here he is—black sweater, black jeans, black boots, and he's holding a black leather jacket, too. He has respectfully removed the earbuds of his MP3 player; they dangle back behind his neck like the earpieces of an inexplicably limp stethoscope. Still, a mini-beat emanates from them, tinny and tuneless.

"My name is Lennie." He puts out a hand.

"It's nice to meet you, Lennie."

"Lennie Dow, like in Dow Joncs."

"Nice to meet you," she says again.

The bone picker is so long-waisted and short-legged it is hard not to wonder if he is not part Japanese—the Japanese having occupied Taiwan for so long, after all. He has a kite-shaped face, too, planar. Seeing as how she also grew up under the Japanese, though, and seeing as how she was so often asked if she was Japanese—strange-looking creature that she was—she doesn't ask.

He senses her interest in his appearance all the same.

"People are surprised I'm so young," he says. "I learned the business from my dad."

"And he was old."

"Yeah." No laugh. "I mean, when he got older, he was. And he learned it from his pa, and so on. We've been bone pickers for generations—a great living in the beginning. These days, though, you need other irons in the fire. Especially if you're based in the States, like I am. Kind of the U.S. franchise."

"I would imagine."

"I was born here."

"Is that so."

He shrugs. "I'm just telling you because people want to know. But I speak Chinese—you couldn't really do this job if you didn't speak Chinese. Mandarin, Taiwanese, Cantonese, at least. Fujianese, too, these days. Seeing as how all the bones are Chinese. The clientele."

"English is fine," she says. "*Dōu kěyi.*"

"Can I get that bag for you?"

"Thank you. Though it's very light, really."

"It'll be heavier on the way back," he says, pulling; he's wearing some kind of string bracelet. "It's ashes, right? I mean, we do do bones. That's why we're called bone pickers. Because we do do that, pick the bones out of any flesh that might be left."

Pick 'em out, jar 'em up.

"But your folks have already been cremated, is my understanding."

"They were cremated for the move here, I believe," says Hattie. "It was some years ago."

"Then they'll fit in your bag okay," he says. "Good thing you're on wheels, though. The ashes don't weigh much but the jars weigh a ton."

He wheels. He does not go so far as to put his earbuds back in, but as they head toward the door, he does begin to bop his head to the beat coming from them. His shoulders jiggle, too, like something you'd want to have a handyman come fix if it was in your house.

Outside, the air is brisk, and the sky above the treeless glare of the parking lot almost as huge as the sky Grandpa Amos described. Lennie dons his leather jacket, inserting his player-bearing arm into its sleeve first. She tells him she wants to stop at a florist.

The graveyard is not what it was in Grandpa Amos's time. The little fence is still there, though, and in good repair; and, contrary to the predictions of Hattie's Chinese relatives, someone has been keeping after things. The whole affair is larger than Hattie remembered, too—an acre or so, with what look to Hattie like some lovely old elms. Leafless, but never mind. They're something a body doesn't see too often, what with Dutch elm disease—that distinctive vase shape. Maybe these are a replacement cultivar? They seem, in any case, a miracle. Less miraculously, a shopping mall has sprung up since the last time Hattie visited, so that the oldest gravestones face loading docks and dumpsters. Gaping doorways, containers. Trucks. The word "façade" has never been Hattie's favorite; but how far preferable a façade to this bald fact. She focuses on the enormous bunch of roses in her arms, bringing them to her face as she begins walking the grassy aisles between the graves. The ground gives underfoot; has the weather been as weirdly warm here as it's been in Riverlake? Men hurl objects into a dumpster—*bong!*—as she begins placing a rose in front of each gravestone. A different color for each; she did clean the florist out. The older gravestones pitch and lean. They are of thinner, darker stone than the newer ones, elaborately lettered and irregularly spaced. The newer ones, in contrast, are both more monumental and more organized, the family having grown better at anticipating its space needs with time, it seems—less apt to find themselves with an extra body to work in, or a no-show. How is that? Anyway, the ground, too, grows slowly more even, until it begins to resemble a putting green. And here come, among the many names she doesn't know well, some names she does. Her great-great-grandparents. Her great-grandparents. Their many siblings and cousins and spouses and children—so many children, grown up and not: This one age seven. This one age two. Baby, three weeks. Baby, six weeks. Baby, one week. Babies, babies, babies. Though how many Amoses and Samuels and Jeremiahs and Joshuas, too! The female names are also mostly biblical—Sarah and Mary and Ruth—but with some family names mixed in: Hattie, like her. Georgia. Caroline, like her mother and grandmother. The men are born and named by the Book.

Overhead, amid the thickening clouds, a biplane drones by, its propellers spinning. Loud, but not nearly as loud as the loading at the shopping mall. *Bong!*

Distractions. And yet as Hattie moves down the line, she feels a dawning orientation all the same—an awareness, not so much of what her mother would have called her *ultimate dependence,* as of the vastness of death—its unreasonable, infinite creep. Of what a different scale people are in comparison—mere nano-things. And how improbable our ability to absorb energy and use it, much less to reason and dream and imagine one another—one another's thoughts, even, one another's feelings.

Testimony to something, her mother would say. And, *Must not there be a giver of this gift?*

Hattie only wishes she were as sure, as she goes up and down the rows, her flower bundle lightening. Must there?

A snow sprinkle. Tiny flakes melting as soon as they hit the ground. Or, no: They disappear even before that, midair. Turn into mist. So the ground must be warm, then—from retained heat or microbial activity, or both. It's a comforting idea, somehow.

But is she driving Lennie crazy, lingering like this? No, he has his music. Boxes to unload, too. An athletic boy, his stiff hairs bending, now, with moisture. Hattie can feel drops on her face, in her hair; she wipes them away.

How quickly the clouds have piled up, thick and gray; what a brilliant light must shine above them. But down here, it's just the changeable midwestern weather—not unlike what they see in Riverlake. The nimbostratus clouds bringing real snow, now, and a hush she appreciates as she comes to the newest stones, with the sharpest carving: Grandma Caroline. Grandpa Amos—her sweet grandpa Amos. Uncle Jeremy and Susan—she stands before these last gravestones a good while, too. On his, their children wrote, WHO WANTED TO UNDERSTAND WHAT IT MEANT TO BE HUMAN. And on hers: WHO UNDERSTOOD.

Two flowers for each of them. Uncle Jeremy and Just Susan, Hattie used to call them because Susan did always insist on being called that—just Susan.

And here: Hattie's mother's grave—lying just where it should. And next to it, Hattie's father's grave. Lying just where it should, too, as if everyone knew her parents would end up here.

Māma, Bàba.

Their headstones are the only ones with Chinese characters, of course—her parents' Chinese names, Gě Kǎilìng and Kǒng Lìngwén, carved, top to bottom, along the right edge of the stones in red. And in one corner of each stone, a clump of bamboo. Bamboo done by chisel! Amazing.

Bamboo, which bends but does not break.

Māma, Bàba.

She closes her eyes. It seems to her she has been painting her way all along to this moment—retreating that she might inch forward, like a snail. How sorry she is to have missed their old age! And how can they never have met Josh, or Joe? She wishes she had been there when they died—together at least, she heard. Not long after they finally escaped the Mainland; of his 'n' her tuberculosis. The end of their story is unreal to Hattie. Far easier to picture are her parents as she knew them: young and modern and rebellious. They were never going to grow old; they were never going to weaken; they would sooner have been dead than be buried in a Christian cemetery.

Or in Qufu, either, probably—*Fallen leaves return to their roots* notwithstanding. But would they have minded being reburied there? Or, more accurately, re-reburied—?

No one more agreeable than the dead, Lee used to say.

More trucks. The rest of the flowers. Hattie catches Lennie's eye. He leaves his earbuds to dangle as he maneuvers a large cardboard box over to the graves. Out of this comes an aluminum folding table, on top of which he places a large red silk square that threatens to fly or slip off, and two smaller squares of shiny gold that, though of a heavier weave, are likewise too slippery to stay put. He anchors them all with dishes: a fried fish, a pork knuckle. A poor roasted chicken with its neck skewered and wound into an S. Dried fruit; fresh fruit; candy; cake. Cups of wine. In front of the food, he places two pillar candles and a jar full of sand in which to stick incense; and in front of the table, to one side, some long sticks of sugarcane. Then he starts to cut through the grass. Jabbing a half-moon spade into the ground, stepping on it, rocking it. He fashions a kind of trapdoor, then rolls this back, snipping the grass roots with a pair of clippers as he goes. Does he really know just where Hattie's father's urn lies? It does seem so, for in goes the shovel and out pops the jar without fanfare, the dirt raining away. Next, Hattie's mother's jar. The jars are sturdy white ceramic with blue markings—two feet high or so, maybe fifteen inches in diameter. Sealed, pockmarked, a little dirty, and quite extraordinarily unextraordinary; they could be for pickled vegetables. Hattie can see where there might once have been writing—her parents' names, presumably—but the writing is too faint to make out now. How to keep them straight? She stoops to pick one up, but Lennie signals her to wait. Some rummaging and, ah—he produces some wet naps from a plastic tub and cleans the urns with these. Then—sparing her the bending—he presents the urns to her.

"In China, women aren't allowed to touch anything," he says. "But this is a free country, right?"

She accepts her mother's urn, kissing it lightly; the jar is cold, the glaze pitted and clammy. Lennie takes it from her and presents her with the other urn, her father's. She kisses this, too, coming away this time with a little something on her lips. Grit. She wipes it away.

Twins.

Lennie sets the urns on the gold silk squares on the table. His hair drips as he leans forward; he flicks it back with a snap.

"Bones, not ashes," he says.

"How do you know?"

"See how tall the jars are?"

"Yes."

"The tall jars are for bones."

"Ah."

"They're put back in the same way they were originally."

"Originally?"

"In the womb."

"Ah. In fetal position, you mean."

He nods. "If you want, we can open a jar and see how they're doing."

Open a jar?

"No thanks," she says.

"It shouldn't smell," Lennie reassures her. "It's only when we open graves, you know, that things are—" He gestures with his unbraceleted hand.

"You mean there's still flesh?"

"Sometimes. You wouldn't believe the smell. That's the hardest part of the job, the smell. My dad used to say I'd get used to it, but I never did. He says that's because I was born here. He says real Chinese can get used to anything."

Bong!

The trees are frosted white now, and the ledges of the tombstones. Lenny's shoulders and hair, too, and his collar, and the flaps of his jacket pockets. A world of the ledged and ledgeless.

"You pick the bones out of the rotting flesh?" Part of Hattie wants Lennie to shut up, but she's curious, too.

"Only if there's no choice. Mostly we pour in some rice wine and leave the body to steep. Crack the lid for air. That speeds up the decomp rate. Even better's if you let the insects and animals do their thing, but most people aren't into that. A lot of other bone pickers use chemicals these days, but we do things the old-fashioned way. It's not as fast as the chemicals, but hey. It's organic."

"Good for you."

Lennie rakes the dirt back into the graves, then rolls the grass back down and stomps. By spring the cuts will have knit themselves up; it will be hard to tell that any of this went on. But does that make it all right? Is this what her parents would have wanted?

Do you not see how people want? Do you not see how people hurt?

Lennie begins to wrap the jars in the damp yellow squares.

"Can we mark them first, to keep them straight?" asks Hattie.

"Sure." Lennie searches through his box and finds a blue marker. "Permanent ink?"

He nods.

She writes the characters for *Māma* and *Bàba,* as neatly as she can, on the bottom of the jars. *Māma, Bàba.* Thinking as she writes how she had not known before Joe and Lee died that you could see life leave a person—that you could see their color drain away, and the light leave their eyes. But there it was. Their hearts stopped, then their brains stopped. And then never mind that their bones and skin cells went on a while longer, nonsensically. Long before their bodies cooled, they were gone.

Māma, Bàba.

Now Hattie sees Greta and Grace and Sophy, all in jars. Chhung and Mum and Sarun and Gift. Carter and Candy and Beth and Ginny; Everett and Judy Tell-All and Jill Jenkins. Tina and Johnson. Flora. Herself. In fact, if Josh pots her up, it will more likely be in ash form. Still, it is everyone's bones she sees, in white jars with blue trim, on a long table. Reveille and Annie. After all that walking, all that talking, all those experiments and cookies and e-mails. Their names are in blue magic marker; their silk squares ripple under them.

"Leaving the headstones, or taking them?" asks Lennie.

Taking them?

"We can arrange relocation if you like," he goes on.

"Leave them," she says. "Please."

"You want firecrackers?"

To advertise what they're doing?

"No, thank you."

"How about offering respects? You're supposed to kneel and *kē tóu*"—he pulls the pillow out of the box and begins to demonstrate. But Hattie grew up in China; she doesn't need to be shown how to stand in front of the table, or how to raise the incense sticks high in the air, or how to step forward and place them in the incense holder. She backs up, kneeling a bit creakily on the cushion—the damp—then touches her forehead to the wet grass.

Māma, Bàba.

Tears, snow.

She bows twice more.

Lennie offers her a hand up and a handkerchief for her forehead.

"When I was little, we had chants," she says, after a moment. "A monk or two, sometimes more."

"Those were the good old days," says Lennie.

He wraps the yellow bundles in bubble wrap, fastening the wrap with packing tape. The ripping of the tape is loud and harsh.

"You should put them in your luggage and check them," he says. "If you carry them on, you might have trouble getting through security—these days, especially. Unless you have their death certificates? That can be a help."

"I don't."

"Well, then, you should check them. Some people feel the bones should stay right with you; but others think the spirits understand that these are modern times. And your parents have been stuck here for so long, they're probably willing to do anything to spring the coop."

"Okay." She nods. Whatever.

"These going to the Mainland?"

She nods again.

"Then you'll want to have them cremated. Otherwise you could have trouble getting them into the country."

"Thanks for telling me."

"Of course, there's almost always someone you can pay off. As I'm guessing you know."

"I'll have them cremated."

He turns his collar up. "If you're going to have them cremated, I should probably point out that we can take care of it, if you like. That is, if you don't have a local crematorium you'd prefer."

"I'll use our local facilities, thank you."

He hesitates. "I didn't mean to pressure you. It's just that my dad would be mad if I didn't point that out." He toes the ground, boyish.

She smiles. "Tell your dad you did a good job. Real Chinese."

"Thanks." He looks thoughtful. "Though maybe you'd be willing to fill out a customer satisfaction survey? If you're satisfied? Then you can tell him yourself."

"I'd be happy to."

"It already has a stamp on it. All you have to do is pop it in the mail."

"That's great."

"I appreciate it."

"No problem. Fathers can be hard on their sons, I know."

He frowns. "Think so?"

It's snowing harder now, the flakes large and light; they pile up quick and high as Hattie pockets the form and Lennie crams the bubble-wrapped urns into backpacks. He helps Hattie put her arms through the shoulder straps of one.

"It's better to wear it frontwise," he says.

"Like a marsupial," she says.

"A what?"

"A kangaroo or some such. An animal that carries its young in a pocket."

"Whatever," he says. "This is heavy. You have to lean back."

"Okay." She supports the weight with her hands, the way she used to support her belly, sometimes, back before Josh was born. It's like being pregnant again, only with her mother.

Your mother turned bowling ball.

Lennie bears the other urn back to the car, one earbud in. In a show of respect he does not add the other bud until the car's out of the cemetery and on the main road. He bops his head with a pecking motion, like a chicken.

The urns seem much larger in Hattie's kitchen than they did in the graveyard and, next to Hattie's computer, older—as if they hail from another reality. *The time of the large jars.* And as if with reverence for that ancient dispensation, Grace and Greta stand now, like the jars, side by side, a pair. They're about the same height; they both fold their hands.

Twins.

"It's a beautiful thing you're doing," says Grace.

"A compassionate thing," says Greta.

Hattie shakes her head. "I think my relatives are nuts."

Grace examines the glaze. "May I touch one?"

"Of course."

"Is this your mother or your father?"

Hattie tilts the jar; she's still surprised how heavy it is. "My father."

"I'll touch both."

"I'm sure they'd like that."

Grace stretches a finger out. Greenhouse gardener that she is, her cuticles are rimmed with dirt such as seems to befit the occasion as she touches the side of the urn, then lays a palm on its top, her fingers flat and splayed. Her eyes are squinched so tight her eyelashes flip up at the corners, but her face is serene.

"Thank you," she says at last.

"You're welcome," says Hattie, though why is Grace thanking her? She asks if Greta wants a turn.

. . .

Sarun is home! As he's still in a neck brace and supposed to stay still, he mostly watches TV or plays with his PlayStation, which he isn't usually allowed to hook up to the TV but is now. What hair he has is not blond but black and enough like Mum's that they're quite a sight together. *Mother 'n' son buzz cuts!* Lee would have said. It's pretty wack. Mum lets him smoke marijuana in the living room, why not—everyone did it in Cambodia, it seems, and she likes the smell. In fact, when Mum has the energy she is going to make him chicken soup with marijuana in it, Sophy says. Hattie does not encourage this. All they need is to get busted, she says. But Mum is far more worried that Sarun will be charged with arson. Because someone must be upset, Sophy says. Like probably Everett is upset. And fair or not, people do think Sarun and his friends set the fire.

"But why the fuck would I burn down the mini-mall?" says Sarun.

He would shake his head if he could. As it is, he can only move it enough to jiggle his pirate earrings, which Sophy and Hattie have cleaned and fixed for him. The earrings rest lightly on the padding of his neck brace, around which is wrapped his gold chain, though it is barely long enough; it looks like an absurdly delicate dog collar.

"And fucking plywood!" he goes on. "That be low, man."

Anyway, Sophy volunteers, even if he's charged, he'll get off, because she knows who really set the fire.

"Oh, really," says Sarun. "Who?" His pupils are huge, his face alive and amused.

"Me," she says. "I set the fire."

"You!" scoffs Sarun. "You can't even strike a match."

"I can so." Sophy takes some kitchen matches out of a drawer that could be the very drawer Hattie rescued long ago. She lights a match then immediately blows it out, dropping it in the sink.

Sarun laughs. "You see? You afraid of fire."

"I did it!" she insists all the same, smiling.

"And why'd you do it? Please tell us."

She pouts prettily, her lower lip protruding.

"Spit it out, now. What was your mo-tive?"

"I did it so they'd pin it on you!" She sticks her tongue out at him.

"Because you wanted me locked up?"

She plays with her hair. "Because you were upsetting everyone."

"This was your grand plan?"

"I thought it was God's plan. Because . . ." She wrinkles her nose.

"Spit it out," says Sarun again.

"Because you were doing Satan's work!" She juts her chin out.

Sarun laughs so loud Mum pokes her head out from her bedroom; Gift claps his hands but then stops, confused.

"Was it God's plan that instead of going to jail I went to the hospital?" asks Sarun.

Sophy looks as though she might cry. Still, Sarun laughs some more as Gift climbs carefully onto his lap—knowing, it seems, that his brother is hurt. Knowing he has to be careful. He pats Sarun's brace and gazes at his face.

"That be some kind of miracle, all right," says Sarun. "And what about the old man?" He hugs Gift with one arm, gesturing out the window with the other. "Tell me, mastermind. He going to be sitting outside all winter? What's God's game plan on that?"

Chhung sits by himself in the guard chair—smoking, drinking, brooding. Falling asleep. Mum is afraid he is going to die out there. She thinks he has been taken by *k'maoch* and that they need a *kru* to fetch him back; she just wants to know where they can find a *kru*.

Hattie calls the hippie Buddhist temple.

"*Kru?*" says the man. "Can you spell that for me?"

Hattie sighs and hangs up.

Mum goes on praying and praying, her hair shorter all the time, her carpet square tucked under her. Her shrine grows more elaborate, spawning bowls of fruit and incense.

"She says he has to come in. She says he's going to freeze to death," Sophy says. "But he says why should he come in when that's what he wants. When he wants to freeze to death."

Hattie shakes her head. "Has Sarun talked to him?"

"No, and he doesn't want to," says Sophy.

And sure enough, when Hattie broaches the subject, Sarun says, "That asshole almost killed me."

Hattie checks his eyes to be sure he's not high, then turns down the TV with the remote control. He leans forward to hear what he can of the show anyway, the cuffs of his sweatpants riding up.

"You're right. He did. He did almost kill you. But you know, he's sorry," Hattie says. "He was worried you did something wrong. And he was worried that because of you the police were going to find out about Sophy's having broken probation, and about the possible 51A on him in your old town."

"If he's so sorry, why don't he say so?" Sarun scratches in under his collar with a chopstick. "If he's so sorry, why don't he come tell me how he knows I'm innocent? If he's so sorry, why don't he come tell me how he knows he beat me up for nothing? He beat me up when that cop had nothing on me, and now he can't even say he's sorry. You know why?" Sarun gestures with the chopstick. "Because he is crazed. That's why. You know what he said when you first showed up? He said you were Khmer Krom."

"Is that Vietnamese Cambodian?"

"Yeah. Or a *k'maoch*. He thought you were a *k'maoch*." He looks back at the screen; he's watching some sort of police drama.

Hattie sighs. "Your father should tell you how wrong he was. He should. He should apologize for overreacting, and for almost killing you. But he's not well, Sarun."

"Yeah, well, I'm not so well, either, thanks to he almost fucking killed me. Like you said. And why should he get off scot-free, tell me? While I'm on the spit for something I had nothing to fucking do with?" Sarun's eyes flash with challenge; he wields the chopstick like a baton.

Hattie plucks it out of his hand. "That is an excellent question." She stashes the chopstick down under her thigh and turns the TV off altogether.

"Hey," he protests.

"Did anyone ask you about this in the hospital?"

"About what."

"About what happened to you."

"Someone did, yeah."

He stares at his reflection. In the blank screen his brace looks bigger and brighter than any other part of him.

"And what did you say?"

"I said I never saw my assailant."

"So you covered up for your father."

"I didn't like the asshole they sent."

"You covered up for him. First you let him do it and then you covered up for him."

He looks out the window as if there might be something new to see, and not just the same old trees. His skin gleams except for the crater that is his scar.

"Why'd you never hit him back?"

He puts his hand out for the chopstick; and when she returns it to him, says, "He's old. I could've killed him." He sticks the chopstick back down his neck brace.

"You showed forbearance but then he almost killed you."

"He's not even my real fucking father, all right? I fucking hate him but he's what I've fucking got." Sarun grinds his jaw. "I probably would've died in that fucking camp if it wasn't for him, but now I've done as much as I'm going to for that asshole. Because first he saved me but then he almost killed me. Like you said."

"Did they ask about 911 being called to your place before? At the hospital?"

"Yeah."

"And you said?"

"I said that was different. An unrelated incident."

"And they believed you?"

He gives a half-shrug, a little calmer. "Knowing him, he probably wishes I'd turned him in. Knowing him, he probably wants to be locked up."

"He wants to kill himself, Sarun."

Sarun taps the chopstick on his knee, holding it loosely, like a drumstick. "People were freaked out by the van, weren't they," he says, finally. "They thought it was, like, a gangmobile."

"Well, it was a gangmobile, wasn't it? I mean, it had your gang in it, and it didn't just drive around. It kind of snuck in and out of town."

"So my old man wouldn't flip."

"Well, that attracted attention. Forget about thieves and arsonists—some people thought you were terrorists."

"Terrorists!" Sarun leans back theatrically. "You mean those salamis with the mad hair?"

Hattie nods.

"You got to be shitting me." He makes a twirling motion with the chopstick. "That is *muy loco*."

"Well, that's what people thought."

"And now you think the old man wants to kill himself."

"I do."

"That is *muy loco,* too."

"The word I'd use is 'sad,' " says Hattie. "It's *muy* sad."

Sarun purses his mouth up and puts out his hand, wanting the remote control. His hand, though, is cupped and uninsistent, like a monk's.

His gang friends come visit. It is strange to see the white van drive down to the trailer and park in the open; and how strange, too, to finally behold its occupants. Hattie counts seven of them. Who knows if this is the whole gang or just a contingent, but they're mostly dressed in black like Lennie Dow the bone picker, with black hair; and all of them are short, and keep their hands in their pockets. Are they armed? Hattie can't help but wonder, even as she recalls Josh's fourth-grade winter assembly and how every single boy did stand there on the bleachers with his hands in his pockets, too. It could mean exactly nothing. None of these boys has blond hair the way Sarun used to, but most of them have gone either super-long or super-short—some of them super-short with super-long strands—no Confucian moderation, extremity is all. Oversize jackets and sweatshirts; pant legs that puddle at the bottom like Gift's; baseball hats facing to the back or side—most of them with do-rags under them, but not all. Tattoos. Gold chains and earrings like Sarun's but also big rings on some of their fingers and, of course, earbuds. Unlike Lennie Dow, though, they not only remove their buds as they enter the trailer, but shut their MP3 players off, besides—a mannerly bunch. In fact, they enter so respectfully—so swaggeringly shyly—that Sarun has to wave at them to take off their jackets. They take off their sneakers, too, and repeatedly refuse Mum's offer of snacks; she has to offer three times before they finally accept a bag of chips. To the extent that they look at Sophy at all, it is furtively. Still, Sophy quickly disappears. Mum slides Hattie a plate of vegetables to chop as if this is Hattie's job; they work side by side in the kitchen, keeping watch as the boys settle in. The living room is too small, and there aren't enough seats, but never mind. Some lean against the wall; others sprawl on the floor. They sniff the air—the marijuana—laughing when Sarun explains, some of them openly, with a *ha-ha,* others guardedly, with a *heh-heh.* One of them covers his mouth, like a girl; none of them sits straight. Instead they relax and sprawl—engaging, Lee would say, in *a little male splay display.*

These gangs, Hattie knows, are not just social clubs. Sophy has told her how they steal computer chips out of video parlors; they deal drugs and steal cars, too, and now they're trafficking in bear parts. Sophy has told Hattie, what's more, about what's involved in getting jumped in—initiated—the beating up for guys, the serial sex for girls. And how prickly the gang members are—how easily disrespected. How quick to retaliate, how violent. Hattie knows all this. She knows that even their own Sarun has "wet" people before; Mum is right to be concerned.

Yet none of this is evident as the boys rib one another. Rainbow of browns that they are, they all appear to hail from Southeast Asia in some way—their differences, as best Hattie can tell, forming the basis of many jokes. It's hard to tell at first because of the way they talk: *He's 'ite*, she remembers, is "He's all right"; and *Whaazup nigga?* she gets just fine, too, unfortunately. It takes a while for her to realize, though, that *Sowegit i'de caaw* is "So we get in the car," and there's much she simply cannot catch. Still, she's picked up teen talk before; no one had a better ear for the cafeteria than she did, once upon a time. And so slowly now she begins to make out jokes about Siem Reap, for example—a Cambodian city whose name apparently means "Trample the Thais." She hears them call a Lao kid *Lao Dang,* which she is pretty sure is like calling him Khmer Rouge—a Communist. And everyone jokes constantly about the Vietnamese—the *Youen*— the one group explicitly excluded from this gang. Much else seems less worth deciphering.

Sarun, in any case, presides over all of this from his kitchen chair. His stiffness lends him a regal air, but he slurs his words with the best of them, ragging good-naturedly on different *puak maak* until, watching him, Mum begins to enjoy herself a little, too, it seems. As if it's nice to have company for a change, even this company. She does not abandon her post. However, she does shoo Hattie with some force out of the kitchen. Hattie protests, but when Mum brandishes a kitchen knife at her—treating her like family—Hattie surrenders, smiling.

She knocks on Sophy's half-open door; Sophy pulls forward her red bookmark.

"Don't stop," says Hattie. "What are you reading?"

"The Psalms." Sophy closes her Bible. She is sitting on the mattress, back against the wall—her knees pressed together, her bare feet splayed. No toenail polish today, but she's wearing lipstick and eye-liner, and a gold metallic headband with her T-shirt and jeans.

"Which one?" asks Hattie.

Sophy hesitates, but finally waggles her head, opens her book back up, and reads, " 'For I am poor and needy, and my heart is wounded within me.' " She closes the book again.

"Psalm 109."

Sophy nods. Her face is a little pale, as if she is coming down with something; she does not seem bothered by the noise in the living room.

" 'I am gone like the shadow when it declineth; I am tossed up and down like the locust,' " recites Hattie.

Sophy opens the book back up, hunching her shoulders like a beginning reader. " 'As the locust,' " she says.

" 'As the locust,' thank you."

Sophy looks thoughtful then—as though she could ask Hattie something—but she picks her book back up instead. Her forefinger moves; she puzzles; she crosses and uncrosses her toes. Hattie watches for a moment, then plunks herself down on the mattress, too, leaning back against the opposite wall. She means to ask if that's okay, but the wall is warm with sun, and before she knows it, she is taking a nap.

A makeup-less Sophy comes to visit the next day; Hattie shows Annie off.

"Sit," she says.

Annie sits.

"Stay," she says.

Annie stays, sort of.

"Stay," Hattie says again, and—giving up—"Lie down."

Annie lies down, her tail sweeping back and forth as if the real command had been Sweep!

"She is, like, all grown up!" says Sophy, kneeling down to pet her; her hair glints almost silver in the sun. "Just like that!"

Hattie smiles. "*Guā mù xiāng kàn,*" she says.

"What does that mean?"

"It means 'You're rubbing your eyes to see someone!'—amazed as you are at her progress."

"*Gua—?*"

"*Guā mù xiāng kàn.*"

"Guā mù xiāng kàn."

"Excellent!" Hattie claps but then says, "This may be the last dog I train."

"How come?"

"Oh, I don't know. I met someone the other day who doesn't train her dogs because she doesn't like how it distorts their personalities. She says she doesn't like how the dogs are always looking to their masters for cues, and I thought she had a point."

Sophy rubs noses with Annie, who bows, tail wagging, wanting to play. "Only you would ever say something like that," she says.

"That's not true. I'm just repeating what this other woman said. And I should add that some people think dogs like training—that they're bred for it and uncomfortable without it. So I don't know."

Still, Sophy insists, her eyes wide, "You know everything. You do."

And as Annie suddenly dashes off—a squirrel outside the window!—Sophy asks Hattie how to turn her father in. "Can we file a 51A on him? Do they have that here?"

Hattie makes her sit down. Pours some coffee; puts out some orange slices, not having any cookies.

"There is probably something along those lines," she answers, finally. "But are you sure you want to do that?"

"My dad wants us to."

"He wants you to turn him in?"

"He says he's an animal, and should be in a cage."

An animal who should be in a cage.

"And what does Sarun think?" Hattie cradles her coffee mug, trying to encourage Sophy to drink by example.

"Sarun was too mad to think anything before. But now he thinks it might make my dad feel better."

"And your mom?"

"She thinks he might kill himself otherwise."

"Is that what you think?"

Sophy blinks. "Maybe. His face is, like, so shattered."

Shattered.

"Does that matter here? With no other Cambodians around?"

"I don't know." Sophy does not even frown. "But if he kills himself, I'm going to kill myself, too."

"Don't say that."

Sophy stares. Where is Annie to rouse her?

"Don't even think that. Please. Look. I want to show you

something." Hattie stands and takes one of the urns down from the bookshelf. Her mother. Sliding the plate of orange slices aside with her elbow, Hattie places it on the table. Then she turns and retrieves her father. Sophy frowns as Hattie explains; her lips part.

"Wow," she says, finally. "That is so wack."

"It is. It is wack. But this is what you're talking about, when you talk about killing yourself. This is what you will be. So please don't."

Sophy moves her head.

"It would be so wack of you. It would be—" Should Hattie bring up what Sophy's sisters would say? No. "It would be a terrible choice."

Sophy nods, her color rising.

"It's not as though this is all your fault. You made some bad choices, yes. But you had help, don't forget. And the person you hurt most is Ginny's husband. Sarun and your dad were hurt"—Hattie thinks—"incidentally."

"Do you think Everett will do something?"

"Press charges, you mean?"

Sophy nods again.

"I don't know."

"Would they definitely be against Sarun? Could they be against me?"

"I doubt they'd be against you."

"But could they be? Since I'm the one who set the fire?" Sophy lifts her chin.

"I suppose that could be arranged. But if you want to end up in a girls' group home, you can just go back to your old town and skip the trial, you know."

Sophy slumps. "Do you think it would make my dad feel better?"

"If you were charged and found guilty?"

She nods.

"No. I think it would make him feel worse. I think he would only blame himself even more if you were in trouble again. But you know him better than I do."

Sophy touches an urn. With just her fingertip, and just for a moment. Then her finger lifts up like a drawbridge.

"Honestly, I think"—Hattie improvises, the way she does with Josh—"I think it would be selfish of you to take all the blame, when only one part of it is yours."

Sophy reaches for her coffee as if just for a warmer ceramic surface.

"You did contribute, but it was your father, finally, who injured your brother."

"He had a choice," she says.

"He did. Yes. He's a damaged man who might not have understood his choices as well as he might have. But he had a choice."

"He reacted."

"Overreacted, we might say."

"If I had never gone to the church, none of this would have happened." Sophy leans back a little, resting her mug on her stomach; it rises and sinks with her breathing.

"True," says Hattie. "Although many people go to church without anything like this happening, either. You know how many people have kitchen knives, but only a few threaten others with them? Some people find that churchgoing increases what we used to call *rén* when I was little—our human-heartedness. But with other people, it seems to have the opposite effect. So I suppose it depends on the person, and on the church." She tries to be delicate. "On what the church teaches."

"And if I turn myself in or kill myself, that will just be what my dad calls a reaction."

"Is that what he calls it?"

Sophy nods after a fashion, balancing her mug with one hand so she can chew a hangnail on the other.

"As opposed to—?

"An action."

"I see. Yes. It will be a reaction. And wrong, do you see?" Hattie has an orange slice; she spits out the pit. "It will not help anything— it will just say how bad you felt. As if this is all about you. And who knows, it could well lead on to something else bad."

"One reaction after another."

"Exactly."

Sophy frowns. "But what would an action be?"

"How about apologizing to Everett?"

"How can I do that? I mean, I can't exactly, like, walk up to him."

"We'll find a way. How's your guitar these days? Is Carter still giving you lessons?"

"I quit."

"Too busy cleaning, I guess."

"I guess."

"Why don't you start playing again? That would be an action."

Sophy waggles her head.

"An action that might lead to more action," says Hattie. "That might increase your capacity for contributing to better days."

Annie reappears and, when Sophy just looks at her, preoccupied, sits.

"Good girl!" Sophy pets her automatically, then has an orange slice. She spits out a pit.

Sarun goes to talk to Chhung after all. Hattie and Mum watch as best they can out the bedroom window, as does Sophy, leaving Gift to toddle around busily. If only Chhung would move his chair a little, they say. Why doesn't Sarun get him to move his chair? They draw a curtain against the worst of the glare; the lilac curtain shines pink.

Finally Sarun returns. He reports first to his mother, tersely and quietly, in Khmer. She nods. Then he turns to Hattie and Sophy and, in a louder, more measured voice, gives his English report.

"I told him he was a great dad. I told him I was looking forward to Father's Day already. I told him I'd dig him the biggest pit he ever saw, if he wanted. I told him I'd dig night and day and that I wouldn't take a break until this place was the Sahara Desert." He stares at the TV, though it's off. "I told him I wasn't mad at him, and that I wished he'd come in. I invited him, in fact, to come in. Fucking begged him. But, you know, he never even looked at me, the asshole."

"Silence."

"Did you tell him you forgave him?" asks Hattie, finally.

"It just made him feel worse," says Sarun.

"*Bong*," says Sophy patiently. "It can't have made him feel worse."

"He was using me!" Sarun's face is contorted and red except for his scar. "To make himself feel worse! I'm telling you, he was using me, my forgiveness, everything! To make himself feel fucking worse!"

No one thinks he can be right, but that night Chhung refuses to come in even to sleep. Sophy goes out to talk to him, then returns with the wheelbarrow.

"For blankets," she says, throwing bedding down into it from the front door. She trundles back off, leaning hard into the handles; Hattie recognizes that squeak of the wheel.

It's a cold night.

And in the morning, when they find Chhung curled up at the bottom of the pit, Sophy wishes she hadn't encouraged him. "His hair was iced up," she cries.

"He would've stayed out there anyway, the asshole," says Sarun. "Believe me. He would've stayed out there so he could freeze to death."

Gift squeals at something on TV, but no one looks to see what it is.

"What would happen," says Hattie, "if you stopped bringing him cigarettes and alcohol?"

"Whatta you high?" Sarun bugs his eyes.

"It's just an idea." Hattie proffers a chopstick.

Sarun takes it—his neck—but Sophy is outraged.

"That would be, like, starving him," she says.

By day, Chhung mans his station. By night, he heads into the pit. Mum keeps him company, huddling beside him as he lies there, though he refuses to open his eyes or speak to her. He does, however, allow her to help him go to the bathroom, and thanks to his diabetes, Sophy says, he does pee and pee.

"Diabetes?" says Hattie.

It's the first she's heard about that—how worrisome. Although, yes. At least it gets him up. At least it gets him to drink. At least it gets him to let Mum stay with him. Mum prays and prays, her white shawl wrapped around her jacket; Sophy brings Mum blankets for the night, too, and warm drinks. Hats for both of them; the temperature at night is in the twenties now. And crates, to make it easier to climb in and out.

In the morning, Sophy brings Sarun and Gift along with her. Hattie watches, moved, as the whole family helps Chhung out of the pit for the day. Mum supports one arm, Sophy the other, as he steps slowly up the shaky crates; they pass him on to Sarun, who, awkward as he is in his collar, manages to help Chhung up onto solid ground. The family works together, too, to settle Chhung in his chair—Mum and Sophy on arm duty again, Sarun supporting his back. Even Gift grabs a leg, trying to help. And there—mission accomplished. Chhung is seated. Never mind that his hat is on funny, or that his

jacket has hiked up, affording a bright glimpse of his brace. He's
seated.

Father 'n' son braces!

Sophy runs off to get breakfast.

"We have to help him because of his back," she says later. "We
don't want his back to get worse." Elbows in the air, she gathers her
hair at the nape of her neck as if getting ready to put it in a ponytail—
having forgotten it's not long enough, it seems. "I don't think starving
him is going to help," she adds, letting go.

G reta and Grace stop by the pit with doughnuts.
      "Are you all right?" asks Grace, her hair blowing.

Mum looks to Hattie for translation though she should really
understand this. Hattie suspects she is just being shy but, after a
moment, translates.

"She's asking, How are you?"

"I'm fiyne," Mum tells Grace.

"You're fine?" says Greta.

Mum nods enthusiastically, accepting a jelly roll. Then comes a
puff of wind; confectioners' sugar powders her mouth and jacket. She
looks down, horrified, and disappears into the trailer.

Greta and Grace knit their brows. Their hair flies sideways,
aviator-style; Grace clamps hers down with a hand to either side of
her face. She looks to be holding her head on. Greta, too, her braid
notwithstanding, pulls strands out of her mouth.

"This can't go on," she says. She gestures at Chhung, asleep in his
folding chair at the other end of the pit. "What can we do?"

Hattie tightens her jacket hood and thinks. Would it be too crazy
to tell Chhung that Greta and Grace are from the Department of
Social Services, and that a complaint has been filed against him? It
would seem an unlikely way of helping, except that Sophy seems to
think that if no one punishes her father, he'll punish himself. So
maybe it's worth a try? Of course, the game will be up if Chhung recognizes anyone. But luckily, though Greta and Grace have both
dropped food off at the trailer at times, they say it was always Mum
who took the deliveries.

They turn now into the wind; Hattie wakes Chhung up.

"You have visitors," she says.

He opens his eyes.

"We're from the Department of Social Services," says Greta sternly. "We've come to inform you of a complaint filed against you."

"Declaring you an unfit parent." Grace is trying to look stern, too, but it's like watching Santa Claus trying to play Hitler. "We thought you'd want to know."

Silence. Chhung's eyes are sunken and his pupils enlarged, his eyes and face as disconcerting as ever. He's only half awake; his chin is sprouting wires. And yet his backlit hair, blowing forward, frames his face in an oddly flattering way.

"Someone will be coming to question you," says Greta.

"You will need to prepare yourself," says Grace.

A raft of brown leaves suddenly levitates, then just as suddenly settles, like something live. Chhung gives a social smile, as if practicing already for his interview.

"When?" he croaks.

Greta and Grace look discreetly to Hattie.

"In a month or so," says Grace—the pitch of her voice far lower than Hattie would have believed possible. Removing her gardening gloves, she zips up her parka with authority. "I believe." She puts her gloves back on.

"After Thanksgiving," supplies Greta, squaring her chin and throwing her braid back. "You'll be receiving a, ah, summons in the mail."

Chhung nods again, and as Grace and Greta leave, half stands to see them off.

"No, no, don't move!" they insist, abandoning their roles. "Don't get up! Please! Stay!"

"Tank you." He gives a jaunty wave but frowns as he sits down and, the next day, begins to refuse food. Though he still smokes and drinks, his meals come and go untouched.

"He can't wait a month," says Sophy, leaning on the kitchen counter. "Maybe I'll tell him the hearing's been moved up."

"Good idea."

"I'll tell him he has to eat so he'll be strong enough to talk at the trial. You know, to defend himself and stuff."

Hattie heats up lunch. "It's definitely worth trying."

Sophy looks at her. "You look, like, exhausted," she says suddenly.

Hattie bangs a cooking spoon on the edge of a pot.

· · ·

What can I do?" says Carter. "Tell me what I can do."
He has at least knocked. Without waiting for Hattie to answer, though, he has marched in, taken off his jacket, hung it up on a peg and, ignoring the dogs' barking—ordering them, in fact, to sit— seated himself in a chair next to her. It's the way he used to enter her lab cubicle, only here they are at her kitchen table, his knees jutting out to either side of his elbows—*a little male splay display.* Hattie even recognizes that old blue-green sweater, or thinks she does. Can it really have lasted this long? Its cuffs and collar are frayed, and there are several out-and-out holes, but the subtlety of its colors is still something. All those heathery hues, every one of them difficult to name; *kingfisher blue,* she had thought one, when she first saw it. The others were beyond both her Chinese and her English. Not that she has cared much for such things—for things in general—but where did sweaters like that even come from? She had always thought she'd know one day, but realizes now that she never did find out. The dogs gather around him. He pets them, strokes their brows, cradles their heads, then raises his gaze, which, intensified by the sweater, is simply unnerving. She cannot reconcile it with her chock-a-block kitchen— how cluttered her counters! She closes down her computer, straight- ens up some papers. Is there not something unfair about this visit? This visitation, she wants to say. She feels intruded upon, delighted, stricken; she wants him to leave; she is afraid she is going to cry.

"I want to know what I can do."

She jams some pencils in a cup.

"Can I make us some coffee?" he says.

"Sure." She tries to sound offhand, though in fact no one but her has made coffee in her kitchen since Lee died, and that was not even in this house. As the dogs seem to know. They watch intently as he puts the kettle on. Now this is strange, their bodies say—even Annie's says it's strange, though maybe she is just picking it up from Reveille. And Hattie's state; their tails are high. How glad she is, meanwhile, to be presented with Carter's back, for a moment. This tallish, deliber- ate, familiar man. Not huge; and yet the kettle is too small for him. The sink sits too low for him, also, and the windows.

All these things reinforcing what her heart has already guessed: He would never fit here.

"Do you want me to talk to Sophy?" he asks as he fiddles with the gas knob—noticing how the flames lap up yellow and, with a little stoop, looking to get them right.

"You could ask if she'd like to restart guitar lessons."

"Done." He turns and roughhouses with the dogs. "What else? What are we going to do about Chhung?"

"I don't know."

"Still keep your coffee in the freezer?"

She nods. Really she should stand to help—get some cookies, something—but instead she beholds herself in her blank computer screen: Why does she wear two pairs of glasses on her head? She takes them off and lays them on the desk.

"I'm so sorry about this whole affair, you know." He takes some mugs from the dish rack.

"It's not your fault."

"I won't claim that. But I contributed. I could have talked to Sophy. I should have talked to Sophy."

"We all contributed."

"It was . . ." He hesitates. "Perverse. Perverse and stupid and confused." He clears his throat. "Now I would like to contribute to a solution." He trains his eyes on her, standing close enough that she can see her silhouette in them, tiny but sharp. "How about Everett? Can I talk to Everett?"

"Find out if he's planning to press charges?" Hattie's mouth is talking without her. "That would be a help, yes. And it would be nice to verify that the state won't investigate. People assume there was a problem with the wiring, but the electricians might contest that, and then what."

"I'll look into it. Talk to Lukens, maybe."

"Also, Sophy would like to apologize to Everett."

Carter nods his subtle nod. "I'll see to that, too, when I see him. There's only one thing."

The dogs lie down at his feet.

"You have to come with me."

"Why?"

"Why?" He pours. "Because I didn't move to this damned town to teach yoga and make boats, I've realized. Slow as I can be and possessed of apparently formidable powers of repression. Two-percent, no sugar?"

"I'm drinking Lactaid now."

"Of course. Your paternal ancestors not having raised cows."

"Exactly."

"So that they did not evolve to keep the lactase gene turned on after infancy, as did some other populations. A classic case of a cultural trait becoming a genetic characteristic." He stops, his hand on the fridge handle. "Hattie?"

"Yes."

"Do I see tears?"

"No."

"Hattie." He sits back down. "Hattie. Come on." He squeegees the lower edge of her left eye with his thumb. "Hattie." He does the right eye. "Hattie." He cradles her face in his rough hands, the way he had the dogs' a moment earlier, and suddenly it leaves the rest of her body; all her being is in her jaw, her cheeks, her eyes, her lips. "Hattie. Hattie. Come on. Can lactose intolerance really be that bad?"

She laughs, crying. The palms of his hands are strafed and wrinkled now, but his fingers are as supple and intelligent as ever; he inhabits them still. And when he pulls her up out of her seat toward him, she finds that she remembers their touch and tease. She remembers his shoulders and ears and smell, too; she remembers his mouth and press and—goodness—his incorrigible stealth.

"Don't you have any damned tissue?" he says.

"No," she says; but of course she does.

"Hattie," he says. "Miss Confucius."

She blows her nose.

"I've missed you."

"Well, I haven't missed you."

He laughs and kisses her again—his tongue, like his hands, full of sly provocation. "That is completely *bú duì.*"

Of course, even now, if she thinks about it, she is not sure she can forgive him that *I don't see what more I could have done.* And what about Jill Jenkins? And why would she want to be involved with a man who seems to fight with every woman he's with?

But that would be, *like, rational.*

She is standing between his legs; he is nuzzling her neck; she is exploring some of the new territory that is his great smooth scalp. Her fleece is riding up. He has found her soft place. And whatever she remembers or doesn't or wants to say or can't, her every afferent nerve is on fire—her every Meissner's corpuscle. They're leaking neurotransmitters by the bucket, and not one synapse cares what she thinks anyway.

. . .

Grace and Greta come to visit again, bringing—surprise!—Beth and Candy, who got the report from, who else, Judy Tell-All. They've brought casseroles mummified in tin foil—Candy's enchiladas, as well as a miso orzo thing.

"Kind of an experiment," says Beth. "To tell you the truth, I have no real idea what miso even is."

"I'm sure they'll love it," says Hattie.

Everyone's cheeks are pink; and how is it that they all wear hats with pompoms? In any case, they are still exchanging cushiony hugs—all that winterwear—when an enormous piece of machinery starts slowly down the drive. Its link belts leave tracks in the hoarfrost.

"Is that a backhoe?" asks Grace.

Sophy is already out on the driveway, with Gift—Sarun, too. Mum is on the crate steps with no jacket on.

"It's an excavator," says Candy. "A backhoe's got the bucket in the back."

And so it is—an excavator, with Carter at its controls. He sits forward in the seat, his green jacket tenting behind him, and manages to steer the thing around the end of the trailer. He stops opposite Chhung's station and slowly raises the bucket; the thing looks like a Tyrannosaurus rex missing its upper jaw. Just as people start to smile, though, the bucket comes slamming down; Chhung, brace or no brace, jumps clean out of his chair. Carter swears. He raises the bucket once more, but down it comes slamming again, hitting the ground with a clank—rock.

"Damn!" he says.

Anyway, no one is hurt and the engine is off now, and by the time people gather at the pit, Carter and Chhung are chatting so amiably, they hardly seem of different heights.

"We're going to get this ditch of yours dug," Carter's saying.

Chhung looks ready to pass out with weakness and shock. His eyes ricochet as Carter, leaning down, puts a hand out to steady him. Then, another. Chhung rests his gloved hands on Carter's sleeves for a moment; his blue knit hat matches, oddly, Carter's eyes.

"Eq-sca-vay?" says Chhung, regaining his balance. "How you say again?"

"Ex-ca-va-tor," says Carter.

"Eq-sca-va-ter," says Chhung.

He sways, his eyes going; Carter extends an arm again, but Chhung doesn't take it. Instead, he suddenly rallies and says, "We have that in Cambodia, too." Everyone stares, stunned, as he proceeds to take off his gloves, stash them in a jacket pocket, and nonchalantly produce a pack of cigarettes. He offers one to Carter, who doesn't smoke but gamely takes the thing and puts it to his lips nonetheless. Chhung lights it with a lighter, then lights his own. Both men coolly puff, the picture of camaraderie; their motions sing a kind of song. Chhung's eyes are steady. Then Carter starts to hack and cough; Chhung, reaching up, pounds him on the back with a fist.

"Too srong?" He grins.

Carter hands back the cigarette, lit end high. "For me, yes," he says, his face scrunched up. "Way too strong. How do you smoke those things?" He waves at the air.

Chhung, amused, pounds Carter on the back some more. "Easy," he says. Then with bravado he places both cigarettes in his mouth and, a cigarette dangling from either corner, smokes them at the same time.

"Most impressive," says Carter.

Chhung emits an enormous cloud of smoke. He does not seem to intend this for Carter's face; still, Carter has to step back.

"Sor-ry!" laughs Chhung. "O.K." He pats Carter on the shoulder and looks around—belatedly registering the crowd, it seems. Then he removes the cigarettes from his mouth—a two-handed operation—taps the ashes from their ends, exhales another mighty cloud of smoke, replaces them, and, to everyone's surprise, gives a clap. No one reacts. He looks around again and raises his hands a little higher; the tips of his cigarettes flare as he claps a second time, loudly, looking around.

That's when people realize it's a cue. A third cloud of smoke emanates from Chhung as he takes Carter's arm; they raise their hands up high, like the Cinderella doubles champions of a most fantastic tennis tournament. And finally, with a small amazed roar, people start to clap and hoot and cheer.

Success! The whole town is giddy. Not that Chhung won't need support; already people are talking about an anger management course that addresses substance abuse, too—kind of a twofer. It's in the city, but people are organizing rides for him via a sign-up at Millie's. As for the holidays, Grace volunteers for Thanksgiving, Hattie for Christmas; other people plan to teach them to make wreaths and gingerbread houses, and to take them caroling. Sledding, too, if the snow ever comes.

"Only in America," crows Greta.

"People have always been reborn here, but not people who've been reborn before," says Hattie. "I mean, generally."

The walking group laughs. Beth hangs two toothpicks in her mouth, one in each corner, like Chhung.

"Though it's always been a question, hasn't it," says Greta. "Whom America can be America for. And who keeps America, America."

Hattie would love to hear more about what she means. But other people want to talk about whether Carter can be made mayor. River- lake's never had a mayor before, but maybe it's time to change the town charter, they say. Greta shakes her head: Would they be talking this way if Carter were a woman? Well, never mind. In the mean- while, he has a new nickname—Professor Excavator.

Hattie laughs.

Sarun's still in his brace, but when Hattie goes to drop off some food, he starts talking about what he's going to do when he's out of it—get a job, maybe. And Sophy's making plans, too. She asks, in a mysterious voice, to borrow a turkey roaster; Hattie diplomatically doesn't ask why. Another few days, and it'll be time to raise the sub- ject of school. In the meanwhile, Sophy's tuning up her guitar in the living room, so that Hattie hears, as she leaves, not only Sophy play- ing and singing, but Sarun laughing and crooning, too. He sounds pretty wack.

All of this renders Hattie more or less completely unprepared for Everett's obstinacy. *A horse lost may be better than horses gained*, her father used to say—warning her, as he liked to, not to be lulled by apparent reality. One must always be prepared to find one- self unprepared, he taught; and yet Hattie, his slow student, finds her- self both unprepared and unprepared to be unprepared for the climb to Everett's hut.

She has to stop to rest every ten rungs or so—her ankle; Carter, too, shakes his head. It's true Everett has a good ten or fifteen years on them. Still, only a madman would live atop such a climb; he might as well be living on a fire tower. They unzip their jackets. At the top of the ladder is a makeshift pulley and a platform piled with firewood. The door has a deer antler for a handle.

A Robinson Crusoe charm to it all, anyway.

They knock, perspiring.

Huge as he's always seemed, Everett appears even huger in his doorway—so huge, Hattie wonders if this is a standard-size doorway he's got, or a made-up size. Anyhow, he fills it—has to duck a little, in fact, so as not to bump his head.

"Well, well," he says. "Thought I had me a bear." Nothing cherubic about him today. He has a stubble you could scrub an oven out with, and his wiry half-gray hair, too, looks like something with a practical application.

"Do you mind?" asks Carter.

"'Course not," says Everett. "Come on in. Don't mind the mess."

The hut is lined with foil-backed insulation, and there are frying pans hung up neatly enough on nails along the studs. Below these on the fiberboard floor, though, sit a chair, an unmade camp cot, a folding table, and a camp stove, as well as scattered stuff: Everett's clothes, his hat, his dishes, a jar of peanut butter, a loaf of bread, some cereal, some water, some coffee, the remains of various casseroles, and numerous bottles of liquor. The place reeks of smoke, since his woodstove will back up, he says, depending on the wind; that's why he has a window propped open even in the cold. Hattie nods—she knows what a woodstove can be—even as she glances out the other window, which really does look right straight at Ginny's window shade, sure enough. Carter and Everett chat. It's late afternoon; a whiskey bottle's open, but Everett seems sober, if subdued. He is wearing two wool lumberjack shirts—one white-and-black check, one red-and-black—a layered look, with a blue sweatshirt underneath. REX REALTY, reads the sweatshirt, COME SEE THE KING. The I in KING is dotted with a small gold crown.

"Hold it right there," he says. "You're telling me you want to pay the damages?"

"I am," says Carter.

"But you didn't do nothing."

"Good point." Carter's nod is less cursory than usual, more congenial. "Maybe we should sit down."

"Be my guest."

Everett sits on the chair, spilling out over its arms; what with the chair legs so skinny, his legs look to be holding them up rather than the other way around. Carter and Hattie perch on his cot, slipping their jackets off and nesting them around their bums.

"I'm only doing it for a girl," says Carter.

"Hattie?"

They all laugh.

"Do I look like a girl?" says Hattie.

"I wouldn't have guessed boy," says Everett.

More laughter.

"'Course, I've done a few things for her myself, now," says Everett. "Shoveled her out every now and then."

"All the time," says Hattie. "You shoveled me out all the time."

"Well, if I'm not an official member of the Hattie Kong fan club, please sign me up," says Carter. "But the girl I meant is Sophy Chhung."

"The Cambodian girl?" says Everett.

"Precisely."

"She need help?"

"She lit the mini-mall fire."

"No kidding." Everett looks surprised but not entirely. "What for?"

The wind shifts; the window shuts; ragged sheets of smoke leak out from under the top plate of the woodstove. Hattie rubs her eyes.

"She seems to have gotten the idea that she could pin the crime on her brother and get him locked up in jail," says Carter. "Where she wanted him, for some reason." He coughs into his elbow.

"She thought it was God's plan," supplies Hattie, starting to hack, too. She can feel a rawness in her nose and throat. "She thought Sarun was ruining things."

"What things?" Everett props the window back open; the air clears. "Sarun's her brother?"

Hattie nods and explains about the Chhungs, as well as about Sophy's conversion, and her relationship to Ginny.

"So Ginny thought, Great. Use the girl to bring me down, what the heck." Everett nods a bit to himself.

"Exactly," says Hattie.

"But now what, right?" says Everett. "The girl's guilty, but you don't want her charged. You don't even want Sarun and his friends charged. 'Cause in the course of their getting cleared the truth might sneak out."

"Exactly," says Hattie again.

"On the other hand, we're trying to make sure you get your damages," says Carter. "Because your site was burned down and you definitely deserve compensation."

"But Ginny's the one who owes me." Everett's jaw tightens. "Not you. Ginny."

Carter glances at Hattie. "At some level," he says, but then stops.

And Hattie, too, hesitates. Should they start explaining how they owe him, too, actually—Carter, especially? On the one hand, they certainly contributed to the situation—hedging as they did, hemming and hawing when they should have been intervening. On the other, Ginny's sins were sins of a different order—sins of commission. And truth to tell, Hattie feels it, too—that Ginny was wrong, that Ginny should pay. *Kept you around when it was convenient but kicked you out when it wasn't,* after all.

"Ginny should pay," says Everett, as if reading her mind.

"Probably," allows Carter.

"But you're hitting for her. What for?"

"Because it'd be hard to prosecute her successfully," says Carter.

"Much as we wish we could," says Hattie.

"Why?" demands Everett. "Ain't she guilty?"

"Because she didn't actually do anything," says Carter.

"She was just an influence," says Hattie.

"An influence," says Everett.

"And influence is hard to prove," explains Hattie.

"All we have is Sophy's word," agrees Carter. "It's 'he said, she said.' "

Everett stands and paces as much as a man his size can in such a small space. His head barely clears the ceiling. "Ginny's getting off."

"Probably."

"She's getting off."

Carter looks at Hattie, who is already beginning to wish they'd taken a different tack. Because Everett, she can see, is heating up.

"It ain't right, Ginny getting off." Everett looms over them, his voice even and low. "It ain't right."

"No," says Carter, looking rueful. "It ain't, as you say. But there's no law to nail her with, sadly."

"Why the hell not? What's the point of law if people like Ginny are going to get the hell off?"

"You want the law to be just," says Carter. "But, as my ex-wife used to say, the law doesn't make things just. It just makes things better."

"Better than what?"

"Better than if we had no law. Better than if we had corruption, which is what they have in many parts of the world, unfortunately."

"You're helping her," says Everett, glaring. "You're helping her get off."

"That might be true," says Hattie, after a moment. "We might be helping her. But we're not trying to help her."

Everett stops.

"Any help she gets is inadvertent. We're just trying to protect Sophy and get you back on your feet, if that's possible. Especially as the situation was complicated." She plunges on. "Especially as a lot of people who could've stepped in, failed to." She pauses.

But if ever Everett could have heard this, he can't hear it now.

"Ain't I on my feet?" he says. "Or is this someone else with my same boots?"

The window claps shut.

"No, no," says Hattie. "Of course you're on your feet."

Smoke spills from the stove. Hattie reaches to prop the window back open with the broken-off stick Everett's been using—part of a paint stir stick, actually, with some white paint still on it—as Everett starts to pace again.

"I don't need your help unless it's to burn Ginny up." The whole hut shakes as Everett starts to pace again.

"Perhaps you should become a Buddhist," says Carter.

Hattie kicks him.

"That some kind of a joke?" asks Everett—swaying himself, now, like the hut.

"Actually, no. Actually my ex-wife felt much the way you did and really did become a Buddhist after a while. Before that she was a judge." Carter stares at the black stove as if at an apparition—Meredith in her robes. "She was mad."

"Sick of the world," guesses Everett. "Sick of a world where people like Ginny get off."

"Precisely."

"She dump you?" asks Everett, stopping.

"She did." Carter looks thoughtful.

"Didn't you just want to kill her?"

"I suppose one part of my brain did, yes," says Carter. "But other parts, happily, thought better of that plan."

"Yeah, well, I just want to kill her." Everett paces.

"Yeah, well, don't." Carter gives Everett an El Honcho look, and for a moment Everett seems to heed him. "Let us help you instead," Carter goes on. "So the world's unjust. You can still get some projects going."

"Don't get hung up, you're saying."

"Precisely."

"I gave her my life."

"That was generous of you, but perhaps it's time to take it back," says Carter, drily.

Hattie kicks him again.

"Take it back!" Everett laughs. "All them years." He shakes his head. "Maybe you have some way of getting them back, now, being a professor. But the rest of us've got to just kiss 'em good-bye, see. *Sayonara*. Good-bye."

Hattie looks at him. " 'Thirty-seven Years Wasted, You Could Say My Whole Life,' " she quotes.

"You got it." Everett smiles.

"Actually," Carter starts, but stops when Hattie puts a hand over his mouth. "You loved her," he says instead, unmuzzling himself.

"Jackass that I was."

"You loved her," Carter says again. And slowly, after a moment: "You gave her your life."

"Wasn't such a great plan, to be frank." Everett yawns. "You probably would've thought better of that plan."

"Probably," agrees Carter.

Everett shifts slightly. "I loved her but, well, now I just want her burned to a crisp, see." He stretches a little. "Now I'm aiming to send her right to hell." He hesitates, then wedges himself back into the chair.

"Everett, we want to help." Hattie sits forward.

"That's kind of you, Hattie. Generous. I always said you were generous."

"We're just trying to help you reach the tacos, if you know what I mean. Pay you back a little for all that snow shoveling you did."

"I can reach what I need to just fine."

"You mean, you don't want help," says Carter.

"Guess I've taken all the help I want to in this life. Guess I don't need any more, no. No thanks."

"You'd rather have your pride. Is that it?" asks Hattie.

"My pa lived his whole life with no pride so's his son could have some," says Everett.

"You'd rather have your rage," says Carter.

"Guess I'm planning to have it for breakfast."

" You plain don't care for a world where people like Ginny can get off," says Hattie.

"Guess I don't."

"Where nobody sees," she goes on. "Is that it? Where you can build a big tower and still have nobody see. Where you can talk and talk and still have nobody hear."

"You got it," says Everett. "You know what I want?"

Hattie and Carter exchange glances.

"You want Ginny burned to a crisp," guesses Carter.

"That church," says Everett, evenly. "I want that whole Christian fucking church burnt up in their own righteous fire."

"Well, whatever you do, don't go lighting any matches." Carter raises his eyebrows and his voice. "You are no doubt uninterested in a professor's opinion, but I will share mine anyway."

Everett waits.

"It is inadvisable."

"That mean it's dumb?"

Hattie sighs. "Can we come back tomorrow?"

Everett laughs.

"Think of your kids," she says. "Think of Brian and Betsy."

He continues to grin.

"Think how they'd feel. Have you talked to them lately?"

He doesn't answer.

"Do you have a phone?"

He straightens a knee. "There some treetop service I don't know about around here?"

"We'll have to do something about that," she says. "That's our step one. In the meanwhile, it's getting late." She stands, putting on her jacket and nudging Carter.

"We'll be back tomorrow." Carter stands, too.

"Is there anything else we can bring you?" asks Hattie. "Besides a phone? Some nice hot bacon and eggs, maybe? Sausage? Hash browns?"

Everett shakes his head again gently, as if he's turning gnomic, like Carter. He does not stand.

"Anything you want me to tell Ginny? If I see her? If she's in town?"

"Nah." He buttons a button.

Cows'll fly before she sees.

And when they come back the next day with a satellite phone and a hot pack full of food, they find him slumped in his chair. The fire is out; the cabin is cold. His skin is blue, his mouth open, his gaze fixed, his pupils huge.

"Oh my god, no," says Hattie.

Guess I've taken all the help I want to in this life.

Carter opens the window, though the smoke has mostly cleared.

"Smoke inhalation," he says.

They sink back down on the bed as if to talk to Everett all over again. Then Carter stands back up, closes Everett's eyes, and puts his hand on Everett's forehead, fingers fanned.

"May you go to heaven if there is a heaven," he says. "You didn't hedge your bets. You gave your whole heart. You were right to be mad."

He puts Everett's hat back on his head, resting his open hand a moment on its crown. Then he sits back down with Hattie. They hold hands.

COME SEE THE KING.

Carter keeps waking in the middle of the night.

"Reedie," he says. "My brother Reedie."

"I remember Reedie."

"They found Reedie slumped over like that."

Reedie with his RBIs and his cotton candy and his, in truth, terrible Chinese.

"Poor Reedie," says Hattie. "Poor, poor Reedie."

"He did all right in the end. He didn't think so, but he did."

She reaches for Carter in the dark, massaging his head. His skull is hard but full of little tensions, she knows, as is hers; he massages hers back. It's a new routine they've developed already, and a pleasure, though Reedie, Reedie, Reedie. She pictures Reedie slumped over like Everett; then Everett himself, slumped over, his eyes open.

Twins.

The room is perfectly black—there's no moon tonight. She nudges Reveille through the sheet with her foot. What with both dogs sleeping on her side of the bed now, it's easy to lose territory, and Reveille's on top of the covers, her foot below; it's hard to get his attention. Still, she tries.

"I'll never get over it." Carter's voice is husky.

"None of us will. Are you crying? Oh, Carter. Come."

She hugs him, their knees knocking in a way hers and Joe's never did. Or did they? She tries to remember but can't, though she remembers very well, she thinks, how Joe snored all night—like Cato, except that Cato only snored when he was lying on his back. Joe snored in every position, as does Carter—who does snore more quietly, however, and more musically, with a little whistle.

And unlike Joe, Carter cries—something else he does quietly, with his shoulders hunched up and his chin to his chest. She kisses his wet eyes, his wet cheeks; she can still smell the cabin smoke in what there is of his hair. That smoke. "Carter." She holds him as she held Joe and Lee toward the end, climbing into their hospital beds to comfort them. Joe. Lee. Everett. Reedie. And Cato—Cato. She's pained for Carter, pained for them all, though she does not cry herself—having no tears left, it seems. *Dá guān*—she's attained some sort of terrible detachment. So that even as she mourns, she's aware how fleshy he is, how healthy and uncolonized. Never mind his hairs and moles and patches of eczema, it is a strange loveliness to hug someone with back muscles over his ribs.

Carter, at least, has come back to her.

She squeegees his eyes. "Reedie," she says.

"Reedie."

"I'm so sorry."

"It was terrible."

"You blame yourself."

"Was there something I could have said. Was there something I could have done. About how he saw the world—about how he saw himself. Of course, to do that, I would have had to see him. And I didn't see him, did I? You said that once. And now Everett. Was there something we could have done about Everett?"

She holds her tongue, or maybe sleep does. Exhaustion. It's been a long day. Her body is a dead weight. A steady thing, though, at least. A thing that can be leaned against, snuggled into. Big as he is, Carter nestles into her like a child, crying himself to sleep, only to wake again.

"Chhung," he says. "It could have been Chhung."

"Chhung?" says Hattie, groggily.

"The only difference between Everett and Chhung," he says, "was you. You saw the Chhungs. Sarun. Sophy. They were part of your picture."

Hattie opens her eyes, then closes them—nothing to see in the dark.

"If only Everett had been as clear to me as the Chhungs," she says.

"Could we have saved him, do you think? Was there something we could have done? Something we could have said? People say you can't stop them. People who are going to kill themselves, that is. That they just have trouble with impulse control. But I still wonder if there's something we could have done."

"Maybe." If only it weren't true! But that moment they could've taken a different tack—maybe it was. And her anger at Ginny, which she sees now was one part Ginny's reminding her of Carter—*keeping you around when it was convenient but kicking you out when it wasn't*. And what about Carter himself? Contributing for better and worse to her life, and to the lives of others. "Let's talk about it in the morning," she says.

Half expecting he'll say, Now, let's talk about it now.

But he turns over instead, taking the covers with him. They recede like a tide in thrall to a moon on his side of the room; she has to pull and pull to keep covered. Yank.

He wakes again.

"I'm not Everett," he says.

"And thank goodness for that." Hattie struggles to wake herself again—that lead apron. "Poor Everett's dead."

"I didn't even know what that was. To be Everett. I was so unable to imagine such a man, I didn't even know that wasn't what I was. I only knew I wasn't Anderson. Reedie wasn't me, and I wasn't Anderson."

"That was hard enough." She opens her eyes out of habit. Blinking, though there's nothing to see.

"He really loved Ginny, didn't he? I gave my life to science. He gave his life to her."

Annie makes a snuffling noise.

"He stuck with her through a lot," says Hattie, slowly. "Too much, maybe."

"A man like that was beyond my ken. Do you know what I mean? He was beyond my ken."

They are lying on their backs. She straightens out her nightgown, which has bunched up under her, then finds his hand. His hand is not papery, as it tends to be, but almost moist. Warm.

"He was a madman," she says.

"He could have used some of your what. Your Confucian moderation," agrees Carter. "If you don't mind my bringing up your sage."

Her sage.

"He was a vet, you know. Everett, I mean," she says.

"Vietnam?"

"Yes."

"Which explains something, everything, or nothing. Something, everything, or nothing."

"Exactly."

"He had my number all the same. What was that he said? 'You'd have thought better of that plan.' "

Hattie hesitates.

"He knew I couldn't love like that. Love you. Another person. In that headlong way. Regardless of the consequences. He knew I'd second-guess myself. Weigh and consider. Cut my own heart out if that was required."

How wrong it would be to cry as hard at this as at Everett's death, or at Reedie's. Yet Hattie feels as though if he goes on, she might.

"What a match we were," he goes on. "Two smart people who cut their own hearts out. What did Everett say? *All them years.* We were as good a match as they were, weren't we. As good a match as they were."

"*All them years,*" repeats Hattie.

Carter snuggles up to her, turning on his side. His arm reaches across her body like a shoulder belt.

"Why did you leave the lab? Tell me. I should have asked you this years ago, I know, but let me at least ask you now. If I may. Why did you leave research?"

How wide awake he is; that Hatch intensity. She should have known he would be this way even in the middle of the night—a train. Whereas her breathing is still slow and rolling, her thoughts still stuffy. "Let's talk about it in the morning."

"No, now," he says. "Now. Don't back away. Don't shy away— that's the word, isn't it? You don't stonewall, you shy away. Maybe as a matter of nature, though it could be nurture, too, of course. All those years as an outsider. As a—how do you say it in Chinese?"

"*Yángrén.* Though today people mostly say *wàiguǒrén. Wàiguǒrén* or *yángguǐzi,* but not *yángrén.*" She should explain the differences, but yawns again instead.

"There was something else you used to say."

"*Wàiláide,* maybe?"

"*Wàiláide,* that's right. 'Come from outside.' You were *wàiláide.* Though it isn't even from everything, is it? That you back away. Only from things close to your heart's wound, as Meredith would say."

You always were well insulated, Hat. Probably you had to be.

She doesn't answer.

"The lab," he says, gently. Not putting her back on track like a grad student—just returning to the subject. Drawing her out. "Why you left the lab."

"I needed a home, and the lab wasn't a home. It wasn't—what did you call it?—an experiment in living. It was an arena."

"An arena."

"That's what Amy Fist called it. She said I could love the lab, but it wasn't going to love me back. And I thought she was right about that."

"But a lab is like a lake, Hattie"—Carter forgoing, for once, a dig at Amy. "You can love a lake, but it's just for swimming. You don't leave it because it doesn't love you. You leave because you're done swimming."

She can feel him breathing behind her. They're holding hands, their fingers interlocked.

"It was about me, wasn't it?" he goes on.

"I suppose you were a factor," she says. "In the final analysis."

"A factor in how you viewed the whole enterprise."

"I suppose. Yes."

"What a shame." He squeezes her hand. "What a goddamned shame."

"It wasn't the disaster you imagine," she says. "I was sick of repeating experiments anyway. You had more stamina for all that what-went-wrong."

"We did have some terrible luck with our samples."

"It drove me crazy. And I was good with kids. I changed a lot of lives—broadened their horizons. Made them see reason." She pauses. "They loved me."

"I'm sure. But did you love it. Did you love it. Did it enlarge your spirit, was it what you were put on earth to do. Did it draw more out of you than you knew you had, did it change your very substance. Was it a gift." His free hand strokes her hair.

"It was satisfying, Carter," she says. "It was worthwhile. I am not going to let you tell me it was a waste of my life, because it wasn't. I gave a lot and got a lot back. You should have seen my retirement party. I had some fifty kids come back."

"But no molluscs."

Molluscs.

"How many people came when you retired, Carter? Tell me. And of the people who came, how many people came who didn't have to? How many came wholeheartedly?"

Reveille parks his head on her foot.

Carter goes on as if he didn't hear her. "And there's something special in those moments of discovery, isn't there. When it's not you and your circumstances. When it's you and the universe, and you feel that. That you're engaged in a most worthy enterprise and have come to stand on some isle of certainty, to boot. Some small, lovely bastion of certainty."

She rolls a little away from him, freeing her hand. "You know, Carter, not everyone can have such exalted work. You've always worn special boots and done special things. Other people have regular boots and regular jobs."

"But you can't deny you know what I mean." He grips her waist. "About the petty world we deal with every day but that we can hardly bear calling our lives. And the feeling that you've escaped, and are finally in the right precincts. The precincts we were made to inhabit."

She hesitates. *The precincts we were made to inhabit*—no. That *you and the universe,* though—you and the universe, you and the unknown, which you were helping to make known for now and forever: Maybe it was just a web of significance, but it did seem like more than that. You did feel that you were adding a brick to an important and immortal edifice—to a cathedral worth building. Who knew what its final meaning was? Who knew but that its truths were as partial as any the mind perceived? Still, it was far larger than you, and descriptive, too, of something yet larger and more beautiful. Beyond you—it was descriptive of something so far beyond you that you could see why some people believed it divine.

Yet still, she asks, "Were you loved?"

"Hattie, listen. What you did was worthwhile. It was a reasonable way to spend your life. Or more than that. It was noble. It was a noble way to spend your life. You had fifty students come back for your retirement, and I'm sure there were five hundred more whose lives were changed by your class. They were lucky to have you—that's a fact. Very lucky. And they loved you, I'm sure. Loved you as no one in the lab ever loved me, probably. So, all right. But what went on in the lab through this time period, Hattie—can you not admit it to have been something special? Can you really not admit it?"

His breathing body presses against her back.

"It was extraordinary," she says finally.

"Wasn't it?"

"A religious experience, in a way. An experience to which you could attach religious feelings."

"Interesting."

"To which your whole family attached religious feelings. That hall where you hung your father's picture was your chapel."

"We were like patrons in the Renaissance, you mean. Except that we hoped to attain immortality with brains instead of money."

She nods. "Something like that."

She can feel him nod back. "That being our web of significance. Well, perhaps you are right, or partially right. My guess is that we accrued earthly advantages from our quest as well. Stimulation such as resulted in the growth of new dendritic spines, and so on. Status. Things that could well ultimately contribute to our longevity and quality of life."

"If it didn't kill you, you mean."

He is quiet a moment. "Touché. But what about you." He props himself up on an elbow; his head moves in closer, his voice. "You've followed the field, haven't you? Who knows but you've been reading the papers coming out of my lab all these years."

It is her turn to be quiet.

"What a time you missed, Hattie. The explosion. Thanks to computers and fMRIs and all the rest. Do you remember how we used to record everything from the oscilloscope onto film? No one knew what neurobiology even meant, what it was. Do you remember? When it was the 'Nerve-Muscle Program.' Remember?"

"You went on to work on plasticity, didn't you."

"The generation of new synapses, yes. Can you imagine? To have built from the isolated synaptical transmissions you worked on to the whole live dynamic of synapse initiation and growth? It was extraordinary."

"Human adaptation at the cellular level."

"Precisely."

"Change and growth. What learning does to the brain—how it changes."

"How it stores new ways and new knowledge and is itself transformed."

"How it comes to see differently, even."

"Yes."

"How it blinkers itself in new ways."

He laughs. "If you want to put it that way. How it refocuses, maybe. Re-frames. Selecting in either a narrower or a broader way. Every way, of course, having some cost, and every way limited by our poor prehistoric hardware, but the plasticity itself offering some small hope for benighted mankind, don't you think?"

Hope that even I could become a fool for life? Lee would have said. *Hope that even I could become corny?*

"Fantastic." Hattie shakes her head a little.

"It was, it was fantastic. It was fun. A journey like none other."

"I'm sure." In the cool room, he warms her neck, her back; she is grateful, yes, to have him. And yet, and yet. "Do you really need to be telling me this?"

"Don't be mad, Hattie." He strokes her hand. "I'm just trying to understand."

"Are you?" She slides her hand away. "It was my own fault I left, Carter. As Sophy would say, I should've made different choices."

"Are you denying me my contribution?"

"I had a husband and a child and a career, Carter. I had a life."

"You married a misanthrope. You got yourself some dogs and moved away north."

"I moved after Joe died. And he wasn't a misanthrope, by the way."

"An antisocial introvert, then."

"Carter."

"You retreated, and worst of all, you never developed your capacities."

"Developing one's capacities being, of course, the point of life."

"It's as close to a definition of the good as we're likely to get, Hattie. You can say this is just another web of significance that I've spun, but it's a hard one to shake, don't you think? The notion that it's good to develop our capacities and bad to waste them. That thriving is a matter of developing those capacities. That thriving is good."

"Doing good isn't thriving?"

"You can argue, but you can't tell me it wasn't a goddamned shame for you not to have at least had a choice, Hattie."

"And what if one person's development comes at the expense of someone else's? Then how much of a good is it?"

"An excellent question." He stops. "As in our case, you mean." He reaches for her hand again. "Listen, Hattie. I promised I would help you and then failed to, just as I failed to help Reedie—Everett, too. Sophy. And, even worse, I failed to even though I knew how vulnerable you were. Professionally and otherwise. I didn't want to know, but I did."

Her heart speeds up. "You knew I'd left science."

"I did, eventually. Yes."

"You watched me go."

"No. I couldn't. I couldn't watch."

"You knew what would happen."

"It wasn't a good field for women, Hattie."

"Witness Barbara McClintock."

"Precisely."

"I needed to be in a lab like yours."

"You needed big allies—bigger than Amy Fist."

"And preferably male."

"Preferably."

"But you let me go because El Honcho thought you were in love with me."

"Because he knew I was in love with you, Hattie. Because he knew. And because he knew you might be in love with me, too."

Hattie kicks off some covers, hot.

"He believed lab romances in general to be a grave and ever-present threat," finishes Carter. "As you know."

Annie snuffles.

"He thought it would hurt your career," says Hattie, finally. "He thought it would wreck your advantageous marriage and distract you. Not to say energize people like Guy LaPoint."

"Who might have only been a problem in the short run, of course, but who might have gone on to become the sort of lifelong time-and-energy sink he thought better to avoid."

"Having so many such enemies himself."

"Precisely."

"And I had an outsider's outlook to boot. I raised doubts."

"You were too much like me. Or like one side of me, I should say."

"Half Anderson, half Reedie as you were."

"He thought you could tip me the wrong way."

"And he thought I'd become a gadfly. The sort who brings disorder instead of perspective. Who dismantles but doesn't rebuild. Who fails to understand what it takes to get the simplest thing done."

"Yet he liked you. And thought you had real potential, early on."

"But just as well to let me disappear." She loosens her hand and moves away. "And you agreed."

He lets her move. "Seeing as how I was going to flunk sooner or later," he says.

A surprise.

"You felt on trial," she says.

"I would have loved to have been able to work without ever hurting another, Hattie. I would love to have been a Buddhist, like Meredith. A Buddhist scientist."

"But the world was what it was. Competitive. Backstabbing. Unsparing. Full of Guy LaPoints sharpening their sabers. Like Anderson. Like your father. You didn't want to end up like Reedie."

"It wouldn't have worked out, Hattie. And yet I loved you still."

"Despite your best efforts."

"Some parts of the brain, it seems, are not so plastic." The bed creaks under his shifting weight; he takes her hand again.

"And now here you are. Now that your best years are behind you." She pushes his hand away. "Now that you have nothing to lose."

"Hattie."

"We'd better go to sleep."

"Hattie."

She does not answer.

"All right, then," he says. "Good night."

But a little later, he wakes and says, "You can argue for the dignity of an ordinary life, in the precincts of the everyday, Hattie. And probably you are right. A nobler person than I, in the bargain. But the higher precincts—they do make a person feel his dignity—really feel it."

She opens her eyes and finds that, in her sleep, she has turned onto her back again. Carter is on his side, alongside her again, too, his arm across her body; and somehow he has found her hand. Meaning, she supposes, that she has bent her arm and made it available.

Self-sabotage.

"Probably we're all driven to find some way in which we're special," she says, freeing herself.

"Dismaying as it is to realize that we're not, you mean. Given the indifferent universe. Given the fact of death."

She is waking up faster, now, she notices, as if she's learning this, already—a new pattern. Adjusting to Carter even as she resists him, who knows how she's changing him.

And yet still, she resists. "You're like Ginny in a way."

"Ginny who was so kind to Everett."

"She put Jesus on the throne of her life and you put science on yours."

"The throne of her life."

"That's how Everett put it. How he said she put it. It was a way of saying that it gave her life Meaning, capital M."

"As opposed to meaning, small m."

"Meaning with moderation."

"Giving rise to vision with a small v, you mean. Something more Inuit-like—more oriented toward the living. Something more Confucian."

"Maybe. Confucianism can be extreme, too. And I don't mean to defend mediocrity."

"Hattie, listen. I may be like Ginny in some respects, but in at least one important respect we differ. Because Ginny didn't love Everett, did she? Whereas I loved you all along, you know."

"All along?"

A pause. "Persistently."

"But your work, you mean."

"Hattie, don't."

She stares into the dark. Never mind that it is too dark to see—she stares anyway.

"I hope I at least get credit for honesty," he says.

She stares.

"I never forgot you," he says.

She stares.

"I came looking for you," he says.

She laughs. "Eventually."

"I couldn't not come."

Is that squeaking?

"So, all right, I'm a decade or two late," he says.

"Three."

"Meredith was jealous of you, you know."

"Was she."

Mice.

"My father was right," he says. "I loved you, Hattie Kong, and hoped you loved me."

Words she has longed to hear for fifty years. *You could say my whole life.*

She is grateful for the dark, the focusing dark.

For then she replies, "You have some nerve coming back," and turns her back on him. "With all you've contributed to the lives of others. You have some nerve, Carter Hatch." She toes poor Reveille so hard that he yelps.

Ginny is coming back from her friend's house for the funeral, says Judy Tell-All, and putting her house up for sale while she's here. Since the kids will be in town to help clean it out, and since neither one of them wants it.

"Of course, they were weirded out by the tower," she goes on. "And no phone. They wanted to know why he didn't have a phone." She stamps her patent leather boots in the cold. "I tried to tell them there were things even I didn't know, but it wasn't what they wanted to hear." She looks thoughtful.

"Just think," observes Grace, "in another couple of months he'd have had cell service."

"I think that's what you call irony," says Greta.

"I think it's what you call sad," says Hattie.

Judy nods and, for once, says nothing.

Where no one's seen Bry and Bets for a while, people would love to say hello at the wake. The way they stand with Ginny in a three-pack, though, no one dares.

"Sophy!" calls Ginny. "Come meet my kids."

But Sophy melts out of the room—taking, it seems, something of Ginny with her. Though she fluffs her hair and smooths her dress, her movements seem empty even of vanity.

Bry catches the eye of various townsfolk as he escorts his mother back toward the casket. A chubby boy turned portly man, he seems at once weighed down and buoyed up as he half smiles at Jed Jamison, his old baseball coach. Bets, too, a wiry girl with cornrows, can't help but smile at Jill Jenkins, without whom she probably would've ended the world's absolute worst speller instead of only the second or third worst. They both hesitate as they pass Hattie, too—the last person to have seen their dad alive, they seem to realize, and yet off-limits for some reason. They knit their brows in exactly the same way, giving rise to twin radishes at the tops of their noses.

Everett's body, meanwhile, barely fits his new home. His hair pushes up into the lining; his shoes push down. And his dress uniform likewise strains, its buttons tipped hard; even his skin is too taut and too pink—blushing, it seems, at the sight of Ginny staggering up to him. *The cat crying at the mouse's death,* Hattie's father would have said, as she kneels beside the coffin. And yet Ginny sobs so like a widow—so like someone riven and cracked wide—that Hattie feels for her all the same. She remembers what it is to see a husband, dead, after all; the impossibility of it, the unacceptability—the sheer searing, numbing nonsense of it. If only Ginny did not rummage in her pocketbook as she stands, producing a good-sized cross! But there she goes, placing the thing in Everett's hand; people are still shaking their heads as her children take their turns kneeling. First big Bry, his knees leaving dents in the kneeler when he stands; then thin Bets, lost in her heavy dress. Her many little braids end in shiny black beads; they clack as she weeps, her hands to her eyes.

They leave the way they came, arm in arm in arm—banding together against this evil town, though Ginny does pause as they pass Sophy again. Ginny's face is strangely girlish; her lips part as if she is going to ask something. But then she doesn't; for there stands a stone-faced Sophy, so solidly closed that Ginny involuntarily looks to Hattie as if for reassurance or explanation. Their eyes meet; and for a second time Hattie feels sympathy for her fellow teacher: a woman displaced, after all. A woman betrayed, a woman widowed.

And yet *all she's contributed to the lives of others*. Hattie closes her face like Sophy and turns away.

For thine was the power and the hogwash.

Ginny and her kids pass through the front door. There is a long pneumatic wheeze as it shuts automatically behind them; people stare at its glossy white panels. Outside, Ginny's car motor turns over and over—a weak spark.

"Where is she going to live?" wonders Greta. "Where is she going to go?"

No one knows, but there is Grace, kneeling by the casket. Her old black dress has gone brown; the banded tops of her knee-highs show.

"Forgive me, Lord," she murmurs. "Forgive me."

And as she stands, she takes the cross back out of Everett's hand, and pockets it.

It would've made him madder'n hell to wake up in heaven with that thing in his hand," says Beth the next morning. "That is just a fact."

Candy cuts her pancakes into sixths; her maple syrup shines. "It was an act of mercy," she agrees finally.

Greta grins. "It was brilliant."

Only Grace worries. "Is that stealing? I hope it wasn't stealing," she says. Her snowflake sweater is all wrinkly, as if she just took it out of storage.

"It was perfect," says Hattie.

As for what to do with the thing, no one thinks Grace should return it to Ginny. On the other hand, she can't just throw it out; it's a cross, after all.

"Maybe send it to one of the kids?" says Candy. "Or keep it yourself?"

But in the end they agree that Grace should ship it off to a cloister she knows.

"Maybe it can get a new start there," says Beth.

"Kind of like a retread," says Hattie.

Everyone nods solemnly until Grace starts to laugh. Then, one by one, they allow themselves to smile.

To smile, perchance to gloat just a little, Lee would have said.

The honor guard ceremony takes place at the town cemetery. The kids don't have winter coats, only incongruously bright ski jackets that contribute, oddly, to the gravity of the occasion: Their faces are so sad and pale in comparison. They cry during the folding and presenting of a flag to Ginny; they cry during the playing of taps by a real bugler. (How lucky they are not to have gotten a recording, people say.) They cry as they throw handfuls of dirt into the grave. Then they bury their hands in their jacket pockets. Their heads are bent; their eyes are swollen; they are surrounded by people and yet alone, it seems, with the coffin. They do not want to leave. The crowd parts, though, finally, making way for them; and though they look at no one, they do proceed tearfully down the path granted them—accepting it with sad grace. People wave as their old Ford turns over a few times but finally starts, and heads down the street. It stops at the stop sign by the field, then takes a left. Headed somewhere—Florida, say some. Others say Arizona.

It is an overcast day.

Hattie stops with Carter at the new extension to the already huge Hatch family plot—a stand of pines, really, in which the family has placed a small stone wall with a bronze sitting ledge that Hattie remembers from Dr. Hatch's burial. Dr. Hatch's stone—engraved with his name, John Wiktor Hatch—was one of just two markers in the patch then. Now it is joined by a number of rocks and names. The ground is covered with needles; a small metal stabile, made by an artist cousin, twirls and tumbles, then switches direction, then switches direction again, a masterpiece of indecision.

"I wish Reedie were here," says Carter, perched on the ledge. His elbows are bent, and his shoulders raised up. One hand sits to either side of his hips.

Hattie folds her arms. "You'd be a fool to have your ashes anywhere else," she says.

"Sheila wouldn't let us have so much as a pinch of him, that niggardly Ignoriah." He scratches his head.

"Couldn't he have a rock here all the same?"

"You're right. Why not. Why not." He gives her a sideways look. "An excellent suggestion." He nods, his eyes warm. What hair he has is neatly trimmed to cleave close to his head; he's had a haircut. "You're right."

It is quiet—all the birds having finally gone south—and starting to snow so lightly, the flakes seem to be headed up as much as down. They fly and drift and swirl as if there is nothing the least bit certain about their ending up on the ground; one makes an asterisk in Carter's eyebrow.

"Because clearly Reedie belongs here, doesn't he?" Carter goes on. "As well as there. Clearly. Wouldn't you say?" Carter blinks and clears his throat. "Speaking of which"—he clears his throat again— "is it at all conceivable that you'll want your name on a rock here, too, someday? That is, eventually? I don't mean to be morbid."

He asks casually, and when she doesn't answer right away, leans his head back to catch some snowflakes in his mouth. His asterisk is still there.

She looks around at the beautiful woods. Where are her distance glasses? In truth, she does not see so well without them. And yet, she sees well enough; perhaps it would break her heart to see better: The stabile moves; the pines rise as if to heaven, their bushy boughs interlaced. Everything will be white soon. How she wishes she could say yes. But *dá guān*—she feels she belongs elsewhere, somehow. Nowhere. The pet cemetery, she supposes, or in a flower garden, like Lee. She is not like Reedie. She was always a guest in this family: welcome, then—as she will always remember—welcome to leave.

Carter tilts his head back down; flakes melt far more quickly on his warm bald head, she notices, than they ever did on his hair. Droplets form. Rivulets.

A rustling.

"Look—moose," he whispers.

And sure enough, a full-grown bull moose with an enormous rack is making its way toward some young-growth forest not far from them. He stops a moment, and looks straight at them with his small eyes and camel face, but then goes on eating. How Hattie misses her distance glasses now! For what an ungainly, knobby-kneed wonder he is. His dewlap is preposterous, and his coat unkempt; he is fantastically humpbacked and graceless. An anti-weasel, an anti-cat. He appears to have no tail. Yet his pace is his own, his peaceable ways; he is a walking event, with his own strange command. A beast.

"Moose can move their eyes independently of each other, you know," offers Carter, once the moose turns away. "They can see two directions at once."

"Is that right."

"And they're tamable. People've harnessed them and gotten them to haul carts and logs."

"Really."

"The astronomer Tycho Brahe had one for a pet. One day the moose drank too much beer, though, fell down the stairs, and died."

Hattie laughs, delighted—isn't that just the sort of thing Carter would know. She dries off his head a little with her hand. And yet she finds she cannot take his arm as they leave.

"Maybe I'll try taming a moose myself," he says, nonchalant. "When I've completed my boat." But he has drawn his elbows in toward himself, and when he tilts his head back and opens his mouth to catch some more snowflakes, they all seem to land in his eyes.

The church holds a reception, with cider and coffee. Hattie and others have brought hermits and penuche and chocolate-chip meringues; there are gingersnaps and fudge puddles, too, and Russian snowballs and chai mousse bars and Oreo-decorated cupcakes, made to look like owls. A treat feast, such as should not go to waste. People do their duty.

As Beth is organizing the Cabin Fever Follies this year, she's giving everyone who doesn't have one already a kazoo, including Sophy and Mum, of course, and Gift (who loves his), and Sarun, too; a neck brace, Beth says, is no excuse. He looks nonplussed, but Greta immediately starts to play a duet with him, then ropes some high school kids into taking her place. This, naturally enough, brings a change of tune—"When the Saints Go Marching In" giving way to some sort of kazoo rap.

"I want you kids to do a number of your own in the show," says Beth. "Would you do a number of your own?"

As they're not too crazy about the idea, she has to bribe them into it—she won't say, later, with what. Even Beth is hesitant to approach Chhung, though.

"He just looks so dazed," she says. "Doesn't he look dazed?"

"As if he's realizing how lucky he was," says Greta. "As if he's realizing how close he came to a different fate."

"Or how he's just gotten reborn again, maybe?" says Grace.

To which Hattie nods, explaining to whoever doesn't know how Chhung always believed he was reborn into his brother's life after Pol Pot.

Candy frowns. "Does that mean he thinks he's been reborn into Everett's life this time?"

"Oh, no no," Hattie insists. "That's not how it works."

And yet she worries that that is exactly what Chhung is thinking even as, sneaking up behind them, Carter breaks in with, "We are going to have to keep that man busy."

All agree. Beth blushes but stays in the huddle as Greta lays out how Chhung could contribute to the town hydro dam project; and when Judy Tell-All comes to report that Jed Jamison's wife has left him, no one elbows Beth until Judy is safely across the room. Neither does anyone comment on the redheaded boy doing card tricks for Sophy, though who doesn't notice? Sophy is careful to stay out of Chhung's line of sight; but what a lot of tricks that boy knows! And how many faces Sophy makes as she laughs. She's folded up her arms demurely in front of her, but her breasts spill over them as if out of a corset; Hattie smiles.

It's only the second town function the Chhungs have attended— the wake being the first—and yet already they seem to have always been there. People pour them cider and play peek-a-boo with Gift; and when the eats unaccountably run low, Mum volunteers that she's brought something for the party, too: whole wheat baguettes! With chocolate in them, no less. By the time things break up, there isn't a person in town who hasn't tried them. Baguettes with chocolate! Made in a turkey roaster! How did she know folks up here like whole wheat? And is that a Cambodian combo? A French? Anyway, what's clear is that it's a new town tradition; already people're talking about next year's farmers' market. And can Mum make other things? Do Cambodians do stir-fry? Or if that's too pigeonholing, here's another idea: What this town really needs is a good bagel. Can Mum do bagels?

Hattie pulls Sophy over to translate; Mum nods.

"A-nih-ting," she says.

And Hattie beams, though she knows the Chhungs've been talking about maybe moving. Mum needs a temple and misses the holidays "like really bad," Sophy says. And they all miss other black-hairs, and Cambodian food, and Chinese food, and the Asian super-market; and Sophan has e-mailed to say she is not sure she could ever get used to the cold. Sopheap, though, knows at least one other Cam-bodian family willing to go anywhere. And if that's true, and if they really do move to Riverlake, well, even that would change things. Though what if after that family comes another family, and after that, another? Then, the Chhungs know, there could be trouble. Or that's what Hattie's told them—not wanting it to be true, but telling it like it is anyway. Especially as there are more Mexican workers up here all the time, she says, some of them legal and some of them not; the dairy farms can't run without them. Which might not seem to have any-thing to do with the Chhungs, says Hattie.

But of course they already know from their old town how nothing having to do with the Latinos has nothing to do with them.

"The Goyas thought we had it easy," says Sarun, "coming in as refugees. You know, with a way to get citizenship and everything. They didn't care we had genocide. If they couldn't get jobs, it was because refugees got jobs. If they couldn't find housing, it was because refugees got housing."

Hattie agrees things are complicated. "Still, you shouldn't call them Goyas," she says. And even though Sarun says why shouldn't he, when the Latinos mutter, "*A-nih, a-nih,*" at the Cambodians— "*a-nih*" being a rude Cambodian phrase—he doesn't argue too hard. Anyway, Sophy says, if they do move, she hopes Hattie will come with them. Even if they move back to Cambodia, she wants Hattie to come! Not that Sophy really thinks they'll do that; her own vote, she says, is to stay.

A n e-mail from Tina:

Dear Aunt Hattie,

We hear from Lennie that you took the bones long time ago, but now no more news. Maybe we should not worry but still we wonder is something wrong. Maybe you change mind. Johnson say maybe you are worried your parents do not like to be moved, you are bring some bad luck to them.

Writes Hattie,

Please don't worry. It's just been busy. I haven't had time to find a crematorium, but I'll find one soon. In fact, I'll look into it today.

Answers Tina,

Why don't you just send the bones here? Let us take care of everything. We have many such places here in Hong Kong, all kinds of choice. Probably it is more convenient for us than for you.

Writes Hattie,

How can I just send them? The bones or ashes, either, now that I am thinking about it. Doesn't someone have to accompany them? That's what my Nai-nai taught us. The oldest male in the family should do it. Though where these are modern times and I am the only member left of my generation, maybe she would forgive me for doing it instead. And for checking the urns as baggage, as I may have to again on the plane.

Writes Tina,

Of course, you are head of family, so whatever you say is right, no one can argue . . .

And no one does ever argue with her, Hattie's noticed.

However, if I may raise my opinion, your Nai-nai was right for that time. But these days people not so strict as before. After all, in the olden days some servants even got burned up to go with their master, right? We cannot follow every way like ancient times. Of course you can bring the bones yourself if you do not believe the spirit will go any other way, but Johnson say he know a monk can do a special prayer, ask the spirit to come along with the remains. Kind of like just follow anywhere the remains go, in a plane or boat, anything. Probably if one day some remains go on the space shuttle, the spirit can go there too. Of course, there is extra charge. But anyway since you do not believe in feudal superstition, maybe you do not mind even the monk take the money and say nothing.

Writes Hattie,

I would mind, but okay. If you are comfortable with it, I will send the bones as soon as I can. Please tell your monk they are coming air mail, special delivery, signature required.

Answers Tina,

Fabulous! Thank you! Thank you!

Hattie stares at the screen, then stands to pour herself some tea; she is drinking more tea these days.

Tomorrow, the post office." Hattie holds a flattened cardboard box up to one of the urns—too small. A roll of bubble wrap rests on the reclin-o-matic.

"Will you miss them?" Carter hands her a box the next size up.

She tries it out. "It's been nice having them here."

"Why don't you keep them, then?"

"I think they would've loved being a help to the living. The whole idea that their bones could bring comfort to anyone, half a century later—they would've loved that."

"The immortality of it."

"I think the word is 'humanity.' "

"*Rén,* you mean. As the Confucians say."

She smiles a little. "Very good. *Rén.*"

A mouse skitters across the floor; Annie retrieves it and, as usual, drops it live. As it starts to escape, though, Carter leans down and traps it easily.

"What do you think?" he says. "Shall we give it the lab snap? We can also make like a local and whack it with a shovel."

Hattie winces. "No shovels, please."

"Or I can let it go like a Buddhist scientist, if you like. Though the house mouse is, of course, a nonnative and notably prolific species that can prove unsanitary and is known to wreak havoc with wires."

"The lab snap," she says.

He pulls down its tail and jerks back its head in one expert move.

"I never did like doing that, you know," he says. He takes the carcass outside.

"Thank you," she says, when he comes back in. And indeed, she is grateful: Annie, she has come to accept, will never be a mouser.

"So the Confucian graveyard is okay?" he goes on, sitting down.

"I think my parents were like the Red Cross."

"Mired in politics and financial impropriety?"

She smiles. "Doctors Without Borders, then. Willing to bring aid anywhere, anyhow, to anyone."

"Even to you? Do you feel they've aided you?"

She thinks. "I know it's crazy, but yes. It's done me good to have them here, yes."

"Some connection to your past, however inchoate."

"Putting me, no doubt, on a road to ancestor worship."

He laughs loudly. "But tell me." He clears his throat. "Have your parents been of aid to us? I ask because, you know, we never did finish our conversation the other night."

His tone is so light, she is surprised, when she looks in his eyes, to see pain.

"Can you forgive me?" he goes on. "Because I know I'm years late with this but I ask your forgiveness, Hattie Kong. I do."

She folds up a second box.

" 'I am poor and needy, and my heart is wounded within me,' " she recites finally. " 'I am gone like the shadow when it declineth; I am tossed up and down as the locust.' "

"From the Bible."

She tries not to laugh. "Very good."

"Your heart is wounded within you."

She puts her hands on the jars for a moment, feeling them. "Yes."

"I was torn, Hattie. I don't know if you can see that."

"I'd have been torn, too," she acknowledges.

"And yet, you were right to be mad."

"Was I?"

She sees Everett, slumped over then; she smells the smoke. *Guess I'd rather have my rage. Guess I'm planning to have it for breakfast.* And there is the breakfast table, with a long line of blue and white jars on it, and a red tablecloth.

"You were hurt," he says.

"I was," she answers—calm but startled: For something light and large has come to her, an ease; she is not herself. And as Carter moves with some emotion to embrace her, she feels, not the bubbly thing she'd always imagined their love would be, but something else—a defining grace, bittersweet and hard-won.

"It would be nice to have some sort of send-off ritual for your mom and dad, wouldn't it?" he says, a little later. What hair he has is flying every which way; his gaze is dreamy; she has never seen such crow's-feet.

"Umm," she says.

"Here we have rituals for yoga and funerals but not this."

"Umm."

He kisses her between her eyes—one of his new favorite spots. "We should invent one."

Nothing brilliant comes to mind, though, so in the end they simply make a nice dinner, and eat with the jars on the table, like guests. Then they meditate a little. And then, though he's a little full for such things, Carter tucks in his shirt and stands on his head.

Josh calls a week after Thanksgiving: He and Serena have broken up. He's not crying, but his voice on the phone is froggy—nothing like his radio voice.

"She decided I was too old for her," he says.

"Just like that?"

"Out of the blue. I don't know why."

"Did someone say something to her? Her parents?"

"Not that I know of. But she did get pregnant and miscarry, so maybe that was a factor."

Hattie clears her throat. "Umm, that might have been a factor, yes. How pregnant was she?"

"Not very. Six weeks and change."

"Still. That sort of thing can be world-changing for a young woman, Josh."

"It was the first thing that had ever gone wrong with her life. I told her things will go wrong because, you know, that's life. But it wasn't what she wanted to hear, I guess."

"She might have needed sympathy."

"Someone to agree it was the end of the world."

Joe's voice.

"Let me ask you. How do you feel now?" she asks.

"Like it's the end of the world. Like I'll never love anyone as much in all my life. But maybe I've lost perspective."

"Or maybe she's the love of your life and you never will love anyone more." Hattie hesitates to say so, but it's true.

Silence.

"Anyway, I'm coming home for Christmas," he says.

"Are you?"

"I owe you a visit, and the station has a backlog. Think you have room? Or have you gotten more dogs?"

"Of course, I have room! But I do have a new dog."

"A replacement for Cato?"

She laughs.

The cold has finally settled in. The lake is frozen solid, and up where Hattie lives, the snow is piling up. Turning baroque, even, in places—the wind chiseling out terrace upon terrace one day, ravines and slopes the next. The sun is so low, it hardly seems to rise in the east and set in the west, exactly. Instead, it seems to rise, then scoot straight across the south sky, just above the trees. From one side of the sky to the other, and then out. Every shadow is a long one.

But never mind. The coming of winter spells the coming of spring spells the coming of summer. Carter's boat will be done no problem, but now that he's making one for her, too, he has his work cut out for him. As for Hattie, she can't remember when she last had a moment to paint, but she's been thinking of moving her operation to Carter's shed. She doesn't mind the radio, and she likes his banjo breaks. And it does get great light. The only questions are, first, is it really as warm as Carter claims? And second, shouldn't she really work at home, where she can see the lake? Because she's sick of bamboo; she's thinking of painting the lake, never mind how Judy Tell-All will laugh.

Most people do do the lake, when they're looking straight at it. Never mind.

Tina e-mails that night.

Dear Aunt Hattie,

I write to inform you the bones arrived here safely. I brought them to the crematorium right away, we will go to Qufu this weekend. The workers all lined up already and we paid some fees too. Of course, we can expect more fees at the last minute. Still we are very happy,

And, a few nights later:

Mission accomplished. We found an auspicious day right away, and even though it is winter, the weather was not so cold. The workers did not overcharge us, and there were not so many fees. As for the town of Qufu, it is changed a lot, I don't know when was the last time you were here. Maybe you would not recognize it. Tour buses all over, everywhere people try to cheat you. But the cemetery is quiet, nobody there. And now our family feel a big peace. We did not hear from our daughter yet but still we believe she will call. Even Johnson says so. Our fengshui is feel something different. I know you are scientific, do not believe too much this kind of nonsense.

True.

Still I hope you will find your fengshui better all the time too.

Such hogwash! All the same, though it's late and she's tired, she writes back,

I am keeping my fingers crossed about your daughter—please do keep me posted.

SEND.

Now she wakes into a brightening dark. Soon Carter will wake and reach for her. He'll jot down some notes—the day's agenda, some other things; then they'll kick out the dogs and set about making love. In truth, it's been a hit-or-miss activity—at times all passion, but at times more entertainment than they'd planned. Not so much because of her: Though she's less interested in the abstract than she once was, she is, in fact, interested—and more or less reliable, too. He's the opposite—alive with interest until certain moments arise;

then sometimes his body is his and sometimes, it seems, someone else's. Oh, youth! In their heart of hearts they feel themselves thirty-five, but the evidence does suggest otherwise. And the waste—*all them years*—she will never accept it. At the same time she is grateful for his persistence and analysis—he wouldn't be Carter if there weren't analysis—thanks which they do seem to be getting at least a few things down. Their timing, their locations, their lines of inquiry. And their aids—their rings, their capsules, their gels. It is a veritable course of study. Though how sweet the fruits of scholarship! She knows it's just her oxytocin levels rising. Still, she's cried every time: For their past and their future, for their happiness and their stupidity; for their finitude; because even now she *thinks things*; because even now, she has to forgive him all over again sometimes, as if forgetting, somehow, that she has already. And because, as much as she loves Carter, he makes her think of Joe. Her dear misanthropic Joe—how can Hattie be missing him all over again? It makes no sense at all. But Carter is so not Joe that Joe seems more present than he has in years. Such a pleasantly bulky man, she is realizing, belatedly; and of course, he will always be younger than Carter, with a younger man's—well. The man, in truth, she sees and feels, sometimes, as she and Carter make love. Oh, Joe! How she wishes Joe could've known, before he died, how he'd stay with her. And Lee—how she wishes she could tell Lee.

The key to my reliability, Lee!

How Lee would laugh.

Shocking, Miss Combustible. Shocking.

Hattie does not tell Carter (who is probably thinking about Meredith, anyway), though she is beginning to understand Chhung—haunted by his first wife, his first life.

If they were even his first.

Ratanak Chhung, the one who lived. And Hattie and Carter, too: the ones who lived.

The ones who live again.

But no more. *Where the water is too clear, there are no fish,* her father used to say. And here it is, in any case, morning in this new life, in this new home.

Carter's here; the dogs are here; and her distance glasses as well, enabling her to enjoy a new favorite sight—Sarun and Sophy, headed to the public school. Chhung they'll have to keep busy, as Carter said; they'll have to find some doctors for him, too, and, if the Chhungs stay, they'll have to find a temple for Mum, and an Asian food market. Which, in truth, Hattie wouldn't mind herself.

But there go the kids in the meanwhile, marching up to the bus stop. Sophy has a new jacket, silver blue, and look how her hair is sticking out the bottom of her hat; by spring she should have her ponytail back. As for Sarun, he's on an anticonvulsant but his prognosis is just fine. If only he would go to school every day now, instead of when the mood strikes him! Then they could call him truly out of the woods.

Well, never mind. For today, at least, here he is, with Sophy. They're wearing backpacks; they're blowing clouds; they're throwing snowballs at the stop sign. The bus—a yellow half-loaf of a thing—pulls up just ahead of them. They run to get on. The wind blows; their backpacks thump. What with the sun so low, their shadows are as big as the mountains. Carter sits up.

"It's been non-trivial getting those kids on that thing," he says.

"Umm," she agrees. And though he reaches for her with intentions, she sits forward for just another moment, hugging her knees. The doors fold shut; the exhaust smoke clears. Snow is lifting in huge spangled plumes from the trees.

"That Sophy Chhung is going to be straight A," she says.

"That is a completely unsupported assertion," he replies.

She laughs—it's good to be watching from a different window. But now she takes off her glasses. "I'll kick the dogs out," she whispers.

"Umm," he says, his eyes already closed; and then, "Precisely."

The ones who live.

They have, by some great gift, all morning.

ACKNOWLEDGMENTS

Many thanks to the American Academy of Arts and Letters for the Harold and Mildred Strauss Living Award that made this book possible; and to the Radcliffe Institute for Advanced Study for its gracious support of 40 Concord Avenue.

Heartfelt thanks, too, to Dan Aaron, Rosanna Alfaro, Jay Blitzman, Lydia Buechler, George Chigas, Eileen Chow, Laura Garwin, Allegra Goodman, Susan Hatch, Nancy Hefner-Smith, Ruth Hsiao, Melanie Jackson, James Jen, Mom Jen, Sue Lanser, Margot Livesey, Sovann-Thida Loeung, Deb May, Stephanie May, Mary McGrath, Markus Meister, Martha Minow, Timothy Mouth, Naomi Pierce, Tony Re-al, Frank Smith, Sayon Souen, Ernest Stern, Anne Stevens, Chhorvivoinn Sumsethi, Boreth Sun, Keto Tan, Lisa Thurau-Gray, Sarun Tith, UTEC, Tooch Van, Mike Vann, and Wendy Wornham for their generosity, candor, and expertise.

As for my extraordinary editor, Ann Close; my patient children, Luke and Paloma; my above-average husband, David; and my great-hearted friend, Maryann: No thanks will ever be enough.